The Stone Cutter

Entrance To the Siq, David Roberts, 1839 (public domain)

The Stone Cutter

—a novel by Brock Meier —

book one of the series

≈ *Waters In the Desert* ≈

The Stone Cutter

This book is primarily a work of human invention. While the characters, dialogue, and events mostly sprang from the author's imagination, they were informed by significant and methodical research.
Some of the characters were drawn from actual persons of factual history: Yeshua, Sha'ul, and the protagonist (fictionally named here Nahor/Shamir), the demoniac of Gadara.

Cover art: excerpt from "Young Man In Reverie"
by John Singer Sargent, 1876 (public domain)
Cover design by: Etward A. Pieranse
Editing by: Toosty Ebbening

This is the first edition of The Stone Cutter, published September, 2023

ISBN-13: 978-19-58902-01-1

Contents

Prologue

She was the New Atlantis—rising not from the mist and mythic waves of an ocean's dream, but springing full-blown from the flinty forehead of Earth itself. Her founders—survivors, dreamers, pirates, and poets—carved and wrested her proud monuments from solid stone.

The rock. Ah, the rock! She *was* the rock. The Latin-speaking foreigners from across the western sea called her Petra: *The Rock.* But she was not just any rock. Her Nabatu builders named her Raqmu and Reqem—The One of Many Colors; Embroidered One. Her foundations and columns glowed with ribbons and swirls of variegated hue. The colors of wine, cream, and blood banded her breast and loins. None like her had ever been seen, nor would be again.

Always roaming, never resting, these nomad Nabatu first found their fortune in lands of a wilder waste. They made their living traveling from hither to yon and back, crossing the endless, sandy void. On the backs of camels they hauled the stuff of luxury from whence it came, to those willing to pay a dear price. Spices from the far east, the magic of silk from yet farther, frankincense and myrrh from secret places known only to them. They grew heavy and fat from the gold they gained.

Peculiar it seems, that desert wanderers—those Nabatu, *bubbling up from the sands*—should invest their sweat, their fortunes, their lives, in Raqmu's dreams of solid rock, not dunes of shifting sand.

But their truest treasure lay not in frankincense and myrrh, nor the gold they garnered in hawking it to the wealthy and pious in Rome and Alexandria. Their substance of supreme value was water: liquid life in the midst of an unending, arid landscape. They learned the secrets of harvesting and harnessing every drop of the scant rain falling upon their domain. Their complex networks of capture and diversion dams, tunnels, distribution pipelines, siphons, filters, and vast underground reservoirs turned the rock of Raqmu into a lush, well-watered garden: a *paradeisos*. The spectacular capital displayed an extravagance of pools, fountains, man-made waterfalls. And the kingdom flourished with the water-fed agricultural riches of fruits, grain, and wine.

Rock and water, incense and gold, silk and pearls sustained and enriched the dazzling city. Under the benevolent hand of their King Haretat—called *He-Who-Loves-His-People*—the city rose to ever greater heights. And their women enjoyed a freedom and power unknown by their sisters in the rest of the world. Haretat shared equal prominence with his Queen Shuqilat on coinage of the realm. And women of every status shared honor with their men.

But these Nabatu rose too successful for their own good. Among the nations around them, envy grew like noxious weeds. The political and military might of Rome lusted after the economic power that was Nabataea. The intellect and religion of the Hellenes saw a people of primitive philosophy and provincial theology, and so sought to transform the Nabataeans' god Dushara into Dionysus, and their goddesses Uzza and Lat into Isis and Aphrodite.

In the summer fever of a barren land the desert-rose blossoms into brilliant red, only to be plucked by a wanderer passing by. The lush beauty is gathered and carried home, to brighten the spare interior of a nomad's tent. But the next morning its colored petals wilt and fall to the rug-covered floor, to be swept out with the day's accumulation of sand. And so, too, the days of the Nabataean kingdom were numbered.

Part One

—Tale Told—

I

I SET ONE FOOT in front of the other. Then that other in front of the first. Ever leaving each other behind. Always onward, ever striving. Never arriving...

My life stretches far behind, its source lost back there—somewhere—beyond those purple cliffs at twilight's last horizon. With my ninety-nine years already past, can there be any life yet ahead? The dark of night begins to fall on my path, shadowing, obscuring where I might set my foot. I would trust the road, if road there be. Has anyone's footsteps preceded my own on this rude desert path? Nothing to guide—footprints not, nor post, nor sign—no simple markers to align my course with those who trod this way before.

And, oh!, how my belly growls. Hunger gnaws a hole in my emptiness. My last meal, two days past—and that, the merest glimmer of a feast.

I have no tent in which to lay my head. The woman I loved, the children we raised—all their bones now dry in the grave. All seems behind, with nothing ahead. But I know in some peculiar way, more than I know my own name, some hidden joy, some unseen treasure lies beyond my feeble sight. It waits most patiently for my timely arrival—whenever, wherever, that might be.

Yet here in this waste, I feel so lost. Can one be lost, when no destination awaits? When no home longs for one's return? Perhaps I'm not lost—just alone. I would welcome the amity of a single fellow traveler across this desert—a lowly dung-beetle, perhaps. But none there be...

Tonight, in this red valley of sand, the full moon rises at sun's descent, content to fill the quiet, inky span of night with its own pale and ivory light. I see a strange symmetry of bright strength giving way to subtle purity.

Is that the bleating of a little lamb? One lost out here in the wild, like me?

2

Thrust from earth's bowels in the timeless past, maroon and black crags jutted into the clear blue sky. Around their bases swirled an arid ocean of sand, the color of blood mixed with milk. Moisture, the currency of all life, deserted the stone, earth, and air.

Yet hidden in a *thaniya*—a slim cleft in the rock—a flock of sheep meandered up and away from the forbidding waste, to a place of safe refreshment. So narrow was the fissure, they moved along in single file at a slow pace, the nose of each animal nearly touching the tail of the one ahead. Leading them, a man shielded against the sun by robe and head-scarf called them onward. Another, at the queue's tail, watched for stragglers.

A flat-topped boulder of red sandstone lodged in a sharp bend of the passage to block their progress. The lead man waited atop the rock, while the other approached from the rear of the line and squeezed his way forward between the stalled sheep and the rock walls of the thaniya. In the middle of the wooly train an especially fat animal clogged the crevice, forcing the tail man to climb upon and walk over its back. He shouted down a curse upon the animal—

"By the veiled head of 'Uzza, may your fat carcass be food for maggots!"

The other chastised him. "Amru, it is a shame upon shepherds who curse their own flock. Recant!"

Amru blasted back, "My brother, if *you* walked behind them all day, seeing nothing but their brown-stained hind-quarters, tasting their dust, and treading upon their dung, perhaps you would curse them yourself!"

"Still, Amru, it is your shame. And your shame falls upon us both—and upon our family and tribe."

"So be it, Timrah—and if you think you would do better than I, even now I stand ready to exchange places with you. Shall we? Shall I be the head, and you the tail?"

He waited for a response, and hearing none, concluded the conversation. "I thought not..."

Finally reaching the base of the boulder, Amru lifted the first sheep and Timrah pulled it up and onto the flat rock. It scampered farther on, into the thaniya. The pair of brothers repeated the process twenty-nine times, until the whole flock, including the fattest, had passed the blockage. They proceeded without words.

At great length they exited the cramped confines of their path and emerged into an open and airy place, full of the lush-green of growing grass, the tinkle of trickling water, and the smell of moisture—the aroma of life.

The clearing was a natural-formed *paradeisos*—a hidden, wild garden. The thaniya here widened into a small canyon, its floor a carpet of green, well watered by the constant seep of a spring. An orchard of a dozen apricot trees bordered the grazing, with fuzzy unripe fruit decorating their branches. Beyond the meadow the canyon terminated in an acutely angled, narrow space serving as a perfect rock-walled *dira*—a secure resting place for the sheep when night would fall.

In the remains of the day, the flock fed and drank. While Timrah mended a tear in his cloak, Amru dozed in the grass. Neither man spoke to the other, as if, each lived in this place alone.

The sun fell behind the high, black rock and they began ushering their sheep into the natural pen. A final count as each passed through the gate would confirm that all were safe, and they could attend to their own repast, and then to sleep.

His robe stained with sweat, Amru put a shoulder to the hindquarters of a contrary sheep and forced it into the narrow opening of the fold. He followed with the sole of his sandaled foot to squeeze the animal through the chute. Timrah, of the same age and face as Amru, looked over the flock, re-counting heads to compare the result with his brother's count. He shouted to his twin, "Amru, we are missing one—the little black-face."

In disgust, Amru shot back—"We are not! Count them again, Timrah."

"I will not! Wasting daylight by counting them yet again will not change the fact that you missed bringing one in. See to the little one's return."

Amru's eyes rolled like balls of sheep dung and he said, "Since you are certain it was left behind, perhaps *you* should go back out and find it yourself. If I am not competent at keeping track of sheep, and cannot be trusted to count with accuracy, I will likely fail to find one that may—or may not—be lost."

The two stood up straight and eyed each other. It was as if one man looked at himself in a polished bronze mirror, so alike were their faces.

Timrah felt heat rising in his cheeks and he said, "Your impertinence toward your elder is not becoming of one born into my family."

Amru bristled. "You call yourself my 'elder' because you preceded me from our amma's womb by no more time than it takes a fresh mound of camel dung to cool on a wintry day—and this would make you my superior?—my lord?"

The sneer on Timrah's countenance could have wilted a desert rose. "I knew I should have slain you when I had opportunity, those nine moons we were crammed together within our amma!"

Amru laughed. "You should have slain me? Pray tell, with what, you dreamer?"

"I should have wrapped my own life-cord around your scrawny neck, and strangled the life from you!"

Amru chortled. "That limp and puny cord of yours could no more have stopped my robust heart from beating, than the one that dangles limply between your two legs is capable of fathering sons!"

The hue of Timrah's face now matched the purple of his brother's. "And those six ne'er-do-well male offspring *you* spawned, you count as *sons*? It is far better that my own wife's womb remains barren, than if I had *sons* such as *yours*!"

Their faces approached so close they felt the puffs of each other's breath.

"A woman's womb cannot be properly described as 'barren' if it has not yet been planted with adequate seed. Were I to inherit your marriage bed after your demise, you would soon see her womb is not so 'barren' as you think."

Timrah spun around once, huffed and puffed twice and then spewed out, "My wife has told me she nearly retches, to smell your stinking breath, and should any misfortune cause my early demise, she would rather join my rotting flesh in the tomb, than have you in her bed!"

"My breath may stink, but you, dear brother, grow bald."

"Bald, am I? Have you not seen your own reflection in the waters of a cistern?"

They both tilted their heads one way, and then the other, attempting to gain advantage in their glares.

"*My* reflection? If the image of your own face fell on the cistern, its waters would turn to sheep's urine!"

"Sheep's urine, eh? But yours would turn it to swine's urine!"

"Would not..."

"Would so!"

Their faces drew yet closer, noses nearly touching. They both sucked in the air sharply and held their breath, staring at each other's reddening eyes. Their faces blue, they finally let the stale air exhale with a *whoosh* from their lungs. With the light beginning to fail, both men knew continuing their argument could only lead to losing the lamb.

Amru said, "Brother, brother—if there is, indeed, a lamb yet straying in the wilderness, he will surely die in the jaws of a wolf if we remain here, our horns locked."

"You speak the truth, brother. May we both release our talons from each other's flesh, that the young one might live?"

"Yes. He needs us. Let us go to him and find him together. He may not be far."

Timrah said, "I will secure the gate of the fold so the flock will be safe in our absence."

"Thank you, brother. Don't worry about the little black-face—we will bring him back with rejoicing!"

3

THEY LEFT THEIR FLOCK in the security of its confines at the head of the little gorge and set out into the desert to find the stray. The sun dropped behind the great rock to the west of the Valley of Red. The sky faded from its deep azure and started to blush. Indigo waited just below the eastern horizon, eager to rise and claim the night sky.

Both men called out to the lost lamb and strained their ears, listening in vain for its desperate reply. And to no avail they strained their eyes, hoping to see it running to them. Amru's voiced cracked as he admitted, "I am afraid we, I mean *I*, have lost our little one, Timrah. It is my fault. I should have earlier recognized my error in counting, and should have set out to find it while there was yet daylight enough. We should return to the flock before night swallows our path. To punish my stupidity, you should break my staff upon my back, and take my share of the meal tonight."

Timrah consoled him. "No brother, instead of foolishly insulting you, I should have left you in charge of the flock and gone in search of the lamb myself—such is the responsibility of an elder shepherd —if *elder* I be."

In silence, they stood in the twilight, taking a final look into the darkening waste, hoping against all odds to catch a glimpse of the little black-face.

Heat from the desert floor rose into the cool evening air above, rippling and distorting the view of distant objects. The far, rocky cliffs waved and undulated in a mystical dance of dusk. And at the base of the cliffs, something dark seemed to swing and sway in the dance.

In hushed tones, Timrah said, "Do you see as I do, brother, that waver and wobble out there? Could it be our lost one, finding his way back to us?"

They waited yet more, and watched. Amru said, "It must be him! Let us run to him and carry him home!"

They ran as fast as they were able on the loose, vermillion sand, calling out to him as they went. Just fifty steps closer, they stopped in their haste. They saw, not the little black-face approaching them, but a figure much taller, and swathed in gray. The gray billowed and rippled in the evening breeze as the figure swaggered and staggered toward them. Timrah whispered, "It is not the lost one, brother—what is it?"

Amru gasped and said, "It is...a *djinn*! A spirit of the desert! It has come to punish me for my foolish ways—I have dishonored you and our family for stupidly losing the lamb. I will go to it and give myself up that our honor might be restored. Pray to Dushara for me, brother!"

Timrah grabbed Amru's cloak and held him back. "No, wait! I think it is not a ghost, but a man. Look—he walks on the earth like us, not floating on the wind."

Amru pulled free from his brother's grasp and shouted, "It *is* a spirit! The Gray Avenging Spirit of all lost sheep—coming to take its due! I will give myself into its hands, if hands it has, and remove our shame!"

"No, listen, Amru—he calls out to us..."

The shadowy figure continued to grow in size as it approached them. They could hear its voice, shouting in the distance—"Halloo, brothers! Halloo!"

Amru trembled and said, "Do you hear it? The spirit pretends to be one of us!"

The figure came closer, stepping forward out of the waves of heat and into clear view.

"Brothers, have you lost a lamb?"

He was certainly a man, an ancient man, cloaked in gray against the heat of the desert—and carrying a lamb upon his shoulders.

"Timrah, he is found! The little black-face is found and my shame is erased!"

The two ran to the old man and Amru placed the lamb on his own shoulders. They took the man by both arms and directed his way toward their camp. Timrah told him, "You have relieved our distress and replaced it with joy!"

Amru added, "And you have saved the life of this little one! *Sabah*, you must sup with us tonight and share our camp."

The old man said, "I would be honored to share your bread, brothers, since I have not eaten in two days and my navel now chafes against my backbone. To fill this belly again would be a great delight."

"We have no delicacies, Sabah, but what we have is yours."

The man said, "Then let us feast—and celebrate these unexpected blessings of life!"

The three men walked arm in arm back to their camp, to join again the little saved lamb to his amma. As they arrived at the hidden garden spot, night stretched over them like a canopy, embroidered with the sparkle of ten thousand stars.

In the near dark, Amru's memory guided his hands to find and move aside a rough rock a little larger than his head. He lifted the lid of a large terra-cotta jar buried and hid in the ground beneath it.

Stored inside, a cache of dried camel meat, dates, and the beginnings of a fire awaited them.

He retrieved two sticks from the jar—one sharpened to a point, and the other split with two flat sides, a small hole bored in its middle. Amru removed his sandal and placed it on the ground to form a stable base for the making of fire. He laid the flat stick atop the sandal and arranged a small handful of dried grass around the stick's hole. He inserted the sharpened point of the round stick into the hole.

"Timrah, will you help me start the fire?"

"Certainly, brother."

The two sat on opposite sides of the sticks that were positioned on the sandal. Amru held the pointed stick vertical, pressed between his two palms. He rapidly rubbed his palms back and forth upon each other, as if warming his hands, while pressing the stick's point into the hole. The stick whirred and whirled. Just as his hands reached the bottom of the stick, his brother immediately started the action at the top again, the stick never stopping its twirling. After half a dozen such handoffs, the stick's tip and the hole glowed red. Amru pushed some of the dry grass into contact with the tiny ember and it burst into instant flame. He added more grass to the little fire and then dumped the flames onto a small mound of fragmented, dry camel dung. In short order, a meager campfire lit the faces of the three men.

Sabah thanked his hosts. "This is a wondrous camp, my brothers! The breeze tonight takes the smoke down the thaniya and away from us. And I thank you for your generous hospitality in sharing your camp with me. Things are no longer as they once were..."

Amru asked, "What do you mean, Sabah?"

"You call me '*Sabah*' correctly, for '*Old Man*' I surely am. I approach a hundred years of life. One more—or is it two?—I need to claim one hundred. You asked—what do I mean? I mean that long ago, before the Hellenes and Latin-speakers were among us—before we *Nabatu* built houses of stone, before we planted vineyards and made wine—all the Nabatu floated through desert wastes, as do you. We made our home on the wind, between sand and stars. And every wandering man that came under our tent was our honored guest—our 'Father.' We would have given our very lives for him if required. But no longer. Men now live for themselves alone, storing up food and wine, and turning the wanderer away from their doors."

Timrah said, "It is not like that for us, Sabah. We yet hold to that old code of hospitality. A man found stumbling in the desert is our brother, indeed—even if he did *not* rescue our lamb. Our fire and food are his own. Our tent and bed would be his as well, if tent and bed we had."

Sabah said, "Yes, I suppose the old code still lives out here—away from the cities. Living in motion, from one camp to the next, has a way of trimming our lives down to what matters—living and breathing, smelling the desert-rose by day, seeing the starry heavens at night. Enjoying the fellowship of a campfire, and sharing tall tales of the past."

"And what of you, Sabah? Have you tall tales of the past? Your hundred years must have planted within you the seeds for such epics. Have you known men of renown, or heard of their adventures? Do you have stories of the men of old?"

The old man raised his eyebrows and stared into the glowing fire. "Yes, I have certainly seen and heard much. But there were not many heroes. We men are a flawed and rebellious herd. Our aspirations are high and lofty, but our doing is mired deep in the troubles of our own muddy mess."

"Surely, Sabah, you must have at least one tale for us? One story to make our imaginations soar, our dreams to take flight this night?"

"I do have a single tale. It is a story of love found and love lost—of ambition and madness—of paradise and torment."

"You would do us a great service to tell us such, Sabah. Already in your debt because of the lamb, we would be even more indebted if you regaled us with this epic. May we hear it?"

The old one pondered the request carefully, and wondered if he had the strength to finish it, once started. "My mind and memory are so cluttered with the dust of my many years, it may be difficult to unearth it. But I will try."

The brothers encouraged their guest—"Here, Sabah, have some meat to refresh your strength. And when you are sated, we have dates to sweeten your face with a smile. Rest with us, and let your memories grow within you. Let what was long ago become like it happened this very day."

Timrah passed strips of dry meat to the old man and to Amru, then took some himself. But before the old man bit off the first piece he held his to the dark sky, and looking up, said—

"To the One who made the stars, and who gives us meat and drink. To the One who makes old things new…"

The old man's words stopped both twins in mid-bite, then Amru resumed chewing. Timrah pulled the meat back from his own mouth and asked, "To which of the gods do you speak, Sabah? I have not heard this address before."

Sabah chewed the meat with great satisfaction. Deprived of food for two days, his mouth exploded with a gush of saliva. The dried camel meat was a feast, indeed, and he savored every morsel with appreciation. He took more meat, and at length said, "My brothers —the story begins to float toward the surface, from the cold depths of memory where it sank so long ago. Perhaps some of those dates would coax it yet all the way up and into my throat, that my voice might give it life."

"Yes, please have some of these sweet dates. Take all you want, that they might smooth the path for your voice."

He took one, chewing it slowly and let it dissolve in his mouth. The syrupy liquid trickled down his throat. He took another and did the same. After consuming eight dates he felt drowsy and said, "Forgive me, brothers, but my life's blood rushes to my stomach to gather the goodness of this sustenance. I must rest—just a bit—and then I will begin."

"Yes, Sabah, take your time. We will be here when you are ready."

The old man lay back on the ground, a flat rock his pillow. Before long, his snores echoed from the rock walls. The brothers waited a long time, and then tiring, they lay back and fell asleep themselves.

Not knowing how long they slept, they both jerked awake at the same time and sat up. The fire barely glimmered with a few red coals, but they added more fuel and breathed it to life again. The low flames illuminated the old man's face, his deeply creased mouth hanging open.

Timrah said, "He snores no more, brother. I wonder if he will yet wake tonight and regale us."

They both watched him intently.

Amru's eyes widened and he said, "Look—not only does he not snore—I fear he no longer breathes! He has died while *under our tent*!"

4

THE REGULAR RISE AND fall of living breaths no longer filled the old man's chest. A full century of life now seemed just beyond his reach. The twins debated about the course they should take. Amru closed his eyes, raised his face to the black sky and blurted, "My shame yet returns to us, brother—our honored guest has died in our care! Perhaps the food we shared with him was tainted, so by our hands he was poisoned! A dark fate by the dreadful hands of Man-awat waits to befall us in repayment..."

Timrah put his hand on his brother's shoulder and took a more measured approach. "Don't despair, Amru. We don't know for certain that Sabah lies dead. And if he does, it was certainly not our intent. I will touch him, and see if he stirs."

Timrah reached over and gently laid a hand on the man's chest. His touch confirmed that he was still, and breathed not. With a finger he softly nudged the bony ribcage and waited for a response. The old man lay inert. Amru, nearly anguished to tears, hoarsely whispered, "He is dead...I know it!"

Timrah prodded him more forcefully, slightly rocking the still body.

The body jolted upward into a sitting position, his eyes sprang open, and words erupted from his mouth in mid-sentence—

"...and then Ashmedai raised his eyes from the prize pierced within his black-iron talons and he saw a cloud of red dust arising far off. The host of his enemy-brothers swept across the desert plain like a flood, marching for the final clash—The Great Conflict pitting the brass of Ba'al against demonic iron—sledge upon edge—hammer and chisel! Onward came the thousand, thunder pounding, to slay defiant Ashmedai and claim his treasure trove. Unflinching stood the demon-giant, gripping ever-tighter the flint heart of Shamir. Lightning brash, flashing light to blast and blind his wicked kin! His scarlet eyes spewed forth..."

"Stop!"

"...molten hatred, with vile curses foaming from his..."

"Stop! Stop, Old Man!" the brothers cried.

"...foaming from his putrid maw! The host..."

"STAAHHHHP!" they screamed in unison.

The old man's mouth hung open but no more words came from it. He blinked his eyes twice and shook his head, before saying,

"I graciously beg your pardons, my brothers—what?"

Amru pulled hair from both sides of his beard and shouted at their guest, "We thought you were dead!—and now we get this story in the darkest hour of night?"

Timrah said, "We understand nothing of what you are saying! Who is Ashmedai, and who are his wicked brothers? Who is this Shamir, and why does he have a heart of flint? What happened to the beginning of the story? Why did you not start there?"

A gentle smile graced the old man's wrinkled face. He spoke slowly, instructing his audience, "My brothers, this is the way of all serious epics—Homer, Virgil, Qaimu, and all the others. The Latin-speakers have a phrase for it—'in medias res'—'in the middle of things.' The teller of stories starts in the midst of fury and storm, to guarantee the attention of his listeners' ears. You would not want me to start with the feeble cry of an infant, born in the middle of nowhere. Would you?"

Relieved because the man breathed again, but greatly disturbed at his mode of rebirth, the brothers stared at each other. Their mouths hung open in disbelief. They counseled their guest to launch the story again.

"Please, Sabah, start at the beginning..."

The old man modified their request. "You mean, '*nearer* the beginning'..."

"No, start at the *very* beginning! And leave *nothing* out."

"I warn you, my brothers, this will take a long time. Are you not sure you would like me to skip over to the exciting parts first? Otherwise, this will take much talking, for it is a long story."

"Sabah, we are two shepherds, moving our sheep by day, from one lonely patch of grazing, through an empty, forsaken sea of sand, to another remote pasture. We sleep each night among these stinking sheep, lying down our own stinking bodies next to each other. We dream of nothing but sheep, and sand, and sky. We've told each other every joke and story we know—a thousand times over. And you want to skip over the beginning and rush to 'the exciting parts?' Sabah, the flavor and savor is found in the chewing, and in the tasting, not simply in the filling of a belly. Have you not learned this in your hundred-years of living?"

The old man stroked his grizzled chin as he listened intently to Timrah, and after a pause in the conversation said, "Ahhhh—I hear wisdom in what you say! And '*may the younger instruct the elder.*' Yes, yes...it is as you say."

Soothed by the man's concession, the brothers' shoulders hung loose again, and Timrah continued. "Two shepherds, doing nothing of much importance, in the remotest corner of nowhere, have all the time you could possibly imagine—and more. So please, give us *all* the words the story wells up within you—and *please*—start from the beginning."

Sabah squinted one eye and asked, "The *very* beginning, you say?"

Together, the twins insisted, "The *Very*..."

He acquiesced to his hosts, "It will be as you wish..."

Sabah screwed up his face, and his features contorted into a knot as he dove inside himself, headlong into the story that swirled in the deep waters of his heart. He searched for the beginning, picking up phrases here, lyrical stanzas there, a name, or two, or three, and dropping each one in turn as he saw they were not attached to the *very* beginning.

Then his eyes lit up, he pointed a finger into the night sky and exclaimed—"Ah-hah!" Then moments later his countenance dropped to the ground before him and he uttered, "No, no...that is not it."

Three more such episodes ensued and the brothers' patience stretched tighter than the tether of an angry ram. Amru's body tensed and his hands knotted into fists. Timrah grabbed him, holding him back from their guest, and he began to say, "Old man, we cannot..." when a sharp jerk of Sabah's head cut him short. He cocked his ancient head askew, like an inquisitive dog. A quizzical pleasure glided across his face, then a bright smile replaced it. And he opened his mouth—

5

UNDER THE BLACK VAULT of the night sky, Amru stoked the fire of dried camel dung with a rare luxury of the desert—a branch of deadwood as thick as his forearm. Rapidly catching fire, the wood popped and crackled, sending yellow sparks weaving heavenward where they seemed to lodge as new stars. The brilliant flames now clearly lit the faces of the three men gathered before it. Amru, the younger twin, watched the sparks fly upward and then his eyes flitted back and forth as he anticipated Sabah's story. Timrah studied the old man's face, curious how the story would unfold. And, having never told it before, Sabah, himself, wondered about the revelation of the story's mystery.

As he prepared to speak, a phrase kept stealing forward in his mind—*And so it was...and so it was...*

So he opened his lips and his voice gave life to the words—

*"And so it was...*that in the fifteenth year of King Haretat, King of the Nabatu, the King Who-Loves-His-People, that Geram son of Dayan went unto his wife Elanat, and lay with her. She previously

bore Geram six fine sons—the eldest, seventeen years before. And so she conceived in her womb another child.

"Now Geram was a trader in fine, cut stone, often working around Hegra, the region frequented by Geram's family and tribe. Hegra lay a month and six days south of the King's capital at Raqmu. The stone of his traffic was not that for building palaces, or temples, but precious materials to be worked into jewelry, small statuary, and other fine things. His buyers, from all corners of the Latin-speaking and Hellene empires, lusted after lapis, malachite, and turquoise—the stuff of luxury. He offered his buyers the finest stone from mines in Egypt, Anatolia, and Persia."

With the epic, at long last, bubbling its way to the surface, Sabah took a deep breath, held it a while, and let it out again, slow and easy. He grinned, marveling at how, of their own accord, the words seemed to form themselves in his mouth and then, without effort, escaped into the air to enter the ears of Timrah and Amru.

The twins sat speechless and leaned closer to the old man. Having caught his breath, he opened his mouth once more.

"Now it happened that nine cycles of the moon later, Geram pitched a tent for Elanat near the caravan stop at Hawara—the 'Place of White'—just a few days from Raqmu. The child she carried greatly burdened her, and her time drew near. Their tribe's *mulda*—the midwife—had been called away to other matters, so Geram hired the local birthing-woman, named W'Shu, to assist in the birth. She entered Elanat's tent and tended to the pregnant woman until the days of her deliverance were upon her.

"Now W'Shu, reputed to be an oracle as well as mid-wife, was old and bald, save for the dozen long, frizzled white hairs sprouting from the crown of her scalp. Toothless on one side, she had just four on the other—a pair above still meeting their pair of mates below. Her right hip frozen, she dragged the leg below it like a log. And she had only a single ear, the other torn from her by a wolf while she was yet a child.

"But Elanat, even now carrying her seventh offspring, lay on her cushions as a vision of loveliness. Her face possessed a soft comfort —drawing in all who looked upon it. Long, thick lashes bordered her clear, green eyes and her flawless forehead rose above noble dark brows. Her soft, full lips reminded one of ripe pomegranates and the perfect rows of white teeth seemed like two flocks of sheep, fresh from their washing. To see the hag W'Shu hovering over Elanat, tending to her needs, it was hard to imagine these two were of the same feminine race.

"On the night the moon waxed full, Elanat crouched upon the birthing stool, overpowered by birth-pangs. W'Shu placed the palm of her bony hand on Elanat's trembling belly and gently kneaded the swelling of new life. The old woman's half-closed eyes sprang open and she jerked back her hand, holding it to her mouth. A low, coarse whisper escaped her shriveled lips—

> *'This one is fated*
> *—thanks be to Manawat!—*
> *for something great,*
> *this one with heart of flint.*
>
> *May he fall on the stone*
> *and so be broken,*
> *lest the stone fall on him*
> *and crush him to dust.'*

"Elanat's womb convulsed three more times, expelling its fruit into the cold night. W'Shu placed an obsidian knife in the hands of Geram, who cut the life-cord of his seventh, and last, son. He briefly showed the infant to his amma in the wavering light of an oil lamp and then carried him outside Elanat's tent. A feeble cry slipped from the infant's mouth as his father held him up and presented him to the stars as '*Nahor*'—a Lamp."

Sabah slumped back, his strength drained from the telling. Amru and Timrah looked at each other, and then at the old man. Amru sputtered, "You are not stopping, are you? You cannot be finished with the story—you *must* continue!"

The aged man weakly lifted himself onto one elbow and sighed, "Not the end...just a respite."

He lay back again, closed his eyes, and slept. Above them a radiant star blazed an arc across the sky, winking out behind the great rock to the west.

6

THE DAWN'S BLUSH, LIKE that on ripe apricots, just tinged the sky above the canyon meadow, stirring the twins from their fitful slumber. Timrah rolled to the right, expecting to see the old man, but not even his shadow remained. He called out, "Sabah? Sabah, are you here?"

Only a ewe in the rock-walled pen answered with—"meh-h-h-h—meh-h-h-h."

Amru sat up, blinked his eyes and yawned. He looked over at Sabah's empty sleeping space near the smoldering campfire. He trembled and then shouted at his brother. "I told you it was not a man, but a spirit! And it has vanished into the air at morning's first light—thanks be to Manawat, we still breathe and have our souls intact!"

No sooner had his words finished echoing in the gorge when a voice greeted them from the pen.

"Brothers, our morning already stands full of mercies—the sun paints our sky above and now we shall break our fast with this milk of three ewes!"

They jerked their heads toward the voice, to see Sabah returning from the penned flock, their leather bowl in his gnarled hands and full of fresh milk.

"We thought you left us, old man. My brother thought you were a spirit and vanished into thin air."

"Not yet, my young brothers—but some day. Here, refresh yourselves." He extended the bowl to them. Timrah received it and took three deep draughts of the rich, warm liquid. He grunted his approval and passed it to his brother. With one hand Amru brought the bowl to his lips, and with the other he pinched the thin, wrinkled skin of Sabah's arm. Amru poked and prodded their guest, until finally satisfied the man was not a ghost.

"Yes—I am made of skin—and bone—and there's blood and guts inside here, too."

Timrah said, "So you know how to milk a sheep, old man? I would not have guessed you to be a shepherd."

"A shepherd I am not, but I have spent enough time around a flock to know how to keep the dung and urine from the milk. It is a trick learned the hard way."

"Yes, you seem to know your way around a ewe's udder and to know her ways."

Amru said, "Since you seem to be a genuine man, what of the story? Last night you left us hanging from the edge of your words, and then you slept!"

"Right you are—and I beg your forgiveness for that. But I am strangely refreshed this day, and will continue the telling as payment for my portion of the milk. Does that suit you both?" They nodded their heads.

The twins opened the pen's gate to release the flock to pasture and water. The three men sat on a rock ledge at the base of the canyon wall and passed the bowl between them. The old man opened his mouth and the words flowed like a spring of fresh water...

*"And so it was...*that the babe Nahor grew in health and vigor, and was weaned by Elanat at his second year. His father bought a bullock and slaughtered it for a feast to celebrate the weaning of his seventh son, and his other sons celebrated with him.

"Now Nahor's brothers were all of age and gainfully employed. Only a year separated the ages of each of the six. Elanat, like a fertile ewe, had dropped her lambs one-by-one each spring, but after a pause in childbirth of a dozen years, Nahor was finally born. His brother closest in age, Wahab, was fourteen and tended his own large flock. The young man entertained thoughts of searching for a wife. The three middle brothers—Amand, Adnun, and Walu—followed in their father's tracks, dealing in stone with him. They had married and their wives awaited their firstborn. The two eldest, Ausos and Nashgu, bred fine horses, and their wives already bore them sons.

"Before Elanat carried Nahor, she thought her womanhood dry and lifeless. She believed Geram's seed would no longer quicken her womb. Nahor's arrival seemed to her a gift from the gods, so she raised him in the shadow of her own tent. She instructed him in the history and poetry of the Nabatu, teaching him to read and write in both the official language of their people as well as the common tongue. She trained him to perform calculations in the manner of the Hellenes.

"Geram began teaching Nahor the rudiments of his own enterprise. He taught him the art of negotiating to gain the upper hand, while convincing the opponent *they* had come out ahead. He explained the complex mental processes that committed to memory a detailed listing of his suppliers, his clients, and their orders. Finally, he revealed his secret system of knotted linen cords—the tangible record of his inventory.

"With each new moon his amma encouraged him to recite, word-for-word, the prophetic riddle pronounced by old W'Shu at his birth."

Sabah paused and took the bowl again from Amru. He slurped in a mouthful and rolled it around with his tongue, savoring the rich, creamy goodness of the still warm milk. With an audible gulp he swallowed, and then licked the white sheen clinging to his lips. He belched loudly and continued...

*And so it was...*when the boy reached his fifth year, Elanat conceived again and birthed her final child—an only daughter. The birth nearly killed Elanat, with a great loss of blood, followed by a fever lasting many days. She never regained her vigor, confined to lie in her tent the rest of her days. Her younger sister was called in to nurse little Talia—a 'Lamb.'

Her seven sons were a delight to her—a strong sign that 'Uzza and 'Lat favored her, lifting her and Geram in the estimation of their kin and friends. But in the privacy of her own heart, her daughter was her greatest joy. For twenty-four years only children bearing a 'quiver of arrows' below the waist passed through her tent. Now, her daughter would share in knowing the ways of womanhood. She would teach her the wisdom and secrets of women.

But her infirmities never passed, limiting her ability to effectively raise Talia. At two years, the child was weaned and the aunt returned to her own family. Elanat called Nahor to her tent and said to him— 'My son, your sister must find her life outside my tent, since I grow yet weaker, not stronger. Your brothers all build their own families and fortunes away from here. I would send Talia to them, so they would count her among their own children, but I cannot bear to part with her. You will now become her guard, her protector, and though you have only seven years of your own, you will be to her as a father."

She drew him close beside her and kissed his cheek. And he hugged her neck. She spoke quietly and tenderly to him.

"You know how you have been requesting of Geram a few sheep to begin your first flock?" He nodded in silence. "Your sister Talia—'a lamb'—shall be your first. Will you promise me to watch over her, to guide and protect her?" He nodded again and said, "Yes, Amma."

Relief filled her soul and she lay back on the cushions. She touched his black hair and said, "I will pray Dushara gives you strength, and Geram will pour out libations to him for you. And since an older brother can only do so much, I have arranged an older sister for her. Geram once had a partner, Arwas, who remains his friend and lives just over the next ridge. His wife Hamilat was like a sister to me long ago, but she died birthing her daughter Qainu, two days after my own womb ceased to be your home. Qainu will be to Talia an older sister—even her amma. Geram has proposed the arrangement to Arwas and he has agreed."

The boy's dark eyebrows crowded together as he considered the arrangement. He tilted his head, weighing the situation. He asked her, "Amma—since, to Talia, I will be like a father, and Qainu will be to her an amma...does that mean I must make Qainu my wife?"

Elanat laughed out loud for the first time in many months and assured him, "No, my son—you need not marry Qainu...unless, when you come of age, that is both your desires."

"Good, Amma—I do not think I am yet ready to take on both a daughter *and* a wife on the same day!"

"I think not, Nahor."

The boy kissed his amma and left her tent. He watched Geram place his god in a groove cut into a flat rock of pink sandstone, not far from their tents. Geram believed the betyl—a rectangular block of dressed, black basalt, two handspans tall, one wide, and half a span thick—to be a throne of Dushara, even the presence of the god. Upon the top of the block he poured a full bowl of cheap, sour wine—for what do gods care about the taste of wine?

7

SABAH RESTED HIS VOICE, and the twins gave him pause. They inspected their animals and found one wounded by a sharp rock the previous day. While Amru held it immobile, Timrah cleaned the wound on the sheep's hind-leg and dressed it with a poultice of crushed willow-bark mixed with urine. The three men rested during the heat of the afternoon, in preparation for moving to a new pasture the following day. In the dregs of the day, the old man cleared his gravely voice and readied himself to speak again. The twins sat up and looked toward him...

*And so it was...*that a handful of stars hung onto their early morning vigil, reluctant to yield their place to the dawn's first rays. The sun poked its nose over the ridge of white sandstone above Hawara and banished those pinpoints of light to the next nightfall. Already, the summer's heat chased scorpions under their rocks, and any snake with a thimble-full of sense challenged them for the shade.

That morning, the seven-year-old Nahor herded his flock of one tiny girl toward the communal cistern. Talia toddled ahead, widening the gap between them. Nahor learned to give her free rein on the way to the cistern, depleting her strength, so on the way back, when full water-skins weighed him down, he could keep her in sight.

They topped a little knoll halfway to their goal. At its foot waited Qainu. She stood erect in the golden-morning sunlight, dressed in a dark blue robe to her bare feet, and her hair covered in a white veil. An empty water-skin hung on her back. Though a few days younger than Nahor, she stood a hand-span higher than he. But the disparity in height never bothered Nahor. He always felt at ease when he was with her. He could say things, and do things, in her presence he would never consider with anyone else.

As they met her on the path, she asked him, "You have two skins today—are you expecting visitors?"

"No. Amma would like to bathe today. She said I should ask if you would help her. Will you?"

"Yes, but I must take my own water home to Abba first. Then I will come to her tent."

Nahor paused, and said, "She thinks of you as her older daughter."

Qainu looked to the ground and smiled, pleased that Elanat felt the same as she. "Please tell her I will come as soon as I am able. I know she dearly misses swimming and bathing in the large pool. I am happy to help her."

A remarkable complex comprised Hawara's water system. Various dams and walls diverted the runoff of seasonal rains at higher elevations into the system, to feed a large, rectangular pool—nearly 30 by 45 paces and as deep as a man is tall. The pool was tiled around its upper edge and smoothly plastered within to prevent any loss of water. To supplement the seasonal supply, natural constant springs, a full day's journey to the north, flowed through ceramic conduits to Hawara's pool. Overflow from the large pool fed the rest of the system, including downstream cisterns carved into solid rock at a lower level.

The three children arrived at the first cistern below the large pool. Talia ran circles around the cistern, to her obvious delight.

Nahor took all three water-skins and descended the stone steps to the water's surface. He submerged a skin and began waving its open neck through the water, filling the volume. He closed the neck with a wooden plug, secured it with loops of a palm-fiber cord, and passed it up to Qainu. He did the same with the other two while Qainu pretended to chase Talia, wearing her down with six more circuits around the cistern. Their task complete, Nahor slung two full skins on his back, and Qainu, one on hers. As they left the cistern, Nahor grinned as he told her, "I will show you something—follow me."

They diverted from the well-worn path on which they arrived, and took a barely-discernible, sloping trail, strewn with rocks. After some time Qainu asked, "Where are we going? This water burdens me!"

"Just a little further—see those three large rocks? We shall leave our water-skins in their shade and pick them up when we are finished."

"When we are finished? With what?"

He ignored her question as they came to the rocks. They dropped their skins at the foot of the boulders and he led her to the other side. The darkness of a deep hole excavated into the bedrock yawned before them. Cool, moist air poured out of the cavern's mystery, bringing refreshment to the hot day. A sense of awe came upon Qainu and she whispered, "Is this the entrance to Gehenna?"

With confidence, Nahor said, "It is the rock-cut cistern that stores the greatest volume of Hawara's water. They say it holds enough that one man could not drain it in a hundred years." Qainu took hold of his hand and stooped low to look into its blackness. Seeing nothing, she shuddered. He told her, "The water is deeper than a man is tall, and it has pillars carved out that hold up all the rock above it. It is longer and wider than the large pool we swim in. And the water is nearly cold—it feels so good when the day is hot!"

She looked at him with suspicion and asked, "How do you know how it feels?"

He grinned at her again and announced, "I have been in it—swimming!"

She backed away from the hole and said, "I do not think we should be here. We should leave and return to our homes."

"Does its cool breath not refresh you? And does its mystery not speak to you? Will you not descend its steps with me, and swim in its waters?"

"No, we should leave now, and go to our homes!"

"I did not think of you as a trembling-girl. What is to be afraid of? Can you not swim?"

"Of course I can swim—and I do *not* tremble! I am *not* afraid—but what if we are caught?"

"No one will ever know we were here—no one comes here, but the cistern-man just twice a year to clean out the settling basin. And just three days ago I watched him do that."

"But what about Talia? What would we do with her?"

"She is worn out from all her running. We can put her in the shade of these rocks. Talia—you can sit in this shade and play with your doll, can't you?"

The little girl nodded her head and sat on the still-cool sand, leaning her back against the rock. Nahor assured Qainu, "See? It will be fine. To be sure she does not wander off, I will tie the long cord of this water-skin around her ankle—she has not yet mastered knots."

He secured the cord around her ankle, took Qainu's hand and led her back to the cistern's open mouth. He told her, "This is going to feel so good in this heat—you shall see."

As he dropped her hand and began removing his robe, she turned away, looking at the sunlit backs of the boulders. Shortly, she heard a loud splash and Nahor shouting—"Ohhh, this is so cold—it is wonderful!" She turned back to see him paddling about, just beyond the stone steps descending into the water. She watched as he swam further into the cavern's darkness, and out of her sight. His words echoed from deep inside, "Qainu! Jump in! You will enjoy it!"

She hesitated, thinking,

What good can come of seeking my own pleasure—leaving Talia out here—and being someplace we ought not be?

His words echoed out to her again, "I knew you were a trembling-girl!"

She shouted back to him, "I am coming in—if you turn away so you do not see me."

"Yes, I am looking away now..."

Qainu looked all around her, removed her robe, and last of all, uncovered her hair. She carefully stepped down the first three steps, feeling the cold stone on the soles of her feet. She pinched her nose between a thumb and forefinger, held her breath and leaped from the steps into the water, a great splash erupting. When her feet touched the smooth, plastered bottom of the tank, she pushed herself back to the water's surface. As her head popped out, Nahor laughed, and said, "So, you are not a trembling-girl after all!"

She swept her hair back from her face and looked around as she paddled to stay afloat. Nahor swam closer to her and she said, "It is so dark in here, how can you see anything?"

"Your eyes will soon adjust to the dark, and you shall see every-thing. Follow me!"

He began swimming away from the entrance, and to avoid being left by herself, she swam, following the noise of his splashing. The farther they swam, the darker the cavern became, yet just as he said, she could now see the large, stone pillars as they passed them. And, looking up, she could see light flickering across the plastered ceiling as the sunlit brilliance behind her reflected from the water's moving surface.

Finally they reached the far wall of the cavern, where Nahor grasped a small ledge just below water level. Qainu did the same and they rested there, panting and catching their breath.

"See, I told you this would be wonderful! And you did not wish to come in. Are you not glad you jumped?"

She said nothing, but nodded.

The walls of the cistern were perfectly flat, and smoothed with the same plaster that waterproofed all the cisterns of the Nabatu. And they saw the ranks of stone columns, their arched tops extending smoothly into the stone ceiling they supported. At what seemed to them a great distance off, they could see the brilliant light of the summer morning penetrating into the cistern's entrance pit and illuminating the interior with a subdued glow.

Qainu finally spoke. "We should go—my Abba will wonder why I tarry."

Nahor finally took notice of his companion's appearance. "I never saw your hair before—it is light—like the sun! I always thought it was dark, like mine. Why do you keep it covered so?"

His question perplexed her and she said, "Do you not know?—that *all* women's hair is to be covered outside their home?"

"But, not so carefully as you—and you are not yet a woman."

She hesitated in answering him. "It is because...because Abba says...it is my shame."

"Your shame? I do not understand."

"It is because no one else in our family, or our tribe—or any tribe —has such hair. He said my amma had no such hair, and that it is a disgrace that I must bear in secrecy—that I should always keep hidden."

"I still do not understand. Your hair is like the bright, golden sun —something not to be hidden. It is a special gift. Since your hair is like the light, I shall call you 'Nura'—My Light!"

As Qainu heard such a positive view of her appearance, a slight smile briefly drifted across her lips. But it quickly evaporated and she looked back toward the entrance. She said, "We must go back— Abba will be angry." She turned and pushed off from the ledge, swimming back from where they came. He turned and followed, soon outpacing her. Passing column after column, they at last approached the entrance, the bright light from outside nearly blinding them.

With Nahor emerging from the water as he climbed the steps, Qainu turned away. She said to him, "When you are dressed, call to me and then turn away so I may..." But a shrill cry, as from a wounded animal, interrupted her unfinished words. Nahor threw on his robe and rushed around the rocks to his sister.

The terror of the sight before him cast his heart into his throat, and his mind tumbled in confusion. Black as tar from the Salt Sea, and glossy as a wet stone, a desert cobra seized upon the flesh of Talia's right arm with the fiery kiss of cold death. She waved her arm wildly, attempting to shake it free. Her face contorted in frantic fright, and she looked to her brother for deliverance.

Panic and anger wrestled for dominance in Nahor, but he ran to her and gripped the viper's head, to tear it from her. As he took hold of it, the serpent coiled its muscular body around both their arms. The harder he pulled, the tighter its coils encircled, and the deeper it sank its fangs into her tender flesh. She squealed like a hare caught in the jaws of a wolf.

Now dressed, Qainu hurried around the rocks and screamed in shock, seeing the violence. Desperate to save his sister, Nahor yanked his *janbiya* from its sheath and attacked the cobra, slashing at its neck. Scales, muscles, and bone yielded to the keen blade, blood spurting, running over its body and dripping from Talia's little fingers. He separated the body from its head and, at long last, pried the jaws from her arm, the fang-holes oozing blood. He unwrapped the coils and cast the still-writhing snake's body as far as he could.

Nahor shouted, "We must get her home! Amma will know what to do, and Abba will pour out an offering to Dushara. Let us hurry!" Qainu lifted Talia to Nahor's back, and leaving the water-skins at the rocks, they sprinted to Elanat's tent.

Sabah dropped his head to his chest, drained from the telling of the story. The twins looked at each other, pain crowding their brows together, and their lips stretched tight in grimace. The story, stopping at such a place, distressed them, but they knew their guest could not continue. With great patience they waited for Sabah to compose himself, and he started again.

8

AND SO IT WAS, that Nahor's eyes birthed tears, but he forced them back as he watched from the entrance to Elanat's tent. She dressed her daughter's wound, applying a poultice of myrrh and dates moistened with a little wine. A blank grief darkened her face, foretelling the outcome. She could not bear the weight of losing her only daughter.

Nahor bit his lip until it bled. He whispered to himself, "How could I let this happen? My sister will die—and it should be me. *I* brought this grief to my Amma."

Qainu stood behind the boy who spoke to her the few words of kindness she ever heard. She laid her hand on his shoulder to bolster and console him. She whispered into his ear, "You are not to blame —how could you know the snake was near? They wake at night and should be sleeping in the daylight."

Geram ran up behind them and, pushing them aside, burst into the tent. He shouted, "Is it true? Is our only daughter on death's journey from the bite of the black-devil? How could this be so?!"

He lifted Talia's limp body from her amma's lap and cradled her in his arms. He looked into her sightless eyes, rocking her to and fro, and humming to her. He took her to Nahor, and stooping down, showed her blank face to him. His voice cracking with the emotion, he said, "Look upon the face of your sister, for you shall no longer see life in it! How could you let this happen to your little lamb? It is *your* shame, and it is now ours as well!"

A pang jabbed through Qainu to hear Nahor so shamed by his abba. She moved Nahor aside and, keeping her eyes to the ground, said quietly, "Sir, it was not Nahor's fault, but my own. I dared him to jump into the hidden cistern and swim in it. I said he would not, because fear was his master. But I was wrong. And the snake struck before he could leave the water."

Geram glared at the boy and rasped, "My son, is this true?"

Nahor could say nothing and his father turned back to Qainu. "I shall speak to Arwas and tell him what *your* shame demands, that it might be covered!" He laid his daughter back in the lap of Elanat, that her tears might fall upon the child's face and ease her final breaths. Geram hurried from the tent carrying his god and a skin of wine and ranted, "I will pour out this *good* wine to Dushara—perhaps that will gain his favor, and yet save my daughter!"

Elanat and the children watched Talia expire. Near the end, her eyelids fluttered and her mouth moved as if speaking, but no words came forth. Her little chest rose, and then fell, never to rise again.

Crushed by her daughter's death, Elanat beat her breast with the little strength she had and she wailed in desperate grief. Nahor could no longer bear his amma's state and turned to Qainu, but she was not there. He walked from the tent and, from a distance, watched Geram pour out the full skin of good wine on the black stone. He threw the empty skin aside and beat his temples with his fists, moaning.

The next day two men and a boy walked in a single line up the long slope to the "Place of Silence." From a distance it appeared little more than a short, flat line in the jagged edge of the horizon, where the clear blue sky touched the white sandstone highlands. A priest led the procession, dressed in a deep blue, ankle-length tunic, trimmed at the neck, wrists, and hem with crimson embroidery. He spoke to Geram behind him.

"My brother, does he know why he carries the load of his sister?"

"Yes—I told him we must place her small body on the platform—to expose it to the elements and the birds, to return it to the earth from which it came, and so release the wind of her spirit to the air and the sky, that it might not be trapped in her body."

The priest nodded and said, "That is good."

They arrived at the sun-bleached rocks and paused at the foot of a stairway carved into the sandstone, ascending to the heights. The priest set his foot on the first step and led them upwards. The steep ascent resembled climbing more than walking. Talia's body, shrouded in blue wool and slung from Nahor's shoulders, burdened him with a great weight. Halfway to the high platform he faltered, and stumbled backward. Geram reached back and gripped his shoulder, steadying him.

After half an hour's climb, and with a final effort, Nahor took the last step up and onto the object of their journey. Long ago the founders of Hawara carved away the topmost pinnacle of this mountain, leaving this level, stone floor of a small platform. The space held room for the three standing there and not much more.

Called the Place of Silence, the space was *hrem*—set aside as especially holy. Unless preceded by a priest, coming here was forbidden. He prepared the area by dropping 'tears' of *lubunah*—resinous lumps of sap from the incense trees to the far south—on the hot coals of his censer. He waved it about, producing a blue-white cloud of perfumed smoke that gently drifted away in the breeze. The incense enveloped the platform in a fragrance both sharp and sweet —aromas full of brilliant light, yet immersed in the darkness of mystery.

At the edge of the space was a grid-work of peeled branches, lashed together with palm cord. The wooden rack lay over the opening to a narrow trench cut into the rock below it.

The priest spoke to Nahor. "Unwrap her body."

Geram removed the burden from Nahor's back and laid it on the stone at his feet. The boy looked up at his father through red eyes, imploring him to take the task from him. Geram nudged the boy's shoulder, urging him to carry it out.

His tears wet the blue wool as he opened the shroud. Her body seemed smaller than he remembered. The naked, grey skin displayed no hints of life, and an awkward posture contorted the limbs. One cloudy eye stared with blind indifference to the harsh sunlight, the other remained half-closed. The mouth hung open, its tongue grey, dull, dry. The image sank deep into Nahor's memory.

The first scent of corruption rose from the little corpse, so the priest swung his fuming censer three times over it, replacing the offensive odor with the divine fragrance, so as to not offend the nostrils of Dushara. He chanted verses of words unknown to either Geram or Nahor.

As the boy stood on the narrow platform at the top of the world —the flat, white stone below his feet, the blue sky above, and Dushara's mountains to the far north—the scene appeared to him as of another world. But how else would it appear, when standing on the doorstep of the gods?

The priest nodded to Geram, who picked up the inert body of his only daughter and laid it on the rack of the exposure platform. They said nothing more, but turned away and began their descent of the stone steps. Nahor folded the shroud, tucked it under his arm, and took a final look back at Talia—his little lamb.

By the time they reached the bottom steps where the gentle slope led to the desert plain, Nahor raised his eyes to the sky and saw the white vultures already gathering above the Place. They would soon land and begin stripping flesh from bones. When the birds finished their meal, beetles and ants would complete the work of devouring the sinews, the joints coming apart, and the bones falling through the rack into the cavity below. For three months, the bones would lie in the desert sun, bleaching and drying. Then the priest, Geram, and Nahor would return, to gather them into a box and place them in the family tomb near Hegra.

Sabah stopped his narration. The story now entangled itself in the substance of his heart, like the roots of a cedar of Lebanon in the heart of the earth. He wondered if he would ever pry it loose again. And it worked its tendrils into the twins, who sat mute.

9

THE TWILIGHT DIMMED INTO deep night and the old man pondered longer than usual the story ahead of him. As it uncoiled itself from deep within, the tale affected him profoundly. He closed his eyes and, in silence, thought about what he would say—and what he would not say. He began again.

And so it was, that Arwas moved his daughter Qainu and his household, away from Hawara. Before he left, he paid to Geram three she-camels, one with calf, and a small flock of ten sheep, to cover Qainu's shame. No one but she and Nahor knew the shame belonged to him alone. From a low hill, Nahor watched Arwas pack up his household, strike his tents, and set off to the north with another small caravan. Behind her father's train of eight camels, Qainu walked with his two servants. She looked back and wondered if Nahor watched her.

In two week's time, Elanat called her son Nahor to her tent. Lying on her bed of cushions, she faced away from him, and spoke to the blank wall of the tent. Her voice sounded thin and dry. "My son, in less than three months you will gather Talia's dry bones and rest them in the hall of your father's father. I cannot bear the thought, and I must be gone myself by then. I have not the strength to live—but I have not the strength to end my life."

Nahor's face fell as he felt his amma's anguish. He wanted to leave and hear no more of her words of pain, but his love for her compelled him to listen. She said, "I have no right to make such a request of you, but...will you...end it for me? By your love for me...will you pierce my heart with the sweet blade of your janbiya? Or if not, will you glide its keen edge across my throat?"

The dire request paralyzed the boy and he could neither move nor speak. When Elanat felt her son's horror at the request, her resolve crumbled and she wept, her voice breaking under the weight of her tears. She finally spoke again, with tortured words. "I am sorry Nahor! I should not have asked this of you. It is a request too severe. Please, do not tell Geram of this."

His amma's pain gripped his heart, and he dropped to his knees behind her back. He laid his hand on her shoulder, and then laid his head on hers. His hand shaking, he slid his janbiya from its sheath. The polished blade gleamed, and reaching over her body, he laid it down before her. His tears fell upon her cheek as he whispered to her, "Keep it under your pillow, Amma—perhaps its closeness will bring you comfort."

She patted his cheek and breathed out a long sigh. Nahor left her tent, knowing he would never see her again.

As Sabah's words faded into the night, he looked up from the campfire he had been staring into, and saw the drawn faces of his two hosts, lost in their own thoughts. Not another word passed between the three and they each lay down on the ground, pulled their cloaks up around them and wondered what dreams might await them.

10

For three days, Timrah and Amru moved their flock often, from one meager pasture to another. Never tarrying, so as to avoid depleting the limited grazing, they stayed in motion, stopping only briefly to eat, drink, and catch a few moments of sleep.

Their invitation remained open to Sabah, so he followed the group, but he had no more heart for telling the hard story. And the brothers had no ears for the hearing. For those three days, the only words they spoke commanded the flock to follow, or comforted a skittish animal in the dark of night.

On the afternoon of the fourth day, Sabah saw his companions increasing their pace. Some destination, known only to them, drew them onward with renewed vigor. They aimed the flock's progress toward the divide between two unremarkable hills, appearing no different than the other hundred they passed in the previous four days. The sheep, too, sensed an inexplicable something, which pulled them toward it with undeniable force. When they neared the passage, the animals broke into a trot and their shepherds could not control their flight. The men moved away from the flock to avoid being trampled, and with grinning faces they watched the stampede thunder up the little pass to disappear on the other side.

As fast as his century-old legs could carry him, Sabah hurried up to the twins, asking, "Is this what I am guessing it is?"

They laughed and said, "That all depends on your guess, old man. Come, and see…"

The three weary men climbed the last rocky slope between the two sandy humps, and at the top gazed down upon a vast, green meadow where the flock already grazed. In the distance they saw another, larger flock, tended by four boys and three men. A rock-rimmed pool of water nestled against the flanks of the hill to the right, and on the lower slope of the one to the left grew a mixed orchard of various fruits. A ring of low hills encircled the meadow, hiding it from the dry plain outside.

His smile nearly splitting his face, Sabah said to his companions, "This is truly a wonder, brothers! And an unexpected refreshment. Are those your brothers out there? Perhaps we should join them and break bread together."

The twins looked at each other, their smiles evaporating in the desert air. Timrah spat, "They are more bastard-cousins than they are brothers. That is one of the flocks of Akyus. His tribe and ours share this meadow—and nothing else. That scorpion snubbed the chief man of our own tribe, and though a contract of two-hundred years continues to join us in this place, we piss in their direction, and while we are here our hands will remain on the hafts of our janbiyas."

"Are you sure the rift cannot be mended?"

"Old man, can you truly tell us that in your hundred years you had no mortal enemy—one who would slit your throat for a small bronze coin, and then capture your soul in a jar of clay?"

"Indeed—I have had such enemies."

"Then, Sabah, we shall speak no more of them. Let us give them a wide berth in this place, and we will feast on its abundance."

Amru applauded his brother's words. "Well said, Timrah!"

The men descended the gentle slope to their flock and they set about the work of inspecting them for any injuries resulting from their stampede. Satisfied with the condition of their sheep, they headed to the shallow pool and plunged their heads in the cool water. With their heads yet submerged, the twins called to each other, the words garbled as blasts of bubbles escaped their mouths. Breaths exhausted, they lifted their heads, water streaming from faces, and they laughed in uproar. The contagion of the hearty hilarity brought laughter to Sabah as well.

Faces refreshed and thirsts quenched, the three lay down beside the flock and reveled in the green luxury surrounding them. As they looked into the pure blue above, Amru asked, "Sabah—this story of yours…it seems only good for the breaking of one's heart. Can you not add a little honey, to sweeten it for our ears? It is a good story… but a hard one."

He considered the request for quite some time before he answered. "That is a good thought, Amru, and I would take pleasure in obliging you. But the story is not of my own invention. It travels wheresoever the truth shepherds it. It possesses no rudder that I might lay my hand upon, to guide it wherever I choose. I am at its mercy, as are you."

Timrah added, "You speak of truth—so this is a true story, then? This is not a fable of your imagining?"

"I did say 'truth,' didn't I? For any story to be worth the telling— or the hearing—it must spring from the truth. If not, it is nothing more than the final flow of the Yorden, as its fresh waters are swallowed up in the undrinkable tears of the Salt Sea."

Amru conceded his position. "So be it, Sabah. Let us have the story, then, wheresoever the truth will carry it. We have the stomach for it."

"Very well. Now where was I? Four long days have come and left us since I last let the story pass through these lips."

Timrah prompted him. "Nahor left his amma's tent, knowing he would never see her again…"

"Ah, yes—thank you, brother…"

And so it was, that before Talia's bones rested in the tomb of her grandfather at Hegra, Geram carried the body of his wife Elanat to the Place of Silence above Hawara. He laid her on the exposure rack above the bones of her daughter. As they had before the girl's birth, amma's and daughter's physical substance would again intermingle.

On the morrow, Geram called his youngest son to his tent and told him, "Your amma lies dead by her own hand. My great grief in losing the wife of my youth is all the greater because of this dishonor she laid upon us. And adding yet more shame to the heap of my troubles, in her hand was found your janbiya—the instrument of her death. I must put you away, and send you among those not privy to these matters, so your shame remains hidden by a dark veil, that your life might not be encumbered by it. You are now my youngest issue —the last fruit of my Elanat's womb. It tears at my heart to send you away, but no other choice is left to me."

Ever since the last new moon darkened his path, Nahor walked as through a shaded dream. He wondered if he would wake from it. Geram's words penetrated his ears, but bounced from his heart. He thought,

Abba says he will send me to those I know not, far away from my family. But in the end, he will not—I know he will bring me back among my own.

The following day, Nahor packed his belongings—a change of garments, and a small box carved of olive wood and once treasured by his amma. He rolled them in his cloak and a wool blanket, tying a cord around the bundle and slinging it over his shoulder. Geram lifted the tent flap and said, "It is time to leave."

GERAM STRODE EAST, TOWARD the edge of Hawara, Nahor several paces behind and struggling to maintain the pace. Already risen before the sun, the skeletal crescent of the nearly new moon grinned down in derision upon the boy. They stopped where two caravan roads merged before heading north to Raqmu.

Hawara was a conundrum, for at this junction in the roads, goods from the east came from the south road, and goods from the south came from the east road.

Goods came from the eastern lands—cardamom, cassia, pepper, and ivory, rubies, diamonds—and from the farthest fringes of the eastern world—engraved swords, quicksilver, and most of all, silk. The stuff of luxury, these caches of merchandise came in the holds of ships of the Nabatu across the wide Erythraean Sea, then up the Avalitic Gulf lying at the eastern edge of Egypt, to finally be unloaded at the port of the White Village, Aila. From there the goods passed northward on the backs of camels, entering Hawara from the south. Most of these goods simply passed through the hands of Nabataean middle-men, but gained for them a great deal of gold and silver in the transaction.

From the eastern road came other caravans carrying goods overland from the far south—the mainstay of Nabataean traders for hundreds of years. From Saba came the harvest of lubunah, and from Hadramawt, myrrh—destined for combustion at altars scattered about the Great Western Sea, in hope that the smoke would find its way curling into the nostrils of a hundred different gods and goddesses.

Father and son waited together at the intersection of these two great roads of commerce. But the son waited alone at the intersection of the familiar and the unknown.

As the morning grew bright they saw a caravan in the distance, and it proceeded toward them. At its head, a contingent of a dozen Nabataean warriors rode their steeds. In the still, cool air the animals snorted, strutting in confident spirit past Geram and Nahor. The riders, with lances at the ready, also slung sheathed, curved swords from multicolored sashes of embroidery, tied about their waists. Hanging from the neck of each horse, small shields flashed in the sun, emblazoned with the monogram of King Haretat, King of the Nabatu, the King Who-Loves-His-People. Each warrior's face carried the severe look of authority—the faces of those not to be trifled with.

After the caravan guard, several strings of a dozen camels each followed. Only one hundred and twenty animals in the entire train, the caravan made no great demands on the caravanserai at which it would rest. Since trade increasingly moved by ships rather than land, the age of great caravans of two thousand animals seemed a thing of the past.

Near the end of the caravan, the shrill whistle of a string's handler pierced the air, and the string of twelve animals halted as one. Sacks bulging with the harvest of lubunah burdened each beast, and the sweet, pungent essence of their perfume soaked the air. The handler greeted Geram.

"Geram son of Dayan—I have not seen you since my camels last calved! I hear you wish transport to the City. I will give you a fair price—a single silver drachm with the royal portraits, for gaining a ride on my best mount, and meals for the next two days. She is already saddled for a rider and carries only a half-load of merchandise, so if you wish the boy to ride with you, I will allow him, free of payment."

The men embraced and Geram tugged the other man's scruffy beard. He pressed a coin into the handler's palm and closed the man's fingers over it. A smile broke across his face as he said, "Thank you, my brother! This will help feed the nine mouths of my sons and daughters."

"Nine, you say, Haritha? The last we spoke I thought you had just seven."

"Yes—it was, indeed, seven at that time, but my beautiful Samsi has since calved twin boys. She is a wondrous woman, Geram, pushing out new children almost faster than I can plant my seed within her! I believe my brood has now passed the size of your own, has it not? Speaking of the making of babies, how is your Elanat? You said before she was not well."

Geram paused and stared at the ground before answering. "She has...left us—for the shadows. And less than a month after our youngest died. I cannot speak more of this."

With a smooth stick, the man touched the front legs of the saddled camel and uttered, *ghin!* The animal dropped to its front knees and then settled itself onto its back legs. He steadied the animal by its halter while Geram mounted the saddle. Haritha lifted the boy onto the saddle in front of Geram and then touched the camel's neck, saying to it *qum!* As the animal rose to its feet, the man whistled twice and the string of camels rejoined the caravan train, heading northward.

With the intersection behind them, the leaders of each string of camels picked up the synchronized chant of an epic poem, to tally the steps of their progress to the next waypoint on the road. Each stanza, verse, and word accounted for a specific distance on the ground, connecting spoken art with the expanse of a journey, and the hard reality of the earth. The epic recounted the tale of one called Gindibu, a farmer-turned-soldier who, singlehanded, fought to avenge the shame of his tribe and regain their liberty and prosperity. The poem required the entire two-day journey to Raqmu to arrive at its glorious conclusion.

12

THE TWIN SHEPHERDS' CAMPFIRE barely glowed, and then snapped, sending a burst of sparks heavenward. Amru yawned and looked at his brother, who nodded half-asleep next to him. Amru said, "This story of Gindibu—I have heard it as a child. Do you remember it, Timrah? Our father's brother could sing it from beginning to end. When our tribe gathered for the spring *hajj*, he sang it after the sun fell, requiring seven nights to complete it."

Timrah shuffled his body and shook his head before answering. "Gindibu? I don't remember..."

"Of course you do—the girl he loved was called Zabibe. And Gindibu fought a rival—and the rival's friends who rode seven elephants. He was victorious, winning the girl's love and her father's blessing."

"Oh yes, I do remember now...and there was something about a spirit clothed in blue, who had the knowledge to find a great treasure —though I cannot remember just what that treasure was."

"Nor I, brother. Do you know the full story of Gindibu, Sabah?"

The old man struggled to stay awake, exhausted from telling his own story. "No, though I have heard about the poem, I have not heard the work itself. And that is a good thing, for if I held that story within me, there would be no room left for my own. I must rest, my brothers, so I can begin again when the sun mounts tomorrow's morn. Peace upon you both, as you gain your rest this night."

The first rays of morning broke the stillness. The sheep stirred and stood to their feet as one. Ewes' udders bulged with milk, and their lambs jabbed the creamy stores with their mouths, demanding breakfast. The flock woke their shepherds with bleating and three men rolled from where they slept on the ground. Sabah surveyed the brightening sky and said, "My brothers, I am strangely refreshed by this new day. Who knows what joys and adventures may lie ahead of us? As you find us food and drink, let me begin my story again, shall I?"

"Yes, please, Old One—it will start us on the best foot today."

The old man began—

And so it was, that fields of green barley waved in the wind on either side of the caravan road which stretched toward the high and purple rocky cliffs ahead of Geram and Nahor. A string of eight camels departed the caravan in this plain called Gaia, east of Raqmu. They carried loads of olive-press-residue to fire the Zurrabah kilns there producing fine pottery. Those potters created bowls and platters thinner than the shell of an ostrich egg, to grace the tables of the wealthy and royal.

The extensive water system in Gaia harvested meager rains falling on the eastern hills, and the constant abundance from local springs supplemented the seasonal flow. The system's stored water efficiently irrigated the lush agriculture of Gaia's fields, in the otherwise arid and barren plain.

The closer they approached the rocks, the higher the cliffs stretched into the clear blue above. Nahor wondered at the course they were taking. "Abba, you say we go to a great city—the royal capital of our people. But we can go no farther than those cliffs. What can be there? I see no sign of a city."

"You will soon see, my son. A city lies before us, as certainly as the sun will fall beyond those rocks. And yes, it *is* a great city—greater than any you've yet seen."

"Greater than Hawara? Or even Hegra?"

Geram laughed. "It is not only greater by far than them, it is greater than anything you can imagine—greater than your richest dreams. It is an even more wonderful city than Yerushalayim—the capital of the Herodians—the Iudaean kings."

The caravan continued toward the cliffs, but Nahor clinched his eyebrows together and pouted his lips in a frown. "Abba—I still see no city—is this a *magic* city? Will Dushara make it appear out of the rocks?"

Geram laughed again. "You are not too far from the wondrous truth of it."

They drew closer to the reddish-purple cliffs, and in the plain before them stood three stone blocks—cut in the form of massive cubes. The blocks were all that remained of carving away the massive rock which once occupied the space. From their sides projected dramatic designs embossed upon the rocky faces, plastered smooth and painted in vibrant colors. The designs blazed with the red of dawn, mocked the sky with their blue, and dazzled the sun with purest white. The sight of them paralyzed Nahor's breath, his mind whirled. When he finally breathed again, he whispered, "Abba! What are those?—colored so brightly?"

"Those are the first thrones you will see of the gods—of his lordship, Dushara—and of her, the All-Powerful 'Uzza—and of his wife, 'Lat. You shall see others of their thrones, but these are magnificent, are they not? And on the mountain peaks beyond them, exposed to the heavens—under sunlight, moonlight, and starlight—are the exposure platforms used by the royal families, that the dead royals might be blessed by Dushara, His Holy Amma, and His Holy Wife."

The camel train neared the throne-blocks and Haritha, the leader of Geram's camel-string, halted the animals with a single whistle. He walked back to the camel on which Geram and Nahor sat, and commanded it to kneel. Geram dismounted and said "The caravan will continue to the city, Nahor, but we must pause here, to pay homage to the gods."

He helped his son to the ground and gave another coin to Haritha, who said, "You are too kind to me, friend. May you go in the way of the gods, and be blessed by them!"

He raised the camel, still burdened with its leather pouches of lubunah, and whistled twice to return the camel string on its journey into the city. Nahor watched the caravan cross over a low dam of mortared, dressed stones and head toward the cliff. High above, a triumphal arch of fitted stones sprang from a large niche carved into the rocks of the cliff on the right. It soared up and over the camels' path, finally descending to a niche on the left. The camel train disappeared into the shadows at the base of the cliff. Nahor gripped his father's hand, wondering what might become of him as they continued toward the city.

They walked to the stone throne of Dushara and met a priest, clad in the same striking colors as the monument behind him. The priest raised his right hand, palm turned toward them, and extended the other to the two travelers. He asked, "Do you honor the Royal Lordship of Dushara, over all the land and people of the Nabatu? And do you bow to the All-Powerful sway of His Amma 'Uzza? And do you depend upon the gracious prosperity and fertility of His Consort 'Lat?"

Geram nodded and placed three silver coins displaying the heads of King Haretat and his first queen, Khuldu, in the priest's palm. From his traveler's bag, he pulled a small wineskin and handed it over, saying, "A holy ablution for the thirst of Dushara."

The priest received it and said, "It is good. Go in His favor, my brother." The man turned away and began walking in a circle around the great and colorful stone block, chanting words unknown to Geram and Nahor.

A smile poured over Geram's face as he looked down at his son. "Now, you shall see the glory of Raqmu—the capital city of Haretat, King of the Nabatu, the King-Who-Loves-His-People." He grasped the boy's hand and led him toward the cliffs, where, at its foot, camels and horses, men and women, seemed to appear and disappear below the high, stone archway extending between two great rocks. Father and son neared the dam, and something like an immense, black snake seemed to stretch its sinuous body from the bottom of the rock-face up to the very precipice. Nahor's knuckles turned white as he gripped his father's hand yet tighter.

The closer they drew to the rock, Geram quickened his pace and the more the boy tried to slow it. The sight ahead loomed higher and broader in his eyes, and he tilted his head back, stretching his neck to see it all. The looming fear in his heart tried to close his eyes, but dropping his gaze earthward, in an instant he saw the snake become a shadowed crack in the immense rock, with travelers entering and leaving the slim passage below the stone archway at its mouth. He looked up at Geram and said, "Abba! Is this the magic way to the city? Or will the rock swallow us?"

"As I said before, you shall soon see."

They left the open plain and green fields behind them, and entered the slender, bending cleft. Deep shadows colored all in bluish lavender. The air grew cool and Nahor shivered. The farther they walked, strings of camels before and behind them, the narrower the rift seemed. The boy looked directly up and saw only a slim band of brilliant blue sky separating the two colossal walls of stone. He dropped Geram's hand and extended both arms from his sides, hoping to touch both walls. Just as he stretched them, his hand brushed the garment of a man traveling in the opposite direction, leaving the passageway. Passing them, the man swiveled his head back and glared at the boy. Nahor snapped his arms back to his sides and tried his best to be invisible.

Nahor saw a long stone box at chest-height, hugging the left wall. With no beginning and no end, the box seemed to follow them as they walked. He lightly tugged his father's robe and asked, "What is in the box, Abba?"

"That is the life—the blood—of Raqmu. The most wonderful miracle of the city is its living water—its flowing water. It not only quenches the thirst of Raqmu, it waters their gardens and fields, and takes away the city's dung and urine. It fills the dry bellies of a thousand camels a week. And you shall see it produce streams pouring from solid rock, walls of water falling from walls of stone, and even water spewing from the mouth of a stone lion clinging to the side of a cliff. This is surely a fitting capital for we Nabatu—we who *bubble up* from the ground. Place your ear on the stone box, and tell me what you hear."

The boy hesitated before walking to the conduit, curving beside the winding path. He looked back at Geram, who nodded and gestured for him to bend down. Nahor approached it with caution and laid his ear on the cold, gray slab of stone. He grinned. "I hear it! —a brook tumbles inside the box!"

They walked on and he asked, "When we reach the city, how long will we stay?"

Geram said nothing for a long time. Three strings of a dozen camels each passed them, before he said, "My business here will take just two days..."

While he drew a long breath to finish his statement, his son interjected, "We shall be home, then, before the end of the seventh day."

"No, my son. I will be home by then, but you are...already home."

Nahor's understanding could not catch the truth of his father's words. Geram stopped walking and stuck his arm out to the side, stopping his son's progress. "We will walk slowly from here—keep your eyes up, straining to see what lies ahead."

"Why Abba?"

He said nothing as they crept forward. Slowly revealing itself between the purplish walls on the path ahead, the twisting form of another snake glared with the brilliance of vermillion and rose. As they walked on, it grew fatter and kinked itself. Nahor suddenly saw they looked through the narrow crack in the rock to an open space beyond—to another, farther cliff—this one glowing in the orange-red warmth of the late afternoon. He saw wooden structures and ropes hanging from the cliff, with men standing upon the beams, working upon a monumental project. The sounds of *clink—clink—clink*—metal upon metal, and metal upon stone—echoed within the space.

13

THEY CAME TO THE end of the twisting gorge, and hearing the staccato raps, the boy asked, "Abba, what is that sound?"

"It is the sound of art and science, of royalty and commerce—that is the sound of something majestic being born."

"Being born? What is born with such a sound?"

The final curve in the path opened a crack of rose-colored daylight beyond. While they continued walking, the majestic birth revealed itself. A ruddy escarpment soared above an open plaza. High upon it, the upper portions of a magnificent edifice projected from the sheer face of the mountain. A complex network of wooden platforms sprouted from sockets cut in the rock, with twenty men standing and climbing about it. Nahor's mouth fell open, and his eyes widened in wonderment.

Men ascended and descended the framework like spiders on a wall. Using knotted cords, a few inspected and measured the capitals of columns springing out of solid rock, growing from the top down. Others struck chisels with mallets, chipping away at various features emerging from the rock face. Near the top, a bald, bearded man had the full attention of two younger men as they began finishing work on the very peak of the monument—a finial knob atop an enormous urn.

The boy and father walked to just below the massive project and stared for a long time at the industry and progress of the work. One of the younger men at the top nudged his master and nodded toward the plaza below. The master shouted down, "Are you Geram, son of Dayan?"

Geram cupped his hands to his mouth and shouted back, "I am. And you are Aslah, son of Aslah?—are you ready for my son?"

With the voice of a trumpet he asked, "What is your name, boy?"

Like his father, Nahor cupped his hands to his mouth and yelled back, "I am Nahor, son of Geram! Are you a mason?"

The man threw his head back and laughed. "Why else do you think I would be up here, boy? Do you think you can break rocks?"

"At my birth, the oracle said I would be hard as a flint. I will try."

Again, Aslah bellowed a laugh that echoed through the plaza. "Small—and hard as a flint, eh? Then you shall be called Shamir!"

"Now I am Shamir, son of Geram!"

The mason continued laughing, looped a hanging rope behind him, and jumped backward without looking, sliding down the rope at a breakneck speed. Before the boy could count to five, the mason stood beside him. He took Shamir's small hand in his bear-like paw and asked, "Will you go up there with me—to cut stone?"

"I have never been that high before—but I will go."

As Aslah led Shamir to the framework, he turned to the boy's father and winked. Then to the boy he said, "Shall we fly to the clouds, then?"

"I see no clouds today, sir."

Aslah clasped one massive arm around the boy's waist, gripped a rope with the other hand, looked up, and said, "Then the clear blue it shall be, to cap this red rock!"

He nodded to one of his young proteges above, who pushed from the structure a large counterweight of stone attached to the rope's other end. The weight pulled the rope through a pulley fixed high upon the cliff, and lifted Aslah and the boy skyward. As they ascended, Aslah felt Shamir tremble and he said, "It is easier at first if you only look up. You forget how far below you the earth falls away, and you learn to make friends with the sun, the sky, and the clouds. Their faces will shine down upon you, and you find they mean you no harm."

When the counterweight touched the earth, the pair arrived at the highest part of the framework. He stepped onto a wood plank beside the two young men and nodded to them. They rappelled earthward, leaving the bear and the boy alone. With his free hand he picked up a mallet and handed it to Shamir, who he cradled in one arm. He then selected a half-beveled iron chisel and held its sharpened end to the surface of the red sandstone.

"Strike the head of the chisel with the mallet, Shamir."

He tapped it, making a *click*.

"Yes, but much harder—we are shaping mountains, not killing scorpions! Take care that you strike it squarely, and avoid breaking my thumb!"

He struck it again, with force, a small chip of stone flying away from the mountain of rock.

"Yes, Shamir, you will do. You will become a mason—at least a stone-cutter, perhaps even a sculptor. Only time, talent, and your own ambition will prove which."

A smile broke upon the boy's face. He turned and looked below for the first time, to tell his father the news. But Geram was no longer there.

"Where is my Abba?"

"This is now your home, Shamir. We are your family. Do you know what it is we carve here?"

He shook his head, forced his eyebrows together, and said, "No. It is big...and it will be beautiful. But I know not what it is."

"This will be a fitting monument for the great king, Haretat—King of the Nabatu, Who-Loves-His-People. Have you heard of the King?"

"I knew there was a king, but I know nothing of him."

"Tomorrow, little Shamir, you shall see him! Shall we return to the earth?"

"Yes—by sliding down the rope?"

"By the rope!"

14

Shamir waited in the grand plaza, below the structure growing from the rock. His new master spoke long with three other men—one in a workman's garb of rough wool, the other two in richly-colored linen tunics and embroidered mantles. The conversation ran its lengthy course, winding through detailed technical explanations, heated arguments, and finally arriving at a long joke related by Aslah. At its conclusion, raucous laughter exploded from the quartet. They slapped each other's backs and said their farewells before leaving the plaza. Aslah started to walk off by himself, but stopped, and pivoted on his heels to look for Nahor-now-Shamir. The boy remained standing in the same place he'd left him before the long conversation.

Aslah laughed, saying, "No, I'd not forgotten you, boy. Even if I'd gone all the way home, I would have remembered that my new boy was still standing in the same place, waiting for me here. Have you seen Raqmu before?"

Shamir shook his head. "Then your eyes and your head will be filled to overflowing in the next days. Never stray too far behind me, and take my words to you seriously—unless, of course, that they are meant to be in good humor and jest. And I confess, sometimes with me it's hard to tell the difference, or so they tell me. Our work is done here for the day. Let us head homeward."

They left the right-hand end of the plaza to re-enter the continuation of the thaniya. Its turning, winding ways confused any sense of direction, but once traveling the narrow, tortuous path, its travelers were swept along at its mercy, and bound to come out at its mouth.

The sun had long since descended behind the high mountains to the west, bringing the purity of the last golden hour of daylight to Raqmu. Scattered over the cliffs of this stretch of chasm were hundreds of rectangular cavities carved into the rock—a few with arched tops. And a featureless, rectangular dressed stone occupied each niche. The blocks reminded Shamir of the small stone god to whom Geram prayed when necessary. Only these were much grander —the size of a man's torso, and even larger. Some stood in inert silence near the path, and they could be seen extending even to the top of the cliff-face.

"You've likely not seen so many *masebas*—the Hellenes call them *betyls*, and the Iudaeans say *beth-el*, meaning the 'god-dwelling.' See those up there? Those are ones of long tradition. Just simple, dressed stone, without features of any kind. A plain block of smooth stone seems a fitting resting place for a god beyond our understanding. But in the last few generations, men have not been satisfied with the ways of their elders. They have added ornaments, like two simple, horizontal bars for eyes, and a vertical bar between for a nose. And see that one? The eyes look like two stars."

Walking on, they rounded a curve. A feasting-hall's facade loomed before them and bore silent witness to its grand purpose. In this place, *marzeahs*—feasts held in remembrance of the dead—brought families together twice a year. The major feast, the *hajj*, occurred in the spring, and the lesser *'umrah* in autumn. To honor those who came before was a sacred duty.

Two colossal columns sprouted from the cliff face, extending upward many times the height of a man. They supported a finely carved gable of solid sandstone. Geometric ornaments of various types appointed the work and plaster smoothed the whole structure. A final coat of paint colored it with rich hues of purest blue and brilliant carmine above the gleaming white.

Two steps behind Aslah, Shamir slowed his pace, turning his face to keep the monument in his sight. As he came abreast of the edifice, he stopped, to gaze upon this thing of beauty and majesty. Aslah no longer heard light footsteps behind him and looked back to see the boy staring in wonder. He walked back and stood behind him, placing his hands on the boy's shoulders.

"It is a thing of beauty, is it not? They say the life of a mason is nothing but hard work and sweat, but when objects like these can spring from a man's mind, and be birthed through the mallet and chisel in his hands—that is not work. It is more like...loving a woman. Come, you must be hungry."

They walked the last curve of the cleft and emerged into the edge of a vast, open space. Though the light was failing, out of the purple shadow of night materialized a high, long wall built of dressed stones. Above the wall projected towers and spires of rock. Beyond it Shamir caught glimpses of an immense, ringed cavity carved out of a mountain. Not speaking to this point, Shamir pointed to the sight and asked in a whisper, "Master, what lies over there?"

"That is one of the greatest wonders of Raqmu. You see not much of it from out here, but that is the great, new theater of our city—cut from what was a mountain. They say ten thousands of people can sit on the pink sandstone seats there, to watch an event."

"A thee-uh-tuhr? What is that?"

"It is a place where poetry is recited, songs are sung, music is performed, and plays are presented. A play is something like poetry expressed in action. You do know what poetry is, do you not?"

"Oh yes, my Abba's uncle was a poet. He often told his poems as we sat around the fire at night. How many is ten thousands?"

"Ten thousands? Let's say men walked in a long line, each man's hand resting on the shoulder of the one ahead. If there were ten thousands of them, for the line to pass would take from noon to halfway to sunset."

Shamir's eyes grew and his mouth hung open to imagine so many filling the seats of the theater. "How did they turn the mountain into the theater?"

Aslah patted the boy on the head and shook his own. "If I answer all your questions tonight, we shall never reach home—and we shall never eat! The day tomorrow will be full. We will need full bellies tonight to strengthen us. And a night full of dreams to feed the passion of our day."

They walked on, but every few paces Shamir turned his head, looking into the darkness falling behind them, hoping yet to see his abba coming through the shadows, to take him home. He suddenly thought he saw something and jerked around, staring into the dark passage. He ran a few steps and called out, "Abba!"

Aslah stopped, but said nothing to the boy, waiting for the echo to die out between the stone walls. Shamir whispered, "Abba?"

Aslah grasped his hand and led him onward. They passed several hills covered by elegant, imposing houses built of stone, their windows glowing with the light of lamps lit within. Another path forked away into a narrow ravine and Aslah took the turn. The boy asked, "Will your sons and daughters hate me?"

Aslah stopped and turned toward him. "Will they hate you? I have no sons or daughters. But if I did, they would welcome you as one of their own."

"You have no wife, then?"

"I certainly have a wife—a wonderful woman. She is called Mashkuya."

"Then why have you no heirs?"

"We had a son, once. Little Aslah. So he was Aslah son of Aslah, just as I am. We have all been Aslah, sons of Aslah, even to six generations. The grandfather of my father's father was the first Aslah. But the little one succumbed to a fever before his first year was complete. And in the twenty-five years since, Mashkuya's womb has not again been opened."

The boy said no more.

The ravine opened to a long, sloping hillside, dotted with tents of black goat hair. Families gathered before their tents for the final meal of the day. Singing and laughter bounced from tent to tent. Aslah answered the many greetings shouted out by his neighbors. He finally turned up the slope and strode to nearly the top of the hill. Shamir struggled to keep the pace.

Arriving at a cluster of large tents he called out, "Mashkuya! We have a new boy here. He was Nahor son of Geram, and now he is called Shamir—given into our safe-keeping by his abba."

A small woman bearing a large smile and a dark woolen mantle threw back a tent-flap and emerged into the open space between the tents. She threw out her arms and ran to Shamir. "Your backbone must be scraping your navel! Sit by the fire and I will bring you bread and meat. And sit beside him, dear husband, so I can feed you as well. You were so late in coming, our other boys have eaten, and retired to the fire of old Akayus, to have their heads filled with his stories."

Shamir ate the food placed before him while the woman looked on. Her smile broadened more, seeing the boy devour her work with zeal. "If your new boy can work anything like the way he eats, he will do well with you!"

Shamir said to Aslah, "I thought you had no sons?"

"We do not. But we have two young men I have raised in apprenticeship to work stone. The tent behind you is their home, and will be yours. Now young men more than boys, they will soon move on to seek their own lives, beyond these tents. For that is the reason they came into this family—to grow, to learn—to fly away and make their own nests. Over the years, Mashkuya and I have watched six boys become men growing beards, and filled with the desire to find wives. They now count among themselves thirteen of their own children—and the eldest among them boasting two grandchildren!"

Mashkuya sat beside Aslah and leaned her small frame against his rock-cut bulk. She hummed to him a gentle tune, her private love-greeting, the intimate, secret words known only to Aslah. Though he had seen well more than fifty years, and she more than forty, the two sat perched together like a pair of young palm-doves, cooing their songs to each other, their necks entwining.

After the man and the boy devoured the last morsel of meat and the last crumb of bread, Aslah said, "Shamir, tomorrow you shall see the city in all its glory. The King-Who-Loves-His-People—Haretat —will ride his white horse along the Colonnade, his hand extending the blessings of Dushara upon the tens of thousands of Nabatu crowded along the way. And I have heard from my contacts at the Royal Court, the King's new queen will accompany his ride. After the tragedy befalling his Khuldu, it is good to hear of the King beginning his life again—to find love, and all the blessings that follow it."

The boy looked up from his meal. "A new Queen?"

"She has taken the royal name 'Shuqilat' and is of the same royal family from which Aeneas arose to become Haretat, or Aretas, as the Hellenes call him. Some said the King would never find love, or a new queen again, after his beloved Khuldu died. To lose the amma of his heirs was a great blow to him."

Mashkuya enclosed Aslah's meaty hand in her diminutive two and said, "I have heard, husband, that many years ago, the King knew Shuqilat as a girl, and was quite fond of her, but since then had not seen her until recently—when she had flowered into feminine beauty."

"Yes, I have heard as much—that while still in the throes of two-years' grief, he visited her family for a change of perspective, and, not even recognizing her as the same girl, he was struck anew by her considerable charm. Within a week, he announced she would become the next Royal Consort, and the only woman to share his bed."

The indigo shadows of night hid the black tents, while, from fires scattered over the hillside, curls of smoke spiraled up into the starry sky. As night descended, the voices heard around fires exchanged their bright, bold garb of daylight for subdued, evening wear. The jokes, coarse rhymes, and laughter faded, and the soft, sweet lyrics of love overpowered them.

Shamir lay back upon the stone bench and yawned. He slipped into deep slumber, and dreamed of his Amma, holding him tight against her breast. Mashkuya tilted her face up to kiss her husband and whispered, "I will carry the boy to his bed. You can find our two story-hounds at the fire of Akayus—tell them a small brother has joined their tent, and not to waken him when they return. When you are finished, you will find me warming the bed in your own tent."

She rose from beside him, and with the strength of an amma's love scooped up Shamir, his legs dangling from her arms. Still sleeping, he snuggled himself closer to her warmth, and clung to her. She laid him on cushions in the tent of his new home, and left a lamp burning on the small table just inside the tent-flap.

Upon Aslah's return, the couple occupied themselves until long after the stars of midnight, continuing their attempts to plant the seed of the next generation in the womb of Mashkuya.

15

IN THE SEMI-DARKNESS of predawn, Shamir woke early, as was his custom. He lay on his back, looking up at the dark material of the tent, trying to remember where he was. He knew it was not the tent of his amma, as it did not carry the delight of her fragrance. And it did not resemble the tent of his abba, made from the finest quality goat's-hair, supported by nicely carved acacia poles.

My Abba?

There was something about his abba he could not quite remember. They journeyed together to Raqmu. He said on the trip he would conduct business, but also it had to do with him—Nahor. He said his son would do well there, with a new life, unencumbered by the shame of his past.

The past? A new life?

Shamir started to shake and sat bolt-upright on the thick carpet floor of the tent. Looking around him, he saw two other figures lying in the tent, and covered with blankets. He could almost make out the face of one near him—a boy older than himself, perhaps thirteen or fourteen. The other, fully beneath the covers, snored more like a man than a boy. He recalled the events of the previous day.

I remember arriving at Raqmu...Abba's oblations...the priest. Then the long, winding cleft in the rock. And the rock being carved—the temple, or memorial. And the man on the cliff...he said he was Aslah? He let me hit the chisel with his hammer. Then Abba was gone. Did the man say I have a new family?

In a panic, Shamir stood, ready to bolt from the tent and run home. But where was home now? He lifted the entrance flap and looked out. Dozens of tents dotted the slope of the hillside, with the haze of morning cooking fires drifting among them. In the distance, scores of stone buildings crowded together, and on the road in the far mist, a few vendors carried their wares to market stalls. He dropped the flap and sat again, waiting for the sun to rise.

With the first sun-rays hitting the hillside, the boy nearest Shamir sat up, raised his arms above his head, and yawned. He clasped his hands above him and pulled them against each other, cracking and popping the joints of his shoulders and back. Blinking in the early light, he looked absently about him in the tent, and spied Shamir— awake and standing at the tent's entrance.

"Wabu—look!—the boy 'Sunshine' is awake—and up before us. You better get up now—you don't want him to catch the sun by the tail before us, do you?"

The other stopped snoring, stirred under his covers and finally pulled them down from his face. He sat up and mumbled, "Heh?"

"I said, look who's awake—it's Sunshine!"

The other boy, sixteen years and with the sparse beginnings of a beard, rubbed his eyes with the heels of his hands and said, "Not Sunshine...I think Aslah said he is Shamir."

The younger boy laughed. "Hah! So you're the Shamir? And no larger than a barley-corn! I suppose you sleep in a bed of wool, hid in a lead box! Well, you better get used to sleeping in a tent now."

Shamir said, "I always sleep in a tent—why do you say a lead box?" And their words remained cryptic to him.

After breaking their fast with boiled eggs and portions of yesterday's bread, Aslah sent his two young proteges to their work in the city. Wabu, the eldest, trained for the finished dressing of stone to be used in royal building projects—at the palace and temples. He would soon be his own man, pitching his own tent, and looking for a mate with which to grow his family. His younger 'brother,' Hartath, apprenticed as a plasterer and fine painter. He hoped, one day, to contract work on the *marzeah* halls of Raqmu's wealthiest citizens, coating the carved halls with a smooth white undercoat and then finishing them with painted murals depicting gardens and vineyards, birds and animals, gods and goddesses.

Only Aslah, Mashkuya, and Shamir remained sitting around the dwindling fire. She looked across the fire at the forlorn boy on the bench and patted the seat next to her, saying, "Would you sit next to me Shamir? Or should I call you Nahor?"

Before Shamir could answer, Aslah said, "He is now Shamir, Mashkuya. While he remains Nahor to the world outside, he will be to us Shamir. We have a new boy in our family, and he has a new name. It is a noble name."

Shamir glanced away from them, and swiveled his head, looking and hoping to see something—anything—he remembered. With nothing familiar, he stared down at his feet. His shoulders drooped and his head hung. He determined he would not cry, but when a tear escaped from his left eye, he resolved he would not make the sound of crying.

I know Abba will come for me again. And he will take me home. Back to my family. Back to Amma...where is my Amma?

Mashkuya stood and walked around the fire to sit on the bench beside Shamir. She sat there for some time, before slowly wrapping her arm around the boy. His body shook with silent weeping, and he leaned over, and into her. She tightened her arm around him, pulling him closer. Her other arm wrapped around him, and he began weeping openly. She whispered to him, "Shhh...shhh...I know...I know..."

He lay across her lap, and she patted and rubbed his back. When his weeping subsided, and his shaking stopped, he sat up again, and drying his eyes, apologized, "I don't remember your name."

"I am Mashkuya. Although that man on the other side of the fire calls me *Shushil*, his 'Little Dove.' Is that not a silly name? What would you like to call me?"

"Mashkuya will do."

"I like that, too."

Aslah said, "Come sit by me, boy, we have much to discuss."

Mashkuya led him by the hand back to Aslah, who held out his arms to him, lifted him from the ground and placed him on his right knee. He said, "There is much we do not know about you, young man, and much you do not know of us. But these things are not as important as what lies ahead. We can know all these other things in due time, if you wish. But today, we have important work ahead. Before we start, is there anything you wish to ask me?"

The boy said, "What is *the Shamir*? And why did your other boys say I sleep in a lead box? And why do you call me that?"

Aslah laughed long and hard. He said, "Those boys of mine will probably find you to be the easy target of their jest. In their own time, they were in the same place as you are now—lost, without a past that continues forward, with a future yet to be discovered. And their elders—the boys before them, who are now successful men— badgered them without mercy. But I think you will find their jollity is merely in fun, and not meant to ridicule or demean you. In time, I believe you and they will become brothers, though their time left with this family grows shorter as the days progress."

"But you did not answer my question..."

Aslah laughed again. "Right you are! The Shamir. Let me think... I believe the Iudaean King Shl'mo, a thousand years ago, sought to build for their god Yah, the temple planned by his father, Da'wid. Their god specified that no sound of an iron tool—neither chisel nor hammer—should be heard at the building site. Since anyone could remember, rumors abounded concerning something called the Shamir—a mystical, maybe mythical, entity that was said to cut the hardest stone by its mere glance. Some say Shl'mo found it and used it to trim and dress the temple's stones."

Shamir's eyes grew and a nervous smile appeared as he whispered, "What was the Shamir like?"

"No one knows for certain. It was said to be much harder than a flint, thus the name. Even harder than the most durable stone. Supposedly, it is no larger than a barley-corn. And some think it was green."

"But what was it?"

"There are those who claim it was a unique substance—a peculiar mineral. But others swear it was something alive, like a worm, able to chew its way through stone."

Shamir asked "Where did it come from?" and then he leaned closer to Aslah, supporting his chin on his palm. He studied Aslah's face as the story continued.

"Whether it be animal or mineral, all seem to believe that when the earth was created—at the last flicker of twilight, on the last day of creating—the miraculous Shamir was made from the final, fragrant fumes of creation."

"Do those Iudaeans still have it?"

Aslah laughed to see the boy's fascination. "No, they don't have it —if they ever did."

"Then where might it be?"

Aslah shook his head at Shamir's naiveté. "It is most likely a myth —an old man's story to tell around the fire at night. But if it *were* *true*, it would be a great wonder, would it not? We could throw away our hammers and chisels and create the greatest works from stone ever seen or imagined—without so much as a drop of sweat!"

Part Two

—Love Lost—

16

AND SO IT WAS that at the age of majority—eighteen years—Shamir followed his master Aslah along the curving pavement that skirted the heights they called *Ni'mah-Attiru*—Prosperity Hill—the neighborhood of Raqmu's wealthy. The hill's proximity to the Colonnaded Avenue, the temples, the nymphaeum, the markets, and most importantly, the flowing water system, made it the obvious location for building grand estates. And with the royal palaces and civic buildings a stone's throw across the river bed, the apparatus of political and economic power lay within easy reach.

The path around the perimeter of the knoll led to a fine row of *bet dzikarun*—while not the largest remembrance halls in Raqmu, they possessed some of the finest design and execution to be found in all of Nabataea. In this valley of remembrance, the two men passed fifteen or twenty such halls—all but a handful active with celebrants. The gathered groups bubbled with conversation, and music floated on the air.

At length, Aslah and Shamir came to their destination, the holy hall of remembrance—or as the Hellenes would put it, the tomb—of their host's family. The wealth of Manotu's family found its most prominent and lavish display in the excavation, construction and decoration of this hall. The hall and its walled courtyard floated twenty steps above the valley's paved path. While the men climbed the steps carved into the sandstone bedrock, Shamir took note of the precision and care taken to form them. Arriving at the upper level, they presented their bronze invitation tokens to the hired gatekeeper, who greeted them and allowed them entrance.

They slipped through the narrow portal in a high, carved-rock wall and entered the open space of a courtyard, a considerable area of about thirty paces wide by fifty deep. Aslah pointed out the court-yard's various features to his young protege.

"Look at these hexagonal tiles of fine limestone—more than a pace across—they cover the entire plaza. And these sidewalls were carved in place from the cliff's sandstone face on both sides of the plaza. They must stand a man-and-a-half high."

Manicured plants lined both walls, their splashes of deep emerald contrasting with the rose and carnelian of the rock. Small fig, willow, and olive trees grew luxuriantly in large, baked-clay pots. Flowers the color of sunrise studded a pomegranate and the fig held small, unripe fruit.

Aslah pointed up the cliff and said, "You cannot see it from here, but far above the hall, a large cistern collects the rainwater running from the cliff, and the mountain above it. The cistern supplies water to the hall by a clay pipeline that ends at the little waterfall splashing into this pool." Iridescent fishes the size of a man's hand swam in the pool's waters.

Fountains also filled ceremonial wash basins on either side of the courtyard. Between the high side walls at their ends away from the cliff, a waist-high wall of balusters and railing allowed a panoramic view of the valley—to the fine estates on the knoll, the busy Colon-nade, and beyond.

Shamir performed a cursory mental calculation and concluded ten skilled men must have worked at this site five years—quarrying and leveling the courtyard, carving the *mashkeba* and the *srihayya*. Manotu's family possessed more wealth than he first guessed.

Aslah recognized Manotu's large frame from behind, and pointed his young apprentice toward the man. He told Shamir, "I would know that bear-of-a-man anywhere!"

He whispered back, "What should I say, Aslah?"

"Just don't stray from what you know to be the truth, and you will be fine."

The sun had not yet set and the sky still waited to trade its azure garb for a veil of lavender, but the Valley of Remembrance already sank into the shadow of the Amma of Cisterns, the large mountain to the west. Only the diffuse vermillion glow from the topmost tips of the eastern peaks still illuminated the plaza.

Manotu stood facing away from the two men, and Aslah not wishing to interrupt the man's conversation, approached from the rear. He waited for an ebb in the interchange.

Shamir stroked his scant, young beard and adjusted his stance from foot to foot as he awaited his master's introduction. As a child he attended such gatherings with his family, but he knew this one would be steeped in serious talk of society, politics, art, even philosophy and religion. If he comported himself well, he might gain favor in the eyes of well-placed people, perhaps the court, or even the royal family. He saw opportunity dancing lightly over the heads of these gathered.

Clad in a Hellenic-styled tunic of fine, maroon wool, Manotu stood beside his daughter. She wore a carmine silk peplos over a white linen chiton to her feet.

The man spoke with animated fervor and passion as one of his guests—Rav'el, the king's architect—listened intently. The conversation concerned economic matters entirely foreign to Shamir's experience. Much of the terminology was unknown to him, and he waited, hoping to not be called into the discourse and so display his ignorance.

In front of Shamir, and directly behind their host, his master waited with the cool patience of an elephant. Shamir thought, *Of course he possesses a bottomless cistern of quiet resolve—how else could he have sculpted the three-hundred and six limestone elephant heads that keep watch from atop the columns of the King's Great Hall?—I will never have such patience myself.*

Manotu and his daughter faced away from Shamir, but she occasionally turned her head, facing either her abba or his guest as they spoke, giving him only brief glimpses of her profiles, both right and left. His skills of sculpting allowed him to mentally combine these partial images to imagine the full-face view with depth and contour. Her face, while not starkly beautiful, beguiled him. The slight asymmetry of her lower lip lodged in his mind. He wondered how accurately his imaginings matched the actual face of the young woman.

The architect then asked her a question, to which she responded. Shamir could not quite hear the words of her brief reply, but it produced immediate and deep laughter from both her questioner and her abba. The architect laughed long and hard, bending over at the waist, holding his sides. As the mirth finally ebbed, he took a deep breath, let out a long, low sigh and wiped the tears from his eyes. He gripped his host's forearm and said, "Manotu, this young woman of yours will keep some lucky man's heart filled with jollity from sunup to sundown! Has she been betrothed?"

"While she has reached that perfect ripeness of twenty years, and has much to offer, she has not yet found her match—her equal."

"I trust you will require a high price for the privilege of taking her hand. She is the perfect Persian peach—one in ten-thousand. If I was a younger man, and yet unattached, I would long to have this woman on my arm, walking into the court of the King."

"Yes, Rav'el, the man who would be her suitor will pay a stiff price for the privilege. But it is not simply a matter of his wealth—for the decision lies in her own hands. The high price is simply a method of weeding out contenders not seriously committed to appreciating her substantial qualities."

"Thank you, again, for your invitation to these festivities, Manotu. We will speak again later, but now I must meet your other guests. Speaking of that, please introduce me to the two behind you."

Manotu and his daughter turned to see who Rav'el indicated. Shamir now saw her face-to-face, and realized how far he underestimated the charms she possessed. Her beauty lay not simply in the proportions and complexion of her features, but her countenance—her expressions—enchanted him. A smile, filled with mischief and delight, danced upon her lips. A playful joy glimmered in her clear, green eyes, and her nose twitched with the nervous excitement of a rock coney. Her lustrous, black hair peeked out from the edges of a purple silk scarf, framing the whole.

"Rav'el, this is one of the master masons of the valley—Aslah, son of Aslah. He has worked some of the most important projects of the past three decades, and was an instrumental consultant for the remembrance hall in which you now stand. Perhaps you know of him."

Rav'el grasped one of Aslah's hands and said, "Yes, yes—of course! I did not recognize you at first, please forgive me. You are responsible for the elephant heads of the sacred plaza at the King's Great Hall and Capitol, are you not? Truly a great work! And if I remember accurately, we worked together a brief time at the renovation of Dushara's temple throne, did we not?"

"Yes, we did. The temple was a worthy effort. It could not have happened without the King's gracious support. And how is he?—Haretat, that is? I hear he occasionally yet grieves for Khuldu, but that Shuqilat now makes it bearable for him."

Rav'el lowered his voice and said, "Only our five pairs of ears need hear this...but it is said among the court he can sometimes be heard weeping and calling his first queen's name as he wanders the palace roof in the darkest hours of the night. But Shuqilat soon finds him in his deep sadness, and with her great love and substantial charms comforts him. Who could be touched by that young woman and not forget all past loves—or even one's own name?"

Manotu answered, "I must agree—she has become quite a woman. Before she wore the crown of the Nabatu, our family and hers were familiar. My daughter and Shuqilat lived nearly as sisters, their hearts entwined. It was difficult for my daughter when she lost her to Haretat and the royal life."

"And the young man?—you have not yet made the introduction."

"Forgive me, brother, this is Aslah's latest discovery—Nahor son of Geram—a protege of which he is duly proud. He says Nahor will soon be the most-sought mason in Raqmu."

Shamir bowed to Rav'el, and with his face to the ground, grinned, hearing of his enviable reputation. He attempted to wipe the smile from his face as he raised again, but was not entirely successful. Rav'el grasped his hand and lifted him to full height, asking him, "Nahor, do you believe this? Will you soon be a great mason?"

"He thought, *I want to be confident, but perhaps I should express humility. Yet if I don't tell him I believe in my own skills, he might pass me over when looking for artists.*

So he said, "I defer to my master's estimation of my skills. He is the master mason and has seen much. If he believes it, I must as well."

Manotu jumped into the interchange. "Well said, Nahor! What do you think, Rav'el? A man of such diplomacy as well as skill with stone might gain favor in the court."

"Perhaps. Some might be swayed by clever answers, but true accomplishments will always outweigh cunning. I look forward to seeing your work, Nahor. And I am sure we will meet again."

Shamir's face flushed red as he felt the mild reproof of his discovered calculations. Rav'el turned away to greet other guests and Manotu excused himself as he clasped their hands. "Brothers, I must attend to final preparations for the feast. Please enjoy yourselves and my other guests. Thank you for coming. Daughter, will you assist me?"

She nodded, and as they walked away, she briefly turned her face again to Shamir and smiled as her eyes met his.

17

THE MASTER MASON AND his disciple joined the others as they gathered before the entrance to the hall. Looking upward, the two men admired the fine facade. Aslah spoke in a low voice to Shamir and pointed out the many details—

"In many respects, this hall mirrors most others carved in recent decades—a vertical and planar presentation, topped by a pair of symmetric, stepped series, representing the divine descent to men, and men's attempts to ascend to the divine. Below that and centered at the bottom, the corniced moulding announces the entrance to the inner chambers. The rectangular portal itself is generous in size— the height of two men and wide enough for three entering abreast. And though not needed for structural support, because of course, the whole is cut from the rock of the cliff, the two pairs of false-columns frame the work with a sense of substance and stability. See how the false-lintel joining the two nearest columns projects the gabled pediment above? And the entire piece is surmounted by a glorious urn, signifying the treasure of honor accumulated by past generations."

He looked back at his protege, making eye contact, and then continued. "But Shamir, what sets this work apart from so many like it is the specific stone from which it was worked. The rock here, more so than anywhere else in the valley, possesses this striking variegated appearance, like multi-colored embroidery—the very reason for the City's name—Raqmu. See how the layers contrast and compliment each other? Rose, pink, crimson and cream curve and snake their way across the face of the cliff!"

He swept his arms in wide, sinuous gestures.

"While most remembrance halls are smoothly plastered and then painted with broad fields and bands of ultramarine, yellow, maroon, and pure white, those who planned and executed this piece relied upon the sumptuous, natural attributes provided by the earth itself."

The reverberation of a small gong captured the attention of those gathered. The officiating priest of the feast stood at the hall's entrance and intoned a prayer, invoking the blessing of Dushara upon the celebration.

"O, Great Lord Of the Sharas, we humbly seek your divine presence at this *marzeah*, this confraternity, this feast for the dead. May you be filled with joy as we honor you, and honor those from whose loins we sprang. The family of Manotu honors you, and these, his adopted kin honor you in like manner. May your Holy Amma and your Holy Consort find joy here as well."

He bathed his arms up to the elbows in the cistern basin to the left of the entrance, took up his censer and dropped onto its red coals, tears of lubunah. As he swung the metal urn like a pendulum before the crowd, clouds of blue-white smoke poured from its perforations, and the brilliant fragrance of lubunah awakened those in the plaza. He entered the hall and filled it with the sacred perfume. As the guests filed in behind him, each stopped briefly at the other basin to cleanse their hands and arms before entering.

Aslah and Shamir entered as the last two in the group of thirteen. Still lit by the reddening rays of the dying sun, the chamber's magnificence overwhelmed Shamir. The room's walls and ceiling had been intentionally carved to maximize the swirl and sweep of the color-banded layers of sandstone. He imagined that a flood of swirling blood and streams of wine immersed him—swallowed him —in waves of crimson and coral, capped with peaks of pink and creamy foam.

A reddish light now filled the interior, bathing the heads and hearts of the attendees with warm anticipation. Like most *tricliniums* in Raqmu, the reclining couches were carved from solid bedrock and lined the three walls away from the entrance. Knee-high from the floor, they sloped slightly away from the serving tables which stood in the midst of the chamber. Brilliantly-colored silk cushions, stuffed with horsehair, lay in luxurious piles upon the couches.

Manotu's daughter, his uncle, and the king's architect reclined at their places of honor along the back wall, leaving spaces for the priest and Manotu. Aslah directed Shamir to their places near the center of the left wall. As the young man lay down on the deep blue silk cushions, he took in the full visual sweep of his surroundings. The sandstone walls pulsed with the glow of the sunset's apricot, peach, and lilac. Looking out the hall's entrance and the two windows beside it, his view included portions of the courtyard, the low wall at its far end, and Raqmu's valley far beyond. He had never seen such a sight, and his head and heart spun with the majesty of it.

Watching his disciple soak in the beauty, Aslah whispered to him. "It is magnificent, is it not? This is why we work. This is why we create such things. You are familiar with the outward spectacle of public monuments, but until tonight, you have not seen such beauty, available to only a few. To produce such a masterpiece requires grand ideas, unswerving commitment to the dream, years of sweat and pain, and the firm loyalty of a wealthy patron. Such beauty does not come cheaply."

In an even lower whisper, Shamir said, "I could not imagine such beauty exists—and made by the hands of men!"

"I think you misunderstand, Shamir. No, the beauty, the magnificence—the majesty—of what you see could only have been made by the hand of *Hayyasa*—The Mercy. Men can only sense the beauty that is already there—frozen and waiting inside the stone—and then cut away that which is not the beauty, to release it into the world so the eyes can see it. So others can appreciate it."

"*The Mercy*? I have not heard you speak before of this Hayyasa. Is this another name for Dushara? Or his All-Powerful Amma, *Uzza*?"

"Look—the feast is about to begin. We will speak of this another time..."

The priest stepped over the couches at the rear wall and stood near the wooden double-doors at the wall's center. He took the bronze gong, no larger than his outstretched hand, and struck it once with a padded mallet. The bright '*clang!*' startled the celebrants out of their conversations, and they gave him their attention. He said, "Manotu welcomes you to this celebration, in the authority of Dushara, the power of his Amma 'Uzza, and the prosperity of his Consort 'Lat. May they bless this joyful assembly and ..."

The priest droned on in a well-rehearsed supplication to the three major divinities of the Nabatu, entirely losing Shamir's attention, as well as that of the others. He scanned the other two walls of reclining couches and observed those lying there. Directly opposite him, a finely-dressed man of middle years conversed freely with a young woman half his age, who punctuated the man's lengthy questions with giddy, two-word responses and staccato giggles. The man's back faced another woman, his own age, also finely-dressed, her face pinched and peeved. The conversation continued, her consternation deepened to disgust, and she turned her own back to the man.

The priest ended his monotoned monologue and opened the two doors into the burial chamber hidden beyond them. Manotu and the priest each carried a lamp-stand with three lights into the dark space, illuminating the spare interior. The room was empty except for two niches carved into the back wall, and three grave-marking slabs on the stone floor below them. At the head of each grave slab, toward the room's center, were three bowl-shaped depressions carved into the floor. The men briefly returned to the banquet room, retrieving the censer, two blocks of black stone, and three bowls. The priest again filled his censer and perfumed the place of death.

Through the billowing smoke, Manotu could be seen placing the stone blocks in their niches. From one of the bowls, the priest sprinkled wine upon both stone gods, pouring the remainder into the floor depression on the left. He poured water from the second bowl into the pit in the middle, and from the last he poured some grain into that on the right. The two men returned to the dining area and the priest announced, "The gods and Manotu's forebears are now filled. Let us eat as well—to our health, and prosperity!"

Manotu's daughter lit the many lights of the lamp-stands in each corner of the room, bringing the room from the fading glow of twilight to a brightly-flickering warmth. Her father stepped to the center of the room between the serving tables, took a large flask of wine, and began filling the small drinking bowls of his guests, one by one. When he finished, he raised his own bowl and said, "I thank you, my family and my guests, for joining me in so honoring those who came before me. May you all enjoy the harvests they reaped, and may we leave as great a legacy. *Dkyryn!*" They all drank together, savoring the fine quality of the wine and responded, *"Ba'ly!".* With the bowls drained, Manotu threw his bowl with force to the floor, its shards shattering and clattering on the stone. The others followed him in the practice, to secure the blessings he pronounced upon them.

Shamir hesitated to throw his own bowl, and whispered to Aslah next to him, "Master, these bowls are of exquisite quality—so thin, and beautiful—I cannot do it!"

Aslah insisted, "Throw it—and with great force!—or you offend our host."

He closed his eyes as he hurled the bowl into the center, where it crashed against the side of a serving table, some of the fragments flying out onto the celebrants. Those touched by the small shards applauded his effort and the vigorous explosion of pottery. A strange sense of cleansed relief replaced his reluctance.

From a small side-room, Manotu, his daughter, and two servants brought large platters of meat and fowl to their guests, serving each one in turn. They left the platters on the serving tables and brought out yet more trays and bowls of food from the small room. The aroma of delicacies filled the chamber, and their substance filled the guests.

Conversation, wine, debate, food, and joking intermingled among those present. For two hours, various courses of culinary delights were brought to them, and in those same two hours, friendships were forged, the past remembered, new partnerships birthed, and romances kindled.

18

WITH THE GUESTS' APPETITES sated, the serving tables were cleared. Some began speaking in hushed tones, and the phrase *"The Song"* was heard more than once. Along the back wall, those in the places of highest honor moved toward the corners, leaving a space open before the burial chamber. Manotu's daughter, with help from the two servants, moved a red-lacquered panel, taller than a man and with gilt designs, to block the space in front of the tomb's open doors. The lamp-stands in the corners of the room were extinguished, save one, which they moved behind the panel. Only the eerie and indirect light from beyond it bathed the room in muted glow.

For a long while, the group remained in hushed suspense. Shamir leaned over to Aslah and whispered, "What is this? For what are we waiting?"

"I forgot that you've not been to Manotu's *marzeah* feasts before. We wait for...*The Song.*"

"Which song is that? I know such feasts have a time of music, but I've not heard there is one, specific song among them. What is the song we shall hear?"

"The question, Shamir, should not be '*what* is the song,' but rather, '*who*' is The Song?"

The young man's eyes narrowed, and his brows crowded together. "This is a perplexing question—*who* is the song? I do not understand..."

Aslah turned fully toward him and spoke deliberately. "Though easily stated, the question is not easily answered. She, whom we shall hear, *is* The Song. And why she is called that, you will only know by your own hearing. Occasionally an experience trumps, and even defies, all verbal explanation and description. On this night, you shall gain your own experience, and form your own memory, of hearing The Song."

While not yet understanding, Shamir asked no more questions.

With all preparations complete, silence stilled the hall. Into the quiet space, three figures stepped from the courtyard's entrance. In the dim light, there appeared two young women and a man. The man held a double-piped *aulos* to his lips and began a slow, melodious tune, the longer pipe providing a bass-drone. The music haunted, and stirred something deep within Shamir. He closed his eyes.

The woman nearest him began strumming a seven-string *barbiton* harp, and the other bowed her single-strung *rebabah*. The simplicity of the strain gave way to rich harmonies, then detailed counterpoint. Each musician took their turn, flying, soaring on dizzying cadenzas, finally coming back to rest with the initial, unison melody. The women joined the tune with their voices, humming the same.

Shamir placed a red silken bolster against the wall and propped himself against it. As the music swelled, in pure, silver voice they sang in wordless accompaniment. The voices soothed and moved him. He heard some in the gathering singing along with the women, and knowing the song, they began adding its lyrics. It was a song of request, a song of longing. They sang,

"Sweet bird, sweet bird of freedom,

The Stone Cutter

Look down upon us, far from rest—

Soar on wind's bright flight
to our fathers' home, Dear Song,
Where in liberty we sang you,
where our freedom flowed
in singing you.

There, under bluest sky,
red sand hides our wealth
There, to desert wind's roar,
our infants nurse and sleep.

Walking, riding, always moving,
no man enslaves us
by his bonds
We rest not at the destination,
Journey is our home
We find not peace at destination,
Journey is our home.

The liquid treasure,
living, flowing,
Lies hid in desert sand
The heartless desert kills all others,
kills our every foe.

They say we have no root
—have no root—
are rootless like the dunes
But our roots are in the knowing
—in the knowing—
Journey is our home

Journey is our home.

Come, sweet bird,
       sweet bird of freedom bright,
Guide our steps
       and guard our night."

The singing faded, and the instruments slowed their melody, dropping out one-by-one. At last, the double-flute played alone and brought the song to a close.

Shamir leaned toward Aslah and whispered, "This was wonderful, but I thought you said it would be one woman..."

Aslah put a finger to his lips, and with obvious intent, nodded toward the red panel in front of the burial space. Shamir followed his gaze and waited. The flute player began again, floating a different melody on the air. The women accompanied him, but this time, with a small hand-drum and finger cymbals. The music hovered through the chamber, solemnity and beauty riding upon it. His eyes drifted away from the red panel, but something moving slowly in the light behind, fixed his eyes back upon it. Shadows played at the edge of the panel.

A metal object—its rim silvery and glinting in the lamp-light—peeked out from behind the panel's edge. It moved with slow purpose in a circular arc, gradually exposing more of its shape. Synchronized to the music's rise and fall, the circles expanded, revealing the object as a silver disc, the size of a serving platter and embossed with symbols suggestive of the moon. Slender fingers held it from behind, and continued moving it in ever-larger, hypnotic spirals.

The motion slowed, and as it ceased, a form glided out from behind the panel—the face hiding perfectly behind the moon-disc. A diaphanous pure-blue silk draped the woman's body. Her free arm and hand undulated like gentle waves on a pool—rhythmic, measured and musical. The timbrel and cymbals continued, but the flute ended its hymn, focusing yet more attention on the figure. The free hand joined its twin at the disc's rim, and together, they swayed and danced with the disc in ever-dilating loops.

The outward-coiling circles gradually revealed her face from behind the edges of the disc. A partially transparent, white veil of silk cascaded over her face from black hair above. Lamps behind the panel lit the gauze in such a way as to mostly obscure her features. Shamir willed his eyes to look beyond the veil, to see the face.

Powdered lapis-stone colored the upper lids of her eyes a vivid sapphire, the lower lids green with malachite, and her lips glowed with the red iridescence of crushed pearls mixed with the blood of pomegranates. Her face, lightly dusted with more crushed pearl, glimmered in the light. Three bright-blue feathers, each the size of a fingernail, adorned the outside of the veil, trailing down from her eye like jeweled tears.

A voice, almost inaudible at first, began to permeate the chamber. Without words, and seeming to have no source, the voice rose slowly, like mist from an oasis on a cold morning. It hovered in the midst of the room before drifting out, to enter and en-trance each ear. Though no words yet graced the song, it whispered with lyrical clarity to each heart.

Slight motions began to stir her lips, and the bodiless voice float-ed toward the woman, finding her mouth and joining it. Word and melody merged as one, and the lyrics of The Song took shape. She sang,

> *"Set me, like a seal, over your heart,*
> *like a seal upon your arm;*
> *For love is strong as death,*
> *for love is strong as death.*
>
> *Its jealousy as fierce as the grave,*
> *Its flashes burn like fire,*

like a mighty flame,
the very flame of the divine.

Many waters cannot quench love;
rivers cannot sweep it away,
nor floods drown it.

If a man—
if a man offered
For Love
All the wealth of his house,
it would be utterly despised.
He would be laughed to shame;
it would be far too lacking
For Love."

The Song flowed on, relating the tale of a woman's pure love for her man, and his for her— a Queen and her King. The stanza *Set me like a seal...* returned as a refrain throughout, proclaiming the peerless power of love.

Shamir forgot where he was, and began moving his body with The Song. He no longer sensed he sat on a cushion, on a stone couch carved from the earth's bulk, but felt himself levitated, hovering somewhere, far beyond the marzeah. He dreamed he danced among the stars, The Song his partner, swinging and swaying before him. Her garments billowed about her, their hems and folds brushing his face, his arms. They not only danced but lived an entire lifetime together, somewhere beyond the milky road, in the indigo of a midnight sky.

He felt a tap on his arm and jerked his eyelids open, to see Aslah looking at him with puzzled eyes. All the guests engaged in conversation, and all the lamps glowed again with flames, lighting the room with a warm brilliance. He blinked his eyes twice and sat up straight, rubbing his face with his hands. Looking over to where he last saw The Song, the panel was gone and he could once again see into the burial chamber. The guests of honor—Manotu and his daughter, the uncle, the priest and the architect—had resumed their places along the back wall. He whispered to Aslah, "What happened?... Where did she go?...Is it over?"

Aslah laughed. "I should have known you would not be prepared for the experience. Between the wine and The Song, you had no chance. This was like throwing a mouse between a leopard and a lioness. Look awake, if you can. They are about to serve the last course. I hear the King has sent over some of the best fruit from his orchards, and the finest of wines from his cellar."

The best of all the best was again served personally by Manotu and his daughter. They drank again to the glories of the family of Manotu, and cast their bowls with vigor to shatter upon the floor. Sweet juice from peaches, pomegranates and apricots ran down Shamir's chin, wetting and staining the front of his tunic. The conversations continued into the night, and the young man felt filled to the brim, in head, in heart, and in stomach.

The priest stepped to the center of the room and stretching his arms wide, pronounced a benediction upon the guests, granting them all peace, prosperity, and happiness. With nothing more to be said or done, one-by-one they left the dining chamber, to mill about on the plaza for a few moments, before finally leaving for their own homes, and sleep.

19

The guests exchanged final farewells and Shamir stood by himself near the low stone wall. He looked out into the black night, lost in sensate memories of the past four hours. On his tongue still tingled the ruby clarity of the last wine, and it yet sparkled in the silver cup of his mind's eye. An incandescent vision of The Song battered his heart. Her pliant hand—waving, weaving at the end of a lithe, slender arm—to cup in its palm a liquid lyric, surrendering it to his aching ears. The fragments of lyric dripped down, deep inside the caverns within, pooling somewhere at the bottom of his soul.

An evening breeze ruffled the hair on his arms, bringing him back to the present moment. The crests of wind wafted the lingering scent of the lavish essence of lubunah. He looked toward Prosperity Hill, and farther, to the very center of Raqmu.

Pinpoints of orange and yellow light flickered to life here and there from lamps in the temples, the civic buildings, and in a thousand homes scattered across the valley. Along the Colonnade, flaming braziers of bronze illuminated the avenue from the Royal Quarter all the way to Dushara's throne. He watched as the curving line of departing guests—from this celebration and dozens of others—lit the paved path with the dim glow of the lamps they held. Numerous, chattering conversations faded as they receded into the night. Aslah, one of the last to leave, concluded his own conversation with Manotu near the entrance to the hall.

Manotu's daughter glided up behind Shamir and in a low voice said, "It is beautiful, yet solemn, is it not?"

The unexpected voice broke his reverie. "What?"

"She stepped beside him, the delicate fabric of her garments brushing his coarse tunic. "See the departing guests? The little splashes of light from their lamps are beautiful falling on the ground, as they bob and weave along the path's curve. But it is all so solemn because they are leaving—they are going away. And perhaps we shall never see them again."

"Yes. It is as you say—beauty and sorrow, mixed as one."

Aslah prepared to exit the portal from the courtyard, stopped, and turned to catch Shamir's eye. As he did, he nodded to his protege and said, "You need not accompany my return—hah!—I think I can find my own way home! I will see you tomorrow then, for our meeting with the King's man—after the sun's zenith. A goodnight and good-morrow to you both."

In an unexpected unison, the two answered "And to you, Aslah." And they both laughed.

He slipped through the gate, nodding to the guard as he left. They heard the *slap-slap* of his sandals descending the twenty stone steps to the path, and watched Aslah and his little lamp weave their way out of sight.

She touched her index finger to her chin, then pointed it at Shamir and said, "I've seen you before, with that master mason Aslah—when he discussed terms concerning remodeling the royal palace. I did not remember your name earlier, nor remember seeing you before, but now it comes back to me. You are Nahor, son of Geram. You are *Nahor*—a '*lamp*'—is that correct?"

"Yes, that is the name given me by my Abba. But you have me at a disadvantage, for I know not your own name. Only that you are the daughter of Manotu."

"So, Nahor, you are a *lamp*...in search of your *light*, I would wager."

Knowing he would not answer, she waited...an uncomfortably long time. He squirmed within himself and averted his gaze from her, pretending to look out over the city. She probed deeper. "Have you found her?"

Another awkward silence compelled him to stammer an answer. "No...maybe...I don't know..."

She laughed, music in her mirth. "For being *one to light the way*, you seem not to know much."

He attempted steering the conversation away from himself. "I have heard you know the Queen—is that true?—that, as children, you were close? What is she like? Is she as gracious as she seems from a distance?"

"You've not done this before, have you?"

Shamir's eyes sprang open and his mouth gaped as the conversation pointed again to him. "Done what?"

"...spoken intimately with a woman—trying to gain her favor. Because it is a man's errant attempt that brings up another woman in the conversation..."

Sheer instinct compelled him to look away from her as this unadorned truth stunned and silenced him.

"...but this flaw is forgivable, because I see the error is one of ignorance, not callous negligence, nor an attempt to goad jealousy. You are simply inexperienced in the mystery of—as our neighbors the Iudaeans call it—*the way of a man with a maiden*. They liken this mystery to that of *the way of an eagle in the sky; the way of a snake on a rock; the way of a ship in the sea*—all things defying simple explanation, and remaining a wonder."

They both stood in silence for a time. Finally, Shamir said, "If it pleases you, daughter of Manotu, tell me your name."

"It does please me. My Amma named me Margani—*The Pearl*."

He uttered the name again, slowly. "Margani—'The Pearl'—a more beautiful name to frame such a beautiful woman, I cannot imagine—the perfect match!"

Again, she laughed, her eyes sparkling with reflections of the lamps lighting the courtyard.

"Now you are beginning to grasp *the way of a man with a maid*, my lamp!"

Together they watched the lights shimmering in the distance, and the sky-full of stars glimmering above. She moved her hand on the low, stone wall closer to his, but did not touch it, and then spoke again. "Nahor, my Lamp, what impression did *Zummar—The Song*—leave upon you this evening?"

His mouth clamped shut, and he stared at her. His mind raced for an explanation. *Why did she bring another woman into the conversation? Is this a test? Or a trap?!*

His contorted brows and lack of an answer prompted her to allay his fears. "Do not fret, My Lamp. It is acceptable conversation if the woman herself brings up another. You may answer the question...in complete candor."

He thought long, before answering. "I now know why they call her *The Song*. She is far more than a songstress, or even *The* Songstress. She is nothing less than...*The Song* itself. Before tonight, I had never heard such music. I could not expect to hear such again, even in the heavenly courts of Dushara—or his amma, or his mate—may they be blessed. The Song touched my heart to its core. I felt swept away to somewhere I've never been, as her pure melody and silver lyrics washed over and through me!"

His eyes sparkled with passion, but seeing he exposed too much of himself, he dropped his gaze to the stone tiles on which he stood. "I am sorry...but that is the truth."

"Why should you be sorry for the truth? Oh—you think I might be envious of such talent, of such feminine attraction and charms. To show you I am perfectly confident of my own—what would you say if I could arrange a meeting between the two of you? Would you like to meet her?"

Shamir's eyes blinked and then bugged out from his face. *This woman greatly perplexes me! Again, is this a trick? A snare?*

"Please answer my question—with all candor—would you like to meet her?"

He paused long before speaking. "Yes...it would be a great honor."

"Thank you for such honesty. It is difficult to find this trait so strong in a man. I applaud you for it."

Holding his breath, he looked at her, waiting, as she drew out the pause.

"Arranging the meeting will not be necessary...for you speak with her now. I am she, whom you so admired."

Hearing that these two women, who both so powerfully attracted him, were one and the same—and he now spoke with her, in this private place—his heart hammered the stone of his ribs. Seeing he was unable to speak, she said, "Abba waits within the hall, to walk me home. I must go."

Finally prying the words from his throat, Shamir asked, "When will I see you again?"

She laughed and said, "When? Perhaps you meant to ask—*'will I you see you again?'* Yes, you will see me again—and before the night is complete. Go to your home and wait. I will send you word of the meeting place. But first, I must take Abba home, and then offer my oblations before 'Lat."

"Oblations? Please forgive me, but you do not seem to me a particularly devout woman."

"You are correct, My Lamp. I am not religious, in the strict sense of the word. But it makes Abba happy to see me fulfilling tradition. As I said, I will send word to you—until then..."

She touched two fingers to his lips, then turned to find her father. As Shamir left the remembrance hall, his feet floated down the twenty stone steps and his head nearly sailed from his shoulders. Though the heavenly display of countless stars pierced the moonless night, he found himself entering his tent without remembering how he arrived.

He lay down on his cushions, wondering how long he must wait. Every few minutes he imagined he heard footsteps, and jumped to the entrance of his tent, throwing back the flap, hoping to see the messenger approach. After a dozen such false starts, he dozed for an indeterminate time, finally jerking awake, running again outside, hoping he didn't miss the word she sent.

He finally despaired of the message ever arriving, and believed she only toyed with his inexperienced ways and boyish emotions. Perhaps the promise of a late-night tryst was only a cruel and calculated joke at his expense. He began to hate himself for his raw naiveté and clumsy incompetence.

20

A BOY'S VOICE CALLED out, "Nahor, son of Geram?"

Shamir stopped punishing himself and ran to the entrance of his tent. A boy of about ten years stood outside waiting for a response.

"Yes, I am Nahor! Do you bring me a message?"

The barefoot boy stood in his threadbare tunic and announced, "She, who they call The Song, sends word for you, to meet her in the royal garden—near the Great Audience Hall of the King."

Shamir wondered aloud, "How will I gain entrance at this late hour?"

"She says to tell the guard, '*The Song has sent for me.*' He will let you in."

Shamir beckoned the boy to follow him into his tent. "Come, I will give you a bronze coin for your trouble in bringing me this word."

The boy smile broadly and said, "The Song has already rewarded me handsomely, but I thank you anyway."

"Then, Dushara go with you, and guard you on your way home." The boy turned and ran into the dark night.

Shamir put on a clean tunic and rubbed a dab of pure oil of nard through his hair. He secured the flap of his tent and hurried to the garden along the nearly deserted colonnade. Two beggars slept at the nymphaeum, and a stray dog approached from the creek bed, but he shooed it away.

As he neared the garden, a coarse "Stop!" echoed through the Colonnade. The entry gate's guard tilted the sharp iron tip of his pike toward Shamir. "These grounds are closed to all, until the sun returns. Move along now!"

"But...I received an invitation...to the garden..."

"Again I say, the grounds are closed to all. You must move along, or be taken into custody!"

He pleaded with the man blocking his way. "But the invitation was specific..."

"Then state your business clearly, but punishment will surely ensue if I am not convinced."

Shamir's heart pulsed in his throat as he struggled to remember the exact words stated by the boy. "I...she...The Song...has sent for me."

At the last word, the guard snapped his weapon upright, then touched his hand to his heart and extended it again toward Shamir, saluting him. "You may pass." He remained at rigid attention and waited for him to pass through the gate. His stance returned to a vigilant rest as the gate closed between them.

Within the walls of the secluded garden, the world outside now seemed remote to Shamir. The fragrances of flower, fruit, and herb swirled around him, further isolating him from the outside. In the subtle, silvery starlight he stumbled along the unfamiliar paths, searching for the one who invited him.

"Margani—are you here? I came as soon as I could. The guard was troublesome, but he finally let me enter. Are you here?"

Well familiar with the garden, Margani followed Shamir in silence the moment he stepped through the gate. He continued to quietly call out to her, "Margani—where are you?" Not receiving an answer, he stopped in the path, considering his next move. He looked up, into the dark, summer sky, its stars brilliant and pure. *I never noticed how each star is colored differently from every other. They are magnificent!*

While he watched the heavens, a meteor flashed from directly ahead to the far horizon, leaving behind a thin streak of glowing green. An awed "Ohhhhh..." spontaneously slipped from his lips.

Margani stood immediately behind him and said, "It is marvelous, is it not?" as she gently laid a hand on his shoulder. The voice and touch jolted him out of his reverie and he jumped two steps forward. His heart jabbed him, and he jerked around.

"You—you're here! Why did you creep up on me so?"

Not answering his question, she said, "That was only the first we shall see. I heard that the king's star-watcher predicts a falling of many stars tonight—that in the darkest hours after midnight, they may fall like rain."

Shamir drew a deep breath, held it a while and let it out slowly to regain his composure. He said, "I have never been here at night, and just briefly during the day—Aslah showed me the sculpture in the garden's center."

"Yes—the marble figure of 'Lat. My Abba, and others of his generation, believe it is a sacrilege, representing the divinities in human form, as do the Hellenes. And some even now call 'Lat by the name Aphrodite, or 'Uzza by Isis."

"And what do you believe, Margani?"

"It matters not what I believe. Whatever the truth may be, my own beliefs will not affect it, one way or the other. Do you see this tree towering above us?—with its green fronds and ripening dates? The Hellenes call it the *daktylos*, the Latins call it the *palma*, and our neighbors the Iudaeans, the *tamar*. But it remains what it is, regardless of what anyone believes it to be."

She led him farther along the paths, showing him dozens of botanical specimens, and explaining to him their nature, their required care, and their uses. Arriving at the upper end of the garden, along a high stone wall, she plucked a ripe apricot and fed it to him. While he savored the sweet fruit, she asked, "Can you swim?"

"Of course. My brother, Wahab, taught me as a boy in the large, open pool of Hawara...and..."

She waited for the end of his thought, which did not come. "Nahor, you leave your words hanging in the night air—I hear in your voice you want to tell me more."

"...and...I swam in the cistern carved beneath the rock, as well as the pool."

She grinned. "The cistern?—buried within the desert? That was bold of you! Come, we shall swim tonight."

She took his hand and led him up the stone stairs to a footbridge. The bridge connected the garden with a man-built island of stone blocks, located in the center of a large, rectangular pool. On the island stood a grand pavilion constructed of stone, as high as three men, its width and length the same. Its walls were plastered and painted in horizontal bands of maroon and indigo, its cornices white. At the end of the causeway, the pavilion stood open on that side, its interior gleaming in the light of many lamps. The opening revealed a large, black, stone, dressed smooth and in the shape of a cube—a golden crescent poised on its top, and bowls of flowers and wine at its golden base. The pavilion extended open through the far wall.

She led him to a closed side of the pavilion, where it stood in darkness, and she disrobed in the shadows. The act stunned Shamir, and he shouted in whispers, "Margani! What about your father?"

"Abba?"

Lit only by starlight, she dove into the pool, cleaving the water with little disturbance. Surfacing, she continued, "What about Abba?"

"You could lose your standing with him, and your family—and your dowry…"

Her laughter echoed around the darkened pool. "I was twelve years old when my Amma died, and my Abba received her financial holdings. But I inherited her real wealth—her family's silk trade and reweaving enterprises. Her younger sister trained me in the business, and assisted me in managing it until I came of age. Hellene women, and even those of Rome, are subjugated by their men, but my Abba is more beholden to me, than I to him. I am waiting, My Lamp—can you dive?"

He looked carefully in both directions before stripping in the starlight, she not turning away, and he dove—but not as elegantly as she. As he broke the surface he sputtered out water. She laughed at him and said, "You enter the water like a bull! But perhaps your swimming is better. To the far side of the pool, and then to the pavilion?—underwater, without taking a breath until the finish. The winner shall gain bragging rights—you are not afraid of losing to a woman, are you?"

"I fear no woman in the water!"

Her laughter echoed again. "Strong words, My Lamp!"

Without giving a signal, Margani submerged and began stroking toward the side of the pool, Shamir behind her. As she touched the smooth plastered wall and turned, he was at her heels. Midway, he passed her and reached the pavilion first, a length ahead. Within an arm's length of each other, they both clung to the stone wall at the water's edge, their lungs heaving.

Between gasps she congratulated him. "Until tonight, neither man nor boy has ever bested me in this challenge. I like your style. I've something more to show you. First, enter the pavilion to dry and dress—you will find towels there. Then meet me at the pool's upper gate."

He climbed from the water, retrieved his clothes, and entered the pavilion. Lamp-stands of seven lights each brightly lit the space from the corners. At the ceiling hung garlands of fresh flowers. And large, bronze censers still fumed with the scent of lubunah. He walked around the black stone, half-wondering if it truly was one of the thrones—the physical manifestation—of Dushara's presence. Under a lamp-stand in one corner, soft towels of Egyptian cotton lay folded and waiting in a pile. He dried, dressed, and made his way up twenty stone steps to the gate. While he waited, more stars fell from the same place in the sky. *This night is like no other. I shall never again be the same. Perhaps it is only a dream and I will wake as Aslah calls me to work.*

Shamir saw her form approaching him, and while he could not make out the details in the dim light, he knew she now dressed differently—her garments waving, blowing, fluttering in the light breeze. He told her, "I have already tried the gate. It is latched from the inside."

"You think I did not know that?" She produced a bronze key, saying, "The Queen's chamberlain is indebted to me, so for this night, I have the key, and we possess what lies beyond." She inserted the key in the gate's latch-hole, turned it and pushed to release the gate. It swung free on its hinges and the two entered.

Shamir whispered, "What is this place?"

"The vineyard and private garden abode of the royal couple."

"They are not here, are they? And if we are discovered…?"

21

She closed the gate behind them and reset the latch, ensuring their private world remained so. The stars fell with increasing frequency. Shamir saw they entered a vineyard that sloped upward. Recent irrigation of the vines now rose as a mist from the ground, softening the dim view before them.

"Take care where you walk—the vines are planted in the manner of the Sabaeans. They grow upward from pits dug chest-deep, with their branches trained on lattices laid over the pits. They say *he who digs a pit will fall into it*—but you may do so, instead!"

Though Shamir took note of her warning, with the increasing level of starlight he found himself watching his guide, her garments flowing around her in the breeze. The slope steepened and they soon arrived at the foot of the first terrace. Four stone steps lifted them to the next level.

She said, "At harvest, the king's vineyard supplies the royal house with fine food for his table—fresh grapes and raisin-cakes. And for drinking, it produces three different wines, and strong spirits from his Egyptian stills." She bent down to the low vines, saying, "These grapes they call the Blood of Persians. They are near their peak with ripe fruit. I find them the most remarkable in the vineyards." She found a cluster, picked it, and handed a few berries to Shamir. "Take, eat, and tell me what you taste."

He popped them into his mouth and burst their skins with his teeth. The flavors tumbled upon his tongue and palate, their complexity defying simple description.

"I taste...I don't know...pomegranates? But these are grapes..."

"Very good. You *do* taste pomegranates. But here, taste again— there is yet more."

He chewed and swirled more berries in his mouth. "Behind the pomegranate...I find apricot!...and, how is it?...the thorn-berry from Dushara's mountains to the east? I have not tasted them in many years—and all in a grape!"

"My Lamp, you are well on your way to being the King's royal taster. Your palate has a keen sense."

"But how can this be? Should not a grape just have the flavor of a grape?"

"There are many varieties of grape, each with a unique flavor. Just as some men have learned to breed certain traits in horses and camels, other men have the knowledge of breeding grapes."

The two continued climbing the terraced slope, and he now led her by the hand. At the terrace below the top, they stopped and turned to see from where they had come. In a vivid flash overhead, a star-burst lit up the lower slope of the vineyard, the pool and garden below, and 'Lat's temple-of-the-winged-lions on the facing hill beyond the Colonnade.

The waxy, lunar crescent peeked out above the summit of the mountain of Khubta, which looks down upon the Grand Thaniya and the theater at its end. And a light-colored, cubic structure loomed above the man and woman at the top of the vineyard's terraces. In the spare moonlight, the building displayed three narrow, horizontal stripes of indigo, painted upon the white plaster exterior. In the windows, a bronze lattice-work of diamond-shapes barred the secrets contained within. Shamir whispered to his new companion, "What is this place?"

She snickered at the attempted stealth of his question. "You need not whisper, for no one but us is within two long bow-shots of this private place. And the only ones allowed here are fast asleep on the far side of the Colonnade—in the royal beds of the Royal Palace."

He looked left and right, and in a slightly louder tone, whispered, "What are you saying?"

"*I'm saying,* this is the private place of pleasure for Haretat and his Queen—loaned to us for this night."

He stood between her and the building, blocking her way and no longer whispered. "Should we even be here? What do you mean, *loaned to us*? What if we are caught here?"

She touched his shoulder, slid her fingers down his arm, and took his hand. "I told you, the Queen's chamberlain was indebted to me, and besides, Shuqilat herself knows that I have come here on occasion. Your worry does not flatter you. This is a place of splendor and rich delights. Enjoy it with me!"

A peacock, roosting in a peach tree nearby, called aloud to its mate —*eeeiu!-eeeiu!-eeeiuuu!*—startling both the man and woman. Shamir scratched the back of his head, drew a deep breath, and exhaled. He took her other hand and looked into her face. "Do you never lack for surprises? *You* are the rich delight! Yes, I *will* enjoy it with you!"

Margani said nothing more and led him to the portal of the refuge. She took the same key she used at the vineyard's gate and inserted it in the door, unlocking it. She pulled him into the black volume within. The sound of falling water tinkled and burbled from the far side of the room. Fragrances—fruity, floral, and savory— drifted on the air. A delicate chirping greeted them from the darkness. She dropped his hand to search for something just inside the doorway.

"Here it is...we will soon have some light."

He heard sounds of rubbing, scraping, then, a *click*. A sharper *click!* accompanied several flying, yellow sparks, astonishing Shamir. More vigorous strikes followed, with showers of sparks briefly illuminating Margani's hands and an oil lamp sitting on the small table before her. He held his breath, beholding the sight.

A small flame finally ignited at the tip of the lamp's wick, and soon grew to full size, lighting the table, the doorway, and the couple. She used the lamp to light several more on a nearby lamp-stand. With the illumination growing, the room's secrets, one by one, revealed themselves.

Shamir found his voice and said, "What *was* that? By what magic arts did you light the lamp?"

She playfully mocked him. "For a man who uses skill and the sciences to shape earth's bulk, you seem to not know much! This is a flint and striking steel. Struck sharply, the hardness of the flint conveys its spirit of motion to the steel, ejecting tiny embers from it. The burning sparks then ignite the oil in the wick. I should think that you, My Lamp, would know of such matters."

"Where did this come from? I have never seen such a wonder!"

"It was a gift to the King from the farthest East, brought by an emissary of the Serai—the Silk Ones. These are used in the palace as well."

"Iron, I know well, and with flint, I am familiar...but what is this *steel?*"

"They say it is a special type of iron. Smelted with the burned bones of sheep."

His eyes bulged and his mouth bloomed into a grin. "May I try it?"

His giddy fascination with the tool charmed her and she grinned as she answered, "Certainly...amuse yourself with it while I light the remaining lamps."

He picked up the flint and steel and touched them together, taking care not to break such a marvelous invention. From the far side of the room, she glanced back to see him struggling in his effort to produce sparks. He frowned and examined the two pieces, trying to understand the mystery. She said to him, "If the flint is to make fire, the two must be struck together with great speed and impact. It is in the collision that light and burning come forth. Pretend you are hitting your chisel with the mallet. Use the vigor of a stone-cutter and you will make sparks."

He added muscle and quickness to his efforts and uttered 'Aaahhh!' when flickering sparks streamed from the steel. The process fascinated him and he almost could not tear himself from it. But he finally remembered where he was—the private, royal sanctuary—and who he was with—The Song.

He laid the fire-starter back on the table and looked up to see the entire room now glowing with the incandescence of more than twenty lamps. Shamir's eyes widened as he scanned the scene before him. Near the table by the door, stood an aviary the height and width of a camel. Made from bronze wires, the cage imprisoned a dozen small birds of vibrant hues. They looked as if they had been sculpted from lapis, malachite and cinnabar. With the birds' home now lit with an artificial dawn, they awoke from their slumber and hopped from perch to perch. Beyond the aviary, two lush, green trees, taller than a man, grew from terra-cotta pots the size of barrels. Among their glossy leaves hung ripening fruits, akin to the citron, but the color of the setting sun.

At the far corner of the retreat, and like a small waterfall in the rocks above Raqmu, a fountain streamed from the wall, arcing over and into an indoor cistern. The pool was circular and at least six paces across...if a man could walk on water. A low wall of dressed and polished black stone ringed the pool. Gentle ripples expanded across the water's surface from where the stream entered it. He put his hand to his mouth and stroked his chin in wonder.

A large octagonal table of garnet-colored rosewood occupied the middle of the space—its width so great, a man could not easily reach its center. And at its center stood a white ceramic urn, two cubits tall and a cubit in diameter, filled with branches of pink-flowering almonds, Persian irises of deepest purple, and the creamy, open blossoms of rose. Below the flowering splendor lay two large bronze cornucopias, the symbols of abundance and prosperity adopted by the Nabataean kings for two hundred years. The open mouths of the horns were wide as a man's waist and out of them tumbled all manner of delicacies: peaches, pomegranates, walnuts, raisin-cakes, figs, and more.

Also on the table, waited platters and bowls of the finest Nabataean pottery—eggshell-thin red ceramic, decorated in finely-executed geometric designs and patterns. Honey-cakes sprinkled with poppy-seeds and sweet leavened breads glazed with honey covered the platters and filled the bowls. Between the bowls crowded numerous white vials, filled with a variety of wines—from Nabataea and beyond—each type indicated by inscribed gold medallions hanging from the vessels' necks.

Toward the far corner of the secret haven lay a large couch, also of carved rosewood and inlaid with ivory. Its width would easily accommodate two, lying side by side on its thick cushion, upholstered in silk the color of flame. Royal blue pillows and bolsters, also of silk and embroidered with the monograms of Haretat and Shuqilat, sprawled across the couch.

22

MARGANI STOOD AT THE final lamp-stand near the couch, lighting the last few lamps. Her back faced Shamir and presented him with a waking dream. In the dim light of the vineyard terraces, he had not seen what the lamps now revealed. At the garden-pool, she had exchanged the peplos and mantle she wore at the banquet for a white, silken cape that flowed from her shoulders to her knees.

Raising her arms as she worked with the lamps, the two painted wings of a huge bird blazed on the back of the gleaming fabric, each feather defined in exquisite detail. The lowest row of primary feathers glowed with a ruby dye; the next row of coverts in a deep sapphire; and the uppermost row of marginals, an intense emerald. Silken loops at the upper corners attached the cape to her wrists, and as she extended her arms to the sides, she seemed poised to take flight. The vision suspended his breath.

With all the lamps now lit, she turned back to face him. In the front, a long rectangle of carnelian silk hung from the shoulders of the cape, sheathing her form. And as she folded her arms in front of her, it seemed a magnificent bird enwrapped her in its wings, cradling her body. The Song spoke to him, in a more serious tone than he'd yet heard from her.

"There is a great love between the King and Queen, though he is nearly a generation older than she. This place we are in is a special place of their love. While they have not yet produced a male child together, it is certainly not for the lack of trying. This chamber bears witness to their joyous attempts. Shuqilat has told me of the abandoned pleasure and delights they often share here."

While his companion, and the wonders of this place enraptured his heart, a disturbing concern again crept into his head. *Should we even be here?...in such an intimate site?* She clasped his hand and said, "Come and sit, that we might enjoy ourselves," and led him to the royal couch. He sat on the cushion and she glided to the other side, sitting opposite him.

At the head of the couch on each side, stood a matched pair of end-tables. Their tops, slabs of ivory, rested on the upraised trunks and tusks of rearing elephants carved of ebony. Their tables displayed an array of ruby-colored glass goblets, jars of three types of wines, and golden plates piled with raisin-cakes, and honey-cakes made with walnuts. She filled a goblet with wine, tasted it herself and then raised it to his lips. She told him, "Taste—it is like the grapes of the vines below, with the essence of apricot, pomegranate, and mountain berries, but more so, and with the added aromas of cinnamon and myrrh."

As he sipped the wine she said, "Roll it around your mouth with your tongue, releasing the flavor. Then swallow, and breathe the aromas." He did as she instructed, and the intensity of the sensations overwhelmed him. She held a raisin-cake to his lips and said, "Try this portion of sweet perfection—it is wonderful, is it not? And feed me a honey-cake, please. I love the flakiness of its rolled pastry."

He had never fed another person, but to share food intimately with such a beautiful and delightful woman was a surpassing experience. With two fingers she traced his lips, caressing them, and asked, "These have not yet touched those of a woman...have they?"

His eyes caught hers and he said, "Only my Amma's...when I was a child."

"My Lamp, the kisses known by a boy have no kinship with those tasted by a man. Close your eyes."

Margani's lips brushed those of Shamir. Lightly, briefly at first, then longer and deeper. His soul seemed to unravel before him. He began to lose the sense of where his own body and life ended, and where hers began. Their lives and hearts seemed merging—becoming one. The experience was to him at once, terror, mixed with indescribable pleasure.

She stopped, and said, "You may open your eyes." Though illuminated by only the twenty small flames, the chamber now sparkled and flared with the brilliance of daylight. As he looked again to her, he felt he was falling into the deep green caverns of her eyes. Her eyelids slowly, gently closed while his remained open. She waited for him. He brought his face again to hers, and caressed her lips with his own. He curled one arm around her back, and then the other. His mouth devoured hers, like a delectable fruit. His passion rose, his hands exploring more of her, and she whispered, "Please, stop. We must not wander further down this path, as we are not yet betrothed."

Did I really hear her say 'yet?' Could this be so?

She placed her hands on his chest and tenderly pushed him from the close embrace, and said, "If My Lamp is to be a great sculptor, it is necessary you know something of the mystery of women. How else will you faithfully represent them in stone? You have no such knowledge, do you?"

Her questions paralyzed his voice and limbs. She whispered, "Stay where you are...," then rose from the couch. She crooned a strange and sweet melody, and danced in grace before him—the silk cape and sheath rippling, billowing about her. The outer silks slipped more, and more from her form, finally drifting to the floor. Covered only in the knee-length chiton of sheerest Coan silk, she continued to dance. A crimson, twisted strophion gathered the garment below her bosom. She danced like a flame—a tongue of fire—flickering, floating, fluttering, to kindle the tinder of his heart. The prancing flame reflected in paired-miniature from the dark eyes of Shamir.

Her dance ended near the cistern, where she stepped onto the low wall encircling it. All her motion ceased, and for an eternal moment, he saw her as a sculpture, frozen in time.

If only I could sculpt such a form!

She finally broke her pose, laughing and saying "You told me you once swam in a cistern, and so shall I...," then turned and dove into the waters. A wave sloshed over the stone wall and she disappeared into the pool's dark depths. He ran to the edge of the cistern, peering into the pool, but a crowd of bubbles rushing to the surface hid her form. Her head finally broke the surface on the far side.

Excitement burst across her face and with a girlish grin she shouted, "I want to find you something!" Diving from the surface, she flipped her body in the water, feet rising above, kicking, and submerging again. In the dim depths of the cistern, he could see her movements and nothing more. Then he saw the top of her head, and her hands pulling her back to the surface. Her head popped free of the water, within his reach. Streams of water washed her long black hair, flowing down from her head, clinging to her olive neck, conforming to the round curve of her shoulders, hiding her breasts. She took several deep breaths, saying nothing, and then dove again.

She remained below, far longer this time. He watched the last bubble rise and break, escaping into the air. The ripples finally died away and the surface smoothed to polished glass. He saw her moving at first, but after a time, all motion ceased and he could barely make out her form on the bottom.

When she did not return, he paced from one side of the cistern to the other, desperate to see if she was in some distress. Panic forced his heart into his throat.

Should I dive in and bring her back up?!

As soon as the thought arose, he saw her stroking again to the surface, turning his terror to relief. Her head blasted out of the water, breaths coming in rapid spasms, desperate to satisfy her body's craving for air. When she could speak again, a toothy smile burst upon her mouth. She held one hand high out of the water, something small within its grasp.

"I have it!" exploded from her mouth.

She swam to the low wall near him, resting her arms upon it, and showed him a fine ring, made of a light-green stone. In a giddy mood she blurted "Is this not glorious? I have seen it before—on the finger of Shuqilat. She said it was a gift to Haretat from an emissary of the Silk Ones—intended for the Queen's hand. The ring must have slipped from her finger as she bathed or swam here. I have often found such treasures before, diving here at night, but never one like this!"

She placed the find on the tip of her thumb, and slowly turned it with her index finger. Their faces nearly touched as they examined the ring together. He smelled the aroma of cassia still in her hair, not yet washed away by the waters.

The light-green stone was carved thinner where it would band the finger. On its top, where a jewel would be, the stone possessed a nodule of much darker green, naturally embedded in it. A delicate, incised pattern of geometric designs encircled the thin part of the ring, and a cryptic symbol embossed the dark nodule. She said, "Hold out your hand.'"

He did as The Song requested, and she placed the ring on the last finger of his left hand, saying to him, "It is now yours."

He protested, but she would have none of it. "The Queen has far more rings than she has fingers, and toes, for that matter. She thinks nothing of this ring, but perhaps you will. And rather than drowning in the cold, dark reaches of this cistern, it will certainly appreciate riding in the sunlight on your own finger." He glanced at the ring, never imagining he would possess such a treasure. He looked back at Margani's face, beads of water still clinging to her eyelashes, one hanging from the tip of her nose. He thought,

You, My Song, are the true treasure, not this ring, but I will keep it, to always remind me of you...

She interrupted his private thoughts, saying, "The sky turns pink, My Lamp...my love. We must leave this place before we are discovered. You can climb the fig tree behind here, and slip over the back wall. I will extinguish the lamps, set everything as it was, and leave alone by the front gate."

He grasped both her hands with the strength he would a mallet and chisel, and his voice nearly breaking, he asked—"When will I see you again?"

She pulled one hand from his, pressed two fingers to his quavering lips, but for the first time that night, no words escaped her own. A thought lodged in her throat and would go no further—

I know that, after tonight, I will never be the same again!

23

HE ROLLED LEFT. ROLLED right. Sat up, then lay down again. Took a breath. Let it escape, slow and uneasy.

Shamir fought with himself for control of his thoughts—and these new feelings—

The sun already climbs into morning, and here I lie awake—like a nervous fox in my tent. Sleep is futile, but I must rest to be fresh for my meeting with Aslah this day. And yet, her face floats before my own— those eyes—like two perfect emeralds in settings of pearl! And her lips, her mouth, consumes my heart—I love the mouth of Margani! I have never known a woman remotely like her. Is there another like her? And did she say she waited for betrothal to me? My heart pounds at the thought! Her form, in all the glory of its perfection, possesses me. I must see her again, if only for a moment!

His body catapulted from the cushions where he lay. From an urn, he poured a basin full with cool water, splashing it on his face, chest, arms. The polished bronze mirror reflected his face, full of bemused excitement, mixed with the strange fear he would never see her again.

What if she is not home? What if she has no attraction to me? What if she lives only in my delirious dreams?

He changed the tunic he'd lain and sweated in for three hours, for a fresh one. A final glance in the mirror revealed his doubts.

Could she—the Pearl, The Song—ever love a face such as this?

He shook his head to dismiss the thought and bolted from his tent.

The young man's feet beat clouds of dust into the air as he walked with haste to the road leading to Prosperity Hill, the neighborhood of Manotu's estate. Thoughts of seeing her again, surprising her at her home, renewed his vigor and he broke into a run. While his fleet feet flew over the pavement, his head and heart flew ahead of his body. A child and her amma stepped back from the road, barely avoiding collision with the chaotic flight of Shamir. Again, doubts troubled him.

Does Manotu even have a daughter? Perhaps he will look at me as a deranged man—maybe I am. Not maybe...I know I am deranged! Thoughts of her derange me...

He arrived at Manotu's home, not remembering how he arrived. The gate stood before him, and the entry guard stood to attention as he approached.

What will I say? I should just return to my tent. What if...?

"Stop! Who are you? State your business!" barked the guard.

"I am Shamir, I mean Nahor...son of Geram. I wish to speak with Margani...the daughter of Manotu."

"I *know* who Margani is! She speaks to no one without prior appointment, or Manotu's approval. I have not been told of an appointment."

"No, I have none. May I speak with Manotu?"

"I will inform him you desire his ear."

"I would be most grateful."

The guard opened and entered the gate, slamming it behind him, but he left its small window open. Shamir put his face to the peephole, longing to see Margani's home. Beyond the gate sprawled a large courtyard, including a central pool with a fountain bubbling into it. Raised beds of blooming plants ringed the pool, with a colonnaded porch at the courtyard's periphery. Silk draperies in blue, lavender, and rose hung from the colonnades, wafting in the puffs of breeze. Chairs and lounges of Hellene design waited in the shade. He imagined he saw her there, lounging in the shade, the draperies blowing over her body, touching her. He thought he could see her sitting on the low wall of the pool, splashing the cool water with her toes, her hair blowing soft and light like the wisps of smoke from incense.

The guard's face popped into the little window, so close Shamir could feel his breath, and startled him back to the reality at hand.

"He remembers you from the marzeah last night, and will speak with you."

Two clicks and a thud announced the guard's unlatching of the gate. It swung open.

"Follow me."

He entered the courtyard and waited for the guard to latch the gate behind him. The man strutted ahead of him while Shamir looked around, taking in this private view of her home. They entered the house, and the guard said, "You may wait here," and returned to his post.

The entrance hall to the extensive home contained a long, narrow reflecting pool. Its bottom featured a complex, geometric pattern of mosaic tiles—indigo, white, and some coated with burnished gold. More mosaics covered the floor beside the pool, exhibiting rich renditions of ostriches, oryxes, stags, and other animals too far away to identify. Numerous chairs were scattered about the entry room, awaiting guests.

What will I say to Manotu? Can I see her? Can I have her hand? I love your daughter, Manotu! I...

"Nahor, son of Geram!..." He jumped as the man came up behind him and greeted him. "...I had not expected to see you so soon, but this is a great pleasure to have you in my home!"

"And greetings to you, sir, and to the whole household of Manotu."

"I heard from Aslah of your meeting this afternoon with the King's building adviser. A propitious occasion, is it not? May the smile of Manawat be upon you both."

"Yes, it is a wonderful development."

"I have some sway with those overseeing the project. I will see if I can sweeten their disposition toward you. It never hurts to take whatever advantages come your way, does it?"

Why does this man prattle on so? Can he not see it is his daughter I wish to be with, not him? "No, it does not. Thank you for your kindness in that. But it is not..."

Manotu interrupted him. "Please forgive me, Nahor...where are my manners? You most likely did not come to my home this morning to speak of business. How can I help you?"

I cannot tell him the truth, that last night in her presence, my face became all eyes, and my eyes all hands...

"Manotu, I wish...that is, can I...may I...see your daughter—*Margani?*"

"Oh, yes, yes. I should have known that was why you were here. I noticed the two of you talked long at the feast last night. She is quite a young woman, is she not? But..." His words faded and he looked somewhere beyond Shamir.

I know, she already told him to send me away, as she could have no real interest in a man like myself—a stone-cutter. She has a prosperous business of her own, and probably a thousand wealthy men to vie for her hand. He finally managed to speak a single word: "But?"

"She did not tell you last night?"

"Tell me...what?"

"That she leaves today."

"She leaves?...for where? Can I see her before she goes?" Panic thrust Shamir's heart from his chest to behind his Adam's apple.

"She leaves for Bostra. The King has plans to make it the new capital."

"Please tell her…I wish to speak with her before she leaves!"

"I am sorry, my brother…but she has already left."

Shamir's head spiraled with the news. "She is gone? When does she return?"

"She will not. This is no longer to be her home. The Queen desires her assistance in setting up the new royal household, and she moves the center of her silk trade there as well. Bostra will be her new home—a new life awaits her there."

The young man's stomach felt as if kicked by the hind hoof of a strong camel. He could neither breathe nor speak. Manotu apologized for his daughter. "I am sorry she did not tell you last night."

Shamir turned away, and forced his feet to take him back to the gate. Manotu called after him,

"She left this morning to prepare the horse she keeps at the royal stables—not far from the King's marzeah halls. She was to meet there with a company of a dozen others from the royal court—to journey together to Bostra. Perhaps if you run to the new works being carved north of the rock they call *Resa Gmel— The Head of the Camel*—you can catch sight of her as they round the west end of the north wall, taking the highway up to Bayda and beyond."

He did not answer, and continued walking from the house.

I knew she could not love one like me. I am a foolish dreamer…always looking for what is not possible, what is not mine. And yet, her face still floats before me. Did he say she would take the sharp bend in the road at the north wall? Fool or not, I still desire to see her face one last time. I may catch sight of her if I climb the scaffolds on the cliff of the new work there. I must hurry!

Not knowing precisely when she left, his dragging feet picked up the pace and began to sprint. Though it seemed to him hours, he arrived at the western tip of the wall before his strength flagged or his lungs burned.

24

AND SO IT WAS that the chatter of mallets-on-chisels-on-stone echoed from the cliffs beyond the Head of The Camel. A dozen men worked high on the cliff. Some clung to the working framework, others dangled from ropes. Shamir scampered up the ladders and lattice work like an Ethiopian monkey, making his way to the very summit of the work in progress. As he ascended, workmen stopped their chiseling to watch the oddity of this man so consumed with rushing to the top.

Shamir stood on the topmost plank of the framework, shielding his eyes against the harsh glare of the morning sun. He looked first to the north, along the road to Bayda, to see if Margani and her entourage were already leaving the city. But he saw only a small train of a half-dozen camels headed toward him, plodding into the city.

He looked toward Raqmu, over the top of 'Lat's temple, where her priests performed the morning sacrifice in the open courtyard before it. Their robes of royal blue matched the color of the sky, and their crimson embroidery mimiced the red blood spurting from the slit throat of the ram. The animal appeared entirely unconcerned with the process, the priests making the incision with razor-sharp, painless, practiced precision. Beyond the temple, the Royal Quarter spread to the far cliffs, with its palaces, gardens, banqueting halls, and stables. This was the road Margani and her fellow travelers would likely take. He saw no one on the royal road, save a dozen pedestrians scattered along its length, headed for a morning of shopping at the markets. So he waited and continued his watch.

Standing so long on the narrow top rung, Shamir's feet finally began to cramp, and he prepared to descend—back to the earth, back to his life, his dreams of the last twelve hours evaporating with the rising heat of the day.

He looked once more and saw a little puff of dust rise at the far end of the road. A cloud of red dust stirred up from the hooves of animals. The cloud grew in size as it passed the temple and approached the tight turn on the road below. In front of the cloud rushed a roan horse, and behind it three blacks and a dappled gray, racing to keep up. Toward the rear of the group loped a dozen camels, burdened with baggage and riders.

He watched the lead horse approach the sharp curve. The rider slowed the horse, and he knew it was her—shielded from the sun by a hat and light veil. Her riding cloak streamed out behind her and fluttered in the air. She rode low, against its neck.

He watched her navigate the bend in the road with expertise, to join the highway heading north, away from Raqmu, away from his dreams. He closed his eyes and called out—

"Uzza—O Great Power—let me see her face once more!"

At once, she sat up straight in her saddle, reined-in the steed, and turned to look back, not knowing why. She lifted her veil to better see through the cloud of dust behind her. Shamir's heart jumped, as he saw her face, and he thought, *Her eyes are red...from crying?...from the dust? Or do I imagine it?*

He opened his mouth to shout her name, but desperation strangled his voice. Seeing nothing of note behind her, she dropped her veil, turned back to the road, and urged her mount with haste.

She disappeared behind the rising dust, and the rest of her retinue made the turn, the camels close behind. The group faded behind the red cloud. The dust settled back to the earth from which it came. Shamir stared at the empty road.

He returned home at a dragging pace, taking the wrong turns, streets and paths more than once. With the sun now high in the late morning sky, he finally recognized his tent and entered, flopping onto the cushions. He felt tears preparing to storm his eyes, but he won the battle and forced them back inside his heart.

Before long, he knew Aslah would call him from his tent, to join him for the afternoon meeting with the King's court. Not sleeping since the night-before-last, fatigue dogged his body, and his time with Margani depleted his mind and emotions. He wanted desperately to fall into peaceful slumber, but knew he would not. As the moments dragged on, the beats of his heart raced ahead.

His hours of restless tossing upon his bed seemed days. Just after noon, he heard Aslah's hearty greeting outside. "Halloo to Shamir, harder than flint! We go to the King's man to seal the contract. An auspicious day, indeed!"

He rolled from where he lay, and stood in the subdued light of the tent. Lazy breaths of breeze opened and closed the tent's flap, flashing sunlight at random inside the tent. He looked for water to refresh his face, but his water jug was empty. The flap flew back and Aslah poked his head inside.

"Are you ready? We should go now and not leave the King's man waiting. Why, you look like a body of death on the exposure platform—the result of last night?"

In an economy of words, Shamir explained his condition to his master. "When she was with me, we stayed up all night, and now that she is gone from me, I shall never sleep again. These twin insomnias shall destroy me."

A half-smile crossed Aslah's lips, he scratched the back of his head, eyebrows arching, and said, "I am not surprised, my son. I should have warned you more than I did, as I could see this coming. The outcome is as much my own responsibility as yours. Your heart will never rest if you leave things as they are. Perhaps you should go after her...and hear from her own lips how she feels about you. Or you will always wonder."

"But what of the King's manager? I should be at the meeting."

"The worry should not be yours, but mine. I will make excuses that seem valid to him. Your place in this work will not be at risk. Go to the one you believe you love. How else can you proceed?"

Shamir embraced his master, kissed him on both cheeks, and said, "Thank you for your great kindnesses to me. For now, and for the countless others. You have been a great father to me—*my Abba*. But how will I proceed?"

"I know a man at the royal stables—Dan'el—who will loan you a mount in my name. Go there in haste, and pursue your love. You can do no more than that."

Shamir clasped Aslah's hands and ran from the tent, to make his way to the north.

25

KNOWING SHAMIR WAS BARELY familiar with riding, the stable master gave him not his fastest, but his surest mount. The filly knew the roads better than her rider, and took him northward at a fast clip.

With only two-day's worth of food and water, he was mindful of where he was and how far he should travel. He doubted he would catch Margani's entourage in two days, but he prepared to go the distance and needed to overnight along the way. To avoid wasting the horse he rode not too fast, but briskly enough to not waste time.

While they proceeded northward, the sun fell rapidly in the sky to their left. They slept in the open and rose at dawn to put more road behind them. The afternoon of the second day in the saddle, he began to weary. Not an experienced rider, his jostling on the back of the horse took its toll on his tender flesh, pounded between the bones of his pelvis and the hard saddle. It became deep misery to him, and only his pursuit of her carried him forward.

Far ahead, he saw something clustered along the road. When he drew near he could see a good-sized train of camels. Large loads hung from their pack-saddles. He slowed his horse as he came to them, and called out to the lead man, "Where are you from and where do you go?"

The man called back, "I hear from your speech that you, also, are Nabatu. We carry bitumen from the depths of the Salt Sea—the Sea of Death. It goes to the ships at Rhinocolura, for sale in Alexandria. They say the Egyptians use it to wrap their dead. It is strange, no? But who can argue with the value of their gold? And where does your own journey take you?"

"I know not the certain end, but perhaps as far as Bostra."

"Bostra?! That is a world away from here! The King's new capital they say—to replace the wonder that is Raqmu. But who cares about capitals? This black tar we carry—*black gold* they call it—is where the fortune is to be made. Why do you seek the King's capital?"

"I seek not the city itself, but someone who travels there ahead of me. I look for an entourage of the royal court. Probably a young woman in their lead—on a fine roan horse. Blue riding cloak with white stripes. A veil and hat. Have you seen them?"

"Ay, we've seen them...if she keeps riding as she does, the horse will never make Madaba, let alone Bostra! Do you seek her for good, or for ill?"

"For good—I hope. When did you pass them, and what is the best way I might reach them?"

"They passed us in haste, kicking up a mighty cloud of dust, two hand-spans of the sun ago. The camels straggled behind them, loaded down with baggage, just a 'span' ago. To catch the horses, take the first road after three black rocks—that look like men standing. It is rougher, but much shorter than the road they take. You will come out on the road ahead of them. At the junction lies a caravanserai—small, but adequate for yourself and the small company you seek."

"Thank you for your assistance. I will not forget it. May Dushara reward you handsomely."

"Dushara? You are far from the Sharas now, young man—Khutby rules this land. It is by his hand we will be blessed!"

"So be it then. May Khutby bless your steps, and may you fare well."

"And you!"

He rode away from the train bearing asphalt, and at their tail, their escort of Nabataean warriors glared at him. He continued on his way, looking for the three black rocks. The journey dragged on and the sun continued its arc across the sky. He wondered if he missed the sign. *Perhaps I drowsed off briefly, not seeing the rocks, and woke just after. Or maybe I looked on the wrong side of the road, just as we passed them. Perhaps the man wished me ill and misled me, hoping I die out here in the desert.*

He rode on, but slowed the horse, not certain of the way. On the verge of turning back to Raqmu, a group of black rocks appeared ahead. When they came abreast of them, he slowed the horse, and stopped. Three black rocks, indeed, stood near to each other, but they looked more like a camel, a tree stump, and a rock—only a wild imagination could see them as men. He urged the horse on and soon came to a cross-roads. A rarely-traveled road diverged from the one he was on, both to the right and to the left—east and west.

Did he say to the left? Or to the west?—but that would be the same. Maybe it was to the east. I certainly remember he said the road was rough. To the right looks as smooth and level as this, but to the left it heads into those low hills. That must be it—to the left, it is.

The road curved left and right, into the hills, then out again. Across dry, stony creeks and unending fields of jagged rocks. The farther they proceeded, the longer the road stretched ahead. Wearied of hanging in the hot sky, the sun began its descent. The horse's strength ebbed, and Shamir knew he would not catch Margani.

Ascending yet one more hill, he dismounted the fatigued animal and led it by the halter. The journey had entirely depleted Shamir's body, and the failed pursuit drained his heart. Cresting the rise, he saw the Sea of Death stretching to the far horizon, its featureless surface glaring like brass in the setting sun.

At the shore nearest him lay a group of small boats and rafts made from bundles of bound reeds. Black tar smeared their sides and bottoms. Three huts of mud and sticks slouched at the hill's foot, and from the one near the path hobbled a hunched man, wearing naught but a filthy loincloth over a dark-bronze body. From a leather string around his scrawny neck hung a copper medallion, smooth and polished like a mirror.

He raised a hand in acknowledgement of Shamir's approach and waved him closer. His skin, wrinkled and deeply creased like that of an elephant, hung in loose flaps from his rattling, bony frame. The man's spine curved forward in a severe arc, bending his head down to the level of his shoulders. He grinned, revealing a lone tooth on the bottom, just fitting into the gap of the single pair above. The man shouted out enthusiastic greetings: "My brother—good seeing you! But you be lost—none come here, but for black-tar. And you've no camel!"

"Yes, I am certainly lost, old man. I looked for the short road to gain time heading north, but this is not the way. The traders I met, with a string of camels hauling bitumen, told me of the route, but I must not have understood the way. I am far from anywhere, with a fading mount. And I know not what to do."

"Yes, yes—tar-men leave at dawn. Loads of 'black-gold' they say it. They take from here. They pay me food, water—to watch sea. When stink bubble up from sea out yon, I wait—till no more see my face in shiny copper. Soon tar float up from deep. I walk to road and leave sign. They look for sign, wait twenty-day for all tar, then come. Paddle out boats and rafts—to take black-tar. Load up camels. On they go.'

The sun's disc bulged as it sat on the horizon at the sea's far edge. The bridle slipped from Shamir's hand. Fatigued himself, he dropped to the salt-crusted sand and sat. He hung his head and said, "I am lost here, without hope of reaching the one I seek, or even returning home."

"You hungry? Tar-men leave plenty food. Barley bread, dry meat! —camel, goat. Come my house—we eat!"

"But what of my horse? She cannot eat meat and will fade and perish—or die of thirst."

"Oh no! See store-huts? Tar-men leave plenty fodder and water. For camels and horses when come back. You eat—horse eat. Then sleep. Go home on morrow."

The stooped old man scurried to his hut, while Shamir led his horse to the storage huts. He removed the saddle and bridle, then fed and watered the animal. By the time he finished, the man returned, skipping along with his hands full of dried meat. His old eyes sparkled in the twilight, and the bright grin on his face brought a faint smile to Shamir. He extended his arms to his unexpected guest, saying, "Eat, eat, my brother! Fill belly—it be good!"

He took the meat from one hand, but the old man extended the other toward him and said, "This too—you eat all!"

Shamir and his host ate their fill. After the night sky stretched across the sea, both men lay down on the hut's packed-earth floor. Stars awoke and rained down their faint light, to glitter back from the salt waters. The old man snored in deep peace, but Shamir rolled onto his back and struck his temples with the heels of his fists. Throughout the night he scolded himself—

Why am I here?—except for my gullible ways and fantasy-dreams? I may be lost no longer, but I'll return home, in defeat and shame. I dishonor not only myself, but my master. I'm a fool—and a failed dreamer!

The last-quarter of an onyx moon rose over the low hill and poured its pale beam through the hut's doorway. Shamir felt the stone ring on the small finger of his left hand, and turned it with his thumb. He held his hand up in the feeble light, the ring glimmering as it turned. Its beauty and perfection mocked his witless folly, and somewhere up on the hill a laughing-dove called to its mate with hysterical titters. Anger and shame forced him to his feet and he left the hut.

The moon behind him, he walked to where the land disappeared into the sea's bitter waters. The stone ring burned on his finger, so he pulled it off, looked at it once more, and cast it as far as he could into the sea.

The sky flushed pink, and with the old man still snoring, Shamir saddled his mount and retraced their steps to Raqmu.

26

ASLAH STOOD IN THE path of his protege as Shamir headed to the quarry behind the Head-of-the-Camel. The young man looked steadily at the ground in front of him, mumbling to himself and not looking up. He collided with his master, reeled backward a few paces and blinked his eyes.

"Please forgive me, sir! I was lost in my own thoughts and did not see you there. Please forgive my pig-headedness."

"My son, it has been two months since you returned from the north. You've eaten little, and said less. I did not want to pry into the private matters of your life, but it is now affecting your work, and your health. So I must ask the questions that will penetrate your silence—I take it your encounter with the daughter of Manotu did not go well?"

The young man looked again at the ground, and after an awkward length of silence raised his head, his eyes filled with a mixture of pain and anger. He said, "Though I can think of nothing but my failures, I find it difficult to speak of them."

Aslah chuckled. "Your failures? Please excuse me for laughing, but you are, perhaps, the most gifted young man I have yet tutored in the ways of my knowledge. You mean your failures with this woman? I have spoken recently with Manotu, and have come to the conclusion that this failure—if you wish to call it that—is not simply your own, but perhaps more so, that of the one who so captured your attention. Manotu said he has always known any suitor for his daughter would probably pay a hefty price—not in the monetary terms of a bride-price, but in the demands her character might put upon their affections. The daughter of Manotu is certainly a remarkable woman—her many arts and talents, and personal charms, are above any of the feminine race I have ever known. But the powerful attraction of these same virtues could be the downfall of many who would love her. And it may, in the end, result in her own tragic fall."

Shamir pouted his lips and shook his head. "I hear the truth in what you tell me, and yet, I still feel the fool. How could I be so blind to fall for my own dreams? To think such a woman could ever care for me?"

Aslah locked his gaze on the young man's eyes. "Perhaps I should tell you no more, but Manotu further said to me that the morning his daughter left for Bostra, something unexpected clouded her mood. Something he'd never seen in her. He said her usual blithe spirit eluded her, replaced by some great conflict warring within. She fled their home that day, attempting to escape something besetting her—haunting her. As Manotu and I spoke at length, he came to the belief that you had left a deep mark upon her heart; a mark she was not prepared to acknowledge, or succumb to. Perhaps your effect on this woman was not so small as you think. Her flight to the north may be evidence of such effect, rather than proof of its absence."

Shamir raised both hands in exasperation. "My master, how can I ever trust my feelings again, when it comes to women? How can I ever find my way through what seems to me a maze? I feel lost in this, before I've even begun!"

The older man scratched the back of his head, squinted his eyes a little and chuckled again. "My son, the ways between a man and a woman cannot be fathomed. And you are right, they are like what the Hellenes call a 'labyrinth'—an unsolvable puzzle. But the very mystery of it makes it all the more attractive, and powerful, when it is fully engaged. One of our poets once said that *the whole business of love is to drown in the sea*, and that *in its embrace, the whole sea becomes full of pearls*. That which is simple, and easily mastered, is also that which is of little value or import. But give yourself a rest from these matters for the moment, as you will certainly come back to them at a future time. Let us head to the quarry, where there is stone waiting for us—stone, which is not fickle, or mysterious in its ways. It may be hard, but it will certainly, and predictably, yield to a mallet and chisel!"

In silence they walked the road leading to one of the main quarries of Raqmu. Tucked away behind the small mountain called the Camel's Head, men worked the substance of the earth. They cut fine-quality blocks to build free-standing construction in the city. Larger blocks suited the carving of ornamental architecture for the wealthy estates on Fortune Hill and the Royal Quarter. This morning, men swarmed the blocky outcrop, searching for material of the proper color, constitution, and flawless character that their specific projects required.

At the edge of the quarry stood two stone pylons, four-sided like a pyramid but narrower, and sharper at the apex. They stood twice as tall as a man, and rather than free-standing as most columns, they were carved in place—still attached at their bases to the bedrock. Shamir asked his master,

"I have heard you call these carvings a *nephesh*—but what soul could they have?"

"When we say *nephesh*, we mean not simply a man's soul as he lives, but we speak of his continuing essence—the remaining trace of all that man is. These two carvings memorialize the two workmen who died in this quarry in the last fifty years or so. Their bones were dry long ago, and were gathered into their families' tombs. But here, where they worked daily, where their sweat and blood stained the ground, we yet remember them—Utaih and Abdmank. At the tremendous labor of carving away a large portion of this mountain's rock, and leaving only these two obelisks, we grant great significance to their lives, to remember who they were. Every time we enter the quarry, we see, and can reach out and touch, a portion of the essence of these two men."

Shamir said, "These men must have made a mark for themselves in the lives of their friends, to be so honored."

"Yes, it is as you say. This is akin to the betyls—the featureless stones to which we ascribe the presence of the gods. Through the great efforts required in producing such geometrically perfect blocks, when men look at them they give their honor to the one whose presence sits upon such a throne."

Aslah waved to three quarry-men near the mountain's top. They acknowledged his presence and began leaping from surface to surface on the tops of blocks yet embedded in the mountain's face. In short order they made their way to the bottom near Aslah and his apprentice. The lead-man called out, "Halloo and good health to you both! We heard you seek top-quality material for special projects at the Royal Palace. What, in particular, will you need?"

"The King's manager contracted us for a new fountain and pool, to be added to the garden at the Queen's private residence. We will need block for building a wall for the pool which we'll carve with fine details—the wall to be about a cubit thick and two in height, with a running length of fifteen. It will be laid with two courses of block. The fountain will consist of a sculpture standing within the pool. Finished, it will stand four and a half cubits tall, including its attached base. The sculpture's block must be flawless, of greater strength than required for the wall, and an unfinished size of two cubits wide, by one and a half thick, by five tall. The wall's blocks can be either variegated or pure, as it will be plastered and colored in the end. But the sculptural block requires a pure, light tone—the lighter, the better. Can we see what you have?"

"Follow me to the north end over there. The block for the wall is standard, of course. We can easily meet your requirements. We will pull two extra from the matrix, so any mishap at the site or unexpected flaws will not delay your work."

Arriving at the uncut block at the north face, the man pointed out the particular material he proposed to fill the order. Aslah directed Shamir, "Take a close look at the material—what do you think? Is it sufficient for royal projects?"

He bent down and slowly stroked the raw surface of stone with open palm and fingers, lightly dragging his hand one way and then the other. He ran it over all the exposed faces of stone, and then rested it on the rock, considering it. He said, "It is not precisely perfect, but it will do—even for royal work."

The three quarry-men looked at each other, pursed their lips and rolled their eyes. Aslah told them, "You heard the man—this will do. You can deliver the blocks directly to the site. We will expect them within ten days. The guard at the gate will show you the place. And the large block for sculpting?"

"That will be high on the face, and toward the south end. If you don't mind climbing, you can follow us up and see it yourselves."

"We don't mind, do we, Shamir? We haven't been up in the rocks for quite some time, so we shall thrill to get our heads back in the clouds and the blue again—lead on!"

The five men hiked to the foot of the south face. The quarry-men clambered up the cliff, expecting the two masons to fall behind them, but the older man and his young charge quickly outpaced them, scampering over the angular rock faces like a pair of coneys. They waited near the top for the others to catch up.

"Old man, you climb like a man less than half your age! You've obviously spent some years in the quarry—you know your way around the blocks! Come over here and I believe you'll find the stone you seek."

They traversed the horizontal course of uncut block, arriving at a mass protruding beyond the rest. The lead-man said, "This material has been long untouched, as harder than the rest, but its strength is also superior. And the size is more than twice what you need. Shall we take it?"

Aslah evaluated the stone himself, looking at it closely and running his hand over it. He said to Shamir, 'Well, make your own judgement of it. What do you think?"

As before, Shamir ran his hand lightly and carefully over the entire exposed surface of the mass. He then picked up a fist-sized rock lying at his feet, and knocked the mass with it in several locations, evaluating its sound and feel. Finally, he held both his palms on the rock face, and stood there motionless, his eyes closed. Satisfied he found the truth, he opened his eyes and stepped back from the rock. He asked Aslah, "How does my master evaluate the piece?"

"An absolutely perfect stone will never be found, but this one should suit the project—even a royal one, such as this. And your own sense of this block's character?"

The corner's of Shamir's mouth turned down like the first crescent after the new-moon. "I find it difficult to contradict the findings of my master, but this stone—this first block—is no good. It appears near perfection at its surface, but within lies a fatal flaw. It is so far within, it might evade detection until the sculpture's form is nearing completion, and then the work will finally fail—not just the appearance, but its structural integrity. All the work will be lost, and we shall have to begin again. No, pull this first block and reject it, then pull the one behind it, which *is* near-perfect, and deliver it to my master's shop. That is the block we will take."

The three quarry-men shook their heads in disbelief, and Aslah narrowed his eyes. But he told them, "You heard what the young man said. We will pay from the King's budget for both blocks. We will pay standard price for the first, but will not take delivery, and premium price for the second, which you *will* deliver. We will expect it in my shop within six days."

27

TWO DAYS LATER, WITH the evening sky fading to peach and violet, Aslah poked his head into Shamir's tent. His slanted smile colored his face with barely-disguised excitement. "Have you heard? The quarry-men came to me earlier, saying they pulled the first block— the one you rejected as unsound. As soon as they moved it away to provide space to work the second,—*snap-crack!*—the block failed of its own, falling in pieces—split into three! From the time you were a slip of a boy, I knew you had some uncanny sense of the integrity of stone—until now, I never knew the extent of the gift. While I can glean some idea of how sound a stone is, I can only see what lies on the surface, what is visible to the eyes in my head. You have a rare, and unexplained knack to somehow see into the depths of stone—to know whether flaw or perfection lies within!"

Aslah's praise of Shamir's gift embarrassed him. He looked to the ground, and said nothing in response. Finally he said, "I always knew I could see, or whatever it is, inside the stone. Maybe I feel it...I don't know. I always thought others had the same sense, but as time went on, I could not understand why they always neglected the obvious. So then I thought, maybe to them it is not so obvious."

"As I said, my son, this is a rare gift. One that I have never seen in another. While your talent of working the stone is a remarkable skill, it is something that can be taught, cultivated, and raised to a high art. But the gift you possess is an entirely different matter. Some would say, it is a gift from the gods."

"Is that what you think? That Dushara or 'Lat—maybe Manawat—has somehow blessed me with this? What do you think of the gods? I remember at the *marzeah* in Manotu's hall, you mentioned something about—*Hayyasa*, I think you called it—'*The Mercy*'? You said we would talk of this again."

Aslah fully entered the tent and sat on cushions near its far corner. He motioned for Shamir to sit near him. The older man scratched the top of his nearly bald head, raised his eyebrows into high arches, and tugged at his red beard.

"Ah, yes. The Mercy. I must first say I am something of a rebel, in this nation devoted to Dushara—to his wife, and amma—and to all the rest. Like you, I was brought up in the worship of all these gods and goddesses. But life has tempered my devotion to them. Much that I have seen and known—and felt—has seemed to pull me from the old faiths. Many would probably stone me for such heresy, and unbelief. But even now, in this current generation, you see the gods of old diluted with the names of the Hellene and Egyptian pantheon. Dushara becomes Zeus, or Dionysus. 'Lat becomes Aphrodite. 'Uzza becomes Isis. Or some say 'Uzza is Aphrodite, and 'Lat, Isis. It is all confusing. And these new gods all seem like mere men or women, albeit with vastly greater powers. They are petty, and tragically flawed—like all the men I know—like myself. Could these really be the powers responsible for all the glory I see, revealed in the heavens above, and in the earth around me?"

Shamir took a small skin of wine from the tent's corner, removed its plug and handed it to him. He took a swig and handed it back. Shamir plugged it again and laid it aside. He said, "I see what you mean. I often felt something like this, watching my Abba pour out his cheap wine on the black stone he said was the presence of Dushara. And how could one as powerful as the Lord of the Sharas live in a rock…a rock cut and dressed by a mere man?"

Aslah leaned toward the young man and lowered his voice. "My son, I have not told this to anyone until now—not even Mashkuya—but, at times, I have roamed these rugged mountains in search of a new and perfect stone, or to work out the details of some difficult design. And I have sometimes sensed up there…a great weight pressing down upon me. I cannot see it, but the immense bulk is beyond my reckoning, and its perfection and beauty so far above any understanding, it throws me to the ground and crushes me. It crushes me so—I cannot even draw breath. But while it is such a great and solemn oppression, I sense it means me no harm. That if it did wish to kill me, it would merely puff on my small life like the wick of a lamp, and extinguish it in an instant. But along with its holy perfection, the great weight is filled with an equally vast mercy for me. It not only wishes me no harm, but holds within its heart all things for my greatest benefit. This is why I have come to call it 'The Mercy,' for it—or he—is surely that."

Shamir cocked his head, attempting to make sense of the man's cryptic words. "Is this not just Dushara? The Lord of these Shara mountains? When you climb into his realm, would he not make his presence known to you?"

A skewed smile crossed the older man's lips, at a loss for how to better explain himself. He scratched the back of his head and said,

"This is no god-of-the-mountains. Though Dushara has his devotees throughout the land of the Nabatu, beyond this land they know nothing of him, and they worship a thousand other gods, with a thousand other names. No, this one is higher than the highest heavens, and for whom the entire earth—in all its rocky bulk—is but a grain of dust. At night when I cannot sleep, I leave my tent and look up, to see numberless, glorious stars swimming in the endless void of midnight. Are they pin-pricked holes in the black canopy, letting the light of some holy-lit place beyond shine into our night sky? Perhaps they are countless suns like our own, burning with unending light, shining on their own uncountable worlds like this one? No one knows these things, and yet, I believe I know with a certainty beyond anything else I ever thought I knew, that all of these wonderful things we have seen are simply play-things created by The Mercy for his good pleasure. He was before, and outside of all that we can see, or touch, or know. And while he is so grand and unfathomable, in some strange way he stoops himself down to where we live, and touches our tiny lives with his care, with his compassion for us."

Shamir shook his head and blinked his eyes. "My master, your words cause my head to swim, and spin. I cannot wrap my thinking or understanding around such ideas. Does this one have a name by which he can be called? Is The Mercy his name?"

"No, though I use that word in reference to him, I don't know that he has revealed his personal name to me. Our neighbors the Iudaeans say their god is so far beyond our own experience it is foolish to desecrate him by speaking his name—if he has one. I once worked in Yerushalayim alongside a couple of Iudaean stone-smiths. They had labored on Herod's great temple for their god. They told me that one of their prophets long ago had encountered their god far out in the desert, somewhere just south of here, and the prophet asked his name. The god replied not so much with something we might call a name, but with a name-like description, summing up who he was. He told the prophet simply, 'I AM...THAT I AM.' I take that to mean he claimed he was the 'self-existent-one'—the one who was before anything else, and through whom, all that we know of has its being. These men said this 'sacred name,'—if you want to call it that—was so holy that their priests said no one should even attempt to pronounce it. That to say it aloud would defile it.'

"Are you saying, Aslah, that this great weight you have met, or felt —that you call The Mercy—is the god claimed and worshipped by the Iudaeans?"

"I don't know. But there are striking similarities. I have read some of their holy writings, and their descriptions of the all-surpassing might and glory, and yes, mercy, of this god of the Iudaeans, reminds me much of the one I have encountered. Whether they are, or are not, one and the same I cannot swear. All I know is that, for me, devotion to Dushara, or to those deemed his wife and amma, and all the rest, no longer holds for me anything of value. And the farther these old gods are diluted by the mannishness of the Hellene pantheon, the less truth seems in them. I believe this *one-who-is-higher-than-the-highest-heavens* is touching my life in some way. And, perhaps, he will touch yours as well. You asked me about my words concerning The Mercy—and there you have it. I can say no more."

28

AND SO IT WAS that the brilliance of mid-morning sunlight glared from the great rock called the Camel's Head. Disturbed from their roost on the far side, a flight of ravens flew over the rock and sped away, above the city's central Colonnade. Almost halfway to the quarry that lay behind the rock, Shamir stopped to watch them pass directly overhead. They continued fleeing their place of rest, toward the mountain Qubta, and the Grand Thaniya at the eastern outskirts of Raqmu.

After he watched the birds disappear into the city's narrow, twisting entrance, he turned to hike the last stretch to the quarry. With the imperfect block at the quarry's face now removed, the quarrymen labored to free the high-quality block behind it. The piece would provide Aslah and Shamir the material for creating a sculpture for the Queen's new walled garden. By the time he met Aslah at the quarry site, he estimated they should be near the point of detaching the stone.

He rounded the north side of the Camel's Head and entered the valley passing between it and the quarry on the next mountain—still in the shade of morning. A boy in ragged clothes, and out of breath, ran up the path, pointed back and shouted,

"Rockfall!—rockfall! Two men lie trapped—go help them!—I will find more men!"

Shamir lifted his tunic above his knees and sprinted to the rock-cutting face. Half a dozen men—some standing, some crouching—crowded together at the far end of the quarry—in the vicinity of where he and Aslah selected their stone. The area now looked nothing as it did two days previous. Above their block, the once flat and vertical stone face had collapsed, strewing a chaotic rubble of large, jagged boulders across and beyond their block.

His pounding heart rose into his throat, and the hair on the back of his head stood up. He yelled ahead to the men—"Who is it? Who lies trapped?!" But no one answered or looked back.

When he arrived at the scene of destruction he shouted again, "Who is it?!"

One of the crouching men turned and yelled, "Waliqu has been crushed to death and we cannot even find him. But we are speaking with Aslah, who yet lives!"

He shoved his way through the crew. Aslah lay face-up on the ground, his skin pale and cold as alabaster. The man kneeling next to him gripped Aslah's hand.

Shamir fell to his knees near his master's face. Only the man's head, shoulders, and torso were exposed—below the waist, his body disappeared under an immense slab of rock. He leaned toward Aslah and told him, "We will pull these rocks away from you, and get you back to your tent. You will be alright!"

Aslah looked up at him. "Is that you, Shamir? We almost freed our nice block of material for the sculpture. But there must have been a weakness in the overburden above our piece. It failed, and fell so fast we had no escape. I don't know what happened to Waliqu. They cannot find him. He must be crushed by the same mass holding me. I know there is nothing left below my waist—I am surprised I feel no pain."

"No! You will be fine! After we remove these rocks, we will take you home and Mashkuya will patch you up."

In a slow, calm cadence, Aslah said, "At last, everything comes to its own end—it will wear out, decay, or otherwise suffer final corruption. All things must die. The heavens will be rolled up like a scroll, and time itself will be closed like a tomb."

Shamir looked up at the others, but they were shaking their heads. He stood and repositioned himself to roll away the large boulder trapping Aslah. With all the strength he possessed, he attacked the rock, but it made not a pretense of moving. Looking toward the men, he shouted,

"Help me! Together, we can move the rock from Aslah!"

But they shook their heads again and said, "The man is gone, and beyond all help. And the rock is still unstable—if we disturb it, injury or death may come to us as well."

"Help me!—or I will do it myself!"

He seized an iron pry-bar lying there and thrust it between the bedrock and the boulder pinning Aslah. The muscles in his arms, back, and thighs bulged, and their veins stood out from the skin. His groan of great effort became a muffled scream as he strained to move a mountain.

With a ringing *clang!*, the iron bar shattered at its middle, and Shamir pitched forward violently. The great force of his effort drove the dagger-like broken shard of iron through the center of his left wrist. It pierced through flesh, sinew, and bone, the ugly prong exiting the other side. Shamir shrieked as fiery pain shot up his arm and flooded his body. A barb of the broken iron prevented his desperate attempts to yank his wrist from the source of pain.

One man took up a hammer and chisel to shear the barb from the shaft, but another interceded in the effort and yelled a warning at him—

"This man incurred the wrath of Manawat for daring to overturn her fate for Aslah—and now *you* would intervene in *this man's fate?* Leave him to his sad destiny—or tempt the goddess at your own peril!"

Paying no heed to his words, he shoved the man aside and placed the point of his chisel at the base of the barb. With two, sharp strikes of the hammer the barb sheared away. He helped Shamir extricate his wrist from the agony, the jagged metal scraping audibly as it passed back through the bone.

In abject misery, he collapsed to his knees. Blood ran from the gaping hole in his wrist and dripped to the ground, where it mixed with that of Aslah's seeping out from below the crushing rock. Aslah's face looked up into Shamir's, but he said nothing. His unblinking eyes possessed a vacant peace, and his face displayed an absence of concern for his mortal condition.

Shamir wept unconsolable tears.

"I cannot help you—but you cannot leave me! To whom shall I now go? No one is left for me..."

In Aslah's tent, Mashkuya laid aside her own severe grief. She stirred myrrh into a bowl of wine and then divided a handful of clean, raw wool in two pieces. She soaked them in the drugged wine and then applied them to each side of Shamir's tortured wrist. A long strip of linen wound around them held them in place, and with another band of fabric she fashioned a sling around his neck to immobilize his wrist near his heart.

Holding the bowl out to Shamir, she said, "Here, my son—drink it all. The myrrh will dull your pain."

Mashkuya helped him hold it to his lips, and he swallowed the drug. When he finished it, she set aside the bowl and then stroked his hair, smiling at him. But the smile soon faded from her face, her brow furrowed, and the gravity of the moment pulled the corners of her mouth downward. Her lower lip quivered, and her face looked as though it might shatter.

She turned away from Shamir and a muffled cry escaped her lips. He wrapped his good arm around her waist and pulled her closer.

Beginning to weep himself, he told her, "I tried to save him...but could not. I wanted to tell him *goodbye!*, but I was too late—he was already gone. Now, what will I do without my master, my friend?—my *Abba!*"

She patted his back and then touched her cheek to his.

"Lie back, Nahor, and let the myrrh and wine do their work. We will fare somehow. Perhaps this great Mercy my husband spoke of will find its way to our tents."

He lay back on the cushions and Mashkuya kept watch over him as he fell into something like sleep.

He felt himself tumbling, falling in the dark. And a voice began ringing in his ears. It was the words of the midwife at his birth, saying,—

This one's heart is harder than flint, and he must fall upon the great rock, to be broken to pieces, lest the rock fall upon him and crush him to dust.

Then he saw a great rock—a mountain of pure, white alabaster—which fell with great calamity, falling upon his master, crushing him. Shamir cried out, "No, *fall on me!*, not my master—he has done nothing deserving this—I am the one to be crushed by the stone!"

He ran toward the great stone, but the faster he ran, the farther it receded. He ran yet faster, and the mountain disappeared beyond the far horizon. He sat on the ground in fatigue, and defeat. He wept.

"*Amma?* May I call you that?"

Shamir sat on the wood bench next to Mashkuya. She cooked a pot of lentils on the fire outside her tent, and plucked feathers from a pair of doves given her by a neighbor. She dropped the birds in her lap and leaned against him. Mashkuya looked up at the young man and with the soft, downy feathers yet clinging to her fingers, she brushed his curly hair from his face. Tears pooled in the corners of her eyes as she answered,

"Ever since you arrived that first evening with Aslah, you have been my son. And I have always longed to hear you call me *Amma*. I could never replace she who birthed you, but I hoped to mother you with her grace. I knew you grieved your loss of her, and so I grieved with you."

He wrapped his arm around her shoulder and hugged her to him. Her wet eyes spilled tears over the dark arcs below them, running down the sallow, hollow cheeks. He said to her,

"From the time Aslah took charge of me, he always saw me as a young man in progress. He constantly challenged me, pushing me forward—he saw something of great value in me, and encouraged me to find it for myself. But I always treasured the end of the day, when I could come home and sit by your fire, to have you fill my belly with the love you put in your cooking, and to have you wrap your arms around me and ask me what I learned that day. So many times my heart wanted to call you *Amma!*, yet I felt it was not my place here—that I was not truly your son, so how could I take such liberty?"

She lay over, across his lap, and he could feel her tremble as she quietly cried. He patted her back and told her,

"The quarrymen told me today they began work on excavating a portion of the quarry for carving two *nephesh* pylons—to the memories of Aslah and Waliqu. Their memorial stones will join the other two who gave up their lives there in years past. And they have barricaded the quarry's far end—where the rockfall occurred. Because it is remote and high in elevation, they have made of the area an exposure platform. A priest has sanctified the location where Aslah fell, and his body will remain there for the allotted period of exposure. Then I will gather his bones and we will inter them in the hall near the entrance to the Grand Thaniya—to join those of all his fathers named Aslah, and his son Aslah. The family of this great name will then be complete."

She sat up again and said,

"After we celebrate his life at the marzeah, my own life here in Raqmu will be finished. I cannot forever lean on the good will of my neighbors. And with your own bad injury restricting your work, I do not wish to be your burden. So I am sending word of Aslah's death, and my need, to our eldest boy who lives and conducts a successful business in Obodas. I know he will take me into his family there."

He said,

"Though I cannot bear to let you go, I know it will be for your best. You need to be among a large family who loves you. You should dandle your children's children upon your knees by day, and at night, tell them stories of Aslah, and of long ago. I have no such children to bring you joy. And who knows if any woman will ever consent to be my wife?"

She was silent for awhile and then said,

"I know a woman waits for you somewhere, Nahor. Do you remember Aslah's fondness for the poets of old? He often quoted one to me, late at night. He would say—*Lovers do not finally meet somewhere, they are in each other all along!* You will find that one who is already in you."

Part Three

—Flight Beyond—

29

AND SO IT WAS, that Shamir journeyed four days south from Raqmu, to the Nabataean port of Aila. It terminated the arid rift called the Arabah and crowned the head of the saltwater gulf that led to the world beyond: to all the lands of the distant east. At Aila's docks, fleets of ships unburdened their loads from those eastern lands: spices, ivory, rare woods; gems, muslins, and silk. Merchants' laborers loaded the cargoes onto the backs of camels for transport to Raqmu, Gaza, and Alexandria; destined for the luxury markets scattered about the Great Sea to the west.

But the day's work was long gone and it rested with the sun. Now in midnight's blackness, a huge ship's deck hovered near Aila's pier like an island of light. Four lamps glowed yellow at the bow, four at the stern and a dozen scattered amidships. The faintest breath of breeze from the southwest left the water's surface barely ruffled—like dressed blackstone.

After tossing his satchel aboard, Shamir stepped onto the teak deck from the pier. Out of nowhere, a massive, horizontal tree-limb appeared at chest-height, barring his further progress. But rather than bark, coarse hair covered the limb, and the trunk barked, "And where do ye think ye be going on this fair barque?"

The brusk manner of the ship's night-watch caught Shamir off-balance, and he tried to right himself. "I...I've already paid my passage onboard. I have the token in my bag here somewhere. I'll find it..."

He started to open the bag, in which he stored all his earthly goods, but a huge hand at the end of the hairy tree-limb grabbed his wrist and extracted his hand from the bag. The tree spoke again.

"I'll be searching the bag, not ye! Ye wouldn't think I'd fall for ye pulling your janbiya on me, now would ye?" He thrust his rough hand in the bag, rudely rummaged around in the clothing, and finding no threat said, "All seems fair in your holdings. Now find the token, and be quick about it—we don't take lightly those what slither aboard in stealth, attempting to steal passage. I'm waiting..."

Shamir dove into his bag with both hands, searching through the now-chaotic state of what once were carefully folded and packed clothing and other effects. At the bottom of the satchel he felt the weighty, bronze medallion, guaranteeing his passage to the farthest shore of the Hindi. He pulled it the from the bag and held it out to the night-guard.

"Here is the token—my journey takes me to Muciri, of the Cherans. Though I am paid as a passenger, laboring with my hands has been my life, so with joy I would hoist ropes alongside you and your brothers."

A hearty laugh erupted from the tree-trunk. "To hoist ropes would be your joy? Had the midwife dropped ye on your head at birth? Halfway there, we shall see if ye still count it joy! Come aboard, and join this merry bunch of goats and mongrels—ye shall be fit company!"

The tree-limb swung away from blocking his path and welcomed him with open hand. "By what name are ye called?"

"My Abba named me 'Nahor.' But no longer in the shade of his tent, I am called Shamir. And yours?"

In the lamp-lights' glow the man seemed a large bear standing upright on hind-legs—but strangely dressed in a *zeira*, the long flowing robe of white, bound by a wide blue belt at the waist. In his dark face glimmered the white of one eye, and a strange, sparkling glint in the other. The black, curling hair of mustache and beard guarded his lower face.

"I am Zabibe—and before ye offer opinions on the presumed girlish-nature of my name, let it be known that in my own country, to the south and east of the Nabataeans, this be the honorable and mannish moniker of many a man. Upon this ship, I hear unending coarse jokes at my expense about a supposed lack of ballocks swinging 'twixt my legs—not to mention improper advances of crewmates mid-voyage. But be forewarned—no eunuch am I! And constantly prepared am I, upon this fair barque, to defend my manly honor."

The massive *bhaglah* boasted a crew of forty-seven men, who would hoist clouds of tapered sail on the three masts. Rope of white coconut fiber stitched together the ship's wide planks of Cheran hardwood timber. And in letters of Nabataean script on one side, the ship proclaimed its name—'*Sarandib*'—and on the other, '*Halad-vipa*'—both meaning '*Dwelling of Lions*' in the respective languages at both ends of their seafaring journey.

In the cavern of its hold, the ship held ten-thousand talents of lubunah, myrrh, gold, wine, barley, ceramic fineware, and bronze statuary. At the Malabar coast of its Hindi destination, the ship would belch forth its precious cargo, to be traded for earthen jars filled with the spices cinnamon, cassia, and cardamom, and precious gems like pearls, rubies, and adamant. Also, teak, ebony, and rosewood logs would fill the hold alongside tusks of ivory. And they would take on board the greatest treasure from even farther east:

rolled bolts of woven luxury—the *serai*, or silk—fabric of the gods and birthed in mystery.

Zabibe examined the new passenger and shipmate closely, squeezing Shamir's biceps in his grip, pounding between the shoulder-blades with his fist, and striking the belly with open palms.

"I see ye have great strength above the waist. Ye will do well here on the deck and in the shrouds. The *Sarandib* is a proud ship, and does not put up with being handled by weak or sloppy hands. If ye mistreat her, she will cast ye from her masts, or slip ye from her sheets, and so disgorge ye into the depths of the sea. And coils of seaweed would ensnare ye and drag ye to the bottom—or some great fish may swallow ye up, to be dissolved in its evil belly. Even calling upon your gods, whoever they may be, will not save you!"

The sailor's wild gestures and dramatic facial expressions punctuated his words. He paused in his theatrical performance and said,

"The build of your arms, shoulders and chest make me wonder— what occupied your labor before joining us this night?"

"I was a mason…in Raqmu."

"Ye were quarryman…or artist?"

"I was well on my voyage to becoming a master sculptor."

The massive man stroked the curls of his beard and squinted one eye.

"A sculptor, ye say? And now ye would be a sailor?—a dog adrift in the belly of the sea? Ye should be rubbing shoulders with royalty, my brother!"

Shamir's countenance dropped to the deck, but in the dim light he felt no need to mask it.

"I once entertained such thoughts. Except for an accident, I would be there today."

"Ahhh. But of course, there are no accidents, are there? Does not she of the Nabatu—the Great Manawat—see to that?"

"If so, she is a cruel, divine mistress, not only taking the subtlety from one of my hands, but stealing my profession—and all those who could love me and make my life a delight."

"Ah, yes...cruel, indeed. But each of us sailing these waves together be brothers in such cruelty. Look up, ye are among brothers here! We all have such tales of woe. And sure I am, ye will hear each one a dozen times over before this voyage be done."

He retrieved a slim, copper ampoule from beneath his white robe, pulled the stopper, and held it to the night sky. In a profound bass, he sang, more than recited,

"Let us drink, my brother, to the Great Manawat, and the woe of destiny she brings—the stuff of great tales and songs to sing! Let these travails be the seed of epics, to dampen the sting!"

Tossing his head back, he put the copper bottle to his mouth, drinking the salute. He sucked in the drops which clung to his lips and passed the strong elixir to his new shipmate. Shamir drank the salute in like manner and extended the bottle to Zabibe, who turned his palms out, rejecting the return of the liquor.

"No, my Dog-Brother, take another—a deep draft—for the voyage will be long..."

He obeyed his compatriot, putting the bottle's lip to his own, and tilting its rump to the night sky.

30

WITH THE ARRIVAL OF favorable winds, they sailed the narrow and treacherous gulf south from Aila. For three days, they gingerly tacked their way toward the narrow, southern passage—the Straits of Phocae, near the isle of seals. The half-loaded ship then entered the larger, Avalitic Gulf separating the east coast of Egypt and the Hejaz. They continued southward to the port of Muza. There, they anchored just off the coast, to secretly take on raft-loads of lubunah tears from Saba and myrrh from Hadramawt, plus fresh water and victual stores. While the days grew longer, the southwest winds called *Liba* arrived, promising to blow ships eastward across the vast and empty expanse of the Erythraean Sea, and on to the Malabar coast.

With a following wind at their stern and fair skies to the horizon, the sails were set, and only the tiller-man worked at their progress. Shamir found Zabibe near the bow, leaning on the rails, staring into the two clear blues beyond.

"What do you see out there, my bear-of-a-brother?"

The man straightened up, hearing his compatriot's voice behind.

"What do I see? Two fathomless roads of blue, I see. And between them we glide."

He held one hand level, palm down and fingers together, the thumb barely separated below it—looking like the jaws of a crocodile, barely open. Into the open slot he inserted the fingers of the other hand, saying, "We slip through that narrow space where sky touches sea—where the dry kisses the wet, and high embraces low. The blue waters buoy up the great weight of this ship, lifting her hull above some unknown bottom, and the blue winds on high reach down to breathe upon her sails, driving her wheresoever they will. We lie here, sliding between the heavens and the sea, leaving our old port in the past, farther behind, and ever approaching our port ahead, yet in the future. We sailor-dog-brothers stand on deck to weigh anchor, hoist the sails, and climb the rigging, but no choice have we in our destination—or even the tack we take. We stand at the mercy of those owning the ship and the captain they hire, while they stand at the mercy of the elements. Is this not the life we live, caught between heaven and earth?—leaving our old port of the womb, and traveling at the behest of Manawat, to our port of destiny at the tomb?"

Zabibe turned away from the sea and sky to face his brother. His one eye glared fierce and dark with sober understanding. The other, an eyeless socket, held a silver tetradrachm, minted by the king of Syracuse and displaying the beautiful face of his city's divine feminine guardian—Arethusa. The sunlight glimmered brilliantly from the coin, its owner removing it nightly from its sheltered home, to clean and polish it with care. Shamir winced at the harsh reflection from the silver surrogate-eye. He joined Zabibe at the rail.

"I hear the voice of a philosopher in my dog-brother—and I thought you to be a sailor."

"No man of letters lives in this rough husk. But when the days and years stretch on, riding these galloping waves—whether they be spent at this rail gazing into the blues, or hauling in a rope of white-coir—a man's thoughts can dwell upon the state of the cosmos—the way things are."

"And where, my big brother, have your thoughts been dwelling since we left Muza?"

The sailor leaned his back against the gunnel, stretched out his arms and gripped the bleached rail with both his massive hands. He stamped his bare feet on the greyed teak of the holy-stoned deck, and looked up to the peak of the mid-ship mast raking the blue sky.

"Me thoughts have been bouncing around this rig we sail. Every day we work at keeping it on course and in ship-shape, but we often miss the nature of what it truly is."

"And what truly is it, my friend?"

"A remarkable artifice is a ship. It is a specific space—but without a place. A floating island, as it were. It is a whole world folded in upon itself, yet committed to the endless, open sea and sky. It plows the waves from tack to tack, ever moving from port to port, brothel to brothel, always seeking other worlds and their most precious treasures, hid within their walled gardens. If a people be without ships, their dreams fly away; revelry replaces adventure, and bureaucrats replace pirates. There is much to despise in the life of a sailor, but I would have none other. And you?"

"That is plenty to chew upon, brother. My first footsteps on such a floating world were stopped by the bulk of your hairy arm a fort-night ago. While I have spent many a day bobbing on the humps of ships-of-the-desert, the only body of saltwater I'd seen was the Sea of Salt—till I wandered into Aila and waded into the great gulf. And now, to see only blue water to all the horizons, is more than I can take in. It is truly a marvel to know nothing but the blue below and the blue above—and us floating between. And we go to a place yet a mystery to me—to see things I never dreamed."

The two men, silent for a time, watched the sea flow by them. Zabibe then peered deep into Shamir's eyes, attempting to see the life inside.

"Tell me, my brother, why do ye sail with us? Ye hide the true nature of your journey. For as the sun rises from the sea ahead of us each day, I see your eyes looking far beyond the place from which dawn sprang. There is something far beyond which ye seek. Many join us on these voyages, running to escape what lies behind. But it seems ye strive for what yet lies ahead. Do ye seek the love of a woman, or wealth, or adventure?"

Shamir wondered himself what he sought.

"Perhaps I seek all those—or none of them. Maybe, I look for something which never existed—except in the words of an old man's story. Or maybe I search for something yet unknown to me. Can that be? Can we strive to find that which we've never seen, or heard of, and have never named?"

The sailor lowered his head, and a low, slow whistle escaped his lips. The tremble of awe rattled his words.

"Aye—ye *do* seek that which lies beyond the horizon. I now hear it in your voice. I recognize it, since I once chased this myself. I sought a kingdom said to lie above the highest clouds. A kingdom where neither infirmity nor death reigned—whose king was Life itself, freely bestowing his never-ending vitality on all his subjects—even those who drank from his sacred fountain. But those were only the words I gave it. I know it could not be truly described by human tongue. With what words do ye call the end of your own search?"

Three white clouds, appearing no larger than a man's hand, sat upon the eastern horizon. White wisps like cobwebs floated far above them, and Shamir wondered if such a kingdom floated invisible, even farther above. He said,

"I have not yet told another of this. I seek something called…the Shamir."

"Yes, like your own name. Of course, I have heard of it—said to be fashioned in the mist of the earth's founding."

"So you already know of it? What else can you tell me about it?"

"They say it is small in stature, but it can split mountains, or melt the heart of the coldest woman. But if I possessed it, I would prefer the latter over the former!"

"I had not yet heard of its effect on women."

The sailor grinned.

"I just now added that—but if it can bring down a mountain, surely it could pry apart the iron barring a woman's heart!"

His grin faded and he said, "I am sorry, my brother, I should not make sport of the object of your quest. I know little more than this. The wrinkled and wizened sailors who spoke to me of this Shamir said it was gained by a great king to the west. But a man I once hauled rope with, swore on the name of Dushara that a king of the *east* possessed it. East—west—who truly knows if it even exists?"

He slapped Shamir on the back and said, "Maybe its existence matters not. If it compels ye to sail beyond the horizon, or to fly above the clouds, perhaps that is enough."

The ship's bow cleaved the waves before it, spreading apart the green-blue waters to the right and left, bubbles and white traces of foam riding on the wake's crest. Shamir stared into the depths.

31

THIRTEEN DAYS BEYOND THE port of Muza, the Dwelling of Lions ran with the wind. By then all hands had their sea-legs under them, and they settled into the constant, gentle rhythm of the ocean's broad swells. With the ship's posture and course steady, the sailor's routine shifted from actively working at the ship's progress, to maintaining rope, caulking leaks, and mending clothes. And when no more work presented itself, they filled their waking hours with singing, gambling, the reciting of poetry, and the telling of lies.

Several days previous, the last glimpse of land slipped below their aft horizon. While shore birds no longer accompanied them, black porpoises now played and leapt before the ship's bow. Their sleek bodies glistened in the sunlight as they left their watery world for brief moments in the air. The crew cheered them as companions of good fortune and praised Manawat for her swimming servants.

The boldest men on board indulged in a sport they called 'plunging.' They set a long spar in a pivot at the rail, and the one to become 'rider' grasped with both hands the tapered, long end. If he was less adventurous, he tightly entwined both arms and legs around it. Depending on the weight of the rider, three to five of his comrades hauled down the spar's short end, lifting the rider above the deck. To start a plunging pass, they swung the long end and its rider over the rail, forward of the fulcrum and above the sea. When the men released the spar, the falling tip would plunge the rider into the water, dragging him in a long arc below the waves. The ship's motion swung him toward the aft hull, when the haulers would jump as one, to again catch the spar and lift him from the sea. A single dunking was sport enough for most, but a few stout-hearted men took as many as a dozen plunges in a row. Though rare, a man occasionally lost his grip on the spar, or collided with the hull, and was lost at sea.

Halfway from noon to sunset one day, four men had already received their exhilarating immersions. In the midst of their sport, the ship's cook ran forward from the aft deck, where he had been butchering one of the goats. He flailed his arms like a sapling in a high wind, and in a high pitch chattered in panic. The crew paused in their sport to witness the scene.

"The entrails—the entrails! Seven black spots! Doom now follows us—our trailing wake is her dark path! She claims one on this ship!"

He returned to the goat carcass to finish his butchery, muttering "She follows...she follows..."

The frivolity of the sailors evaporated in the cook's dread warning. The few words heard on deck were now ones of quiet alarm.

Shamir sat down next to Zabibe, who chewed a fat wad of *qat*. The man's jaw jerked with jittery unease, and the veins in his temples protruded. Shamir asked the large sailor, "Do you believe the omen? Do seven specks on the intestines of a goat truly announce harm creeping upon us?"

Zabibe raised his one eye and flicked it back and forth on those of Shamir.

"Ye have now been a sailor for what?—three entire weeks? When ye have sailed these seas as long as I, ye will learn to respect the signs of misadventure. The signs may be found in the stars of the black void above, or floating among the waves. Or sometimes in the loops and tangles of bowels spilled upon this deck. These signs have passed from old dogs to pups like ye for generations unknown. Ye would do well to heed them."

The blood drained from Shamir's face.

"Then one among us is truly marked...and bound for calamity?"

"For a certainty. But we know not which. Not even Manawat herself knows his name or face. Just as the knuckle-bones are fated to roll a certain way as they are cast, no one—not even our harsh mistress—knows the count till the bones stop rolling. She acts in the outcome, but with a blind eye."

Shamir's eyes widened and the pitch of his voice raised. "So none on this deck are safe?"

Zabibe lowered his gaze and spoke in a half-whisper. "There is a way. A way to stretch a shield of protection over this crew."

Shamir's breathing quickened, and he gripped the older sailor's forearm. "Then let us apply this way of safety—this remedy!"

Zabibe shook his head and said, "Though the way is known, it has never been tried."

Shamir stood, waving his hands, and he raised his voice—"Then let us try it now! So we might all be saved!"

Zabibe pulled him back down and rebuked him. "Lower your voice! Ye do not understand what the remedy requires. And not *all* will be saved..."

"What then? Tell me!"

He sucked in a deep breath and said, "She knows not the one marked for the fall. So if one of us chooses to throw himself into her fearsome embrace, she will suppose he is the one, and take that one in payment for the rest. Then all else will be safe."

The explanation stunned Shamir and he could say nothing. Zabibe finally broke the silence.

"So, will *ye* be the one to throw yourself into the cold, iron talons of fate herself?—to save the rest of us?"

Silence drenched the air. Shamir felt his blood pulsing in his ears. Zabibe said,

"I thought not. None has yet been found to so act on behalf of the others. Each is willing to be saved himself, but not to save others by submitting himself to certain death. And so it goes…"

The other conversations on deck were few, and subdued.

For the first time in weeks, the southwest winds diminished. The sails hung slack. They lazily flapped in the slight breeze. Behind the barely moving ship, hung a somber, orange sun in the afternoon sky. The orb vanished behind clouds tumbling down from the north. The ship drifted without direction and slowly turned broadside to the storm. The air chilled and all on board hushed to watch the storm gather.

The clouds looked like jumbled heaps of black granite piled on layers of blue slate. They soon swelled to great hills and then mountains. An immense, gray wedge formed at their front and advanced toward the stalled ship. Below the wedge and between the clouds, the sky glowed an unnatural blue-green. In the still air the Dwelling of Lions lay dead in the water. In silence the huge wedge overtook the listless vessel. Each man raised his head and stretched his neck, watching it coast high above them. The hair on their necks stood at grim attention.

Momentarily awakened from his spellbound state, the captain screamed out, "Men!—Reef all sail!" The crew scattered across the deck, climbing rigging and pulling ropes to limit the sails' exposure to the imminent gusts. Before they could fully act, a great wind struck the ship broadside with violence. Sails ripped in tatters and the blast nearly capsized the ship. The boat heaved and threw men from the rigging. Their bodies thumped the hard teak planks of the deck. A few in the crew narrowly avoided being swept overboard as they collided with the downwind rail. The ship rocked three times before finally settling in the wind-whipped sea.

The rudderman fought to guide the barely-moving ship into the wind. The gale abated nearly as fast as it arose, only to be replaced by a downpour. In moments, the rain soaked the men through as if they had pitched into the sea at the end of a 'plunging' spar. And then it was over.

The blue-greenness widened and deepened, surrounding them in its unholy light. Heavy air pressed down, making breathing difficult. Not one spoke a word.

Tink...plink...thunk...

Hard, white, stones began falling from the churning mountains of storm above, hitting the deck, bouncing from it. Balls of ice, the size of grapes pelted them from the heavens. The flurry of hail grew in number, and size, until hundreds—thousands—of ice-stones fell upon the ship. As large as apricots, even peaches, the hail bounced or shattered on impact. Men cried out in terror and pain as the dangerous missiles struck them. They ran for cover, flinging themselves down hatchways, for safety below deck.

Hailstones of various size cluttered the deck in treachery. Zabibe rushed toward the nearest hatch, but lost his footing. He skated on the icy balls across the deck's crowned surface, toward the ship's rail. The impact pitched him headlong, his flailing arm catching the rail. Dread contorted his face and a shrill cry erupted from his mouth.

Shamir saw him dangling from the fragment of safety and ran to rescue him, but as he neared the man, the top of the rail split with a loud *crack!* Zabibe lost his grip and slipped into the sea's turbulence. Shamir's heart jumped into his mouth, and slipping on the icy deck himself, he rushed to look for his friend. He searched the waves for sight of the man overboard. Then the sound began—a buzzing— like the sound of ten thousands of hornets swarming from their hive.

He looked about him to locate the sound, and then he saw *her*, descending from the green sky. She twisted and twirled, dipping from the dark clouds, lowering her lithe, slender form to the sea.

Though having neither arms nor legs, she danced a sinuous dance, gyrating and flexing her bluish-white body. The sight entranced Shamir. The long, thin tail of her serpentine form touched the dark seas, roiling them into a white foam. A spray of water erupted in a ring around the tail's tip and was carried aloft around the twining body. Extending skyward, the spray clothed her in a white sheath of shimmering silk.

Shamir broke from the seductive spell. *Manawat claims his life— she takes my brother! I must either save his life, or forfeit my own.*

He glanced about the deck and saw a rope coiled at the foot of the middle mast. Stumbling and slipping over hailstones, he ran to the rope and secured one end to the mast. He returned to the rail and searched again for some sign of Zabibe but could not see him. He looped three coils of rope over one shoulder and dove into the dark waters.

His head broke the surface of the sea and he rose and fell with each wave. Rising to a peak, he briefly spied Zabibe struggling at a distance, aft of the ship. He swam for the man, straining to reach him. The storm raged around him and as he approached his brother, the swirling, blue-white snake above swept toward them. She reached out for Shamir, and he felt something snatch tightly at his shoulder. The rope pulled taught, its coils pulling him away from his friend. He quickly turned in the water, slipped the coils from his shoulder and flung them back to the struggling man.

"Take the rope!"

It landed behind Zabibe and he could not see it. He flailed his arms in the water, and when the very end floated behind him, his hand felt the rope's roughness and he grabbed for it. The rope began dragging him and his rescuer through the sea.

The voice of a sailor shouted to them from the ship—"Keep a tight hold, men, and we will haul you to safety!"

The rope soon pulled them yet faster through the waves, and they finally slid along the ship's hull. One man at a time, they were hoisted up the ship's side. Exhausted, they collapsed on deck.

The gale diminished and the dancing, writhing column retreated to the clouds. The storm passed on to the south, allowing a brief glimpse of the sun before it hid itself in the sea. Twilight came and went, and the ship's crew fell into an uneasy sleep. Shamir and Zabibe remained awake, waiting for the light of dawn.

On the morrow's daybreak, each man worked at some task in restoring the ship. The carpenter repaired the rail where Zabibe fell into the sea. Most of the sailors mended sail torn in the initial gust. Shamir and Zabibe sat beside each other, stitching sailcloth. They worked in silence until Zabibe, not looking up, said,

"Ye should have left me in the sea...to *her*."

Shamir stopped his stitching of the coarse sailcloth and said, "Left you? You would have drowned—or worse!"

"But I was the one chosen by her. She thirsted after my life. And you denied her the prize."

"You said if another offered up their own life, others might be saved."

Zabibe stopped his own stitching and stared into Shamir's face.

"But ye denied her your *own* flesh as well. There will be fate to pay. Not today. Not tomorrow. But an hour of her choosing."

The men returned to their repairs and spoke not another word concerning the matter.

32

AND SO IT WAS that the ship was restored. And the southwest winds again pushed the Dwelling of Lions toward its port in the east.

Zabibe tapped Shamir's chest with the back of his hairy hand and said, "I will show ye more—now I know my secrets are safe in your knowing."

With one hand he spread apart the lids where the missing eye once resided. And with the other, he pressed in the rim of the silver coin, so it pivoted in the empty socket like a door on its hinges. He pinched the protruding edge between thumb and finger to pull it from the cavity. Holding it toward Shamir, he said, "Here—hold my beautiful Arethusa for me."

Shamir took the coin and examined it, still warm from its residence in the man's face. It had a certain heft about it—the weight of four silver drachmas. He admired the bold beauty of the nymph's portrait—striking in its design and in its realistic portrayal of feminine charm. The coin's face held a three-quarter frontal portrait of the Nereid, Arethusa, who was said to have fled from the amorous pursuit of the river god Alphaeus, and then escaped as a fountain, finally springing up in Syracuse on the far side of the Great Western

Sea. Her eyes boldly met the stare of Shamir as he beheld her. The coiling locks of her hair floated outward in wild abandon, framing her face in fluid splendor. Three small dolphins bent their bodies in streamlined arcs, swimming and leaping in grace through the tumbling waves of her flowing hair. Her name, Arethusa, emblazoned the coin's rim above her head, and the diadem atop her hair proclaimed the name of the coin's engraver, Kimon.

Turning the silver disc over in his palm, he marveled at the depiction there of a chariot race. The charioteer passionately drove his four rearing steeds onward to the finish line, while Nike, winged goddess of victory flew above, delivering a laurel crown to the head of the victorious driver.

He looked back at Zabibe, who, from his eye-socket, extracted a small pouch of red silk, no larger than the end of his thumb. It left the cavity in his head vacant—filled now with only an angry red glower. Zabibe held the little bag in his palm and folded back its flap. He upended it and four bright flashes of pure red tumbled into his palm. He held high one of the gleaming stones—each the size of a small bean—and a ray of sunlight pierced through the gem, staining the light as with blood.

Shamir's excited whisper—"Rubies!"—was heard by no one but his friend.

"Aye, rubies! Some years back I met a man in Muciri, his art, cutting gems, and his business, trading them. Only the gods know why, but he took a liking to this old sailor and tutored me in the appraisal of precious stones—rubies, beryl, topaz, and the like. And he introduced me to the source of such gems—those who work the mountains and rivers in their pursuit. I began in a small way, buying a single stone here and there, and selling them for handsome profit in Raqmu, sometimes Alexandria. Within a few years, selling gems placed more silver in my palm than thrice that of raising sail and weighing anchor on this ship."

33

AT THE END OF forty days, in the late afternoon, the sharp bow cleaved blue water while creamy clouds of sail billowed full. Before them hung the pale, crescent moon in a pure blue sky. The lookout atop the foremast cried,

"A beacon's day-light shines from the tower at the mouth of the River Culli—we arrive at the coast of Chera! Rejoice, and thank your gods for a safe voyage!"

Shouts and hurrahs erupted from the crew on deck, and those below clambered up the ladders to join the merriment. They slapped backs and kissed bearded cheeks. Both fore and aft, men formed circles to dance, clap and sing in celebration. The cook released the remaining goat from its tether on deck to wander among the sailors' gaiety. Its freedom was brief, and its life soon forfeited in sacrifice to Dushara. Then came its butchering for the crew's last meal before tying at port.

The *Dwelling of Lions* plowed through the final hours' swelling of sea waves while the emerald forest fringing the coast grew in size. The beacon's stone tower on shore also began to show its true height. Just to the south of the light, the roiling width of the River

Culli's mouth sloughed its green-gray flow into the surf. Half the ship's crew strained at raising more sail, to increase their progress against the river's heavy flow.

As they pulled abreast of the light-tower, Shamir stood shoulder-to-shoulder with Zabibe at the forward rail, and said, "While I have surely seen remarkable structures, both carved and built of stone, I have never seen a marvel such as this—it must be the height of forty men, each atop the other!"

"Ye estimate on the short side, my friend. It is more like that of fifty men."

He pointed to the tower's top and said,

"The light we saw while still offshore, is formed by the sun's rays reflected from a great, polished-bronze mirror the size of a camel. And at night they kindle a blazing fire at the tower's peak to guide sailors in the dark. I have heard its building required a king's treasure and ten years' labor of five hundred men—and the life's blood of thirty-one. In majesty it is second alone to the great light-tower at Alexandria."

Shamir whistled low. "I have heard of the wonders of Alexandria. Have you seen them with your own eye?"

"I have. And while that city is certainly remarkable in its own style, I yet prefer the wonders of Raqmu. The lavish display of lush, green gardens, and the sparkling flow of waters in the midst of a vast and dry-as-a-stone desert, compels the heart to nearly spring from a man's chest. There be nothing else like it in the world."

"Tell me of our destination—the port at Muciri. I hear it lies yet farther up the river."

"It is not all that far by land, but the river's flow greatly impedes our progress. If it were not for the summer winds blowing at our backs, we could not sail up the river at all, and offshore we'd be forced to anchor, making our way to Muciri by land, or rowed in a *pattamar*, or small *badan*. As it is, two or three hours and we will reach it by river."

After weeks surrounded by only the sea's blue depths and the heavens' blue heights, the deep green forest bordering the River Culli and its equally green flow formed a potent contrast. It was if the ship left a rarified, fluid existence, to plunge headlong into a vivid new world, potent with life and mystery.

Shamir turned to Zabibe and said, "Once we make port, will you sleep aboard ship the four months we layover here? Or will you take a room at an inn in Muciri?"

Zabibe looked away from Shamir with his one eye, watching the emerald tangle of forest glide by. After long consideration of the question, in a low voice he confided, "Not a man outside of Muciri knows this...but my home awaits me there. While I spend most days of the year aboard ship, hauling ropes, holystoning the deck, and raising sail, this is not really my home. And while I was born among the Hadramaut, and raised by Nabataean pirates, Muciri is now my home. Seven years previous, on a layover longer than usual, I journeyed inland, beyond the kingdom of Chera, and found myself among the Pandyans. Though with their war-elephants they wage fierce battle with the Cherans—to seize their sacred images—as an outsider I found them an amiable sort, and befriended by them."

He paused in his explanation, wondering how far he should expose these matters. Shamir waited in patience, not eager to pry into the man's life. He finally began again.

"During the months I spent among them, I met a young woman. Not much more than girl. She took a liking to me—can ye imagine that? Taking a fancy to this stinking hulk of a one-eyed man? I suppose my physical heft and coarse ways were something of a novelty to that delicate creature. I wiled away many hours and days —weeks—with her and her family. I had never before known such bliss on this earth. Though we knew each other's speech but little, with eloquence she spoke to me in the taking of my hand, and by brushing my cheek. As I prepared to leave Pandya, to return to my ship in Muciri, I grieved the loss of such sweet company. And she wept greatly, entreating her father to give her to me as wife. Though I had little to offer the man in return, he granted her request, and retained the local priest to sanctify our vows to each other."

He paused again, and Shamir thought he saw a tear trickle from the man's lone eye. He waited, until his friend prepared himself to continue.

"I moved my sweet Aarunya to the far outskirts of Muciri—to a little hut I obtained for the cost of my silver 'eye.' I loathed to have her see the shame of my empty socket, so I filled it with a ball of clean wool and covered it with a patch of linen, tied round my head with a string. It was a year before I could replace it. My Aarunya and I had the time of one full moon to the next, for the sweet honey of knowing each other to the fullest. In Muciri, from the few gems I'd obtained, speculating for a profit in Nabataea, I selected and sold a fine-quality, uncut ruby for enough silver to keep my Aarunya safe and fed while I was gone. Our farewells before I left were long, and as bitter as they were sweet. I could barely pry the grip of her small hands from my waist."

"But you returned—your reunion must have been rich!"

"It was wealth beyond all words. Not only did I return to the love I never deserved, but when I saw her standing in the doorway of our little home, I saw her belly swollen with the promise of new life! Within two weeks, without assistance from a midwife, she delivered our first-born. In the five years since, my Aarunya has supplied our home with the gift of five more children, so we now have three small bulls and three small heifers—or that was the last tally. I have counted the hours of my last eight months of absence, waiting to see again the precious face of my woman, and if she again blesses me with another new shoot."

Shamir's jaw fell open and his eyes bulged. "I had not the slightest thought you maintained a family—or that you were even married!"

"I know...ye thought no woman in her right mind—even a one-eyed hag—would take up with a worm such as I. Am I right?"

Shamir grinned at the man's self-effacing words. "No, that is not what I meant at all…or maybe it was! Nonetheless, it pleases me greatly to know you have found such happiness. But how can you live the eight months on board this ship, longing as you must be, for your treasure waiting in Muciri?"

The sailor slowly shook his head, and then hung it to his chest. As he took a deep breath, his lungs trembled, drawing in the air.

"Ye cannot imagine the difficulty of such a life. For the most part, I keep to myself and do not mix with the crew. I devote myself to my work, as though it were my religion. And I fix my eyes on the plans I have made of gaining the best trades for gems in Muciri, and then making the most profitable sales in Raqmu or beyond. Each year my brood grows, and I must increase the value of my business. I hope, one day, to have built it enough to watch my children grow and learn each day, rather than seeing them just once a year, not even recognizing their faces. And to lie each night of the year with my Aarunya, hearing the bulbul sing its sweet nighting-song outside our hut. And I will wake with the sun's first rays, lying with my dawn beside me, wondering if I am truly awake, or still living and breathing in some world of dreams. If dream it be, I prefer to remain and die there, rather than return to this life without her—without my children."

The man's words astonished Shamir, his mouth hanging open as he listened. He said, "You once told me you'd have no other life than that to be found on the sea. And now, you disclose to me you do everything within your grasp to live in simple peace with your family?"

"Aye—I say these things to guard my image among those on board. And I once numbered ye with them. I tell them tales that I once held close—as some kind of truth. But ye now stand as more than shipmate, even more than friend. I hear in your voice and your heart you understand the value in these things. My true brother are ye. So I open my life to ye, as unrolling a scroll of sacred parchment. I trust ye with the tender, precious treasures I stumbled upon."

Shamir slapped his dear friend on the back and said, "I honor you, my brother, for finding such treasure without looking for it. And recognizing the gift for what it is, celebrating and cherishing it. And then doing what is within your grasp to solidify and magnify such a fortune. I could only wish for such a prize myself. But there is no map to be had for finding treasure such as this. They are either mysteriously bequeathed by some shadowy, divine hand, or simply the product of sheer, unspeakable luck."

"Luck or godly gift, I know not. But I am grateful for what I possess. And if ye find a tenth of what I have, a happy man ye will be!"

A silence came upon them, and they watched the impenetrable, green forest float by. An unexpected path opened briefly through the trees, giving them a fleeting glance into a glade farther in the jungle, where a tiger lay, holding the limp carcass of its fresh caught prey—a red-deer fawn.

34

THE SHIP ROUNDED THE last bend and a wide bay lay before them. It was Muciri, the port city of the Chera, where the handsome ships, the great works of the *Yavanas*—those from the west—churned white foam from the Culli River. They arrived with gold and departed with pepper, malabathrum, silk, and rubies. The din of commerce besieged this Muciri, overflowing with wealth. Like Raqmu, trade fueled this kingdom.

In the bustling port city domestic and traded goods were exchanged for imported gold. The generous Cheran chiefs, flush with wealth from the prodigious trade, regarded their contacts with merchants from the west as a form of gift exchange more than straightforward commercial dealings. Though speaking a vastly different tongue, they regarded the foreigners more as brothers than clients.

The *Dwelling of Lions* plowed toward its final anchorage in the port, gliding through the city's center. Still standing at the rail, Zabibe laughed aloud, delighted to see his home again. He gestured with outspread hands to the tumult of activity and said to Shamir, "Look! This is Muciri, with its streets, its houses, its covered fishing boats, where they sell fish and pile up rice—with the shifting and mingling crowd of the raucous river-bank, where the sacks of pepper lie in heaps—with its gold deliveries carried by these ocean-going ships and brought to the river-bank by local boats. This is the city of the gold-collared Kuttuvan, the Cheran chief. The city that casually bestows wealth to its visitors, and the merchants of the mountains, and the merchants of the sea. The city where liquor abounds. Yes, this Muciri, where the tumbling ocean roars and the river rumbles, is to me a marvel, a treasure."

The two men launched the skiff, to row from ship to shore, delivering the *Dwelling of Lions'* captain and second officers to the solid earth. Shoulder-to-shoulder, they put their backs into pulling the long oars, and side-by-side they spoke of how to best use their freedom on land. Zabibe extended his invitation to Shamir. "Come with me—to meet my fair Aarunya, and my six little ones. Rejoice with me at our reunion."

The oars made a slight slapping sound as they dipped into the water in unison. The rowers' heaving lungs sucked in the heavy, musty air floating above the river's water. Shamir said,

"I cannot intrude upon so precious and private a moment. This is the exclusive privilege of a family—not an outsider."

"Ye are no outsider—ye are my brother! Ye have shared in my life at sea—no, saved my life—so now share in my life at home. I know my Aarunya would have it no other way."

The little boat's hull had barely touched the gravel of the beach, when they leapt from its side to pull it farther onto shore. They assisted their superiors in disembarking, then secured the boat with a line to the large bronze pin driven into the shore. They stowed all the boat's equipment in proper order and prepared to go ashore.

They walked the wooden pier paralleling the edge of the river's deep and wide bay. Zabibe pointed out matters of interest along the way. When they arrived at the pier's end, he said, "This is where we will either part our ways—with ye to find a room and board—and brothel—and me to go to my family. Or will ye concede to continue with me—to meet those who love my sorry carcass? This is the place of deciding. Which shall it be?"

Although determined to experience the sights and pleasures of the city, without thinking about it Shamir unexpectedly changed his mind.

"I will go with you. But I know it will diminish your sweet reunion with your family."

The sailor laughed at his friend's pessimistic view and slapped his back.

"Ye shall find joy with us, my friend. I know it! Let us head to the forest and find the path which leads to my love."

Following a narrow footpath, they left the clamor of the harbor. A heavy stillness filled the jungle, pressing in on their ears, compressing their chests. The occasional call of a bird cracked the silence, filling it momentarily with a pulse of life. Then all was again quiet. Not the quiet of what might be called peace, it was more the quiet of tombs. For more than an hour they followed the twisting path, with never a straight-ahead view of more than a few paces. The green tangle crowded in around them.

Zabibe slowed his pace through the nearly impenetrable thicket of brown branches, grey vines and green leaves. He whispered to Shamir, "The edge of this forest lies just several paces ahead. Beyond that is the clearing, where her garden lies and our little house stands. We will creep forward to the edge, but remain hidden in the shadow of these trees. I enjoy waiting here, before I make plain my arrival. My heart pounds while I watch them, and my longing to touch and hold them grows. When it builds to where I think my heart will explode in my chest, I burst forth from the forest, and take them up in my arms!"

They moved closer and saw the small house beyond the garden. Zabibe held up his hand as signal to stop, the trunks of only two trees separating them from the open glade. He whispered, "I believe those are the two eldest—my boys cultivating their amma's garden. I am amazed at their size! And look!—the three younger play outside the door. Are their wee, bare-brown bodies not beautiful? The smallest must yet be inside with her amma. I wonder if she walks yet…"

They continued watching in silence. From time-to-time, the two sailors quietly erupted in muffled laughter when either arguments or mirth punctuated the children's play.

At great length, Aarunya's melodic voice called out to her children from inside the house. Within moments, the youngest toddled through the doorway, only to lose her balance and fall backward into a sitting position, her plump rump making a '*plop*' as she settled abruptly on the hard-packed earth. The two men again stifled their laughter.

Then Aarunya's delicate body, clad only in a cream, cotton *mundu* from waist to ankle, appeared in the shadow of the doorway. Shamir thought he could hear his brother's heart pounding for her. A moment later she stepped out from the house and into the full light of day. Zabibe gripped Shamir's arm until the young man thought he would break it. In the coarse whisper of panic, he told Shamir, "She is slim as I left her—maybe more. Where is my seventh baby she was to carry?"

Shamir pried the man's grip from his arm and offered, "She did not conceive. Perhaps for once, in the short time you were last here, you did not plant seed enough for a crop to take root."

They watched a little longer and Zabibe said, "No. Her normal, bubbling spirit is subdued. Something is amiss. Stay here while I go to them. Then I will beckon ye to come out of hiding."

He stood, watched a few moments more, and then strode into the open, calling out the names of his six children. The youngest four near the house only looked up in surprise to see a stranger approaching their home. The eldest two stopped their work to watch from the garden, until they recognized his voice and face, and ran to him with open arms. The others soon followed, with the baby staggering to her feet and tottering behind them. The six swarmed the sailor's towering frame, the tidal wave of small bodies knocking him to the ground. They piled upon him in a chaotic confusion of laughter and shrieks of delight.

The shock of his sudden appearance stunned Aarunya and she froze in place near the door.

Still in hiding, Shamir watched the children's celebration finally diminish. They dragged the one-eyed sailor to his feet and pulled him to their amma. As the children drew him near her, she refrained from her usual welcome of abandoning all restraint, to run and jump into his arms, burying her face in the abundant folds of skin at his neck. Instead, her blank gaze rolled up and back, and her body swayed as a tree about to fall.

Zabibe rushed forward to narrowly catch her under her arms. Her head flopped backward and he pulled her to his massive chest. Dropping to his knees, he brushed her hair back and whispered her name in her ear. He finally sat on the ground and moved her limp body to his lap, rocking her and quietly humming a melody to soothe her.

The scene which played out before Shamir wrecked his composure. *She must have lost the child. My presence here would be an unwelcome intrusion upon the sanctity of such a private and overwhelming tragedy. I will find my way back to the ship...*

He watched a little longer until the young woman regained awareness and buried her face in her husband's chest. Shamir could not hear her quiet words, but would not have understood them anyway. Zabibe stroked her hair and back, comforting her. The private conversation ended and he helped her to her feet. As Shamir turned to leave, the sailor loudly spoke his agreed-upon signal. "Come. I have news for ye, my brother."

An awkward dread filled Shamir, and the desire he once entertained to meet this family now repelled him. *I have no strength to stand with those touched by death. I have no good thing to offer them.*

Zabibe bellowed even louder, "Come, I say! Please, come and meet these I love."

He sucked up the meager courage he could find, and put one foot in front of the other, reluctantly taking him closer to the grieving pair. He stood before them, bereft of any consoling words. Zabibe took his wife's hand and placed it in Shamir's. He said to him,

"I have explained to her that ye are my brother. She thanks ye that my brother is here to share the weight of our grief. She has told me that two months ago, her womb cast its tender fruit far too early. Born hours after the sun's peak, the child breathed until the sun set, and then ceased. Aarunya's lullabies floated over the infant until midnight. Then she wrapped the tiny girl's body in the white linen skirt in which she wed me. She placed our daughter on a pile of bamboo timber and kindled a fire—consuming all. Aarunya buried the ashes under a large stone at the edge of the forest, near where we watched and waited. She gave her the name *Anusha*—bright star of the morning.'

Shamir knew the poverty of what he could offer.

"I know not what to say, my brother. I have tasted the bitter fruit of death myself, and all words to console it sound hollow in my own ears—and in my heart."

"Yes, it is as ye say. But we do not wish for your words. Your presence with us is enough. She sees the concern in your eyes, and your careful reluctance to draw near. She knows ye care about this painful loss, so she thanks ye. As do I, my brother."

35

A MOIST DARKNESS, WITH the fragrance of night-blooming vines, diffused from the forest into the hut. Zabibe and his wife sat on rough, simple cushions scattered on the bamboo floor. The children clung to their abba's frame; the last rays of twilight illuminated the joy on their faces. The smallest curled in the sailor's ample lap, asleep in the security of her home. Although the free expression of grief still creased Aarunya's fair face, to see such pleasure in her children caused a faint smile to cross her lips.

Shamir lounged above them in a hanging sling—a portion of fowler's net suspended between two poles of the little house. This, the bed of choice, was reserved for their few guests. He said, "Zabibe, please tell your dear wife how much I thank her for providing such wondrous flavor from a simple meal. And for sharing the security and privacy of her home. I know how much you must treasure time alone with your family, so I thank you for your hospitality in allowing my intrusion tonight. I will return to Muciri at daybreak and give you back your family."

"It is no intrusion, my brother. Ye be not only guest here, ye be family. And feel not obliged to leave by morn. Ye may stay as long as ye wish."

"Again, I thank you. But I must be going—to find the rest of my adventure. I know not exactly where it takes me, but I must find its path."

As the last light fled beyond the horizon, the black night embraced them. Conversation slowed, became intermittent, and then faded. In a hushed melody, Aarunya sang a lullaby in Malayalam to her babies and husband—

"I sing to you, my little birds
I sing my peace upon you

So dream your dreams
of silver beams
and gleaming drops
of fairest dew..."

Each one lay back, to fall into the arms of Sleep, to dream her dreams.

Shamir stirred awake in the enveloping darkness. Some faint sound called him forth from his dreams, but left him waiting for its return. Perhaps the dream itself called him out. He turned in the hanging sling. At first he thought it a peculiar sort of bed, but after lying in it for hours, he appreciated the gentle, enclosing comfort it offered a weary body.

And there it was again. The quiet murmur. Too soft for even the hushed nighting song of the *rappati*. He lay there, trying to imagine the small bird perched on a branch at the edge of the dark forest, the feathered coat gleaming greenish-blue in the moonlight, its head purple. And then he knew the trembling mumble did not fit. Fully awake and intrigued by the sound, he listened for it again.

There it was—

It is the muted whisper of the wind, sighing its intimate longings to the forest. But no, I hear tragedy in its singing breath.

He turned again, to listen longer.

And then it revealed its source. Below his swinging bed he heard the gentle weeping of Aarunya. Though the specific meaning of her words were foreign to his understanding, the grief in her plaintive whisperings to Zabibe was plain as the black of night around them. He knew her muted grief intended not to waken her guest, and he felt sorrow for her inhibition.

While he assumed Zabibe must be awake, the man never interrupted her hushed lament. Shamir knew the man wrapped her in the cocoon of his massive arms and clutched her to his chest. Surely, his calloused hands smoothed her glossy black hair, and the touch of his lips consoled the crown of her head. At long last, she could murmur no more and her quiet sobs faded. He then heard the sailor speak gently to her, in her language. In the midst of his words of comfort, the man broke down and sobbed his own tears. Shamir imagined Aarunya touching the sailor's rough cheek, and collecting his tears in the dark palm of her hand.

Zabibe's voice then spoke directly to Shamir—shocking him in the quiet intimacy of the moment.

"My brother, she wants ye to know that while tragedy and pain will surely enter a life of love, it is far better encountering it as one of two, than to suffer it alone."

The words paralyzed the young man's voice. Shamir could not respond, the truth of the matter cutting deep.

Zabibe continued, "As I spoke to ye on the *Dwelling of Lions*, I imagined myself as the philosopher-sailor—trumpeting that the highest and best life one could live was on the sea, as one's own man. But even as the words tumbled from my mouth, I knew them not true. I cannot count the hours I have spent in the brothels of every port in many years past, in the arms of numberless, nameless women, who pretended to be the lover of my purchased moment. To her, my half-drachm of silver had no more value than one held by the next sailor standing in line."

Zabibe choked on his own words and had to recover before continuing.

"It was only in knowing my Aarunya that I understood I had given over those many years to diminishing the power, and diluting the truth, of love. I had given away something far more precious than the silver coins in the pouch at my belt."

Shamir twisted in the dark anger rising into his face, while a desperate longing battered his heart.

It is easy for my brother to utter such words—lying in the embrace of one who loves him so. And to be surrounded by a half-dozen children of his own loins, who laugh with him and call him Abba. How I long for such. But perhaps it will never be...

Below his hanging bed, he heard the soft, moist sounds of lips meeting, caressing. It continued long. The man and woman exchanged brief, simple words—a single syllable at a time, responding to each other. Then, she began faintly sighing, her voice trembling. In the perfect blackness of the hut, Shamir saw not a glimpse of the pair, but he knew he was in the presence of love being made. Perhaps, new life conceived.

And he wept, for himself.

36

D AWN ARRIVED IN A golden mantle, and the half-dozen progeny of
Zabibe's loins already played at the edge of the forest. Shamir and
his hosts lingered outside the door of the hut. Aarunya bowed to
Shamir, saying, "*Rinnal avale kantettum.*"

Zabibe interpreted her words.

"She says she knows ye will find her—the one ye have been seeking all your life."

Shamir half-smiled and said, "I fear I will go to my grave without
love's jewel inside me, but please thank her again, for her generous
hospitality."

Zabibe gripped Shamir's shoulders, kissing him on each cheek.
He looked into the young man's eyes. "My brother, I vowed last
night to Aarunya I will not return to Nabataea when the *Dwelling*
sails again in four months. Instead, I will remain here with my
family. So this may well be the last time I see your face. I wish ye all
peace and happiness, under the fearsome gaze of Manawat."

Zabibe looked deeply into the young man's face, studying it
intently, trying to fix its features in his memory. He continued, "And
I remember your quest—that ye look for your mythical namesake.

To that end, find in Muciri that master gem-cutter named Sariyan, and use my name as introduction. He is the one who tutored me in the appraisal and trading of gems. Long after taking me into his confidence, he once spoke in awe of a thing he called *Zuizhi*. Perhaps he has more knowledge of the thing ye seek. And while he speaks no Aramaic, he has a daughter gifted in discerning all manner of tongues. She will interpret for ye."

Shamir embraced the sailor, saying, "I will never forget my brother! And I thank you for an introduction to the gem-cutter. May Manawat smile upon you and yours, and clear a smooth path before you."

He turned away from the man and his wife and crossed the clearing to the rain-forest's path. The children scampered about him, giggling and chattering. They took his hands in theirs, swinging his arms as they marched beside him. When he reached the boundary of the forest, the youngest ones stopped and watched, while the two eldest accompanied him to the first turn in the path.

They, too, dropped his hands, and Shamir entered the jungle alone, to return to the port.

Back at Muciri, clamor and commotion ruled the waterfront. The massive, floating *baghlahs* and *ghanjahs* from Nabataea, sleek *jahazis* and *sambuks* from Persia, and *pattamars* and *boums*—those noble ships from Bangal—took their turns to tie at the pier and docks. The ships' holds disgorged wares brought from afar. Like trails of scurrying ants, men carried the cargo away in baskets, to pier-side storehouses: figured linens and silk yarns; indigo, spikenard, lubunah, and malabathrum; wheat, rice, and amphorae of sesame oil. Others, under armed guard, moved chests of topaz, coral, and turquoise; gold plate, bdellium and lapis lazuli. With the burdens lifted from their bellies, the ships rose in their berths.

In Muciri, agents of the ships signed contracts and clasped hands with traders on shore, to seal deals for their goods. And they made deals with others, buying their spices, silks, muslins, gems, and other luxury goods—to fill their empty holds with freight destined to bring handsome profits in the luxury markets of Raqmu, Alexandria and Rome.

Shamir poked his head in the door of a shop near the pier. Toward the back, three men argued vehemently with one standing behind a long, narrow table. Shamir waved his arms and asked the one-word question: "Sariyan?"

The shop-keeper shrugged his shoulders and returned to the argument. Shamir moved on to the next shop. Walking in the door, the relative calm relieved him. When he entered, a man sitting on a bench along the side wall looked up at him. Again, he asked, "Sariyan?"

The man responded with many words, all unknown to Shamir. The man punctuated his soliloquy with hearty laughter, and finally ended with an obvious question of his own—"Eh?"—then waited for an answer. After a long pause, Shamir finally said, "I beg forgiveness—I do not know your language. Do you speak Aramaic? I look for the gem-cutter Sariyan. Do you know him?"

The man's eyebrows tilted toward his nose. He glowered at Shamir and pointed to the door, shouting caustic curses after him in Malayalam. The venom of his words followed Shamir out the door and onto the waterfront. Rushing past three more shops, he could still hear the man's curses splitting the air behind him. He stopped outside the last business in the row, wondering if seeking the gem-cutter was a fruitless pursuit. A whimsical voice called out to him from within the shack—

"*Ni vannkkuka?*"

Shamir took just a step inside and said, "I speak Aramaic..."

The man's smile broadened, displaying only a bottom row of crooked teeth. He said, "Ahhhh...from west! You buy...or sell?"

A relieved Shamir said, "You speak my language?"

"Just little. You buy, or sell?"

"I am not trading. I look for a gem-cutter. Sariyan, by name. Do you know him?"

"Ahhh…yes, yes! Sariyan—of jewels, and pearls. Good man! He end of street—edge of bay. Shop built of stones. White-wash outside. You see—white-wash!"

He pointed north, toward the head of the bay, where the river's fresh flow filled it.

"Thank you, sir, for your kind help!"

He left the shabby building, and the man called after him, "You tell Sariyan—I take daughter!"

As he skirted the bay, the white stone shop came into sight, standing in stark contrast to the dark green background of the rain-forest —a pearl set in a brooch of malachite. Before entering, he paused.

Perhaps I waste my efforts here, as before. I should cut my losses, make the best gem trades I can, and return to my homeland aboard the Dwelling. I may as well make all the profit I can.

Tied to the door, a tiny silver bell tinkled as he entered, announcing his presence. A stooped man, in a cream-colored linen *mundu* hastily thrown over his frame, shuffled in from the back room. Shamir said, "I look for the one called Sariyan."

The old man looked up and said, "*Nan Sariyan,*" then turned toward the back room and called out, "*Makal—enikk Aramaya* (Daughter, I need Aramaic)."

A woman's voice called back—"*Nan varunnu* (I am coming)."

A slight, young woman soon appeared, a pronounced limp impeding her progress. She wore a deep blue *antariya* of fine, Sondin muslin in *kaccha* style—wrapped around the waist and then brought up between the legs from behind. The extended panel of muslin then covered her from the waist-up, and gold clasps pinned it together at the shoulders. The fabric's multitude of pleats and folds were artfully arranged. She stood with bare feet on the floor's cool slabs of black slate. Seeing Shamir, she addressed him in fluent Aramaic.

"You seek Sariyan, the gem-cutter? He is my abba. What is your business?"

Surprised at finally finding his friend's acquaintance, he was at a loss to speak. He blurted, "His tutor...my friend...to find you...he said..."

An amused smile broke the earnest expression on her face, she shook her head slightly and asked, "Is Aramaic truly your tongue, or should I speak a language with which you are more familiar?"

"No, no! This is the language I know. I was...not prepared to speak. Yes, I look for your abba. He once instructed my friend Zabibe in the science of appraising precious stones. He said your abba might hold information concerning a certain matter."

Her face beamed to hear the sailor's name.

"Ah, Zabibe! My old 'uncle' from the sea! I was yet a girl when he last carried me upon his broad shoulders. *Acchan!*—Daddy!—This man brings us word of Zabibe!"

Sariyan's business-like countenance broke into the welcome of an old friend. He grasped Shamir's hands and bowed profusely, saying, "Ayyy! Zabibe!"

With excitement, the woman asked Shamir, "Is he well? Is he here in Muciri?"

"Yes, he is in fine health, and with his wife and family at their home in the forest. He now has six children. But I am here concerning another matter.'

"Of course. I will translate for my abba. And the matter?..."

"From several sources I have heard mention of something, said by some to be only myth—the stuff of legends—but some say it exists. The thing is said to cut all materials, even the hardest stone, by its mere glance. A great king of the west was supposed to have used the device to silently trim and dress all the stones for a great temple he built. I seek knowledge that would lead me to the thing."

"I will tell my abba what you have said…but I know, myself, of what you seek. I have spoken with those who claim direct knowledge of its existence. And the name of that western king was Shl'mo."

She spoke at length with the gem-cutter, and then he uttered in a low voice—

"*Avan tetunnu…Zuizhi…Shamirine!*"

"So, he knows of it. You both know of it! Where may I find it?"

A caution entered her voice. "In ignorance you ask this, as if it were a matter of mere location. But I will ask him."

She and her abba conversed a long time before she turned to Shamir.

"He strongly warns you against your pursuit of the Shamir. He says it always comes at great cost. Far greater than you can now imagine. But if you cannot be dissuaded, he will give you the name of a jeweler in the far east, whose family is said to have once possessed the Shamir. The man is his primary supplier of certain pearls he collects."

The young man nearly collapsed, hearing this news—to know the object of his pursuit may be more than just folly.

Shamir gasped a hoarse reply. "Yes, of course! I am prepared to pay him handsomely for the man's name—and his whereabouts!"

The young woman took a deep breath and told Shamir, "He says he will take nothing from you, for guiding you to such malignant knowledge. He says to do so would be like taking payment for feeding you poison. It would be unconscionable. But he does have a different proposal in mind."

"Yes?…"

"Since the time I was a small child, I accompanied my abba on his every-third-year trek to the *dure kilakk*—the farthest east—to build his inventory of pearls that are found nowhere else. He buys them from those you call the Serai—the Silk-Ones. But though he still wishes to augment his collection of priceless pearls, he is old and weak, no longer able to endure the journey. And while I am well familiar with their culture and speak their tongue as well as they, I am lame—and a woman."

Her words puzzled Shamir, and he said, "I do not understand."

She fixed her eyes on him. She tilted her head, studying his face, before proceeding. "You have physical strength, plus a vowed passion to complete the long journey. And...you are a man. However, you are ignorant of the people and their language. You would not reach your goal on your own. Therefore..."

She looked back at her abba and took a deep breath before completing her thought.

"...therefore, he proposes to hire you as my protector, and as his guarantor of transport for the valuable merchandise, while I would serve as your guide and mouthpiece. He will pay your passage and expenses. Will you clasp hands with him over the contract?"

"Tell him I cannot accept payment in such an over-generous offer."

She relayed to her abba the objection, but the old man vigorously shook his head and then spoke directly to Shamir in Malayalam. Though the words were foreign, the man's old eyes penetrated to Shamir's core. The daughter said, "He claims such a payment to you will constrain you to not dishonor yourself by breaking the contract. He believes it will compel you to act honorably."

Shamir raised his eyebrows and pursed his lips. "In that case, I will accept the agreement...on the condition that I will not receive half of the payment until I safely return his pearls—and his daughter."

She passed the compromise on to the old man, who nodded, bowed deeply, and with satisfaction said, "*Atu ceytu.*"

"He says 'it is done.' We wait seven months more for the winds to change, to take us east, and then to the north. Until then, I suggest you make whatever preparations you deem necessary for the trip. My abba will give you half payment now, and the silver for securing our passage on the *Mutalmann*—the *Red Mist*. I will pack my own baggage, as should you, if you have any. And finally, we should meet daily in the time ahead, that I might tutor you in the bare necessities of their tongue. You should not be seen by them as a deaf-mute— nor worse, as an ignoramus. Do you accept all these conditions?"

"I do."

The two men clasped hands, he bowed deeply to the old man, and nodded to the daughter. He nearly danced to the door, and before he exited, Sariyan called to him, *"Entan ninre per?"*

"He says—'Wait, what is your name?'"

Shamir turned back toward them, his dark eyes glittering. He laughed, "They call me Shamir!," and walked out the door.

The man and his daughter looked at each other, their mouths agape.

37

ON THE FOLLOWING MORNING, Shamir left his room at the tavern to head toward the gem-cutter's shop. He walked along the road behind the shops at the waterfront. Warehouses crowded the road on one side. Buildings of mortared stone, their doors barred with iron or bronze, guarded merchandise of high value. Less valuable commodities piled up in bamboo shacks. On the other side of the road, vendors unrolled grass-mats where they arranged their commodities and wares for trade. Even while setting up their displays, they cried out to Shamir as he passed by—

"*Ninnal vinnunna! Kuranna!*—You buy! Cheap!"

Reaching the shop, and in no hurry, he sat on a bench outside the establishment and waited for his language tutor. The shop was the farthest permanent business on the outskirts of Muciri. It was close enough to the dense forest, a boy could easily cast a stone into the lush undergrowth. Shamir thought this a good idea himself, and did just that.

He leaned back against the cool stone wall behind him, to catch a quick nap. Sariyan's daughter appeared through the open doorway and stood there. She watched him—his eyes closed, his breathing progressively slower, deeper. A faint smile crossed her lips and she tilted her head, her pendulous, silver earrings swinging with the motion.

"Do you always sleep the morning away?"

The close proximity of the unexpected voice startled him, nearly knocking him from the bench. He scrambled to an upright position, embarrassed someone caught him unaware.

"Nuh...no...I was simply...thinking."

As she stood before him, her head was not much higher than his as he sat on the bench. She wore a red-madder cotton *antariya,* wrapped in *saree* style about her waist and hanging freely to her ankles. A thin, silver anklet barely peeked out from the edge of the skirt. White-dyed leather sandals kept the soles of her feet from touching the earth, and a wide, embroidered muslin *uttariya,* or stole, covered her above the waist.

"Let me clarify something before we start. My abba hired you to protect his valuables during the journey. And that would include me. If you insist on taking a lackadaisical approach, we should cancel the agreement before the voyage begins."

"No...please...that will not be necessary. I will be ready and alert at all times. I assure you I will not take his, and your, trust lightly."

"I would hope that is the case. Now you have much to learn, and the seven months we have here is scarcely enough to make you barely fluent in the language you will need. Fortunately, on board the ship, we will also have opportunity in the following three months to increase your facility. Shall we start?"

Shamir nodded.

"While I know *your* name—Shamir-Who-Seeks-the-Shamir —I am surprised you have not asked for mine."

He said, "I wished to know it, from the time I left your father's shop. Please tell me—by what name are you known?"

"My abba named me *Ceriya-onn,* or Tiny One. But my amma refused the name and called me according to her own amma's name

—*Tenicca*, meaning Honey-Tongued. Within a year, my abba gave up and called me Tenicca as well. So Tenicca I am."

As she said these few words about herself, Shamir watched her face transform from a pleasant but earnest expression into a warmer, inviting form. He took notice of her tiara. The thin, silver band crowned her jet hair with a row of tiny pearls. And below it dangled an amethyst cabochon in the center of her forehead, hovering above perfect, grey eyes. Her voice interrupted his gaze.

"But enough of that. The land of our destination has many languages, but for the reason we travel, only one will be required. They call it *Gwongjau*. We shall start with learning your name in their language. Shamir will become *Zuizhi*. Tenicca will become *Mi She*.

"'In the three months we are aboard ship, you will be my primary companion. I loathe the thought that I will not be able to speak freely with you in my own mother-tongue. So for my own sanity, I will also attempt to teach you something of Malayalam, the language of Chera.'"

And so the lessons began. Shamir possessed no natural affinity for any language other than the one he learned in his amma's tent. And it proved to be no small difficulty for Tenicca as well as her student. Day by day and from time to time, the lessons often ended abruptly.

Tenicca asked, "Shamir, how do you say 'pearl' in Gwongjau?"

He thought a while before speaking. "That would be 'zehzhun'."

She closed her eyes and took a deep breath. "No. The word is pronounced 'zhen-zhu'."

He sat up straight, puffed out his chest and with a smile on his face, said, "Zhu-zhen!"

"NO! I said, it is 'ZHEN-ZHU!'"

He crossed his eyes and waggled his head back and forth, spouting "ZHU–ZHEN, ZHUZI-ZHENZI, ZHENA-ZIN, ZHUNA-ZIN!"

Her eyes shot bolts of rage, she jumped up from the bench, and with her lame leg, kicked the bench from beneath him. His tailbone collided with the stone pavement, his knees crooked over the upset bench, and his arms flailed akimbo. In a the fury of a whirlwind, she flew inside her abba's shop and slammed the door—its little silver bell tinkling loudly to announce the storm.

She left him contorted in a heap over the bench, while she regained her composure and a semblance of patience. In time, she smoothed her hair, and straightened her garments. Shamir rescued himself from his embarrassing posture. He set the bench back on its feet, brushed off his clothes, and sat again, waiting in silence for the return of his tutor. She took a deep breath, and forced a slight smile, before opening the door and resuming the lesson.

Waiting patiently and in silence, he stood in deference for his teacher to seat herself. She took his hand and nodded for him to sit beside her, and the lesson continued.

Nevertheless, her tutelage was not without success. Bit by tiny bit, the foreign words penetrated his lack of natural ability, and he found himself able to carry on the most basic of conversations with his teacher.

The seasons changed, and the winds shifted from the southwest. Ships prepared to set sail for the east: around the southernmost cape of the Malabar coast, northeast through the tight passage between the mainland and the large island kingdom of Eelam, and across the expanse of the eastern sea to the spice and fabric ports of the Bangal. From there, few ships continued on, crossing the open sea again, to the next narrow strait between the major islands of Melay. Beyond the strait, only the most daring ventured to the farthest east—to the land of the Silk Ones—the Serai.

With the arrival of monsoon winds came word that, within a week, the *Red Mist* would weigh anchor and set her sails for the islands of Melay, to trade gold for spices and precious woods, and then on to the farthest point of the eastern voyage: Gwongjau's Fragrant Harbor at the mouth of the Pearl River.

Because of the baggage and Tenicca's difficulty in walking distances, Shamir hired a *palki*, shouldered by two men, with another pair to bear their baggage to the pier. He also arranged for a small local boat to take them downriver to the *Red Mist*, anchored among three other large ships just offshore.

The *palki* carriers and porters arrived at the gem-cutter's shop just after dawn. Shamir stood outside with them, awaiting the appearance of Tenicca. The weeping of an old man, and of a young woman, floated through the open door of the shop. Their long goodbyes finally faded and she appeared at the doorway.

A red *pashmina* shawl, extending over her head and covering her hair, topped her ivory-colored linen saree. As she stepped out of the doorway, she wrapped a heavy traveling cloak about her. Sariyan tottered a few paces behind.

As she approached the *palki*, one of the men opened its door. She waited before entering, then turned back to embrace her abba a final time, not knowing if he would remain alive for the full year of her absence. Their heads fell upon each other's shoulders, and the old man's withered arms encircled his daughter's fair neck. They wept again, sobbing openly. She pulled her abba's hands away from her and kissed them with tenderness. She looked away from him and entered the *palki*, sitting upon the cushioned seat inside. The rigidity of her lame leg prevented the full closing of the door, so her sandaled foot and ankle extended just outside, and she held it partly closed from within.

Shamir gave the word to proceed to the pier, and they began the long journey.

38

AND SO IT WAS, that the afternoon sun hung low, and Shamir and
Tenicca stood on the teak deck of their floating home of the next
three months. Her substantial collection of baggage, and his single
sailor's sack, lay beside them. Shamir said, "I will stow your belongings in the cabin assigned to you, and then return to assist you
below."

The design of the *Red Mist* accommodated both freight and a
limited number of passengers. The layout of the second deck primarily stowed sailing materiel—sail, rope, rigging, caulking, blocks,
and spare booms—and it also included four small, separate cabins on
each side. The cabins held sleeping berths and very limited floor-
space.

He left her on deck, sitting on her large trunk, while he carried the
other bags, cases, and basket below, to secure them in the little room.
In the dim bowels of the ship he found her cabin, a canvas curtain
serving as its only privacy. On the far wall—the inside of the ship's
hull—hung two sleeping berths, one above the other. He placed all
of her baggage in the upper bunk, and finding her woolen blanket,

spread it on the lower. He climbed the steep wooden steps, more ladder than stairway, back into the fresh sea-air and light.

"I am sorry, but I will have to take your current seat and drag it down to the cabin."

She said "There is no need to apologize for doing the work for which you were hired."

The process of moving the chest proved more difficult than he imagined, and consumed more time. He finished the work and returned for his last task of the day.

"Your cabin is now in order. Are you ready for me to carry you below?"

"Yes, please."

Tenicca had not been lifted by a man since leaving childhood behind. And Shamir had never carried a woman before. He held out one arm to her, and she was not quite sure what to do with it. She came close to him, face-to-face, and then realized that approach would not work, so she turned her left side toward him with her stiff leg on the other side. She raised her arm next to him, expecting to put it around either his neck or his waist, but wasn't sure which was more appropriate. He changed which arm he held out—more than once. There they stood, both waving their arms back and forth. The awkward dance continued until they broke the silence with laughter.

Their laughter faded, and in a single motion, he crouched and held his right arm low—like a seat in which she could sit—and she wrapped her arm around the back of his neck. Standing erect, he lifted her from her feet and placed his other arm under her legs. She felt surprisingly light in his arms, as if he held a young lamb. He carried her to the steps leading to the lower deck, and with his first clumsy attempt, took her below.

At the entrance to her cabin, he returned her to feet, and said, "Is everything in order for your stay here? If not, I will do what I can to make it right."

Greatly perplexed at the state of her room, she said, "*Nothing* is in order here—how will I sleep, with my bed filled with baggage? And I see you have helped yourself to my blanket!"

Her words puzzled him.

"I don't understand. I have your blanket on the lower bunk, so you may sleep and rise from it whenever you wish. And I placed your baggage above, where it will be out of the way."

"Then where will you sleep?"

"I thought I would sleep on deck. And perhaps there will be an empty sailor's berth from time-to-time, whenever all hands are called above."

"Shamir—you are not traveling as my slave. Or even as my servant. You are to be seen by those outside as fully my partner for this endeavor. And since you have been retained as my protector, what good will it be to have you somewhere on deck, while I am down here alone, and helpless to go above? And if your concern is what others may believe of this arrangement—whether they think we are close kin, or married, or lovers—what is that to us?"

He had nothing to counter her argument, and saw it had a certain inescapable logic.

"So you will remove the baggage from my bed and stack it in the corner. You shall sleep in the lower berth, since if any harm comes our way, you will then be in the best position to defend or help me. And you will remove the blanket from yours and spread it on the upper one. Then, we shall pay a visit to the ship's cook for a final meal before retiring. They say we sail with the tide in the morning."

Two weeks after departing the Malabar coast, and having left the strait of Eelam behind, the wind was at their backs and the Red Mist plowed a straight course for Melay. The blue of the sea could be seen in the ship's wake as it trailed out behind them, white foam flecking its peaks. Tenicca and her pupil-assistant sat on a bench by the ship's rail. With the day's instruction behind them, conversation turned in a different direction. Shamir had a question for her.

"Please forgive me if this seems forward, or rude. But since I was called into this expedition *because* of this matter—I have wondered —what is the origin of the infirmity in your leg?"

She closed her eyes and raised her eyebrows, thinking of the far past. The pain of her memories resisted prying them loose. He could see her eyes faintly darting back and forth behind her closed, light-brown lids. Her long eyelashes flicked almost imperceptibly. She slowly opened her eyes and parted her dark lips, saying,

"I was three years of age when my amma entered death's portal, birthing my younger brother. He died the same day. My abba hired a woman to be my nurse and caretaker, and within a year, she shared his bed. Though she became the corner of comfort to my abba's heart, I would not allow her such a place in my own. I could never let another supplant the few memories I still cherished of my amma— the one whose womb was my first home. The next year, the Pandyans plotted an evil war against our people.

"One day, we three traveled to the Cheran capital on my abba's business. I remember the day as heavy, dark. With storms on the horizon. Then we heard the trumpeting cry of the war-elephants. We ran into the forest to hide from the onslaught. In the desperate flight to our hiding place, the nurse stumbled on a steep slope, dropping me from her arms. I tumbled ahead of her, and she then fell upon my right leg. The impact shattered the joint of my knee. For many months, the pain possessed my every waking moment. When the fire in my knee finally subsided, it had fixed in the slightly bent position you see, causing my limp.

"Even now, when the night air is thick and menacing, I imagine I hear the thundering footsteps of the elephants. They raise their trunks high, to shatter the air with the trumpeting of their war-screams. I wake, bathed in sweat from the dream, pangs throbbing in my knee."

She closed her eyes again and shuddered. Shamir said,

"I sometimes have my own dreams of painful times—from my life long ago. In the family to which I was born, dreadful events occurred. The terrible death of my young sister...and of my amma. I dream as if it happened all over again. Upon waking, I can hardly catch my breath. For nights after that, I dread the thought of sleeping again, that the dream might repeat itself. So I lie awake all night, fleeing sleep."

She laid her hand on his wrist, and gently squeezed it. She said,

"I have also noticed the scar, and hindrance, in your own hand and wrist. Like my leg, it lacks fluid motion. You have never mentioned how it came about. Since you have already touched upon such matters, how did this happen?—if I am not prying too deeply."

Shamir never told another soul of the deep wound this event cut upon his life. He looked into her grey eyes, and held her gaze. She never looked away, but he sensed no threat in her long stare. He felt her heart beholding his. Inhaling deeply, he let out a long sigh before speaking.

"I was not always a sailor..."

"I guessed as much. Though when you first arrived at my father's business you wore a sailor's garments, you had not the speech of one given to the sea. I hear in your voice a refined Aramaic—and exposure to both Greek and Latin—you are from Raqmu, perhaps?"

"You have been there?"

"No, but our customers come from the whole of the known world —Rome, Alexandria, and yes, Raqmu. On occasion, as far as the eastern empire—the land to which we journey. But I am sorry, I have distracted you from answering my question. Please forgive me...and continue."

"Someone close to me—a man who became like my abba—died a violent death in my presence. A massive stone had fallen on him, and in my attempts to save his life, my left hand and wrist were maimed. As he lay dying, we spoke of the things which matter most, but on watching him die in my presence, something went out of me. Leaving a void in its place. And because of the injury, I lost my ability to progress in my profession. I found other work, and was paid adequately for it, but the plans and dreams I'd held for so long...were dead. Part of the reason for my quest—finding the Shamir—is to recapture something of what I had before. Maybe even more than that. I know it is probably the dream of a fool, but it compels me to seek it."

Still holding his wrist, she pulled it toward her, and clasped his hand. They spoke no more about these matters, and sat there, watching the blue sea and white clouds drift by.

39

THE WINDS REMAINED STRONG and constant, and the sea swells were moderate and long. Standing on deck was like the motion of sitting in the saddle of a slow-loping camel. The morning's language lessons ended and Tenicca pulled a small, lambskin bag from beneath her shawl and laid it upon her lap.

She said to Shamir, "There is another skill you must learn. In the weeks before we left, my father held your attention, telling you of the history and culture attached to pearls. While the majority of his business revolves around gems wrested from the earth, those wrested from the living bodies of sea-animals are closer to his heart. The mystique of these orbs from oysters and mussels has captured his devotion for many years."

With the drudgery of learning two languages behind him for the day, Shamir's face brightened at the mention of a new direction in their conversation. He said, "Yes, your father's passion infected my own heart. He showed me some of his most prized pearls, and while I still know little about them, their astounding beauty beguiles me."

"He recited to you the poetry of pearls. And he regaled you with tales of these gems. But you will need a familiarity with the appraisal, the science of discerning the quality of pearls. And I will help you with that. My father's particular passion for pearls directs our journey. The gems we seek are the lilac pearls of Gwongjau."

"Pearls, I know. But what is *lilac*?"

"The lilac shrub grows in Persia, and springtime covers it with clouds of tiny, pinkish-blue flowers. Their sweet, pleasant fragrance fills the air, relaxing one who breathes deeply its aroma. The unusual and arresting color of the flowers is the same hue as certain pearls found in Gwongjau. And beyond the striking and unique color they possess, their form can be nearly perfect, and their luster like the full moon. Pearls such as these are found nowhere else."

"So...what do you hold in your hand?"

She untied the drawstring of the pouch and poured into her palm seven gorgeous spheres of radiance. Each the size of a fox's eye, they rolled in her hand and gleamed in the sunlight. Even in the bright sun, the pupils of Shamir's eyes dilated. He shook his head, and under his breath uttered "Ohhh..." His eyelids opened wide, he raised his eyebrows, and looked up at Tenicca, saying, "I thought we were buying pearls, not selling. And how could you sell prizes such as these?"

"No, these are not for sale. They are, instead, the exemplars of what we may find. These are my father's standards for judging the quality and color of those we will find in Gwongjau. And we will be using them for the purpose of training your own eyes and under-standing."'

With her free hand she opened his palm, cup-like, and turned it face up. She began slowly rolling the seven brilliant orbs into his care, but he objected, saying, "No! I will drop them!"

The force of her gaze pierced through him like the spiraled horns of an ibex and she commanded him, "*NO!* You will *NOT* drop them!"

She laughed at her unexpected vehemence, but he didn't smile.

"Then *how* will I not drop them?"

"Hold them...as you hold me...when you bring me up from below. You hold me like I was a quail's egg, that would crush with your slightest grip. And yet, you hold me securely, as though the motion of the ship on the waves would tear me from your grasp and throw me into the sea."

She finished rolling the pearls into his hand, and he took her encouragement. He held them close to his face, examining them. He said, "I am amazed how well matched these pearls are. How identical they appear."

She shook her head, sighed and said, "And that, my stone-cutter, is why you require a tutor. These seven pearls are each different from the others. They represent seven different colors, graded from an overly-bluish to an overly-pinkish hue. The pearl in the middle of the range possesses the lilac color we seek. Also, three are nearly perfect in their roundness, while the others are flawed in this regard. And finally, there is one among them which outshines the others in the rarity of its glowing luster. By learning to discern these subtle differences, you will be able to appraise the gems we will find."

He looked at them again, slightly rolling them around and examining them in greater detail. And yet, he said, "I still see nothing different in any of them. How can I see something that is not apparent?"

"That is why I am here. I can teach you to see the subtlety. And there are certain techniques we will use to try the pearls. The first I will show you is the detection of color."

From under her shawl she produced a small wooden block, no thicker than her slim wrist, and about the length of her hand. She slid back the top cover, exposing the interior. A long, deep groove extended the length of the block, its two side walls being painted a glowing red on one side, a vibrant blue on the other. She retrieved the seven pearls from Shamir and placed them in a line in the block's groove.

She asked, "What do you see now?"

"The seven pearls…still all the same."

She tilted the block until one side wall was just shading both itself and the pearls from the direct sunlight, while the blue wall remained fully lit. She said, "Now the pearls are illuminated by only the light from the blue side. You should notice that some of the pearls appear very slightly darker than others, and that, in fact, you can arrange them from darkest to lightest."

She performed the exercise, and he thought that, maybe, he could see what she meant. She then tilted the block in the other direction, until the blue wall and the pearls were shaded, and only the red side remained in the sun.

"Do you see now, how in the light from the red side, the direction of lightest to darkest is reversed? This technique allows one to compare others with these standards, and understand where they fit in the range. By practice and determination you will be able to reliably compare the colors."

She removed the pearls from the groove, rolled them around in her hands and placed them randomly back in the groove, saying to him, "Now reorder the pearls into a smooth transition from bluish to pinkish."

He worked for several minutes, picking them one at a time, replacing them in different locations, and then, finally satisfied with the result, said, "There, I think I have it."

She laughed and said, "Well, you have three out of the seven in proper order. You should try again."

They performed the test hundreds of times over the next two weeks, until he reliably and properly ordered them each time. They then went on to the tests required for determining perfection of roundness, and comparison of lusters. Before they reached Gwong-jau, Shamir became a master in appraising the quality of pearls, and Tenicca surged with pride to see his success.

40

AT THE PORT OF Gwongjau, Shamir stepped onto the dock from the boat which ferried them from the Red Mist. Though the dock's planks lay perfectly still, they felt to Shamir they moved in rhythmic swells like the sea, the result of having lived the past months on an ever rolling deck. He helped Tenicca from the boat, and when she set foot on solid ground, her own legs and body continued swaying with the phantom waves. It would be days before the earth's stability would steady the way they stood, walked, and slept.

Not far from the docks, a small group of men sat on the ground, waiting. While they waited, they spoke quietly among themselves. They fell silent as Shamir approached them. In the fundamentals of their language, he bargained with them.

"We need three porters. Two to carry baggage, and one to carry the lady...my sister. Are you for hire?"

The six men looked at each other, and then at Shamir. The smallest among them wore a black silk cap, sprouting the long, barred feather of a pheasant. The little man spoke for the group.

"Yes. These two men, and the largest one, will go with you. You will pay me half now, and the other half to them when you arrive.

The two will take your bags, and the large one will take the woman. They can remain with you as long as you wish."

They concluded the transaction, and by gestures the headman indicated to the others to transport Shamir and Tenicca to their destination. The big man picked up a large basket shaped like a chair and placed the two large hooks projecting from its back over his shoulders. Around his forehead he looped a long, leather strap from the chair's top. He squatted, lowering the seat to the ground. Shamir helped Tenicca sit and she gripped the chair's arms. The man stood, lifting her from the ground, and the five proceeded toward an inn.

The morning after their arrival in Gwongjau, a cold wind blew and bullied Shamir and Tenicca as they left the inn. They wrapped their cloaks even tighter. Fine, white wisps of cloud in the lapis sky curled and tangled like loose fibers from a hank of raw silk. On the street outside the inn, the two porters and the man with the wicker transport chair remained where their clients left them the previous night. Shamir told them he would not need the porters for three days more, but they would require the large man and his chair each day. The two men left dejected.

Tenicca took her seat and the three set out for the pearl merchant's shop. The narrow streets meandered and wound like the curves and loops of a long snake. Crowds already headed to market stalls to offer their wares. All manner of foods—raw, fried, roasted, and boiled—poured forth clouds of fumes and aromas, to entice the empty stomachs of those passing by.

Tenicca requested to stop at the stall of an old woman frying mussels in an immense, beaten-copper pan. Shamir purchased enough for himself, Tenicca, and her carrier. The generous offer of food, above his agreed-upon fee for services, surprised the man. The woman served the mussels, pungent with garlic and mustard, and wrapped in the thin, crisp-fried skins of a rabbit. They ate while they continued their journey.

The street made a sweeping bend and then paralleled the shore of the estuary. Elevated well above the water, the land provided a panoramic view of hundreds of boats in the bay—from majestic ships of Chera, Pandya, Eelam, and Bangal, to their equivalents in this eastern empire. From a distance, the eastern ships stood out from their western sisters by their batten-rigged sails. Nearer the shore, a clutter of small fishing boats bobbed in the small waves, their sides nearly touching.

Many of the boats were the floating homes of their occupants and revealed glimpses of the daily lives of those in this watery community. A man cooked his morning catch of two fish and an octopus. While a young amma nursed twin infants, another woman bathed in the next boat. She kneeled at the boat's side, washing her long, black hair in the bay's water.

They stopped briefly, to take in the view and finish their meal. The large man lowered the basket-chair for Tenicca to dismount. She said, "They call this estuary the Fragrant, or Sweet Bay, because its water is kept fresh by the large inflow of the river. Farther upstream, where the bay becomes a river, it is called the Pearl River. The empty shells of long-dead mussels—open and naked with their pearl-like surfaces—cover the river's bottom.

"The pearls found here are quite different from those near Muciri, on our own coast. These are produced by the mussels that live in the headwaters of the bay, where the water is freshest. And in a very few of those beds, the pearls are colored the delicate lilac we seek. The specific location of the beds is a guarded secret, known only to the few who fish them. They expend great effort in subterfuge to hide the whereabouts of their trade. Not even our pearl merchant knows."

Shamir asked, "What is his name again?"

"He is Rongyu Shu. His family has lived and breathed the gem and pearl trade for generations, like my own. This point we have in common. It is what first connected my abba and Shu, and made them fast friends. My abba is grief-stricken he can no longer make the trip to see his eastern brother."

"What is the man like?"

"He has a deep wealth of knowledge concerning pearls. My abba's fascination with the gems stems from this man's understanding and his poetic appreciation of them. You cannot long be in his presence without being touched yourself with a love for them."

His brows crowded as he said, "If you accompany me to his place of business, and you personally know the man, why should I be in the precarious position of selecting the pearls and making the transaction? Your own skill and understanding are far superior to mine."

She looked at the ground and said, "When I last saw Shu, I was a girl of twelve. But in the years since, my monthly blood has flowed and my breasts have grown, making me no longer eligible to enter his place of business. In this land, a woman has even less opportunities than I do in Muciri...and far less than a woman has in your own land. Accompanying my abba as a little girl was one thing, but a full-grown, child-bearing woman is quite another."

He pondered her words for a while and then asked, "What is he like...to do business with?"

"Though he drives a hard bargain like a man selling his last meal—always with his own interest uppermost—he is a decidedly fair man. To deceive or cheat another is, to him, totally foreign and a reprehensible matter. And he is extravagantly generous with his knowledge and understanding."

"Since I am like an infant in this trade, and have never met the man, why should he even consent to meet with me?"

She said, "First, he is a businessman. You have money, and a desire to acquire his product. This is reason enough for him to meet with you. Second, I will provide your introduction. He will be gratified to receive news of his old friend, from his friend's daughter. And to know that both I and my abba have vouched for you will give you a measure of respect with him."

Shamir looked relieved and said, "I thought I would have to be there without you."

"No, we will first meet him outside his business. He will certainly greet me there with great joy. And we will speak of my abba. Then, I will introduce you to Shu. But only you will be able to step over the threshold, to enter the chambers of his trade. It is there that a woman is not allowed. And this is not a matter of his own choice. It is something demanded by the strictures of this culture. To continue to live and prosper among these people, he must follow what is acceptable. To do anything else would bring upon his head the consequences of untold dishonor and shame. We should continue on our way now, since I specified in my message to him that we would arrive before the sun's zenith."

The street leading to the pearler's business was wider and far less crowded than the rest of the city. Rows of shops lined both sides of the avenue, with everything appearing clean and orderly. A few armed guards of Emperor Guang-wu patrolled the neighborhood.

The people rambling along the street presented a wondrous and exotic sight to Shamir. The broad sleeves, flowing robes, and belted waists displayed great varieties of length, form, and patterns. Dressed in the finest linens, muslins, and silks, they appeared as vivid-colored clouds floating along between the array of shops and offices. While a few woman strolled among them, men comprised the majority.

Their unfamiliar forms of headgear fascinated him. Some wore silk caps with various long flaps, either in front and behind, or hanging down over each ear. Some sported dual cones raked to the rear, or a device like a square, flat panel balanced on top. And the most peculiar to him—a cylindrical hat with long, thin ornaments sprouting horizontally from both ears, like bizarre, black horns.

From behind them, someone called out "Make way! Make way!" The man carrying Tenicca instinctively stepped aside to the edge of the street. Eight men, dressed in red wool uniforms and their jackets sporting rows of mother-of-pearl buttons, spritely marched along in perfect step, transporting a sedan. At each of the carriage's corners a pair of men held the long handles. The honored occupant within, hid behind screens of muslin gauze, patterned to camouflage the view from the outside. A man at the rear intoned, "*Tut...tut...tut...*" to keep their pace in synchrony.

After the entourage passed, the three reentered the street to continue to the pearler's shop. While they marched along, Shamir watched Tenicca bob lightly in her seat on the back of the porter. Now accustomed to the rhythm and swing of her porter's gait, she rode admirably, and he imagined his companion swaying in the saddle of a fine camel.

Near the end of the avenue and after passing a large tree, Tenicca said, "We are nearly here. Turn at the next right." Three steps led up to a narrower side street, and halfway down, an elderly gentleman sat on a bench, his lap and legs covered by a blanket. He stood as they approached, saying, "Where is my little Ten-Ten?"

Shamir motioned for their porter to let Tenicca unseat herself, and as soon as her feet touched the cobblestone street, she hurried to Rongyu Shu and bowed deeply from her waist. The man waited for her to rise and then seized both her hands in his.

In the language of Gwongjau, she said, "I am so sorry that my abba could not make this long journey to greet his great friend. But I am here in his stead."

The man's smile beamed from the vertical creases and wrinkles of his aged-leather face.

"It has been eight long years, and I would not have recognized his daughter, had not you first sent me the message you were coming."

"Yes, it *has been* long. We have both missed seeing our Master of the Sea-Gems. My abba is now old and weak—and may not live until we return. But he speaks of you often, and even now desires to add to his collection of the lilacs."

"Is this man your abba's agent?"

"Please forgive me, Rongyu Shu. Yes, this is Zuizhi—from Li-Kan, in the arid lands beyond the great sea west of Chera. His abba is a trader of lapis and malachite, and Zuizhi is formerly a mason and sculptor. He has been trained in my abba's methods of appraising pearls, and so acts in his place."

Shamir bowed to the man and said, "It is a great honor to represent Sariyan in this matter, and to meet one of such high reputation as yourself."

Shu spoke to Tenicca. "I hear, myself, you have taught him our language well. Though he does not yet speak it with your own fluency, it will suffice for the business at hand. Shamir—shall we proceed?"

He gestured toward the open door of the shop.

41

THE PORTAL'S LINTEL AND doorposts, hewn from massive pine timbers, had the look of many generations on them, reminding Shamir of the grand entrances of marzeah halls in Raqmu. The wood, dark and smoothly worn, gave testimony to the countless hands touching them for centuries. Stepping across the threshold, the two entered another world.

The place smelled of old wood, tanned leather, ginger, and tea. On the far wall hung vertical banners of red silk, emblazoned with large characters executed by a bold calligraphic hand in the blackest of ink. In the shop's corner a large, muscular dog with short yellow hair sat at vigilant attention, unmoving. The dog's piercing stare unnerved Shamir, and he froze in place. His host said, "Ah, you have seen my guard. He is quite a specimen of strength and ferocity. But only when I give the command, or when I am not present. You need not worry."

In the middle of the shop stood a curious construction. A step higher than the floor, a platform supported a square table in its center. And directly above the table, a tunnel, or tube, wide enough for a man to crawl through, pierced the room's ceiling and extended upward through the roof. A white-wash coated its inner surface.

Rongyu Shu extended his hand toward the table set before them, inviting Shamir to approach it. As they reached the table's side, Shu grasped the end of a chain extending up into the tube, and pulled it downward. The chain tipped a pivoted cover at the upper end of the tube, filling it with the brilliance of sunlight above the roof. The light flooded downward, illuminating a large set of pearls laid out in patterns on the black linen covering the table. They glowed as if lit from within. The spectacle filled Shamir's eyes to overflowing. Shu said, unhurried and with deliberation,

"The pearls you are about to experience are the pinnacle of these gems mined from the waves. I know you have some knowledge of the signs of quality in these pearls, for the purpose of comparing and appraising them, but please indulge me in giving you my own insight into the truth of what they are."

Shu waited for the sound of his preamble's words to fade, and for silence to reassert itself in the shop. He began again, in hushed tones and simple gestures.

"The pearl is said, by some, to be the visible sign of love, devotion, the perfect union of man and woman. While this is true, it is far more than that. A pearl is a singular and miraculous entity. Some say *the seawater begs the pearl to break its shell.* The first miracle we encounter in the pearl is its extreme rarity. Though no one has made a serious count, only a single shellfish out of, perhaps, tens of thousands will contain a pearl. One could easily collect many mussels or oysters daily, for an entire lifetime, and never find a single pearl. Imagine all of these animals, with their soft bodies protected within their rock-like homes—all ten thousand—giving up their lives on the unfortunate and mistaken expectation that they hid a small pearl somewhere within. And then to be casually cast back into the sea to die, or to be fried up in the molten fat of a pig and consumed in a single gulp.

"The next miracle lies in the origin of pearls. Some believe such rarity must surely involve the heavens above. It is said that in certain seasons, the full moon drains itself of brilliance by spilling its semen —its man-seed—the brightness falling to the earth like shining drops of light. If this glowing dew falls upon certain blessed regions of the sea, the oysters or mussels there open their shells wide in response, the moon-drops enter them to lodge in their intimate folds, and so, beget lustrous pearls."

He waited for the idea to capture Shamir's imagination, and then said,

"While that is a beautiful, poetic view of the matter, I believe the truth of the miracle is far more compelling. I believe it is to be found at the very center of what a pearl is. We commonly think of a pearl as an object of consummate beauty—and that is certainly so. But if a costly pearl were split open—and I shudder to imagine that—we would see at its core, something tiny, and unsightly. A grain of sand, a piece of broken shell, perhaps a small parasite. None of these has a beauty or wonder in itself. They are ugly, malignant, destructive. In the normal course of life, these things may invade the protected home of the shellfish. The invaders work themselves in between the shells and into the soft flesh of the animal's delicate body, producing irritation, disruption, perhaps injury.

"To protect itself from the invader, the animal then begins the miraculous work of containing, isolating the alien contaminant. It uses the same process as for producing its home, its shell. The soft tissue of the animal secretes a substance that becomes the *nacre*— the crystallized essence of clouds, rainbows, and moonlight. The animal wraps the dark, broken, grit and filth of living in an envelope of the highest form of beauty. Month after month, and year after year, it adds layer upon layer upon layer of nacre, ultimately developing a depth of glowing luster that could never be imagined, if not seen first in a high quality pearl.

"This is certainly a miracle of the highest order. I believe that, somehow, whoever imagined and created all that we know has enabled this wondrous process to tell us something wonderful about themselves. It must be a picture in miniature of who they are, and what they are about.

"Shall we now inspect these gems provided by the sea?"

Shu presented dozens of pearls individually, and then the ones for which Shamir displayed the greatest interest, he laid aside to compare as a set. After a few hours of close inspection, discussion, and wrangling over price, he selected a dozen, large, exceptional gems of precisely the lilac hue, size, form and luster prescribed by Sariyan. And with his generous retainer fee from Sariyan, he selected three smaller pearls for himself. Shu wrapped each of them separately in a small, black silk pouch, and then bundled them in a single red bag smaller than a man's fist. After Shamir paid him the agreed price in gold and diamonds, Shu passed the bag into the young man's possession and cautioned him—

"You now hold in your one hand the equivalent of more than three-hundred years of a laborer's wage. Many would not hesitate to end your life for these gems. I suggest you be discreet as possible, and leave by a different path than you arrived."

"I thank you for the warning. But since I came here with our payment of equal value, I am familiar with carrying and protecting such valuables."

"That may well be, but what you have in that one small bag is actually of inestimable value. The pearls you now possess have no true equals. There are none others like them in the world. While I have more pearls here, any I have collected are unique. There are those who would casually kill to obtain such beauty for their own possession."

Shamir loosened the sash at his waist and opened his robe, tucking the bag into a pocket sewn just inside the waist, next to the sheath of his janbiya. Shu pointed to the dagger's handle and said, "Is that your protection?"

Shamir deftly slid the razor-sharp weapon from its home and extended it, handle first, toward Shu. He accepted the weapon, turning it over in his hand, examining it. He pulled the wide, silk sleeve back on one arm and used the blade to shave the hair from his forearm. He pursed his lips, raised his eyebrows and handed the weapon back, saying, "That should suffice—if you know how to use it, and are willing to do so without hesitation."

Shamir slipped it back into its home and said, "I am."

With their business concluded, Shu asked, "Is there anything else in which I may be of help? And if not, may it go well with you and Tenicca on your voyage home."

Shamir said, "There is one matter for which I have heard you might assist me. I am told by Sariyan you have knowledge of something called...the *Zuizhi*. Is that so?"

The pearl trader caught Shamir's gaze and stared long and hard into his eyes while turning his head left and right.

"The Zuizhi, you say? Your namesake? As soon as I heard your name, I thought of it. Certainly I know of it. Most say, '*Zuizhi*'—calling it the 'thing like a flint.' But some have called it '*Sooh*'—a 'thorn.' If you like, we can speak in your own language. You may have some of our common language for getting by day-by-day, and for dealing in pearls, but I fear your understanding does not extend much beyond that. I am, perhaps, more familiar with your language, than you are with mine. I once befriended a group of jugglers and acrobats, sent from your King Haretat to our Emperor Guang-wu's court. They taught me their tongue quite well. Some yet live among us, having taken local wives and produced families. I still associate with them on occasion."

"Yes, that would certainly make discussion simpler for me. Thank you."

Shu continued. "The Zuizhi—or the Shamir, as you call it—is said to be a unique material, or device, small in size but grand in effect. Smaller than the tip of the 'finger-with-no-name,' and the color of mulberry leaves as they first sprout. No other hard substance could remain intact in its presence, and so it could only be kept wrapped in lamb's wool and laid in a bed of barley bran in a leaden box. It could cut, carve, penetrate, or break any material. Able to cleave the hardest stone—the adamant. And it has been used on occasion, more than a thousand and a half years ago, to engrave gemstones with letters and symbols, without cutting a groove in the stone's material. Is this, in fact, the true object of your pursuit?"

Shamir nodded sharply and waited, hoping this would be the deep source of information he sought so long. The man pursed his lips and then let his memory flow through his mouth.

"The stories passed down to me say it was found by a foreign king, to the far west—the kingdom even farther than the place we call Li-Kan, the place of waters-in-the-desert. And they say he used it to trim and dress the stones for building a shrine to his god. After he was no longer in need of its powers, he presented it to a queen from the south, for her consent to be the vessel of his royal seed. Some years later, in her trade for 700 camels-of-two-humps, it passed into the hands of a Persian satrap, whose grandson made of it a gift to the king of Eelam, who finally lost it in a game of chance to the Admiral of the Royal fleet of our Emperor Xuan. It was then that the Zuizhi entered our land."

42

RONGYU SHU PLACED A pair of small, white-porcelain cups on a gilded tray of red lacquer, and poured the aromatic infusion from the dragon's-mouth spout of the pot. Steam billowed up from the stream of liquid. Pointing to the far corner of the room, he gestured for Shamir to follow. The dog followed Shamir and then lay down in a nearby corner, still watching him. Among some cushions stood a low table made of ebony inlaid with ivory, and he placed the tray on it. Motioning for Shamir to sit he said, "Please, recline in comfort and we will talk more," and so they sprawled upon the cushions. Raising his small cup, Shu said "Let us enjoy this liquid art—to our health and prosperity."

They sipped the savory brew, and Shamir, not accustomed to such hot beverages, burned his lips and tongue but hid his pain. He watched his host, and seeing absolutely no indication of discomfort in him, marveled that anyone could enjoy such painfully hot drink. When they had drained the cups, Shu refilled them and said to him,

"It is clear Ten-Ten is no longer the child I once knew. Despite the limitations of her lameness, she has blossomed as a peony in spring.

And I now hear in her voice, the soft, low music of a woman's soul. Does she please you?"

Shamir opened his mouth, but at a loss for words, he simply looked at the man. Shu said,

"I take that to mean she does. Is she your woman?"

Again, Shamir hesitated but finally found his voice.

"No, I am simply her father's agent. She has no interest in me beyond his business."

Shu waggled his head, saying,

"A pity—such a long voyage, and only business between the two of you. And she has become an unusual creature, has she not? The understanding and depth of a man, mixed with the soft beauty and perception of a woman. Ah, well..."

Shu took another sip of tea and thought some before speaking again.

"And tell me—what is your great interest in such a thing as this Shamir, as you call it?"

Shamir looked away from Shu. He truncated the story of his pursuit and only said, "I have heard of it so long, I wish to settle the matter of whether it be myth, or fact." He went back to sipping from the little cup.

The old man raised his eyebrows, skeptical of the evasive answer, but then started his story.

"Xuan executed his Admiral for alleged intrigues against him, and confiscated the dead man's estate. Along with the man's wives and concubines, among the many items that came into his possession was the Zuizhi, accompanied by a small scroll describing its abilities. The Emperor passed the device into the hands of his master jeweler, for the purpose of producing new gems for the Royal family. The jeweler attempted to use it for engraving what was to be a heavy amulet of light-colored jade."

Shamir quickly lowered the cup from his lips, spilling some tea upon his clothes, and said hoarsely,

"It is true then! It exists not only in the stories of old men, and in the dreams of their sons!"

"Yes. That jeweler was, in fact, my abba's abba. I have never seen the object myself, but heard my abba speak of it. He was in his abba's workshop the day these events transpired. As a boy, he watched this affair with his own eyes, and the words I tell you are the words he told me."

Shamir set his cup back on the tray and sat erect, saying,

"It is here, then? May I see it?!"

"Your words betray the passion with which you seek the thing. This is no matter of idle curiosity for you."

"I confess that I have long dreamed of and sought this device..."

"Your answers will be found in the telling of the story's end. As I said, my grandfather received the task from Xuan to finely engrave a certain valuable piece of pale jade. But apparently, the Zuizhi's powers had declined over the few thousand years of its existence. He removed the device from the padding inside its lead box and approached the jade stone with it, to engrave upon it the symbol for 'Life.' As he did, its powers seemed to expire in an instant, accompanied by hissing and crackling. And violent heating of the Zuizhi. It burned his fingers, causing him to drop it onto the block of jade, whereupon the great heat melted the stone where it touched, the Zuizhi sinking down into the molten spot. It sank into the interior of the stone, and as it cooled, it became solid again, trapping the device permanently within. He placed the stone into a locked, bronze vault, where the most valuable jewels of the empire were kept."

Shamir sank back onto the pillows, deflated by the news the device was exhausted, and now lost. He said, "It is still in safe-keeping then, but useless?"

"There is more to the story. Because of his failure of engraving the amulet, on the next day the Emperor had my grandfather's head removed in the courtyard of his own shop—in full view of his son… my abba."

"And the Zuizhi, inside the pale stone—what became of it?"

"For a long time it remained in the vault. But a new Emperor arose—named Cheng. It is said he either had some other item made from the block of stone, or gave it away, or simply discarded it. Whichever is true, it apparently is no longer in the vault."

Fearing his quest may have come to an end, Shamir took a very deep breath, held it a while, and let it out, shaking his head. "So it is truly gone from this land—and no one now knows its whereabouts?"

The old pearl merchant took a long, noisy sip from his cup. He stroked his scraggly beard, pointed a crooked finger at Shamir, and said, "There is one, last point. In the general lore and myths I have heard over the years, concerning this Zuizhi, it has been said that a malevolent spirit—an *emo*, a demon, a *djinn* you might call it—was its original owner. And they say that the king of the far west first received it from this spirit by trickery. Some have proposed that the demon somehow learned of its location in the vault, to spirit the thing away, taking it back into its rightful possession."

Shamir propped himself up on an elbow and asked, "How would one contact this spirit? Do you know his name?"

"I fear you are too deeply fascinated with this device. It died, was buried, and has become the dust of history. Why try to dredge it back up from its grave?"

"I am willing to pay for any more information. I pray you give me this spirit's name."

"This will come to no good end. But since you persist, I will acquiesce. And you need not pay me, as I do not wish to have the responsibility of your life upon my hands."

He tipped his cup and drained the rest of the hot liquid into his mouth. He looked at Shamir—anticipation stoking the young man's keen attention. The old man shook his head, and said, "The name depends on who is doing the telling. Some say '*Asmodeus*,' and others '*Aeshma-daeva*.' But most often, it is called '*Ashmedai*.'"

"And the spirit's whereabouts?"

"He is said to crave the water of a certain well he considers his own—it is called Be'er Sheqerin, the Well of Lies—but I know not where it is. I have also heard he is fond of quality wines—but what could a demon know of quality? And that is the end of my knowledge in this matter."

Shamir rose and prepared to leave, but Shu gestured for him to sit again, saying, "The tea is gone, and now it is time to dream..."

43

SHU OPENED A DRAWER in the table and removed from it a bamboo tube, a glass lamp, and a light-brown wafer of waxy luster, the size of a large coin. The glass reservoir of the lamp contained a thin, clear fluid like water, and a thick wick, which he lit from a nearby lamp. It flickered to life with a fluttering pale-blue flame and Shamir remarked that he'd never seen anything like it. Shu said, "The wick burns not oil, but a pure spirit distilled from strong wine. Yes, the blue flame is unusual, is it not? The spirit burns with a flame that invests itself more with heat than with light. I use a similar lamp for the making of tea."

He placed the wafer on a porcelain saucer and took a metal device from the drawer. Extending from the wooden handle, a thick copper wire a hand-span long ended in a flat spiral, about the same size as the wafer. As he heated the spiral over the flame, Shu said, "I call these my 'dream-coins' and obtain them from a source to the west. While they have no obvious beauty about them, they are quite remarkable in their ability to produce rapture in the one who breathes their essence. And unlike natural dreams, these visions precede the sleep. Would you care to join me?"

"No, but thank you. I have no desire to either dream or sleep while the sun yet remains in the sky. And, before long, I will need to return to Tenicca. But please indulge yourself, and speak to me of your dream, if you can."

"Of course. I remain quite conscious as the visions transpire."

With the copper brought to a dull, red-heat, a few wisps of smoke fumed from its wire spiral. He grasped the bamboo tube and put it to his lips, with the other end directly over the wafer. Without hurry, he removed the glowing spiral from the blue flame and plunged it onto the surface of the wafer. It hissed and squeaked as it fumed with a dense smoke. He drew the smoke into his lungs and held it captive, waiting for the fumes' effect. When he could hold it no longer, he released the vapor back into the room. It smelled darkly sweet and resinous, like pine-pitch melted together with the waxy comb of bees, still filled with honey. He extinguished the lamp's flame and said,

"There is an ancient tale told among my people, and I begin to see it now before me, as in life. There is a remote and mountainous region to the north, where a lowly stonecutter lived and plied his trade. Each morning, as the first light of the new day fell upon the valley of his home, he could be heard whistling a joyful tune as he hiked through the morning mist and into the mountains to find his work. And each day until the sun fell in the west, he happily worked, chipping rock with his chisel and mallet, to free blocks of stone from the mountain's flank. The fruits of his sweat supported his wife— the love of his life—and the five beautiful daughters she gave him.

"One fine day, a merchant in the business of buying and selling stone contracted with the stonecutter to purchase quality marble blocks for finishing the palace of the provincial governor. When the stonecutter completed his work, he sent word to the merchant the order had been fulfilled and he could receive the stone. The merchant arrived with six ox-carts and their drivers, to move the stone to the palace building site. When the stonecutter received the small bag of bronze coins in payment, he thought to himself,

Look at this wealthy merchant—in his fine clothes of silk, woven with threads of gold! I have heard he has a great house in the next valley— where he keeps three beautiful wives and eight concubines. He pays me this pittance for a fortnight of hard work, and yet, without lifting so much as a finger, he will sell my stone to the builder for ten months' of my wages. If only I were a wealthy merchant, like him...

"A deep magic was at work, and as the stonecutter's thoughts concluded, he looked down at his clothes and saw that his coarse wool tunic had instantaneously transformed into a flowing robe of black silk, shot through with threads of silver and gold. The cuffs and neck trimmed with crimson embroidery. An elegant hat sat atop his head, and a gold chain with a large, costly pearl hung from his neck. He realized, to his considerable joy, he had become the wealthy merchant.

"He told the cart drivers to begin transporting the stone to his buyer in the next city. Along the road, while the oxen lumbered and labored before their heavy burdens, the stonecutter-turned-merchant began counting in his head all of the silver he would own after the sale was made. He rubbed his palms together, as they itched for the silver that would soon fill them.

"With his mind still swimming with these thoughts, a cry from behind him called out—'Make way! 'Make way! Make way for his excellency Guang Mi, governor of the province! Make way!'

"All those walking on the road immediately parted to the left and to the right. The ox-drivers goaded their animals repeatedly, driving them from the road into the muddy ditches on either side. The wealthy merchant, too, stepped away from the stone-paved roadway and into the ditch. Twelve men in total, six at the front and six at the rear, hustled along the road carrying the sedan of the governor. The carriage, lacquered in red and glossy black, displayed his crest—a spread-winged eagle in gilded feathers. The sedan was large enough to comfortably carry two, and hidden behind its silk curtains, Guang Mi cavorted with his woman of the moment. They soon passed, leaving the ox-drivers the difficult task of extracting the stone-laden carts from the mud, out of the ditch, and then back onto the road. The wealthy merchant looked at his red satin shoes, now caked with mud, and thought to himself—

Look at that powerful politician—sweeping down the road like an unstoppable tide! None dare defy him by slowing his progress. He would behead on the spot such a man, not giving a thought to it. And he would claim for himself whatever pretty virgin he might see along the road—to enjoy her young flesh for a moment, and then cast her aside when done with her. Who would dare oppose such a man? If only I were a powerful politician, like him...

"And as he entertained these thoughts, he felt himself swaying and bouncing in rhythm. He sat on richly decorated silk cushions inside a cubicle. His right arm encircled the waist of a half-undressed young woman, her pale flesh, supple and enticing. He looked through the gauzy silk curtains ahead of him and saw a sea of people parting and bowing before his entourage, and he knew then that the magic had made him governor. He almost could not believe the great fortune that had befallen him, but he roughly kissed his companion and prepared to satisfy himself with her.

"But the heat of the afternoon grew as the sun proceeded before them. The governor fanned himself, and finally removed his official robes, stripping to only a simple loin-cloth. He could barely breathe in the heat, and to gain fresh air, he tore back the silk curtains of the sedan—thereby exposing the humility of his near-nakedness to the countryside. He heard the tittering laughter of those driven into the ditches at the sides of the road. He cursed the sun, and said,

The sun pays no heed to all those on the earth! All wilt in the fearsome glare of his countenance, bowing before him and removing their hats and robes. The rivers dry up before him and the forests parch into deserts at

the heat of his glance. Who can resist the heavenly might of the golden orb ruling the day? If only I were the sun on high...

"In an instant, the sedan was gone, the road was gone, and the great heat of the day emanated from himself. Now the sun, he floated far above the earth. Far above the blue sky. His light beamed out, reaching to the farthest corners of the universe. He inflated his shining chest and glared down upon the world. But a white cloud, so insubstantial it floated upon the air, came between the sun and the earth, shading its relieved occupants and reflecting the brilliant light back to its source. The sun filled with resentment at the upstart cloud, daring to block his blazing might. He beamed brighter and brighter, but the cloud paid no attention and continued to shade the earth. The sun gave up the struggle and said,

The cloud acts as though I don't exist! He floats along, free and easy, as though life were a trifle, as though nothing mattered. And yet, his quiet strength trumps my own glory and might. If only I were the cloud...

"The magic worked again and he found himself majestic and white, floating above the sea, and land, and mountains—like a great ship of the air, its sails full and trailing a strong wake. His shadow crept over the earth, crossing rivers and deserts, bringing relief to all people. He chortled as he floated, and changed his form with every whim. He became a rabbit, a warhorse, a grand palace—whatever his heart desired.

"But a wind arose in the west and confronted him with its bluster and gusts. It buffeted his billowing heaps of white, tearing him to shreds. Every wisp and particle was dispersed across the sky and he found it difficult to even think in his scattered condition. And he said,

I have no power, no substance in the face of this wind, who blows and bullies from one end of the earth to the other! Who can stand before one who is invisible and invincible? If only I were the wind...

"And, of course, he became the wind. The force of his powerful breath increased, and he worked himself up into a potent tempest, raging through the countryside to destroy the crops of farmers, uproot tall trees, and tear roof tiles from the Emperor's palace. He congratulated himself on his magnificence and set his sight on the north. From a great distance he spied an imposing mountain, and sped toward it, to strike it from the earth. He slammed into the rocky crag with a mighty blast, and then staggered back. He saw the peak was unmoved, so he threw himself upon it again, with even greater violence, but the mountain was not shaken. He admitted defeat, and slinked back toward his home in the west, mumbling,

The mountain—what a repository of inert strength and stability! In a thousand years he will remain standing tall, and unchanged. His durability is without peer, and he laughs at the approach of any storm. If only I were the mountain...

"No longer the wind, he now felt his rocky roots extending downward, into the very core of the world, and he wore a crown of fog and mist upon his jagged summit. He flexed the muscles in his broad, granite shoulders and thunder rumbled across his stone belly. He laughed a hearty laugh, knowing now there was no match for his awesome strength. A deep peace filled his flinty heart and he rested within his mantle of forest green.

"And then, in the valley far below him, he heard a simple, joyful tune, whistled by a lowly stonecutter on his way to work. And the mountain shook to his core, knowing the man's true might...”

The dream ended and the old man's narration concluded. While the story had not been told to shame him, Shamir felt a strange anxiety, his hot blood rising into his face. He turned away from Shu and squirmed on the pillows.

How are the deepest thoughts of my heart laid bare for this man to see? I must leave...now!

He saw the old man's eyelids begin to droop, so he stood and bowed to him, saying "I thank you for your generous assistance in adding to Sariyan's collection. I know he will be greatly pleased. And

I thank you for your generosity in sharing your depth of knowledge and wisdom with me. May you continue to prosper."

He turned toward the door and the dog stood to attention. Rongyu Shu said, "Please set the door's latch as you leave..."

44

HAVING PASSED THROUGH THE narrow straits at Melay and on the last leg of their journey west and south, the *Begum of Bangal* paralleled the Pandyan east coast of the great peninsula, steering to pass through the strait at the island of Eelam. Since the winds blew constant in a favorable direction, the captain filled the yards with sail and gave the ship its head. And so they flew, back toward Muciri.

Shamir and Tenicca stood together on deck, watching the sun bury itself in the waves. The sails towered above them like clouds, amber and ochre in the failing light. Below an acre of billowed sail, the ship lumbered and lunged—a great, wooden sea-monster, swimming the green-blue sea. As it climbed each swell, to slide down the far side, its massive beams and ribs flexed under the strain of its cargo's burden. And with each slight flexure, the volume of the hull expanded and contracted in rhythm, causing the hold to breathe over the cargo of cinnamon, malabathrum, and spikenard, its exhale lading the sea-breeze with gracious and mysterious fragrances of the east.

Tenicca leaned her back into the secure comfort of her protector, friend, and confidant. She said, "I have heard from the crew we return ten days early, and may anchor just off the coast for a few days, awaiting a berth at the pier. When we finally reach Muciri, what will you do?"

He wrapped her slight frame in his arms, to guard her from the heave of the ship, and he enveloped her in his cloak, to shield her from the cool wind and spray. The sun lolled on the horizon, flattening and fattening, to settle in the sea. She looked up at him, expecting his response to her question. The sun's last, orangey rays illuminated her face like burnished bronze with glints of gold.

The weight of her words and the import of the moment paralyzed his voice. His heart restrained him from speech. She said,

"You need not chase your quarry—your Shamir. If you ask my father for my hand, I know he will not refuse you. And if he does yet live, he will surely bequeath you the business upon his death. His gem-trade will be yours, as I am yours. You have said yourself you have no family in Nabataea, or even in this world. Could not your family begin with me, and grow from here?"

He held her closer and felt her heart pulsing with life inside her. His own pulse pounded in his ears.

The mighty ship rose and fell with the rhythm of the rolling swells. As it wallowed in the wave-troughs, sea-spray flew across the deck, wetting their faces with cool mist. And as it rose to the wave-peaks, the strength of their passion rose with it. When the sun finally drowned itself in the sea, it emitted a final, flickering flash of green.

She said to him,

"Please—take me, below..."

She clung to his neck, and he swept her up in effortless motion, to fulfill her request.

During that season of the year, proceeding up the Culli River by sail was impossible with the northeast winds in their face. For three days, the *Begum* lay anchored offshore of the river's estuary. The heavy traffic of ships arriving from up and down the coast forced a short-age of local river boats. So they waited for portage of passengers and freight, upriver to the port of Muciri. Shamir and Tenicca spent those days in tender moments.

The morning for departure arrived, and their collection of baggage waited on deck near the rail. Like the hundreds of times before, he carried her topside from below deck—this time he continued holding her in his arms. The morning sky looked like clabbered cream and pressed down from above.

She asked, "Would you, please, turn us around, so I can see for a final time our home upon the waves?" He granted her desire and spun around while he held her. She said, "I know it seemed a silly request, but this was my first time beyond my father's voice. I won-der if he still lives…"

A small boat from Muciri pulled alongside the *Begum*, and they lashed it tight to the ship. Sailors on deck dropped the baggage, piece by piece, into the waiting arms of those in the boat. Then, a bosun's chair, with a wooden plank for a seat, and walls of heavy rope netting, was brought near the rail and attached to a rope roved over a short spar. Shamir helped Tenicca onto the seat and nodded to the sailors operating the lift. They hoisted their passenger, then swung the spar with smooth precision over the rail, and above the boat. They slowly lowered the seat and Tenicca into the boat, where they assisted her from the lift. They began hoisting it again for Shamir, but he already clambered over the rail and descended the rigging hanging on the side of the ship. He took a seat beside her.

They untied the boat and pushed off, rowing toward the river's mouth. As they worked their way among the anchored ships, it so happened they passed close to the *Dwelling of Lions*, it having arrived from Muza four weeks previous. Shamir caught sight of a sailor on board he'd met the previous year when he first traveled to the coast of Malabar. He waved and shouted to him. "Wahabu! It is me—Shamir. I am just returning from the farthest east. Are you well?"

The man shouted down to him from the deck of the *Dwelling*. "I am, my brother. I see you have gained a companion on your journey! We sail this afternoon for Muza, and then on to Aila. You may join us...if you wish to escape! You still have time...hah!"

He shouted back to the man, "May it go well with you, Wahabu, and may you return to your family in safety!"

"And may you find the desires of your heart, Shamir!"

The hull of the small boat groaned as it rubbed against the pier's brick pollards to which it had been made fast. Shamir lifted the several ox-hide cases, small wooden chests and a lidded basket to the roughened planks of the pier. Returning to the boat, he said to Tenicca, "Shall I take you to the pier?' and held out his arms for her.

As he carried her across the small gangway, suspended above the dark green waters of the bay, she asked, "What is the matter, Love? —you tremble as you carry me."

Stepping onto the pier, and well away from the edge, he placed her again upon the soles of her feet. He stood there looking at her, frozen for a moment, and then said to her, "I cannot..."

But his lips closed and refused passage to the rest of his words. He glanced skyward and then returned his eyes to the world, his face creased with remorse.

"I am not..."

And again his words halted. His gaze dropped to the cracked, weathered planks of the pier beneath his feet. Through the spaces between the boards he saw below them an egret. With invisible speed, it speared a small fish with its sharp bill, and with an upward flick swallowed it whole. He finally said,

"I have...dishonored you...greatly. And I dishonor your father. And I am shamed beyond remedy."

Her mouth opened as if she needed to say something, but the words wedged below her throat. She fanned her face with both hands, hoping to breathe again with a fresh infusion of air.

His voice near a whisper, he said, "My love for you, Tenicca, is beyond my understanding. But I cannot...wake each morning...to see you...yet in your infirmity. It does not, itself, offend me. But it reminds me sharply of my own, and what I have lost because of it. You do not deserve someone lost in the past. Or one who would cast himself carelessly into the future. And if I remained, you would despise me as I wallow in my self-pity. I must complete my pursuit of that...which *may* complete me. Perhaps it does not even exist. But if I lay it aside now, I shall forever long for it."

He slipped his hand into his garment and extracted the small bag of pearls protected at his waist. He placed it in the palm of her hand and closed her fingers over it.

She knew then, she would never wear the *jadanagam,* the serpent-jewels worn by brides to decorate their braided hair. She would not pin at the back of her head, the nuptial *rakkadi,* in the shape of the sun, symbolic of brilliance and power, followed by the crescent moon of calm and peace. And below them, the fragrant *thazhambu* flower, and the ruby-studded divine cobra, *Ananta.* Finally, she would not decorate the long hair braid down her back with jewelry in the form of flowers and buds, bursting out into the three silk tassels encrusted with bells. Even the temple dancers who remain virgins, consider themselves brides of the temple deity and can adopt the *jadanagam.* But her physical defect made her unsuitable even for that.

He left her standing on the pier and entered a boat just leaving for the *Dwelling of Lions.* There he joined himself to the crew. That afternoon they weighed anchor, launching the return trip to their home port of Aila. The sails filling with gusts of the northeast winds, Shamir stood on the deck hauling rope, and he imagined he saw Tenicca still at the pier, watching while he sailed away.

He tore open his robe and yanked his janbiya from its sheath, holding high the gleaming blade. He cried out to the sky, "O, Manawat! Pour out the burning coals of your fearsome curses upon my head...upon my worthless life!" He lowered the dagger and drew the keen edge across his bare chest, trailing an arc of growing droplets of blood. The droplets broke into rivulets and trickled down his chest like red tears.

45

AND SO IT WAS, that upon their arrival at Aila fifty-eight days later, Shamir left the *Dwelling of Lions,* and near the port sought a Iudaean trader of gems and fine pearls. He wished to trade one of his three, small, exquisite 'lilacs' for a substantial stake in gold and silver coin. Although the man's place of business was not much more than a shack of mud-bricks, he had an impressive inventory of valuable gems—rubies, beryl, and saltwater pearls from Malabar; turquoise, emeralds, and amethysts from Persia; and fine coral from the Great Western Sea. A round table, small enough for a man to reach across, stood in the center of the shop, topped with a black silk cover.

Shamir removed his three pearls from the bag hid within his wide belt-band, and laid them on the silk. The man inspected them closely, touching them only with an ivory stylus. He then asked for and received Shamir's permission to pick them up. He held them in the sunlight streaming through the doorway, rolling them between thumb and finger to see them from all sides, and to evaluate their roundness. Shamir said, "I will be selling one of the three. Which do you desire, and what is your best offer for it?"

"Are you certain you will sell only the one?"

"Yes. It will be some time before I settle in one place, so while I travel I will only require enough coin for traveling expenses. Concealing the remainder of my wealth in pearls will be more secure."

Though the dealer disparaged the quality of the pearls throughout the long process of haggling, once the deal had been made, he was greatly pleased to possess such an exquisite gem. In celebration, he poured them both a cup of wine. The man lifted his cup in salute, and said, "L'chaim!'"

They emptied their cups, and the man poured them a second. As they sipped their wine, Shamir startled and ducked as something flew past his ear. It fluttered, hovered an instant, and finally descended upon the gem dealer's shoulder. The bird displayed striking black and white bars on its wings, back and tail. Its shoulders, neck and head had the soft color of a ripe Persian peach. The black beak was long, thin, and sharp as a needle, and as it opened, a long tongue as slender as a thread darted out. From its head sprouted a curious crest, orange as a pomegranate flower and tipped with black.

The dealer laughed at the bird and said, "Would you believe this bird—this *hoopoe*—has taken me as a pet? A month ago she appeared out of nowhere. Every day I bring out for her a single corn of barley. She takes it in her mouth, and then flies away. Before long, she started perching on my shoulder when I did not feed her promptly. I call her *Gannaba*—my Robber."

The bird strutted back and forth on the man's shoulder, and occasionally lifted her crest, extending it above her head into a brilliant-orange feathery crown, topped with round black dots, like dark jewels. A single feather of the crown's twelve bent in the middle, so the black tip bobbed over the bird's face. The man held a barley grain between thumb and finger and the bird deftly extracted it with the tip of her beak. She immediately took flight and sailed through the doorway.

Shamir did not quite know what to say, but after the astonishment subsided he asked the gem dealer for information.

"Sir, I look for one who may have knowledge of certain spirits, or demons, who were known to the ancient kings of your people. Do you know of anyone who might help me in this?"

The man squinted one eye and arched the eyebrow of the other. He twisted his mouth and nose to one side and then asked, "Are you looking for a man with mere knowledge of such history?—or do you seek a man with personal experience in this area?"

"I suppose I will take whichever comes my way. Do you know of either?"

He thought a long time, and then bent low over the table toward Shamir, almost whispering.

"When I yet lived in Hebron, I once met a man—a priest of our religion—who told me of his harrowing encounters with such unclean spirits. He was oft called upon to exorcise such from the unfortunates plagued by these monsters. If anyone knows something of these matters, it may be him."

"Do you know of his name, and where I might find him?"

"His name escapes me now, but I know as soon as you leave, I will most likely remember it. Hah!—that is the way of these things, is it not? But I do know where he lives. He is of the Levite tribe, and some years ago bought the finest vineyard near Mahoza. It produces some of the best wines between Damascus and Timna. You have tasted some of it here today. So my best advice would be to travel to Mahoza and ask all you meet, for the Levite with the fine vineyard. You will find him."

"I thank you for this guidance. And I thank you for your honest dealings with me. May it go well with you."

He leased travel on a camel from Aila to Mahoza, under the protection of a two-hundred-camel train. He turned his back to the sea, and the two years behind him. The path leading to the Shamir, though still not clear, beckoned him onward.

From Aila, his caravan followed the great rift of the Arabah north to Mahoza. He sought the former Iudaean priest, a Levite, who was said to live near the date-palm plantations there. Levites, restricted by religious law from owning considerable property in their own land, formed a sizable community just southeast of the Salt Sea, in a region controlled by the Nabataeans. There they purchased productive tracts of date-palms, pomegranates, olives, and vineyards along the fertile bottom-lands of the River Zered.

While the orchards' owners jealously guarded their legal water rights to the river, water-masters appointed by the Kingdom of Nabataea tightly regulated the timing of access to the liquid resource. They allotted irrigation periods for individual groves in units of half-hours, to be used only at particular hours of the day, and specified days of the week.

He inquired among the farms and groves, about the man retired from the Iudaean priesthood. Shamir finally found the man in his vineyard, assessing his vines. Shamir walked among the rows, picking his path carefully between the vines and a crop of barley planted between the rows. The Levite looked up to see his approaching visitor, and suspicion covered his face. Shamir greeted him. "Sir, I seek a man—a Levite—who was once a priest among the Iudaeans."

The man looked back to his vines and continued his work, saying,

"I am just one of many. And your business with this man—this Levite?"

"I seek information that he may possess—the location of a certain well."

"A well? There are countless wells in Iudaea. But the water in the cisterns of Nabataea is of far greater abundance, though the land is arid."

"I look not for the well's water, but a certain personage said to be fond of this well."

The man looked at the ground and shook his head. "So, you are *looking* for a well—but you are *not looking* for a well. Just come to the end of the matter, young man, and you will save us both much time and pointless conversation."

Shamir hesitated long before saying, "I seek a spirit—some say a djinn—by name, Ashmedai."

The Levite mumbled incoherently, and taking hold of the collar of his tunic, tore the fabric. He stared at Shamir. "Please, do not again utter that name in my presence! And who sent you on this foolish errand? Do you not know this path is fraught with danger?"

"So, you do know of what I speak? Can you direct me to the well it calls it's own?"

"The Well of Lies? It is not really a well at all. Only a hole in the ground. It contains no water. More a cave than a well. Yes, I know of it."

"But I was told he was fond of its water."

"You have, apparently, been told a great many misleading things."

"Please, I have gold coin, and am willing to pay for such knowledge."

"I will take nothing from you. It is a man destined for condemnation, who takes money to send another to his death."

"Then, you will not tell me? Must I wander forever, until I stumble upon it myself?"

"I will tell you what I know—may the Blessed One forgive me—but your fate lies in your hands. I wash my own hands of it."

"Please, tell me, and I will leave you in peace. And may your god not hold you responsible for my decisions."

The old man lifted his face to the bright blue sky, shook his head and moved his lips, but Shamir could not hear his words. He turned again to the young man and said,

"The so-called well you seek lies in a desolate place. You must first go to Be'er Sheba, and then find the dry stream bed which meanders to the west. Follow it for most of a day's walk and you will come to a section which bends sharply to the left. The bend is full of tamarisk trees, and beyond them you will come to a series of white, low cliffs. Near the middle of those cliffs, at their base, is the cave you seek. There is only one. As I said, your blood is on your own head."

Shamir saluted the man's health and prosperity, and turned to leave the vineyard. Then the old Levite called after him—

"Wait! There is something else you must know. He is a liar. That is why they call the cave the Well of Lies. No matter what he says, do not believe him. But he has a single weakness. Through this defect, you may force the truth. On the smallest toe of his left foot, he has a mark—a sign left upon him by the king who once tricked him before—King Shl'mo. He marked the demon with the seal of his own signet, a six-pointed star. And by piercing that spot through, he is your captive and will be forced to say nothing but the truth."

"To pierce his toe?—what should I use, my janbiya? A thorn? What?"

"His spirit body cannot be pierced by anything not living. It is only living, human flesh which may pierce him through. And make no mistake, he will exact his own price from this situation. As soon as he is released, of course he has the power to kill you. Unless—you have already made a deal with him, granting him his own wish— whatever that might be."

Shamir thanked him again, but he walked away puzzled by the man's riddle, and he left Mahoza, seeking the cave.

46

IN MAHOZA, SHAMIR BOUGHT a fine horse and took the northern Gaza incense route—from Hazeva to Zafir, to Mamshit and Aroer, where he obtained a tent and some furnishings. He stopped at Be'er Sheba and pitched his tent, not knowing how long he would spend there. Making acquaintance with the local people, he inquired about the well.

"Do you know of a place west of here, named the Well of Lies?"

"We have seven wells here in Be'er Sheba—why look for one farther? Our father Abraham dug the first. It and all the others have plentiful and sweet water. Why look elsewhere?"

One morning, he set out to find the stream bed mentioned by the Levite. The winter rains long past, the creek's flowing water dropped beneath the surface rocks and boulders, to run through beds of gravel, out of sight. The rocky ravine not suitable passage for a horse, Shamir stumbled along on foot, looking for the bend to the south.

He stopped and sat on a stone to quench his thirst. Having heated all day in the harsh glare of the sun, the boulder nearly burned his skin, but he needed to rest. The small water-skin slung from his shoulder dug a groove in his skin and a wave of relief coursed through as he removed it. He wiggled the wooden plug from its spout and tipped the leather bag to his mouth. Cool water flowed—over the tongue—into the throat. He licked wetness across his lips.

A scorpion ventured from its lair under the rock's edge into Shamir's shadow, a tiny refuge from the blazing sun. Instinct forced Shamir's feet to jump away from the threat. Perceiving danger, the scorpion froze in place. Shamir lifted one foot above the motionless creature, to crush it under the hard sole of his sandal, but he relented, and continued his search.

With the sun well beyond noon, a dense, green smudge appeared on the horizon ahead of him. As he came closer, the green became a stand of willow and salt-cedar. Ahead of the stand, the creek bed split into six rivulets, weaving among the trees. He followed the rightmost stream, to stay near the north bank. Among the green foliage, the dry stream meandered and then sharply veered south. Through the trees, a bright white glared beyond. Shamir fought through the tangle of branches. The salt-encrusted stems and bark slashed at his skin. He tumbled through the last thicket into the open space beyond.

The cliff-face dazzled him as though freshly white-washed. Barren of any green plant, the chalky white wall barred further advance, so he walked along it, looking to find Ashmedai's haunt. He soon stopped and considered the import of what he was about to do.

What if this is simply an old man's tale? What if there is no Ashmedai?—no Shamir? Can I face knowing I have thrown away my only opportunities for joy in this life—for nothing?

And what if it is true? What if I come face-to-face with this Ashmedai? What will I say—how will I stand before it? And if I were to find the Shamir—what will I do if its power has waned—or if it has not?

He kicked hard at a chalk-rock lying at his feet. The friable chunk flew into a spray of particles, nearly breaking his toe in the process. He cursed his stupidity and hobbled on.

The bloody and rapidly swelling toe throbbed without mercy. It occupied his attention and his eyes did not see the salt-cedar sapling in his path. Something near the tree caught at his good foot, flinging him around and slapping him to the rocky ground. He cursed again as he worked to extract his foot from the rope now tangled around it. Jumping to his feet, he kicked the rope for good measure.

The old and frayed rope lay knotted around the base of the little tree and extended several paces beyond it, disappearing into a hole in the ground. Shamir's heart accelerated and his pulse hammered in his ears as he ran to the hole and peered into it. He shielded his eyes against the glare from the chalky-white wall, but still could see only blackness. The rope dangled loosely in the pit, and when he lifted it, nothing seemed attached to the other end. The unremarkable hole seemed nothing more than a small, natural cavity in the earth, and only large enough to accommodate a man descending the rope—not that Shamir felt inclined to do so.

He held a fist-sized rock above the opening, and just after releasing it, he knew the rashness of the gesture and wished he'd not let it fall. The rock rattled from side to side on its descent, but he never heard it hit bottom. The hot breeze of the desert sighed, passing among the trees behind him. Shamir held his breath, and waited for some response to the rock dropped into the Well of Lies. But none came.

The wine-skin bound at his waist reminded him of its presence and he removed it from beneath his robe. If this hole in the ground was no well, and contained no 'sweet water' to lure a possibly-nonexistent demon, would the tale of its fondness for good wine be just as mistaken? He opened the skin's mouth and tasted the wine. Though warm, the fruity elixir coated his mouth with a rush of sweet savor, and its fragrance exploded in his head. If, in the end, the wine would not lure his quarry, he would sit down and drink himself into a happy stupor.

He tipped the skin and dribbled some wine into the open pit. Red drops fell, one after the other, disappearing into the dark void. He waited. With no response, he poured a long, thin stream into the hole. He waited yet longer—again, to no avail.

I knew it all along—the stories of old men—crafted to widen the eyes of gullible boys around the fire at night. So, here am I...and yet a boy. And still gullible.

Shamir tipped the wine-skin and poured some wine into his own mouth. His tongue swirled it around, releasing its flavor. He swallowed it and smacked his lips. He shouted coarsely into the hole— "Are you down there, or not? At great expense I purchased—for the one called Ashmedai—the finest wine between Damascus and Timna! Wake up and smell the wine I have dropped into this paltry hole in the ground—this dank pit you think so grand! Can you even hear me? I thought not..."

Shamir dropped to the ground and swung his legs over to dangle in the pit. He held the wine-skin to his lips and drank a deep draft. The ruby liquid trickled from the corners of his mouth, running down his chin and throat. He picked up another rock and dropped it down the hole. He made it his latrine.

With the skin of wine nearly empty, a distant sound of scurrying and rustling drifted up from deep in the pit. The rope swayed, then jerked and tugged. Shamir yanked his legs from the hole and stood up.

Something crawled and climbed up the rope from the dim depths of the cavern. No larger than a man's hand, the body appeared that of a scrawny rat, its hair singed and skin blackened as if from close encounters with fire. The head and face, though, looked that of a man—an old and ugly one. It squeaked, "I am the Great and Powerful Ashmedai—Commander of a Great Legion! Who is it that disturbs me?"

The unexpected sight replaced Shamir's nervous anticipation with disappointment, and then amusement. His voice loosened by the skin-ful of wine, Shamir laughed, "The commander of a legion?—a legion of rats? You are surely not what I expected."

The rat-man squinted its eyes nearly to slits, tilted its head with disgust and spat back, "So—you prefer spectacle over substance, eh? Then spectacle you shall have…"

The thing closed its eyes, and in the space of two flicks of its hairless tail, began to inflate in size. As it approached the stature of a normal-sized man, the body transformed into something more human. Still clinging to the rope, it stared into the young man's startled face with the golden glare of tigers' eyes. Shamir could no longer withstand the withering gaze and looked to the ground. The demon grew larger than a man, its waist filling the mouth of the cave, its head towering over Shamir.

From some hidden, monstrous drum—its drumhead the hide of an eastern elephant, its mallet a cedar of Lebanon—a thunderous boom erupted and shook the earth. The shock slapped the chest of Shamir, his heart jumping inside him. And a mighty gong, fashioned from the disc of the full moon, crashed and shattered the desert air. Then shot the blast of unseen horns. Horns of bronze and brass— the carnyx and salpinx, taqowa and qarna, the buq and kakaki— blared and wailed the bars of some brazen, demented fanfare. As the drone and din continued to howl, cymbals crashed and *jalras* clashed in percussive clamor and clang. The great drum then began its insistent, incessant beat—a rhythm so brash, and bursting with bedlam, as to smash the howling turmoil of Babel.

Ashmedai continued stretching upward and outward, its belly straining to rupture the dark shaft. It placed both its palms on the ground, either side of the cave, pushing against it to escape its grasp. The demon lifted one leg free, pulling it from the cavern's volume, tearing up the earth, ripping great rocks from the ground. Stamping its freed foot upon the surface, it lifted the other leg to stand erect upon the earth.

The horns, drum and cymbals continued their mad music to herald this great power. Taller than five-men-high stood this Ashmedai, its skin now a smooth and azure-blue from scalp to sole. Muscles rippled beneath the skin as it raised both arms above its head and glowered. It exulted in its mastery and dominion.

An acrid aroma of hot brass and the choking fumes of burning sulphur permeated the atmosphere and assaulted Shamir's nostrils. He looked up to see the terrifying vision of this spirit-man, the color of the sky, and now the height of more than ten men stacked one atop the other. As Shamir raised his gaze from the mammoth feet he could no longer see the great Ashmedai's head, but only the belly and the immense, heaving chest above it. With his strength and swagger drained from him, Shamir fell to the ground as a dead man.

The hellish fanfare that announced the rising of Ashmedai dragged on till every demon blowing a horn turned purple-faced, and no breath remained in all the halls of Gehenna to blow it. At once, the brazen jangle ceased, but the drum's frenetic rhythm continued pounding, pounding, pounding. Inky clouds gathered in the air above, swirling and congealing about the massive, demonic head. They formed as a ring and encircled the bald, blue pate, and descended to rest as a black, vile crown upon the brow of Ashmedai. Forks of red lightning crackled and shot from the dark crown. The demon folded both arms across its chest and looked down upon Shamir, smaller than his foot, and cowering on the ground.

The drum stopped, and a hideous silence stifled the desert.

Then a voice, like the sound of many waters, thundered—

"Well, my little pissant, is this spectacle enough to satisfy your craving for pageantry, or do you demand yet more? I am Ashmedai —The Great and Terrible! A thousand like me bow their knee at my command. I rule over all powers and authorities on the face of the earth! Tell me why I should not step on you and grease the sole of my foot with your puny substance."

47

SPENT FROM THE TELLING of Ashmedai's appearance, Sabah fell backward. He lay on the ground, his lungs heaving, trying to catch his breath. Amru kneeled beside him and offered a small water-skin. "Here, Sabah, quench your thirst. Take your ease, before you pass into the darkness."

Amru put the skin to the old man's lips and helped him sip. His thirst quenched, he said in a ragged voice, "May you be blessed, brother. Yes, I must rest."

Sabah fanned himself, and blinked his eyes. He swallowed hard, his throat yet gripped with fear. Amru helped him sit up against a large rock, and they waited until his racing heart returned to normal. And he continued the story—

And so it was, that Shamir appeared a grasshopper in his own eyes, and he stumbled to speak.

"I...I pray you, forgive me, O Great Ashmedai. I knew not your great majesty and mighty power."

"Why do you bother me...pissant?"

A glory, dark and menacing, shone from the terrible face, forcing Shamir to look away from the glowering guise.

"Please forgive me again, O Ruler. I have but one...humble request."

"I am listening...what do you ask of me?"

Shamir could only fix his eyes on the ground before him, and with great effort said, "Please forgive me...but I ask concerning the whereabouts...of a very small...matter..."

The demon flashed red light from his eyes and thundered down at him, "Spit it out, pissant, as you have wasted too much of my time as it is. Go on...the *very small matter?*"

"I...I seek the whereabouts of that which is called...*the Shamir.*"

Crude laughter spewed long from the corrupt mouth of Ashmedai. After it caught its breath, it said, "The Shamir? *The Shamir?!* You waste not only my own time, you waste your own. Only a fool pissant like yourself would ask such a useless question. There *is* no more Shamir...if one ever existed. And if it does yet exist, its great age would render it powerless by now. Why would you seek such a thing? Whose childish stories have misled you in this? They have played you as the fool you certainly are. Give up this silly quest before you waste your life on this errand of a fool."

Shamir sprang to his feet, and with every muscle called into action, drove the tip of his index finger into the six-pointed, black spot on Ashmedai's small toe, a toe as large as a swine. The finger pierced into the toe's substance—cold as hailstones and with the consistency of soft goat-cheese. His hand and arm followed and the finger went out the bottom to lodge in the soft sand of the desert. He held his finger fast in the sand, hoping the monstrous frame above him was, indeed, pinned to the earth, and captive to his question. He looked up, to see what would happen next.

The blue giant stretched out its arms, opened its mouth wide... and yawned. It dropped its gaze to the tiny man below and said,

"You attempt to injure me? Don't you know spirits cannot feel pain as do men? This trivial matter has extended far beyond my patience, and I feel it is now time to crush you. Do you have any last words?—as if they would matter to me?"

Without hesitation, he shouted up to the massive form above, "Ashmedai, how may I find that which is called the Shamir? Answer me now, without equivocation."

Without thinking about it, the demon said plainly, "The breeze at dawn has secrets to tell you. When you awake one morning, not many days from now, open the flap of your tent. You will see a hoopoe bird displaying, as if for a mate. It will raise its crown three times, and then fly off. You must be ready with a fast mount to follow it. It will fly far, but you must not lose sight of it. When it lands at the location, it will raise its crown three times and nod in the direction of the Shamir. It will not be far off. Yes, you have trapped me and forced the truth from my lips. But before you release me, you know you must grant my own request—or I will kill you when you release me."

"Yes, I know that is the bargain I have entered."

The corners of the demon's mouth curled into a vicious smile. "In return for not killing you, I request only...a *very small...matter*. Something so small it cannot be measured on a balance. Something so immaterial, the wind has more substance."

"Yes?"

"All I ask of you is...your *nephesh*...your soul. And though I ask, this is not a request. This is what I *will take*, in due time. Now release me, and flee. For I may yet find a way to kill you."

48

THE REMAINDER OF THE afternoon, and all night under the gibbous moon, Shamir retraced his steps along the dry creek. With just an hour of darkness remaining, he stumbled into his tent and collapsed upon the rug. His eyes closed, but with his heart still racing, sleep stood at a distance. The sky glimmered a faint carmine in the east and he jumped to his feet, throwing back the flap to look for the bird. But as the sun rose to full brilliance, not one was in sight.

For most of a week Shamir spent the daylight and nighttime lying in his tent, subsisting on dried camel meat and dates, waiting for the next sunrise. And with each bird-less dawn, he retreated again from the tent's entrance, to sulk within.

On the seventh morning, he reluctantly opened the flap, expecting again to see nothing. As he parted it no more than a crack, a bird flew in, flapping and circling inside the tent and causing Shamir to duck his head with each circuit. It hovered over the small table and then dropped to perch on the edge of the water basin. It took several sips of water, raising its beak to let the water trickle down its throat. He gawked at the bird with wide eyes, and it returned his stare.

While the hoopoe bird watched him, she lifted her crown of feathers—something like a miniature peacock's tail—but orange, tipped with black-spots. And the crown had a peculiarity. One of the feathers bent in its middle, so the 'eyespot' did not align with the others, but bobbed about on its own. She raised the crown three times and then flew back through the tent's entrance, still held open by the transfixed Shamir.

He finally realized the significance of the event and tore himself from his fixed position, running outside to spot the hoopoe, circling in the air above the tent. He hurriedly saddled his horse, tied the bag of dried foodstuffs and water-skin to it, and took off after the bird as it flew higher, and straight to the east. It flew all day, only descending a few times to spear small insects from the ground and drink at a small brook. During none of the descents did it lift its crown.

Crossing the ford at the Zered River, his horse raised a spray of water, and on the other side they turned toward the north, following the route on the eastern side of the Salt Sea.

With the sun low in the sky, having expended its strength over a long and wearisome day, the horse and its rider were spent as well. They could go no further and stopped on the road. The bird continued its flight north.

We can no longer follow it. Perhaps this was not the bird. Or perhaps it is. Regardless, we cannot keep its pace. I know not what to do, but I must stop at this stand of grass, to feed my horse, and for both of us to sleep. I will return to Be'er Sheba tomorrow and decide what comes next.

He slept a fretting sleep, with a rounded rock his pillow. He dreamed of a ladder descending to the underworld, demons ascending and descending on it. The night crept on.

His eyes yet closed, he felt the early morning's breeze brush the hairs on his arm. Behind his closed lids, the pitch-dark of night gave way to the dim light of dawn. Shamir's dreams evaporated, forgotten in the crushing reality of the new day. His thoughts dogged him.

I seemed so close—the object of my pursuit nearly within my palm! But no—the one controlling my fate would have none of that. Any future I had flew away on the wings of a bird. What a fool am I!—a sad excuse for a man. I shall return to my tent in yet more shame, and determine what direction my life shall now take. Will I ever learn from the follies that control me?

He rolled from his back to his right side and slowly parted the lids of his eyes to assess the morning before him. Just beyond arms' reach, a bird strutted on the ground. Seeing him open his eyes ever wider, the hoopoe raised her crown, and the bent feather bobbed before the bird's face, nearly touching her long beak. She unfurled her wings and lifted herself into the air.

Shamir scrambled to his feet and watched the bird soar high above him. He ran to his horse, grazing in the tall grass beyond. He whistled to the animal, which raised its head and trotted to him. He saddled it, threw his small pack behind him and mounted, spurring the horse in the direction of the circling bird. The hoopoe flew northward, high and barely within sight.

All day long they followed the bird, which stopped when they tired, and flew again after their refreshment. With the afternoon dragging on and the sun beginning its descent, the bird took a sweeping turn to the left. Another, and less-traveled route soon diverged from the main road, in a direction following the bird's flight. Shamir tugged the bridle to the left and followed his quarry.

They rode up and down numerous hills and crossed dry creek-beds. The bird occasionally dropped from sight behind the next hill, but they never lost her, seeing her again as they crested the hill's summit. The sun fell lower, its color fading from bright yellow to a subdued amber, and then orange as it approached the horizon. The almost-full moon rose above the low hills behind them.

The bird's flight descended, finally dropping from sight beyond the next hill. Nearing physical exhaustion, Shamir's mount climbed the hill at no more than a walk. At the hill's brow, it could go no further. He dismounted, patted the horse's neck and removed the saddle. He shielded his eyes against the glare of the sun, to see the glowing, copper disc poised upon the horizon and ready to drop into the far reaches of the great Sea of Salt. He searched the sky for the bird but could not see her. Worry no longer gripped him, for the past two days convinced him she would reliably lead him to the location of the Shamir.

He finally saw her—strutting back and forth on the shore of the sea. Leaving his horse, he walked the remainder of the path, descending the hill to the beach. An eerie feeling wormed its way into him, as he looked along the shore and saw small boats of reed-bundles, pulled up from the beach and away from the water's reach. Black smeared their sides. Jerking his head the other way, he saw three low huts made of sticks plastered with mud, their roofs thatched with palm fronds. His heart nearly stopped, knowing he stood in this very spot, three years previous.

Shamir walked to the beach, where the bird waited for his approach. Something inside him began to shrivel, and then died. A hollowness filled him as he sat down on the damp, salt-encrusted sand. Now half-submerged in the sea's waters, the sun continued its descent. The bird kept pacing before him, then stood still. She raised her crown three times, the bent feather drooping before her eyes. She caught his gaze and nodded her head sideways—toward the sea —three times. She leaped into the air and her wings carried her up and away from the beach, toward the drowning, dying sun. Shamir shook his head and buried his face in his hands.

In the dimming twilight he sat, knowing his dreams ended there on the beach. Only a shadowy void now hovered ahead of him. His heart desperately desired to weep, but no tears survived within him.

An arm wrapped around his shoulders—violently startling him, and his body lurched away from the touch. He jerked his head toward the one sitting next to him and saw the creased face of an old man. The ancient, bronzed and wrinkled body gleamed in the last rays of the vanished sun, his copper medallion hanging from the cord around his neck. The man opened his nearly toothless mouth and said,

"You come back, my brother. Lost again?"

"I am certainly lost. But not *again*—I am *forever* lost."

The old man's mouth fell open and he hesitated before he spoke.

"I know you come back."

"How could you know such a thing?"

"The One—who hover over water—and dwell in deep—he show to me."

In the lavender glow of twilight the bright evening star staggered toward the far horizon of the sea, pulled downward by the submerged sun.

"Such great treasure. You throw away once. Now you seek again?"

"You saw me cast it into those waters, years ago? I thought that was a private moment—its pain known only to me."

"This my beach. I miss nothing. I see all. So, the bird. She lead here. To your past."

"I thought it would be my future. My past, my future; my pleasure and pain—it all now seems tangled in confusion. Which is which?"

The old man's face conveyed compassion toward his young companion. He said,

"Such a gift! Worn on finger. Held in palm. Cast into deep. Then, seek again. To lose again. A puzzlement!"

Bony, gnarled hands gripped Shamir's arm to comfort him. Old, dark eyes looked into downcast young-eyes, seeing something far beyond. He spoke again.

"The matter not settled. You *will* break to pieces. On great rock —great rock of love. A high price—not yet paid. When times full— true treasure not lost."

Part Four

—Debt Paid—

49

"I HAVE HEARD RUMORS of a great find of new stone in the Decapolis—not far from Gadara. They say it may equal that unique porphyry from Egypt!" The man smiled broadly and drove a fist into his palm to emphasize his point. Barely more than a stranger, he sat in Shamir's tent and shared his host's spare meal of barley porridge.

With his quest of the mystical stone-cutting device at its bitter end, Shamir had returned to his tent near Be'er Sheba and then lost himself for two weeks in skins of wine, and the skin of a woman—both purchased from his rapidly dwindling cache of silver. But he made an acquaintance with this man who traded in rumors. Rumors that tickled his ears. A mason of sorts, the man was one of the few in Be'er Sheba who struck up conversation with him, attracting Shamir's attention with tales of a new cache of the exclusive commodity.

Shamir raised his eyebrows and asked, "Are you certain of the stone's character? The true stone is very hard, and glows with a deep purplish-red—like a bull's liver. And flecked with small grains of white. I once saw a block of it in Raqmu—large enough to sculpt a portrait bust. I heard it was smuggled there by Nabatu pirates operating on the sea between Egypt and the *Hijaz*."

The man's wide eyes underscored his enthusiasm. "That would certainly describe the hand-sized piece of stone I saw, said to come from the Gadara find. It surprised me as it did you. Before that, the only such stone came from that single quarry in the hinterlands of Egypt—the 'purple mountain.' They say a cohort of the Roman army controls it, and they work it with slaves they call the '*damnati ad metalla.*' Their Emperor declared it the Imperial Purple-stone and claims the entire output of the quarry for his exclusive use."

Shamir leaned over toward his guest, lowered his voice and said, "I have heard them say it is like no other stone—and that, in truth, it is *congealed blood and fire!* Could there be a second find of such rare material?"

With his fingers, the man slurped the last of the barley from his bowl and wiped his lips with the back of his hand. "As I said, I have only seen a single piece, and that was small. I have heard there are more than a handful of men there now, searching for the mother lode which birthed these small rocks. If, indeed, there be such a source, those who find it will reap a vast fortune! And, perhaps, incur the wrath of the Empire in the process."

Shamir smirked, and said, "That matters not to me. I have nothing else to live for, and have already encountered dangerous and awesome powers beyond the imaginations of most men."

He thanked the man for the limited information. The next morning he struck his tent and sold the lot of his belongings in the marketplace at Be'er Sheba. He set out for Gadara in the Decapolis with a final hope—

I have long sensed the presence of perfect stone, where others could only know what their eyes showed them. It may be this faculty will lead me to the source of something marvelous. Something only dreamed by other men!

50

AND SO IT WAS, Shamir exchanged the second of his gems of the sea for silver, and for most of a year he rambled through the hills to the north and east of Gadara. He gained a knowledge of the terrain as detailed as that of the lines and scars on the palm of his crippled left hand. But it yielded him nothing more.

In his pursuit of the rumored source of a new find of Imperial Porphyry, he occasionally came upon other men searching for the same. Though closed-mouth concerning the details of their hunt, a certain emptiness in their eyes betrayed their lack of success.

With one searcher, however, Shamir developed an engaging rapport. The man, who dragged behind him a useless leg, had once been a slave—one of those 'damned to the mines'—working the Roman quarry of purple stone in Egypt. He called himself Iohanan of Hermopolis. He had escaped by feigning his own death and then inscribing a porphyry tombstone with his name to complete the ruse. He hid aboard a cargo ship of the Nabatu, made his way to Aila, and finally to freedom in the north.

Always candid about how he expected to find the porphyry, Iohanan told Shamir, "That quarry in Egypt unveiled itself, even from a distance. The scree of eroded rocks below the porphyry outcroppings displayed a certain lurking bloom linked to the softness of the sky and the fine, blue mist that descends from it. The priceless stone could not well hide itself. The peculiar color gave itself away. Only the vastness of the desert could hide it from the outside world. Here, we need look for that same color, toward the base of mountains and cliffs. If the rock is there, the subtle color will lead us to itself."

Shamir thanked the man for his candor and wished him success. He then set out on a final search in an area he believed to be promising.

With the passing of two more full moons, Shamir depleted his stake of food and subsisted on the mountain mallows, the edible red flowers of the *humaad*, and the *yasar*—an acacia tree covered with tiny white blossoms. And by observing the movements of bees on their paths to and from their fields of nectar, he traced them to their hive-home in the hollow of a dead tree. Risking the stinging defense of their swarm, he toppled the trunk. Though his hands and limbs swelled with the stings' venom, he scooped handfuls of the honeycomb into his mouth and gorged himself into a temporary bliss.

But sweet relief fell to disappointment, and then tumbled toward despair in the flint heart of Shamir. He resigned himself to failure in his venture to find the new Imperial Porphyry. In defeat, he dragged himself down from the hills and sulked back into Gadara.

Around Gadara he heard occasional talk of a mineral hot spring west of the city. The *Hammata Degader*, the Hot Springs of Gadara, were only an early-morning's walk away, just across the Yarmuk River.

Again I fail at what I pursue. I am down to a few coins and my last pearl. A hot soak might relieve my bad humors. And perhaps, the spring is home to some oracle, to give me guidance going forward.

Shamir left for the springs before first light blushed the eastern sky. Except for a few stray dogs quarreling over scraps in the gutter, the city still slept in its wine-induced stupor of the night before. He walked past the concavity of Gadara's theater. The semicircular rows of seats lay in silence and shadow. The final echoes of last night's laughter and applause had long since faded into mute darkness. He continued walking along the market street between the parallel rows of vendor stalls, now abandoned and empty of merchandise.

With the city lying asleep behind him, he stood atop the escarpment at Gadara's western limits. The last quarter moon rose behind him, illuminating the steep descent from the hills. In the distance a rich plain of orchards and fields gradually sloped to the valley of the Yarmuk.

Most of the river's course bent and twisted through a steep and rocky gorge. But at this stretch, the valley broadened and opened into a fertile river bottom. Just beyond the lush valley and across the river lay the mineral-rich hot springs.

With increasing presence of Roman interests around Gadara, talk swirled of developing the springs into a commercial enterprise. The prospect of building public baths, temples, and resort accommodations filled their plans. But for now, Shamir's path and destination bloomed with nothing more than natural wonder. He began his descent to the river.

After an hour of clambering down the forested hills, he wound through orchard after orchard—their trees arrayed in neat rows and columns like an army formation of date-palms, apricots, citrons, figs and pomegranates. Another hour's walk across this fruited plain and he arrived on the banks of the Yarmuk, its flow rushing and turbulent with late-spring snowmelt from the mountains of its headwaters.

The waters at the region's only ford surged waist-deep, making for precarious wading. A strong swimmer, Shamir did not hesitate to throw himself into the rushing current, and in short order, stroked to the other bank. He emerged from the waters dripping and cold, but it was a short walk to the embracing warmth of the thermal springs. He craved its comfort.

A small knoll lay between him and the spring, and as he crested the hill, the last-quarter moon stood at its zenith, dimly illuminating the spring's small lagoon. The water looked black in the pale light, and grayish-green clumps of rushes crowded the pool's perimeter. A light breeze wafted plumes of thick mist from the hot water. He sat down to wait for the first light of dawn.

While he waited, something moved on the water. It glided slowly at the water's surface, and occasionally paused before moving again. A dense fog blanketed the water and confounded his attempts to identify the object.

And then he heard it. A woman's voice. A young woman's voice—humming a simple melody. A woman swam in the pool of the hot spring, her movement through the water barely discernible in the layers of mist. And the wordless tune tumbled end-over-end through his mind—

What is that? I know I have heard it. But where? And what are its words?

His hearing sharpened as he strained his ears to listen. Under her breath the woman began mumbling the words of the song. At first, he picked out only a few—

"Treasures...ruins...broken..."

The words swirled, jumbled, and stumbled over each other, his mind adding ones from his child's memory:

hidden...wild...hearts...

As she glided before him, hidden in the moist vapors, the song finally crystallized as she gave clear, melodic voice to the lyric—

> *"Treasures are hidden*
> *among the ruins*
> *in wild, abandoned wastes*
> *The best of treasures*

> *are hid in hearts*
> *once broken by the fates."*

Time's knife slid from its sheath and sliced away fifteen years.

It was in Hawara I first heard this melody—hummed by my Amma! But these words I only heard from the mouth of Qainu—my Nura! Could this be her?—now a woman?

The sudden thought catapulted him to his feet, but he made no sound. He gawked, rocking his head this way and that, commanding his eyes to pierce through the fog.

A light belt of pink hovered above the horizon beyond the spring, a dull blue band between it and the earth. Behind him, the sky colored to peach with the rising sun, and its first rays reached the pool. The sunlight fired the fog with an amber brilliance, further hiding the swimmer within its glow.

Blind to his presence, the woman still lingered in the pool, floating on her back. She rolled face down and lazily stroked toward the shore below him. As she drew near, the sunlight struck her golden hair. A name burst from Shamir's lips—

"Nura!"

She stopped her progress with a convulsive splash, and shrieked. Her screams echoed across the pool—

"No! Who are you?! Leave me!"

She immediately turned and in a chaos of splashes swam to the pool's far shore. She stumbled in the shallows, disappearing behind a stand of green rushes.

Shamir called out—"No—please don't go! I mean you no harm, Nura. Please! Come back!"

With no response to his plea, he hurried from the hill, retracing his path back to the Yarmuk. He rapidly crossed the ford to the other side, and lurked there behind a boulder, knowing she must pass it in returning to Gadara.

Qainu waited a long time before returning from the spring. Caution her companion, she headed back to her abba's house near Gadara, hoping the shocking interruption of her swim was far behind. At the ford of the Yarmuk she looked both directions—up and down the river banks—and stepped into its swirling current. Wading remained a difficult undertaking, but she eventually emerged from the waters on the far shore.

Shamir stepped from behind the rock, to block the path and hem her in against the river.

"Nura—it's me, Shamir! Can I talk with you? Do you live here?"

The jolt locked her in place. Her heart throbbed once and her mouth opened to scream, but no sound came out. She turned and plunged back into the river, straining to cross it, to escape her pursuer. When she reached the river's midpoint, Shamir threw himself into the waves and swam after her. She saw him give chase and she struggled wildly, changing her direction into the river's flow. The torrent carried them far from the ford, and as exhaustion overcame Qainu, she fought to reach the shore. With her ebbing strength she dragged herself from the water onto a large, flat rock. Shamir caught its edge as he floated near, and emerged from the waves.

Drained, and sitting on the rock, she scuttled backwards on her hands and feet, pushing herself away from him. She cried, and whimpered, "Please...don't...hurt me! If you need money, Abba can pay you. Please—stay away!'

Shamir stopped. He caught his breath, and assured her, "I won't hurt you. You knew me long ago—in Hawara. I am Shamir...I mean, Nahor."

Backed up against a large rock, she froze, her eyes white with fright. He said, "I called you Nura—my Light. You once saved me, taking some of my shame. My Abba might have killed me otherwise, but as it was, he only sent me away—to Raqmu. For another man to raise me."

She thrust her hands and arms at him, to block his approach, and turned her face from him. He said, "The man made a stone-cutter of me. I came to Gadara looking for a special stone, but could not find it. And in its place...I have found you!"

The waters rushed and rumbled behind him, careening through the gorge. Neither spoke for some time, as his words raced through the mind and heart of Qainu. He held out his hand to her, but she made no movement toward him. Her voice still breaking with fear, she said, "Hawara? I left there when I was little. Who are you?"

"I am Nahor. My Amma hired you to help with my sister. You live here? You have a family here?"

She slowly turned her face back to him, and said, "Nahor? I remember a Nahor—you are Nahor?"

"Yes. And I called you Nura—my Light. Because of the glory of your golden hair. Living so far from my family, and all that I knew, I thought of you often."

She dropped her defensive hands. The rapid heaving of her lungs slowed and deepened. The quaver in her voice faded and she said, "I remember now...yes...Nahor. My Abba has always felt shamed because of my hair, and he made me feel the same. You were the only one who ever valued me. That is why I lied then—for you—so I would take the heat of your abba's anger."

"Do you have a family here?"

"Ever since we left Hawara, I live as my Abba's servant—along with the slave he owns. I do nothing but wait on his requests. But now he tires of me, and offers me for marriage—longing to spend the bride-price on fine clothes and wine."

"You have no husband?"

"Abba says he will color my hair dark with walnut husks, and pass me off to a man living in a far city, who will not notice it for a few months. Long after the wedding is consummated, it will be too late for him to reclaim the price."

"Do you wish...to be married?"

"I long not only to be far from my Abba's harsh ways, but I want to love a man, and serve him, raising a family in his name."

The two remained motionless on the flat rock, beside the swollen river. An eternity of silent moments passed between them. Shamir extended his hand again to her, saying above the tumult of the river,

"If you will have me—I can be that man—I would ask your abba for your hand. And I will gladly pay whatever price he sees fit."

She sat like a stone on that rock, not moving, not speaking. With the River Yarmuk thundering by them, she haltingly extended her hand toward him. He took it in his own and raised her to her feet. He found them passage out of the gorge, and back to Gadara.

51

SHAMIR STOOD ALONE AT the gate of Arwas and rapped hard on it three times. The man's old female slave, grinding barley meal in the courtyard, went to the gate and croaked,

"Who goes there? And what is your business?"

"I am Shamir, son of Aslah. I am a stone-cutter from Raqmu. I wish to see Arwas—to ask for the hand of Qainu, his daughter."

The old woman hurried into the house to report the message, and quickly returned to the gate.

"My master Arwas will see you. To hear your offer."

The gate swung open and she escorted him across the courtyard. He briefly glanced at Qainu in the corner, twisting carded wool into yarn. Their eyes briefly met and a smile crossed her lips before she averted her gaze.

The old woman escorted Shamir to the main hall and said, "Wait here while I announce you."

She walked to the doorway at the end of the hall and knocked once on the doorpost, before saying, "Shamir of Aslah is here."

A voice grunted from beyond the doorway, "Send him in."

She made a gesture toward the doorway, and as he entered, she turned and left the house.

Though living in a house built of stone, bricks and plaster, the man was clearly more comfortable dwelling in tents. The tiled floor was covered with multiple carpets, and he lounged on a pile of cushions. He held a goblet of Roman glass, from which he drank a dark, red wine—at mid-day. He gestured for Shamir to sit.

"I would offer you wine, but I have little left. Can we avoid the dance of business, and simply come to the heart of it all?"

Shamir said, "Yes, I appreciate coming to the point of a matter, and not..."

Arwas cut him off. "This woman—Qainu—what is your interest in her?"

Shamir raised his eyebrows at the man's brusque speech, but he answered, "Well, sir, I intend to provide for her, care for her—and to love her. And I believe she will love me. We are..."

Arwas rolled his eyes and interjected, "That is only a matter between you and the woman, and of no consequence to me. What I am asking is—what are you willing to pay for her?"

The man's crass and curt manner stymied Shamir's attempts to engage him, but he responded to the man, "I thought you would set the bride-price, and then we would bargain until we reached agreement."

Arwas locked eyes with him and said, "I will be frank. I have contacts in many other cities—from Hegra to Damascus—and some of these men even seem to appreciate such pale hair in a woman. So don't think this flaw will drive down the price. There are no bargains to be had here, and I am not in the mood for dealing."

"What then, is your price, sir? I am willing to pay it."

Arwas looked at the cracks in the ceiling's plaster and at the just-emptied glass in his hand. He stroked his scruffy beard and said, "Five hundred drachma of silver. Four hundred if we avoid the expense of a wedding feast. All in Roman coin."

Shamir threw his hands in the air. "Well over a year's wages? I cannot now match that sum! May I pay you over a period of time?"

Arwas shook his head. "When you first spoke, it seemed you had your heart set on this woman. But perhaps not. Perhaps your desire for her is not as great as you thought."

Shamir began to despise the man. His thoughts raced to find a solution. He finally said, "I will get your payment. I am well familiar with the hill country northeast of here and know how to find quality stone. I will locate a perfect block in the outcrops of marble I have seen up there. And I yet have enough of a stake to hire cutters to free the block, and to retain a sculptor to carve a sarcophagus fit for royalty. Upon sale of the coffin, then you shall have your four hundred in silver. Do you accept?"

The man yawned and said, "Only if you can provide evidence that you will have the money before long. Then the woman will be yours."

And they clasped hands over the agreement.

North and east of Gadara, Shamir again roamed the hills, this time in search of the perfect piece of marble. His previous empty search for a new source of Imperial Porphyry familiarized him with the lay of the land. He had encountered a few sources of marble in his sojourns and returned to each to evaluate their potential.

The first location lay just a day and a half's hike from the edge of Gadara. He remembered it having decent marble, but on closer examination, gray and brown streaks shot through the entire mass. Maybe adequate for flooring, but certainly not suitable for high-quality sculpture.

He headed to the next location, another day's journey away through rugged hills. He found the place much as he remembered— a nearly pure white stone, which sparkled in the sunlight. But something felt amiss there, and an uneasiness accompanied him. Pieces of marble lay scattered about, and he picked some up, to try them. The gleaming white chunks broke apart far too easily in his hands, convincing him the material was unfit for producing a work as large as a coffin.

While the first two sites possessed stone of only inferior quality, he hoped the third still held promise. Another day of crossing deep ravines and climbing steep hills brought him to the place. Though small, it had been quarried in the distant past. Much of the overburden of degraded material had already been removed, allowing access to the pure heart of the mineral body.

He spent a few days camped at the site, getting a feel for the mass. He examined the piles of flakes and shards left from the process of freeing and dressing blocks. He slept upon the cleaved tops of rows of blocks not yet pulled from their rocky home. The stone did not readily yield its secrets, but in time, Shamir's gift of sensing perfection penetrated their secrecy, and he found the flawless piece.

Wasting no time, he returned to Gadara and hired three quarrymen. And he retained the services of a sculptor, for when they had freed the marble. He stopped at the house of Arwas to report his progress in securing payment of the bride-price for Qainu. He handed a fist-sized piece of white rock to the man and said,

"I have found as near a perfect block of marble as can be found. I am hiring men today who will cut it from the earth and a fine sculptor who will carve it into a coffin fit for a king. In three months time you will have full payment, and I will take my wife."

Looking at the rock in his hand, he frowned and tossed it back to Shamir.

"In three months? Make certain you do not extend it by a day, as I am certain other suitors will knock at my gate."

"You have my word."

Leaving the house, Shamir paused in the courtyard to take Qainu's hand and press it to his lips. He whispered in her ear, "I long to hold you—to love you! In three new moons, we will be as one."

Arwas stepped into the doorway behind him and said, "Do not touch her!—she is not yet yours. Get on with your work. And bring me my money."

As he dropped her hand, she pressed something into his palm and closed his fingers over it. He whispered again, "Three months!" and left.

He strutted down the street, humming the melody he heard her sing when she swam in the waters of the hot spring. He opened the fingers of his clenched hand and a thin, silver ring glittered in his palm. He picked it up, rolling it between his thumb and finger, and then placed it on the last finger of his left hand.

52

AND SO IT WAS, that with the final holes bored and feathered, the stone cutters pounded in wood wedges and soaked them with water. Swollen with moisture, they slowly expanded, producing great stress along the planned line of fracture. A sharp *snap!* pierced the air and a deep *thump!* jolted the ground as the coffin-sized mass of marble separated from its womb in the earth.

Cheers erupted from the small crew. They hurried with iron pry-bars to clear the block from its brothers. Shamir crouched behind it to examine the newly-cut face, and he soon declared it without visible flaw. They tipped it over to expose its bottom face to sunlight for the first time.

Shamir ran his hands along all sides, tapping it occasionally with a mallet. "This is as fine a piece as anyone is ever likely to see. The color's purity is absolute, and throughout. I thank you for your work."

Shamir paid the cutters their final wage and sent word for the sculptor. While he waited the few days for the man's arrival, he dared to dream of the future—

I see the sarcophagus, lying complete in its gleaming white. And coiling along its sides, carved vines abundant with perfect leaves and clusters of grapes. Each corner is guarded by an eagle—wings spread, talons extended, hooked beak prepared to defend. On the top spreads the relief of a large palm—the trunk solid and criss-crossed with the diagonal leaf-scars of maturity, its fronds full and luxuriant, with rich clusters of dates hanging in fertility. The tree is bracketed with a pattern of god-steps—the geometric framing the living.

The moon now rises just an hour before the sun—it is nearly new. Will this man I hired create for me a masterpiece in two months' time? Nura must be my bride—and I must be her man! I am finished with following the fables of fools. I renounce them all!

The sculptor Farwan arrived, and for three days Shamir explained the details of his vision for the piece. With sticks of charcoal from their fire, he sketched plans for the design on the pristine faces of the white marble block. They discussed the subtleties of carving leaves and grapes, and the feathers of eagles. The plans solidified, and at dawn on the fourth day, the sculptor touched the cold stone with the sharp end of his chisel and struck it with a mallet. The first chip flew from the marble, to land in the campfire and shatter with a *pop!*

Fifty days later, the team of four oxen huffed moist breaths at the end of their five-day journey from the eastern hills. They remained yoked to a heavy cart behind them, which hid a bulky load beneath a canvas shroud. The ox-drivers waited as Shamir entered a stone building to conduct business with the proprietor.

He soon emerged with Nabat, a broker of luxury items and fine merchandise to wealthy families of the Ten Cities. He sometimes found clients as far as Damascus and Bostra. The man's bald head with bushy beard looked like an ostrich egg in a nest of straw. His large mouth bloomed in a grin as he said to Shamir,

"Of course I have an interest! Shall we have a look?"

With his sculptor standing to the side, Shamir threw back the canvas, revealing the lavishly carved stone sarcophagus. The pure white marble gleamed and twinkled in the late-afternoon sunlight. The stone vines, curling and twining around the coffin, seemed to have grown there, and then froze into ice. The eagles looked ready to leap into flight from their corner perches.

In a low, slow cadence, Nabat said, "By the beard...of...Zeus..."

He scratched his bare scalp while pulling at the curly hair on his chin. "I have never...and I mean, *never*..."

He looked at Shamir, then turned his head toward the sculptor. "Is this your man? Your artist?"

"Yes. This is Farwan—a sculptor to match the skill of my old master, Aslah. While I conceived the work's design, he executed it with precision and flair."

Nabat grabbed the sculptor's hand and pulled him closer to the cart. "Please, show me the details of your work."

Farwan pointed out how the vines and leaves lay at different levels, crossing over and beneath each other at various points, mimicking the depth of reality. And he showed him the fine veining on the surface of each leaf, and the fine-grooved texture on every eagle's feather.

Nabat took three steps back to view the whole, and said, "A wonder...a *wonder!* Of course I am interested. I know rich men in Damascus who will fight for the right to own this tomb-bed, and to one day rest their sorry bones in it."

Shamir said, "Can we forge a deal, then?"

"Yes, yes...of course! You said before you were not interested in a consignment contract, though that would bring you the greatest profit. You wanted an immediate sale. Since I will be buying it outright, and will need to pay transportation to Damascus, and other ancillary costs prior to my own sale, I can only give you half its true value. Let's say...twelve hundred and fifty drachma...silver."

"In Roman coin?"

"Of course."

"I have already paid the last of my finances to the stonecutters, and I yet need to pay Farwan and the ox-drivers. Will you make it an even thirteen hundred?"

"Certainly. We have an agreement, then?"

"Can you pay me now?"

"Of course!"

The two clasped hands over the contract and disappeared into the building to sign the document and transfer the cash. As they emerged, Shamir counted into a leather bag six hundred drachma in tetradrachm coins and passed them to Farwan for his services. He counted out sixty drachma more for the crew that hauled the coffin from the work site. In his own bag remained six hundred and forty drachma—more than enough to pay Arwas the bride-price, plan an elaborate wedding feast to honor his new bride, and the rest to give them a good start, wherever they chose to live.

Nabat slapped Shamir on the back, and laughing, said, "That is a lot of silver for a young man—you should go out and celebrate!"

Shamir's broad smile nearly cracked the corners of his mouth as he said, "That is *exactly* what I plan on doing."

"It is unfortunate you were not here ten days ago..."

"Oh?"

"Yes, there was quite a celebration—singing, dancing, and I hear the wine flowed like water! A rich magistrate from over in Bostra—a Syrian fancying himself a Hellene—married the daughter of that little conniver Arwas. I was not invited, but I heard it was an extravagant affair."

"Yes, I have been consumed with my work until now, and just arrived back in town. Too bad I...what did you say was his name?"

"I didn't. But I believe the groom calls himself by the Hellene-styled name, Anatolios. I have since heard that his given name is Zaidan."

"No—I mean the other man—the bride's father."

"Oh. He's called Arwas. A rather despicable fellow. Came here from way down at Hawara, I think. He is not the most…"

"Arwas? Are you sure? It cannot be!"

"Oh, I am very sure. I have known him for…"

"And the daughter's name?"

"Well, I don't know that I heard. Are you all right? You seem…"

"Was it Qainu?!"

"Perhaps—yes, I think that was it…"

"It cannot be—I am more than a week early! How can he do this to us?—to her?!"

The rage of Shamir's face rivaled the red of the setting sun. He strutted rapidly back and forth, gripping the sack of silver in the fist of one hand, and pounding his temple with the other. He kept repeating,

"He can't!—he can't!—he can't!…"

Nabat watched the mystery unfolding before him, his mouth slowly opening to say something to Shamir, but no words came out. His jaw hung wide open and he tilted his head as he attempted to understand the strange course of events. He watched as Shamir ran down the street and away from his business.

53

WITH TWILIGHT DIMMING THE streets, Shamir ran to the far side of Gadara, to the house of Arwas. No lamplight yet shone in the windows. He pounded on the gate, demanding entrance.

"Arwas! Let me in! How could you do this to us? We had an agreement! Let me in!"

He continued pounding until the man's slave came to the gate. In a gruff voice, she announced, "It is too late. He is seeing no one. He says to go away."

He pounded on the gate again.

"I will not go away! Bring him out here, or let me in—or I will break down his gate!"

She shouted back at him, "I cannot let you in. And if you break this gate I will run to the magistrate—he will clap you in chains!"

He hammered the gate with both fists, and then began ramming it with his shoulder. The gate shuddered but remained intact. He backed away from the gate and, cupping his hands to his mouth, shouted, "Arwas! You thief, and breaker of contracts!—your word is worth less than the dung of a diseased goat! Come out you coward, and I will take my due!"

Arwas came to the doorway of the courtyard, shouting at his slave, "What in the name of everything sacred is going on out here?! I am trying to sleep! Can't you keep..."

"Arwas?! Is that you?—you son of a leprous whore! Let me in so we can '*discuss*' your treachery!"

Arwas shook his head and muttered, "Ye gods!—it's that lame-fisted stone-cutter I sent off into the hills. I thought I was rid of him..."

Shamir staggered back and forth and shouted, "Open the gate to me, or I will open it for you!"

He backed up three more paces and ran at the gate with full force. The gate shuddered again, cracks appearing in the masonry holding the hinges. He made another run, and collided with even greater violence. The gate gave way, crashing into the courtyard, Shamir lying on top of it. He scrambled to his feet and marched toward Arwas, who shrank back into the shadows of the doorway.

Shamir stood before him, his breath blasting from his mouth in short, rapid spurts. His shouting turned to pleading, and he said, "How could you break your word with me? I had another week left! And here is the money—more than enough! How could you?"

He raised the sack of silver and shook it in the face of Arwas, jingling the coins.

Arwas girded up his best imitation of courage, and pouting his lips, said, "Well...time was dragging on...for all I knew, you may have just died up there in those hills. I could have ended up waiting forever! And a well-to-do and respectable man—a far superior match for my daughter—came to me and bested your offer. How could I refuse such an obvious gift from the gods? I would have been a fool to say no."

Shamir followed Arwas into the shadows, and stood nose-to-nose with the man. He shouted, "We had an agreement! I have kept my end of the bargain—and you will keep yours! You will have the marriage annulled! It is a void covenant!"

Arwas laughed. "Annulled? Are you mad, man? The wedding was last week. It was consummated in the bridal tent, while the wedding party feasted and drank wine outside it. I even saw the cloth of virginity paraded among the party—fresh blood-stain and all! The woman is his wife, and the matter is settled."

Shamir remained standing before him, mute—the only sound, his ragged breath pulsing through his clenched teeth.

In a single motion of speed and precision, Shamir slid his janbiya from its sheath at his waist, whipping it to just level with the man's throat. Time froze in an icy moment, the dagger's handle clutched in his fist. Only the twilight's reflection on the polished blade glimmered in the shadowed hallway.

The razor-edge hovered midway between their two throats. It trembled and quivered, not yet discerning whether the hand would command it toward the greasy folds of flesh at the throat of Arwas, or to the strained sinews bulging from Shamir's. His grip tightened on the weapon, preparing to end one life—or the other. The blade shook with violence, then dropped to the tiled floor, clattering, and spinning. Its turning slowed and finally stopped. Nothing moved in the dark hall.

He turned away from Arwas and walked across the courtyard. Arwas shouted after him, "What about my gate, man? Someone has to pay for its repair—and it won't be me. I will rouse the magistrate from his bed, and sign out a warrant for your arrest if I have to!"

Shamir stopped in the middle of the courtyard, turned, and loosened the cord binding the mouth of the sack he still held. He grabbed a fistful of coins and flung them at Arwas. They rang and jangled as they bounced on the stone of the courtyard. He turned again and ran in a sprint. Dark clouds streaked the thin sliver of the moon's crescent, as it set on the heels of the sun. He knew not to where he ran, or why.

His legs burned with fatigue and the raw night air sliced through his heaving lungs. Shamir dropped to his knees, his strength, his heart, unable to carry him farther. The city of Gadara lay buried in the cold darkness behind, along with all sweet hope.

He opened his mouth, to wail, to curse, but the knot in his throat stifled all utterance. Falling forward, he caught himself, his palms on the rough stone path. Drops of liquid pain fell from his eyes, wetting the backs of his hands. Soon, many drops fell, wetting the pavement. A cold, light rain dampened his clothes, then soaked through and chilled his back.

He thrust his fists to the sky, and shouted. "Why are you doing this to me?! Is this because of Tenicca?—or Amma—or Talia?"

A coarse laugh—more curse than laugh—spewed from his mouth. He stood in the dripping rain and trudged on.

The path ahead passed beside a long row of simple tombs, carved into the bedrock of the hillside. Heavy wooden doors protected the silent sanctity of most, but one door hung ajar. The corroded hinges resisted his efforts, but with a creak and a groan it opened and he entered.

The relative darkness of night gave way to a consuming, oppressive blackness within. Unable to see even his hands and feet, he stumbled in the small, dank space and fumbled to feel what lay in his path. His foot stubbed into an immovable mass, and he felt it with his hands. Box-like and made of stone, sculpted reliefs covered its sides. Less than knee-high, the ossuary would make a useful seat to wait out the rain.

He dropped the bag of coins and sat on the box, again running his fingers over the stone reliefs. Unable to see his hands, but feeling the carved details, the peculiar sensation of being separated from his physical body began to overtake him. With his fingertips probing along the carving, he thought he could see in his mind, a face. He saw a vision of the stone portrait of the one whose disjointed bones lay hid within the marble box. It was a man with short neck, prominent brow, keen nose, and a medallion hanging from his neck.

Moving at their own behest, and crawling like a spider, the fingers crept to another side of the box and discovered letters, letters of the Hellene language, spelling out a name: A—U—S—O—S. Ausos.

"So, Ausos—here we sit. You inside the box. Me atop it. You, long dead. Me, as good as. And how I long to join you."

His fingers felt for the handle of his janbiya, but they found the scabbard empty at his waist.

"Of course! As the cruel goddess would have it, I cannot even end it here..."

The rain grew to a steady downpour and Shamir shivered in the cold. The chill crept beneath his skin and penetrated the muscles and blood, to the depth of his bones. His jaw shuddered, teeth chattering. His body shook with violence, nearly toppling him from his seat on the bone-box.

And then...all was calm. No longer freezing, neither was he warm. It was not peace that surrounded him, but a stillness. A still blackness.

It not only surrounded him. He could no longer discern between the edge of himself and the brink of the stillness. It permeated him. Filled him.

I should fear this emptiness. But I do not. I prefer this quiet to the nagging pain that has followed me since I was a boy. I will take it.

He slipped from sitting on the ossuary to lying on the floor of the tomb, and slipped from conscious thought into a dreamless sleep. He floated somewhere in the dark. Hidden from the world. Hidden from the universe.

The glow of dawn spilled through the half-open doorway of the tomb, lighting its interior. Shamir awoke, the red light of sunrise filling his vision. Seeing the tomb for the first time, he looked around to see what it held.

I thought I fell asleep on the floor. So why is the ceiling so close?

Sensing he was at some height, he looked downward, to see the floor at some distance below him.

Did I sleep here on some high shelf, or loft?

He jerked his gaze about the tomb to quell his confusion. But it only increased his perplexity. Along the far wall sat three ossuaries, evenly spaced. And on the center one sat a man. He sat motionless, barely breathing.

Halloo sir! Were you here all night? Were you here when I arrived, or did you come in after I slept?

Though his eyes were open, the man made no attempt to answer Shamir, or acknowledge his presence. He stared with vacant eyes toward the doorway.

Halloo, I said—Have you been here all along? Are you all right?

The moving shadow of something small crept across the threshold and into the tomb. As the shadow floated across the floor, a rat scurried in behind it. The vermin poked about in the corners and then scampered to the feet of the sitting man. It stood on its hind legs, propping itself on its naked, scaly tail. It looked intently into the man's blind stare, before turning its head to look up, over its shoulder.

"Oh—you are floating up there?"

Shamir gazed around the tomb again.

Are you speaking to me? And how can a rat be speaking?

"Yes, I am certainly speaking to you. At least you are awake now. The rupture has strained your ability to focus and perceive."

The shock of the rat speaking to him, and the puzzling nature of its words wobbled his mind, and he felt himself floating around the stone chamber. He scrambled to steady himself but the effort only intensified the uncomfortable effect.

"You will become accustomed to it over time. But no one ever truly likes it."

His mind spun again and he tried to shut his eyes to the vision, but could not.

Who, or what, are you? What evil are doing to me?! What sorcery is this?

"Doing *to you? I* have done nothing *to* you. *You* have done this to yourself. And come, come...do you not recognize me? Your patron? I trust my guidance led you to the great prize of your pursuit. And to think you once wore it on your finger! Ah, well...*easy to own, easily thrown.*"

Shamir fought to set his feet upon the floor and bolt from the tomb, but the attempt merely tumbled him, end-over-end. He saw the ceiling, walls, and floor flash alternately before him.

Why do you make me float like this? Release me!

"I am not making you do anything. That is merely the consequence of your having no weight. And as far as releasing you, I am under no compunction to do so. I fairly traded to you the information you so desperately sought, in exchange for...well...*you.*"

Hearing the words swirled his perception left and right, the four walls and doorway whirling around him.

What do you mean—no weight?

He held his hands before his face, turning them from palms to back, but seeing nothing. Ashmedai said, "Yes, your hands are still where you left them."

It pointed a claw of its ratty paw toward the man sitting on the ossuary, whose hands were barely lifted above his waist and turning slowly from fronts to backs.

"I find a man's body more compliant to my wishes when the soul is not resident."

I am dead, then? You have killed me?!

The rat-demon squeaked out a laugh and held its diminutive sides. "No, no—hah! Why would I intentionally destroy my property? Look closely between you and the man who sits on the box-of-bones."

He did look, and fixing his gaze on the space between them, saw a subtle *something*—a merest glimmer in the gap. The rat shook its scrawny head and sighed. "Here, let me help you."

The rat drew near the man and sank its teeth into an ankle. The man flinched, and the glimmer in the gap momentarily flashed a silvery white—like a silken band extending from the man's belly to the floating Shamir.

"That life-cord yokes you to your body. It can be stretched to some extent, as you see, but if it is broken, your body dies, and I lose my property. You yet have a link to that body, but it is tenuous. As I said, this facilitates your body's compliance with my wishes for it."

The rat hopped onto the lap of the man, looked up at his face and spat in it. The man took no notice of the insult. The rat hopped back to the floor and shook its front paw vigorously, three times. The man rose from the box and, one by one, knocked over each ossuary. The lids clanked to the floor and the collections of bones spilled across it. He kicked the piles of bones with great force, scattering them. When Ashmedai patted the top of its head, the man lifted each of the three skulls, and smashed them to fragments against the solid stone walls.

The rat kicked out its right foot and pointed a paw to Shamir's sack of silver. The man lumbered to the leather bag, drew a leg behind and then kicked forward with such effort the bag split, showering the tomb with a cloudburst of silver. The coins jangled and rangled as they ricocheted from the walls. They rolled across the floor, looping and spinning, finally coming to a rest.

The rat pointed to the open door and the man left, dragging Shamir behind by the life-cord.

54

SHAMIR'S BODY STUMBLED THROUGH the collection of tombs, pounding on doors to break their latch-bars, gaining entrance when possible. It desecrated any human remains found unguarded within. To quench the body's thirst, Ashmedai directed it to lick moisture from the stone walls and floors of the damp tombs. And to still the body's hunger, he commanded it to tear and chew any dried flesh remaining on corpses. When it needed to void, he demanded it urinate and defecate on the coffins. Shamir's soul, drug along behind his body by the silken cord, was bruised, beaten, and wounded.

Though the unspeakable acts performed by his physical self were at the behest of the demon, and counter to his own consent, it still deepened his shame. His contempt for himself grew and he longed to batter his temples with his fists, if he had fists he could raise, and temples he could touch. Day after long day, and night after sleepless night, the desecration and defilement ravaged, unabated.

In ten days, Ashmedai tired of the game, and sated with its craving for irreverence, it retired to the Well of Lies, the hole near Be'er Sheba. Still separated from his body, the two Shamirs rattled about the tombs, at a loss to find direction or purpose in living.

Shamir eventually found that, with the absence of Ashmedai's controlling force on his body, he could gain some slight measure of control. He could make the man sit on a rock, or lie on the ground, or walk at a slow and staggering gait. In time, he helped his body feed itself, plucking papery leaves from trees to fill its gnawing belly, and to chew young twigs from certain shrubs to glean their scant moisture. This was more waking death than life.

Resting the man's body behind a tomb one morning, Shamir heard the voices of men approaching. One said to the other,

"It is just ahead here. Some time ago, a rich widow commissioned it for her dead husband, but the man's family claimed the body from her and buried it in their own family's tomb. She has relinquished all rights to it, so here it lies—waiting to provide food for the worms. You have a coffin, then?"

"Yes. I purchased a particularly fine one from that red-bearded cretin on the east side of the city."

"I hear the old man died in his sleep—screaming out in the throes of some nightmare. Why would you go to such expense, to bury a man you had no love for? He is not even your kin."

"Even my new wife had no respect for the man, who treated her shabbily—more like a servant, than daughter. But I must keep up appearances. The lavish display of my wealth—be it for coffin or a host of mourners—insures that my power and influence will be seen and felt here, like it is in Bostra. I see this as an opportunity, not some begrudging nod to my new wife."

Shamir took note of the men's words and strained his slim influence to urge his body near the tomb's front corner. The seller-of-tombs chuckled and said, "Speaking of your new wife, I hear you are more than twice her age—even older than her dead father. How did you gain such a prize—and her consent? I hear she is quite comely, yellow hair excepted."

"In my circle, consent is of little significance. The man tried to use the old scheme of claiming that some rube offered him a certain amount before me, and I would have to counter with a higher bid. I have no time for such games, and simply threw a bag of money his way. That is all the consent I need."

"So, this young woman has no interest in you? As a lover?"

"In time she will come around. In the interim, her body is young and supple, and a delightful diversion from my wife of many years I retain in Bostra. When Qainu comes to me of her own accord, I will take her to Bostra and divorce my old wife. I will take the new woman to my marriage bed there and she will learn to love me."

The heart of Shamir's soul became a boiling cauldron, and the silken cord lashing him to his body throbbed white-hot. His anger surged through the life-cord, animating his body to leap from beside the tomb, in front of the men. Its sudden appearance, its spasmodic leaping and jerky thrusting of its arms struck fear into them. They backed away, screaming and shouting at the strange figure before them. But Shamir urged his body on, staggering after the two men. Its lungs heaved, breath pulsing through clenched teeth, frothy saliva drooling from the corners of its mouth. He caused the living carcass to lift a large stone and cast it toward the men. They turned and ran, screaming in terror.

Shamir and his body found a scrap of solace in the empty tomb. The night sky let down its curtains, the two slept, and dreamed not.

From the valley between Gadara and the tombs, a mob climbed the hill, armed with torches, clubs, and chains. They shouted encouragement to each other, making their way to the city of Gadara's dead.

"They say he raged with a violent strength, but he is only one, brothers—gird up your loins, and act like men! He is nothing more than a man. He may be crazed by a demon, but we are armed with clubs. He will be no match for us!"

Shamir awoke, and hearing many agitated voices below the tombs, stirred his body back to life. He heard them enter a tomb and shout, "He is not here...keep looking...we will find him!"

They moved on to other tombs with the same result. One at a time, they searched the homes of the dead, drawing nearer to Shamir. Two men stepped into the open doorway of the coffin-less tomb, torches blazing in their hands.

"He is here! We have found him! Come quickly before he is on us!"

They waved their torches wildly before them, and Shamir's body instinctively held up its hands, trying to block the bright light from its eyes.

"Quickly—come quickly! He is moving and about to attack us!"

A dozen more men arrived in a sprint. They burst into the tomb and fell upon the thoughtless form as one. They knocked it to the ground and beat it into submission, their wooden clubs thudding into its abdomen, thighs, and chest. Shamir felt each stroke as a burning, piercing jab through his mind. He lost consciousness.

In the gray light of predawn, he awoke. He looked around and saw his body crumpled, lying in a heap beneath a scraggly shrub. It made no movement, and he wondered,

Is it...am I...finally dead?

He strained his vision and barely detected the faint glimmer of the life-cord. He urged the body to wake, and to move—to no effect. His mind felt slowed, and dragged down by some immense weight. Gathering all of his efforts, he begged his body to move. It quivered, and then rolled over. Shamir saw its hands and feet restrained by iron manacles, bound together by a dark chain.

He scanned the area in which he found himself, and saw the row of tombs at some distance, on the next hillside. A team of oxen pulled a heavy cart up the road that snaked toward the tombs. On the cart lay an elaborate coffin, carved of white marble and gleaming in the morning sunlight. A long line of mourners trailed behind it, wailing in practiced unison of rhythm and disharmony. At the end of the line walked an older man in official robes and cap, and a veiled young woman behind him.

The ox-team reached the tomb and its driver halted their progress. They detached the oxen from the cart and a group of men rolled it to the tomb's doorway. Using long, metal bars they pried the coffin into its final resting place on the tomb's raised platform. Stone on stone made a scraping, grinding sound, sliding along the stone dais. The sarcophagus, resplendent with its vines, and eagles, and palm tree, dominated the drab tomb.

The men re-hitched the oxen to the cart and drove them back down the road to Gadara. The mourners still wailing, they divided and filed to each side of the tomb. The man and woman walked between them, entering the tomb to pay their final respects.

Shamir spurred his encumbered body to lift its bloody self and begin lumbering its way to the tombs. The chains greatly hampered its progress but Shamir's heart yearned to see his Nura a final time. A white flash surged from Shamir and coursed through the silken band. It flooded the body with renewed strength. The grisly and wounded form tore at the chains, and beat the manacles with extreme force against rocks. Iron rang in the clear air as metal struck stone. Manacles broke, chains burst, and the body ran to the tombs.

Approaching the site of the funeral, Shamir ached to call her name—*Nura!*, but only a hoarse grunt tumbled from his body's throat. The mourners turned from the tomb to see the monster staggering toward them, chains hanging from wrists and dragging behind its feet. Wails in pretense of grief turned to screams of true horror. They ran wildly from the tombs, waving their arms.

Anatolios appeared at the doorway, wondering at the commotion. Seeing the demonic man again, he picked up an iron pry-bar and prepared to defend himself. As Shamir urged his body on to see Nura, the man struck it soundly on the side its head. It stumbled backward and Shamir's mind reeled in a dizzy haze. He fought to keep its balance.

Nura stepped from inside the tomb to the doorway and tried to restrain her husband. She pleaded with him,

"No! Stop! I know him—he is Nahor—my Light! Please do not hurt him. My Abba promised me to him—before you paid for me. He loved me, and went into the hills to find a treasure—to buy my freedom. Please! Do not hurt him..."

The old man shoved her roughly aside, throwing her to the ground. Her head struck the stone of the tomb's doorway and she fell at his feet, blood pouring from the mortal wound. Shamir's wrath erupted and he propelled his body again toward Anatolios. The man swung the iron bar low, taking the legs of the hulking frame out from under it. It crashed to the ground, knocking its wind from it, and Shamir struggled to stay conscious.

Having thus made himself a widower, the old man ran back to Gadara and reported, "That demonic *man of the tombs* has broken his chains and slain my new wife! I barely escaped with my own life. He roams up there now, near the tomb of my dead father-in-law. You will find her body there. Destroy him now, before he kills another of us!"

An angry mob armed themselves with spears and swords and axes, and set out to vent their vengeance upon Shamir.

He lifted his physical body to its hands and feet, and crawled to the lifeless form of Nura. He gently rolled her into his lap, and brushed back her bloodied veil. With a tender touch he brushed her red-spattered, golden hair from her face. Tears rained from his eyes, falling upon her cheek, washing away a bit of the blood. He ached to join her.

Curses and threats of violence propelled the crowd of men up the hill, toward the tombs. They needed no encouragement and rushed to find their prey and slay it. Shamir looked up from his grief to see the mob flooding up the road toward him.

I shall simply wait here for their attack. They will beat me. And pierce me through. And hack my limbs from my body. They will disembowel me and behead me. For such I deserve. It will finally be over.

Through the body's throat and mouth he screamed in grief. By his hands he gripped the neckline of his tunic and split the bloodied garment open. He tore it from his body in anguish.

But when the army of hatred approached, something beyond him compelled his body to rise. He laid aside her still body, and stood to flee the mob. His feet raced, and he ran far beyond the tombs, into the hills from where he took the perfect marble coffin. He left his attackers far behind, and he disappeared into the wilderness.

55

AND SO IT WAS, that clear, blue perfection spanned the sky above. But beauty did not accompany it. The sun dripped down its amber rays, but they held no warmth. Deep green forest mantled the mountains to the horizon, but the view did not swell the heart of Shamir with noble thoughts.

On a boulder near the summit of a rocky crag his naked body perched. Shamir's soul hung from the body's navel, suspended by the silken band, twisting and turning in the air.

Aslah could not have been right—where, now, is his Great Mercy? Perhaps it is not so great. Or not so merciful. If you ARE there...shed your great mercy upon me now! I do not deserve it, but I certainly— desperately—require it. I hang here, suspended between life and death. There is no life left behind me. I see none ahead. Nothing of value remains. I would seek death, but even that eludes me.

With a savage tug he yanked the life-cord, toppling the man from the boulder, to tumble out of control down the stony side of the crag. Bruised and beaten, the form finally rolled to a stop near the bottom of the slope. He made the man sit up and grasp a fist-sized rock from beside it. He directed it to pound away at the remaining shackle and chain on its left wrist. Each impact of stone on iron extended a tiny crack in the metal, and hundreds of strokes later the iron split, and the man forced it open until it fell away.

I see the wounds—but I no longer feel them. Where is the physical pain? Where is that sweet sting of affliction that tells me I yet live? To be numb...is death...but not quite.

The man sat on a slope of scree—those loose, broken fragments of rock that erode and fall from above, to pile at the crag's base. Shamir drew near his body, and looked over its shoulder. A palm-size shard of flint lay between its feet. He made the man grasp it and lift it toward its face, the better to see it. He turned it over and the shard glinted in the morning sunshine. The smooth, keen edge rivaled that of his janbiya.

I want to be alive—I want to feel life again! I want to taste that marvelous flame of anguish I deserve.

He ran the fingers across the edge of the flint, but felt nothing. So he lowered the stone to a naked thigh and sank the blade skin-deep. As he dragged the edge slowly through skin, it sliced open a groove the length of a handspan. Still feeling nothing, he marveled at the layers of white, yellow, and pink that opened before him. He watched a dark, red fluid creep into the groove, filling it, spilling over and running down the inner thigh.

He moved the blade over and cut again, a parallel, but deeper groove, from near the knee to almost the crease between thigh and abdomen. The blade sliced through skin and fat, into the topmost layers of red muscle. Blood oozed immediately, and copiously from the incision. And accompanying the cutting, a sweet thrill coursed from the body, traveling through the silken cord, to flood his awareness. He nearly fainted from the delicious sensation and the hand dropped the stone knife.

His body panted, and Shamir trembled with the quickening surge.

Oh! To savor the sweet delicacies of suffering! This is a way to feel—a way to stay alive.

Shamir kept the stone blade clutched in the right hand of his body. He carried it wheresoever the naked man's feet took him. Like a cherished friend, a confidant, the blade remained close to his side. Daily, the rock provided a fresh comfort—a relief from the deadened callous of his heart. And daily, the crusted, scabby wounds accumulated on his body, like a flock of parasites sucking his life.

In the silent depths of night, he lay the man down at a brook to quench its thirst. As his body sucked from the riffling water, a small ratty rodent swam downstream. The rat floated on its back, baring its grayish belly to the stars and stroking toward the man. It spat a jet of water into the air. As it neared the man, it said,

"I have sated my thirst at my well, and have tired of going to and fro upon the earth. It was an entertaining diversion, but I am back to claim my property. I would ask if you have treated it well, but I see it gashed, and covered with festering wounds. You have done this to your own body?"

You left me in a state of death—but without its freeing release. So I found a way to feel again.

"Hmphh. I should have known you would resort to some mischief like this. If release is what you want, I have had my way with you long enough, and it tires me to think of inventing new games to amuse myself with you. So, I am prepared to end it—here, and now..."

You will kill me? How will you do it?

"It will take no more than the bite of a rat to sever the cord linking you to your body."

Ashmedai scrambled from the brook, slicked the water from the dingy fur with its paws, and positioned itself halfway between Shamir's soul and his body. In its two rat-paws, it gripped the glimmering silk of the life-cord, and opened its jaws to cleave the band.

It jerked its head and said, "Did you hear that?"

It cocked its head the other direction and pricked up its two ragged ears. It dropped the cord and looked to the northern horizon.

"Oh, Mother-All-Nightmares! They are at it again…"

Who is it? Are you not going to finish this matter?

"It is that same damned crew I dealt with a year ago. The whore-bastards! Do they have no sense of authority and hierarchy? And protocol? There will be hell to pay here, and it won't be me!"

From beyond the crescent-range of mountains to the north, a tumult of clatter, blather and clamor rushed onward. The noise and discord raised a great cloud of dust, cloaking the horde. The storm rolled forward, gathering momentum, gaining force, and Ashmedai braced itself for the onslaught.

As the demonic host charged their foe, Ashmedai held up a paw and surged in height, and strength, and majesty. Its form changed from that of a rat to a great captain of hellions. The storm of villainy swirled about the demon's legs, like bolts of black lightning, and red, twisting cyclones of destruction. The whirlpool of vengeance slowed, and separated into many foul spirits, like tongues of a dark fire.

The chief incubus approached the face of Ashmedai, and spitting green vitriol, said, "You have lost this man—he now belongs to us! Yield, or suffer humiliation…"

Ashmedai inflated its chest and raised itself up, growling. "You have no authority here. Bend your knee to me, or suffer yourself!"

"We claim this human excrement on the authority of the Sovereign of Abbaddon himself. We be a thousand strong, and will sweep you away to claim this prize."

"You flatter yourselves too much. A thousand strong?—even a hundred would be a boast. Leave me in peace and slink back to the slime you inhabit."

"Ashmedai, you have frittered away your jurisdiction here, and your claim is forfeit to us. Again—yield, or let the wrath of His Greatness, Beelzebub, fall upon your sorry self!"

The storm churned again, with jagged bolts hurled into the torso of Ashmedai. It boiled up into a swarm of hideous hornets, stinging the master demon in a fury. To fend them off, the demon swatted about its head, but they drove it from its standing posture, and chased it far to the north.

Two dozen spirits remained behind to claim and molest Shamir. They stalked around him, studying and scrutinizing their prisoner. Then they hurled upon him venom and gall, beating him into yet deeper submission. They gripped the silken cord in their cruel claws, and by it, swung him in a great circle, to daze and addle him. They repeatedly slapped his soul down to the earth, knocking the last breath of will from him.

All but three of the devils flew away as gray and black streaks, streaming to the west, and leaving a sulfurous wake of stench behind them. They flew to confront another interloper encroaching on their territory. The remaining three brought forward a black iron chain, forged in the furnace of Gehenna, and they twisted its rough links around the silken cord uniting Shamir's soul to his physical form. His life would be secured, and their use of the man guaranteed. In the wake of the others, they goaded him westward with firebrands, and by prods studded with the stings of scorpions. He staggered on at their command, climbing up hills and tumbling down the far sides.

The devils dug their grisly claws into Shamir's body, and forced their way within. With shrieks and howls they entered to inhabit the husk of flesh. Their horrible wills forced out the last shreds of Shamir's volition and he shrank to a dismal corner inside himself.

The twenty-one flying malignant spirits made a hornet's line to the freshwater sea between Damascus and Yerushalayim—the lake known as Kinneret. In the middle of the waters and the midst of nightfall, twelve men rowed a leaky wooden boat eastward across the lake, hoping for dawn, while another slept soundly in the stern. In the sky above them, the nearly two-dozen demons whirled like clouds of corruption. The tempest surged and coiled, to roil and churn the sea below into foaming waves. The gale gusted and blustered, boiling the waters around the boat. The waves swelled and crested, crashing upon the boat and its men.

Driven by the fiery fury swirling within and without, the shell of Shamir's body staggered to the summit of the last hill. All physical strength spent, the man collapsed to its knees, lungs sucking air, fatigue burning thighs. The man's eyes looked down the slope and beyond the plain that bordered the sea. Far from land bobbed the tiny boat in the night—a speck of life lost in the vast stretch of water. The dozen men bowed their backs, rowing in desperation for shore.

Shamir's eyes saw the clear night sky birth the tumbling cloud. Twisting and writhing, it puffed itself larger, and gathered its dark garments about it. Stretching, growing, gaining momentum, it spewed darkness across the sea. The violent and black tangle of storm clouds reached down and tore at the waters. In the middle of the sea it focused its power, blue-bolts flashing from cloud to cloud, throwing down lightning, striking the sea. The wind roared in ferocity, whipping the water to white foam.

Far from shore, and amidst the tearing turmoil, the speck of life still bobbed—thrown from wave to wave, and heaved about by the hurtling mountains of sea. The hordes of menace inside Shamir grinned with his mouth to see such terrors of the sky unleashed upon the sea, upon the speck floating helpless.

Shamir's body again stood to its feet, but as it watched, a moment stood still in the flow of time.

The one who had slept in the boat's stern awoke. He stood to his feet in the pitching skiff and assessed the situation. From his lips then slipped a single, serene word—'*shaynah*' (be still).

From the uttered word, a peculiar peace radiated outward across the galloping waters. From the place of the speck on the waters, a calm pushed out the winds. A clear sky broke through to drive away the warring clouds, and the spears of lightning hid themselves.

In forty beats of a heart, the sea stood still, its surface smooth as polished marble. From the womb of dawn, the rising sun shone on the waters, glinting as from a mirror. A brilliant azure flooded across heaven's canopy, from one horizon to the other.

The shock of such a transformation confounded Shamir's captors. They goaded him on, but he lost his footing, to slide, roll, and tumble down the slope. The scarred and bloody, naked form bounced from stone to rock, tearing more skin, bruising more muscles, breaking more bones.

He rolled to a stop. With no pause for rest, they forced him to his feet and spurred him to stumble-run across the plain to the lake's shore.

56

EXPELLED FROM HIS OWN body, yet bound to it by an iron chain, Shamir floated and tumbled behind himself. He watched his body lumber forward, driven to an unknown and hideous destiny by his conquerors. They neared the final descent to the edge of the great lake, and farther up shore saw the boat about to land. The malignant spirits prodded him onward and he staggered down the rocky pathway leading to the beach. They whispered, mumbled, and buzzed incessantly inside his head—a cyclone of hornets evicting his inmost thoughts.

The wet gravel of the beach crunched under the shredded soles of his feet. The extreme exertion dripped flecks of foamy spittle from the corners of his mouth. On the unstable footing of sand and gravel, he staggered, and flailed his arms. He bit his tongue and lips, screaming curses and blasphemy.

As he lurched onto the beach, just an arrow's-flight off, the boat's hull touched land, making an extended '*sssshhhh*' as it scraped along the grit and gravel. Some men at the bow jumped into the water and beached it on the sand. The rest of them moved forward, rolled over the side, and helped drag the vessel farther onto the beach, to secure it from the waters.

One of their number—the man who had slept, and then spoke—stood confident on the shore. He surveyed the surroundings and then set off down the beach toward its intersection with the path descending from Gadara. The others saw his determined stride and followed several paces behind.

On the sands of that beach, two sets of footprints met. And there were heard two voices—one screaming hatred, curses, violence—the other filled with peace.

Black, turbulent clouds swept around Shamir, confusing his vision. And dark, hideous whisperings crowded his ears with suspicions and accusations—

This man has come to destroy us—and you! If he torments us, or assigns us to the pit, so will be your own fate. By bonds eternal we be bound to you, and you to us—bonds that cannot be broken. Make him leave us!

So Shamir screamed out, through the tempest that blew about him—

"Go away! Leave us be—leave us alone! Stay away from us!"

But the other man, unafraid and unoffended, broke not his stride, determined to follow his intent. Shamir's captors prodded him ever more, their talons piercing his flesh, and he screamed again,

"You *must* leave! We know who you are—the one set apart by that foreign god, set apart as his offspring to do his bidding—to cause us great harm. Do not torture us, or send us into that dark chasm of the earth, away from this light and this air—Depart from us!"

Still, the man walked toward him with resolution and a calm confidence.

They cut Shamir even deeper with their cruel claws, digging them deep into his stony heart, cracking, fracturing it.

Now, on a hill, a distance down the shore and overlooking it, a large herd of swine fed. The scene unfolding before them caught the attention of their herders. Several of the men gathered at the hill's brow, discussing what they saw. One said, "Look!—on the beach—it is that man of the tombs, screaming and dragging what remains of his chain."

Another said, "And a man from that boat walks to him—he must be a foreigner, for he does not seem to know the insanity and violence of the one he approaches."

"Yes, he and his fellows look dressed as Galileans. I'll wager the lunatic will slay him, strangling him with that chain!"

One answered his bet with "No, look at the strength of his fellows—there are ten or more of them, and they have the bearing of fisherman. My half-drachm says they will overcome the wild one and kill *him*."

And yet another said, "They may be a group to be reckoned with, but remember just two weeks back? When those four magistrates, six soldiers, and a brace of bear-hounds were fended off by that demon-possessed man? He killed their dogs and with a thigh-bone from the tombs beat the rest within a hair's breadth of their lives!"

All the while, Shamir's tormentors continued to tear at him—soul and body—compelling him in agony to shriek from the depths of his being—

"Begone! And do not send us into the abyss!"

The society of evil took counsel among themselves, searching desperately for a place of negotiation, a place of strength from which to bargain. The closer the man approached, the stronger he appeared to them, and the weaker their own position. Their dominance slipping away, as sands in an ebbing tide, they unsheathed their many daggers and slashed the bowels and liver of Shamir, causing him to cry out—

"If you must banish us, send us among that herd of swine!"

Through the murky mists swirling and writhing about him, Shamir saw a light—like a small lamp—on the far horizon. From it, a single ray penetrated the cold tumult and clanging voices, and bathed his face with a warm peace. The light came toward him, walking, as it were, upon the turbulent waters. It extended a hand to him, beckoning him to take it.

Refusing to yield their hard-won prize, they clutched his heart ever tighter in a grip of iron talons. Their obscenities and hateful abominations poured from Shamir's mouth—

"Forsaken be you by all men, and damned by all their gods! Now, begone—or send us among the pigs and leave us to our business!"

The man stood fearless, and the truth stood bare before him. Every hidden matter lay open to him, yet, in calm words he asked,

"Who are you?"

Shamir's overlords stretched themselves as high as they could muster, puffed out their hollow chests, and in their most threatening and murderous voices blasted back through Shamir,

"We be *A Thousand!*—no, we be *Two Thousands!*"

In a voice only they could hear, the man responded,

"The Truth be known, you are only two dozen. But then, you have always followed the Father of Lies. And if you *were* a thousand— your fate would remain the same."

Without raising his voice, and in the hearing of those on the beach, he spoke just one word more.

"*Twah*"—(Begone).

Though uttered in calm, the single word possessed the force of a mighty wave of water, as if the whole sea beyond the beach lifted itself and rushed headlong toward that company of corruption. It blasted into the ones gripping the life of Shamir and washed them away, casting them among the swine. The ugly menace tumbled along the backs of the beasts, and dug their sharp hooves and talons into the living flesh, attempting to gain a footing. The animals reacted in supreme confusion, and madness overtook them. So great was that flood, even the swine were carried away and drowned among its violent waves.

In the midst of the swarming waters Shamir still fixed his eyes on the steady lamp. And he stretched out his own hand, desperate to grasp the one offered him. Skin touched skin, and the man's fingers tightened around Shamir's hand, pulling him up through the churning waves. His body jerked and shuddered, buffeted by the whelming current, but the other man's grip never failed. The iron chain binding Shamir to his physical body crumbled away. The shining, silken cord throbbed with new life and pulled him back inside himself. The man continued hauling Shamir toward him—out of the blackness, out of captivity and confusion, and toward a place of light, peace, freedom.

He took Shamir's other hand and drew him yet closer, wrapping him in a secure embrace. Shamir coarsely exhaled the last, stale stench of death. For the first time in what seemed a life-time, he took a deep breath, inhaling the sweet aroma of life. He fell to his knees, streams of tears falling from his face to the sand.

Blessed silence surrounded Shamir, the man, and the others on the beach. Only the lapping of gentle waves on that shore greeted their ears. A dove, gliding above them, cooed its approval.

The man placed both his hands on Shamir's head and simply said, "Be cleansed, Nahor."

Though no one could see it happening, the ugly scars and deep wounds where Nahor had cut himself became new flesh and fresh skin. His body slumped, the constant pain—internal and external—relieved in an instant. To see such a wonder, the man's friends gasped and whispered in awe. He spoke to them,

"Friends, do you have an extra tunic or cloak for this dear one?'

From the back of the group, one of the twelve said, "I have a spare garment," and passed it forward. As it came into the man's hands, he clothed Nahor's nakedness. Nahor stretched out his hands and arms, marveling at the healed wounds. Still on his knees, he wrapped his arms around his benefactor's legs and clung to him. In broken words he asked, "Who...are you? Why...did you...help me?"

"My Abba named me Yeshua. And you were delivered for the glory of the One God—the One called Yahweh—the Always-Existing-One."

Overcome by gratitude, Nahor collapsed to the damp sand and clasped Yeshua's ankles.

Standing at a distance, those who had herded the swine beheld all the wonders displayed on the beach below them. They watched the thundering herd stampede, and had run alongside them, waving their arms furiously and shouting in vain attempt to halt the pigs' madness. Now, the group of herdsmen, about forty in number, gathered and argued about what they should do.

Their fear swelled, for the calamity was great, and they were at a loss to explain it to their employers. They railed at each other, the leaders blaming the lowest among them, and the lowest accusing the leaders. In the end, with countless dead animals bobbing in the surf, they determined the fault should lie at the feet of this foreigner on the shore, this sorcerer who makes madmen sane—this worker of strange wonders. They returned to Gadara to tell the owners of the herd.

They later returned to the lake's edge, a large group of the town's citizens with them. They found Yeshua and his friends, and with hearts full of fear and confusion, entreated him to leave their region. Seeing the madman who had formerly terrorized them, clothed, in his right mind, and seated at the magician's feet, bewildered them. Having no explanation for this great power demonstrated through Yeshua, they implored him to have nothing more to do with them and to leave their shore with haste.

Yeshua said nothing to them but turned to his friends and said, "My work is finished here. Let us return to the other side."

The men shoved the boat from the beach back into the waves and clambered into it. A man in the boat held out his hand to help boost Yeshua into it, but Nahor still clung to him in the water, pleading with him—

"You *must* let me go with you—you cannot leave me! My life is in you alone, and only *you* have power over those who would torture me!"

He gently pried Nahor's grip from his cloak, and smiled at him. "Don't fret, my brother. I will not forsake you, though I go away for a time. Go home to your people and tell them what great things God has done for you. You will meet me again, and our fellowship will be sweet. Trust me, and trust the Great Mercy Who sent me."

His waiting friends hoisted him aboard, and they rowed from shore toward the west. The townspeople ascended the slope to return to Gadara. Nahor, still waist-deep in the waters, watched his rescuer sail away. With the sun falling into the distant reaches of the sea, the boat became a speck on the horizon, lost in the red glare. And then it was gone.

57

THE SKY TURNED VIOLET and Nahor remained in the waters alone, small waves lapping and gurgling at his belly—the cursing, accusing voices replaced by a sweet silence. He lay down on the beach and slept. For the first time in many weeks he slept, enveloped in rest, calm. Peace.

Flying above the shore, birds cried, and Nahor awoke to the morning sunlight. He rose and returned to Gadara, to tell them of the great wonder that intervened in his torment. He walked the western street into the city, past the theater and through the markets. The crowds paid him no attention, and he wondered what he would say, and to whom.

This great thing that has happened to me—this man Yeshua, who cared for my desperate plight, my agony, and who released me from its chains—what will I say of this? Or of him? How can anyone understand what has happened? How can I understand it? Who will care?

A man and woman shopped at a booth selling bronze lamps. They looked up from their haggling with the vendor, and took notice of Nahor's approach. The man leaned close to the merchant and whispered to him as he pointed at Nahor. The seller jumped back from his display of lamps, waving his arms and shouting, "*Mrd'mu! Daywan!*—Madman! Demoniac!"

The crowds walking along the street stopped, and they turned to see the source of commotion. Those nearest Nahor tripped over themselves, backing away in a mad rush, while shouts and shrieks broke out and echoed across the plaza. A man bumped into a pile of *colocynth*, stacked like a pyramid. The bitter gourds fell away from the display, rolling down the street like a hundred green-striped balls.

While the crowd cleared the street around Nahor, young men and youths stepped forward to form a circle around him. Their taunts and screams pierced his ears and pricked his heart. They picked up the gourds and bombarded him. The hard missiles pummeled his body, one striking his head and knocking him to the stone pavement. Dazed, he held up his hands to block the barrage. He struggled to his feet and ran down the street, his tormentors parting before him. He fled the chaos and the screams followed his escape.

"Leave this place, you lunatic!—you maniac! You are polluted by spirits of death. Leave our city and never return! Take your fiendish and vile ways far from us, or we shall torture and kill you. Begone!"

They picked up rocks and hurled them toward the fleeing Nahor. Several found their mark and left their evidence of bruise and gash on his newly-healed skin. A few men gave chase for several minutes, finally stopping the pursuit far from Gadara, as their victim stumbled and splashed his way across a brook.

In exhaustion, he dropped to the rocky path. With his lungs heaving and burning, he turned to see his pursuers returning to Gadara. They wound their way up the hill, where some of the crowd welcomed them back, and thanked them for removing the scourge from among them. He slumped against a rock and took stock of his wounds.

O, Great Mercy—I so wanted to share the wonders of what you did for me. I thought they would share in my joy, rejoicing with me over this great thing. Is this the reception I will always receive—for such a marvel? Can they not understand the good you have done me? Where shall I now go, and to whom shall I speak of this?

For the rest of the day, he lay with his back against the rock, pondering his future.

A light breeze blew softly through the ravine of that brook. And whispered words wafted along the ravine, carried upon the wings of the breeze, into the ears of Nahor.

Do you?...Do you remember?...Do you remember what he said?

The question startled him, and he wondered what it meant. But as he turned it over in his mind, some of the final words of the previous day bubbled up in him. He spoke out loud, though there seemed no one there to hear him.

"He said to me—'*Go home to your people...tell them what great things this God has done for you.*' Yes, he said '*go home.*' But do I even have a home? It is certainly not Gadara. Raqmu? Hawara?"

He picked himself up, and tearing narrow strips from the bottom of his borrowed tunic, he bound some hyssop onto the worst of his wounds. He set out for Hawara, to discover the whereabouts of Geram, son of Dayan.

The streets, tents, and even the sheep of Hawara lay under a red blanket. The previous day a vicious breath from the desert blew in a fury, driving the red sand before it. The storm surged through Hawara and dropped its load of silt and dust, snowing a ruddy blizzard across the landscape.

Nahor entered the city and walked the vermillion streets. Most of the residents busied themselves with getting out from under the layers of grime. One man stood with arms folded, supervising his sons who prodded his tent with poles from the inside, shaking and moving the dust from the tent. He shouted at them to be careful of poking the tent's fabric too hard. At the next tent a middle-aged woman shook a rug vigorously, each motion releasing a red cloud into the air. The pile of red rugs next to her awaited their turn in her hands.

Near the end of the street, an old man sat cross-legged in front of the open flap to his modest tent. Nahor greeted him.

"Sabah—I see the desert has breathed its dusty exhale upon you."

."Yes, my young brother, it was quite a blow yesterday. Just before the sun set. The dust-laden wind darkened the sky to an early night, while the sun yet sat upon the horizon. Those shirkers who left their tent cords unsecured found themselves bearing the brunt of the blast nearly naked. I heard them screaming curses above the roar of the wind, as it blew their homes away. They are out looking for their tents today. But they will never find them. And they will never learn from their follies."

"Yes, some things never change. But then there are others that do. How did you fare last night?"

"I and my belongings are still here. Except my donkey. But if you look inside you will see all is dusted red. And I have not the strength to shake it out."

"Have you no family, or friends, to help you?"

A smirk bent the old man's mouth.

"I have four sons. But they are all busy washing their camels down at the pool. Not that it will do them any good. The water there will be as red as blood until it settles in a few days. But their rides take precedence over all else. What is a young man in the eyes of his peers, if he has not a fast, clean camel with bells, bridle, and saddle to best his brothers? And more importantly, to impress the ladies..."

"I have a strong back and arms, Sabah—I will help you."

"You are no kin to me. And I have little I can pay you. I have a large skin of water, untouched by last night's red plague, and some barley gruel and flat loaves from yesterday. They are yours if you would assist me."

"We will share them together. I have walked for days without a morsel, and but little water. Even now my navel scrapes against my backbone. Sharing this meal shall be a feast."

He helped the man dig out from under the weight of dust covering everything. He turned the interior of the tent again to a pristine, inviting oasis in the midst of a sea of red. The two sat in the comfortable space and delighted in the simple meal.

"And why would a young man like you be wandering these dirty streets? You are not from here, are you?"

"I lived here long ago. While yet a young boy. But I look for someone else who once lived here. His name is Geram. Son of Dayan. He was a trader in semi-precious stones."

The old man opened his mouth and scraped the knuckles of one hand with his two front teeth. He wrapped the curls of his grey beard around a thumb.

"Geram, you say. The name sounds a bit familiar. But the face does not come to me. He certainly is not here now...Son of Dayan... yes...yes. I seem to remember something about his wife long ago. A shameful act—taking her own life that way. Yes, I do remember the man."

"Do you know where he might now be?"

The man closed his eyes, raised his eyebrows and shook his head.

"No, I never knew the man well. Mostly heard things about him from neighbors. I think his clan was from down around Hegra. At least, I believe they had a family tomb there. There might yet be family in the area. I think he had sons, as well."

"Sabah, I thank you for your kindness in feeding and watering me. I must be on my way, and see what awaits me in Hegra. May the peace of the Great Mercy be upon you and your tent."

"What? You leave so soon? What will you take to sustain you on your journey to Hegra? It is a longer distance there, than to Damascus! At least you can fill a small skin with water from the larger."

"I believe my master will take care of me. He provided this meal and companionship already this day."

"If you are a slave, traveling out here alone, I don't think your master will be providing you anything. Wait a moment…"

The old man found a small box carved from acacia wood, and slowly opened its lid. He pulled something from it, and held out his clenched fist to Nahor. He said,

"Place your palm under my hand."

As he did, the man opened his fist, dropping a coin into Nahor's hand. He looked at it, and turned it over. The gold tetradrachm sparkled.

"I cannot take this from you. Our bargain did not include money. And this is far too much, anyway."

"It was to be an inheritance for my sons. Not much of an inheritance, divided among the four, but an inheritance nonetheless. And when my last breath is carried away on the wind, I can only imagine the strife and warring that will erupt between them, as they contend for this small bit of metal. Better that you have it, than they. And you insult me if you refuse my gift to you."

He looked again at the coin. The face of Philistis, queen of Syracuse, graced the gleaming yellow disc. He looked at the old man and said,

"I will take it—as a great gift from the Great Mercy, by the hand of a great friend. I will not forget you."

"Go in peace, my young brother. And may Manawat follow you with a smile.

58

NAHOR PURCHASED TRANSPORT WITH a camel train, southbound from Hawara to Hegra. He swayed in the saddle ten hours a day, for fifteen days. The caravan skirted the northern edge of the Red Valley of Ruhm and then headed to the east. Plumes of pink blew from the peaks of soft, rolling mountains of shifting sand. Halfway through the journey, the caravan turned south, working its way toward Hegra.

He mulled over the last three years of his life, wondering at its meaning. And he wondered what yet awaited him—

Why do I even go to Hegra? Abba may be dead by now. My brothers scattered. And if they are not—what will I say to them? Will they stone me, as did those in Gadara? Or just laugh at my crazy story?

Marzeah halls appeared out of the desert, isolated here and there like islands in a red sea. Much like the simplest tombs of Raqmu, the facades' god-steps and small entryways reminded Nahor of his previous home. But unlike them, the smoothly carved and angular faces jutted from isolated, giant bulbous rocks, extruded from the desert floor. The geometric designs contrasted with the fantastic shapes of the rocks. Traveling on, they paralleled a long cliff face, where tomb after tomb rubbed shoulders with each other. The row of a dozen carved monuments displayed little difference between them—except in height and the coloration of bands painted upon the plastered faces.

An escort of Nabataean cavalry rode out from Hegra to meet the caravan and accompany them to the caravanserai. After reaching their destination, Nahor dismounted while the camel's handlers offloaded their cargo. Each camel carried a weight equivalent to about three men each: eggshell-thin pottery, obsidian, bronze, copper, olive oil, dried figs and wine. With their burdens relieved, the camels waited their turns to find space at the edge of the large open pool. They bent their necks to quench their thirst of two weeks, and each sucked up ten large water-skin's worth of cool liquid, in as many minutes. When the two-hundred and fifty animals finished, the level of the cistern was substantially lower.

At the caravanserai and the nearby city, Nahor inquired about the tent of Geram. Within two days he heard of the man's location and set out to find him.

Nahor stood at the top of a knoll and looked down on the small tent of Geram, son of Dayan. Drifts of sand crept up the windward side of the tent, evidence it had remained in its place for some time. The goats' hair fabric was torn in places and some of the cords were slack, causing the roof to sag. The loose entrance fold flapped in the light breeze. It appeared not occupied in some time.

So...he is either gone, or dead.

Before he turned to walk away, movement inside the entrance caught his attention. The flap opened and a man shuffled outside. An old man.

He carried with him a black stone block no larger than his head, and placed it upright on a mound of dirt just beyond the entrance. With a faltering gate he scuffled back inside and then reappeared with a skin. He waved his arms and bobbled his head in front of the black stone, and then poured water on it from the skin. The water ran over and down the rectangular stone, each rivulet coloring the rock a darker shade of black, and then it dripped down onto the dirt. The man turned and reentered the tent.

Is that old man my Abba? And he now pours water, not wine, on the betyl of Dushara?

Nahor descended the hill and approached the tent. Reaching the entrance, he called out,

"Is this the tent of Geram? Son of Dayan?"

A feeble voice within said, "Who wants to know? Do I owe you anything? If yes, then I no longer live here."

Nahor smiled and shook his head, wondering if he had heard correctly.

"I am Nahor. I am a son of Geram…"

Only silence filled the tent. After a while, a weaker voice said,

"Nahor? Geram has no such son. You are mistaken."

"I am not mistaken. I know who I am. I am Nahor, son of Geram."

Only the tent flapping in the wind interrupted the desert's silence. In a yet weaker voice the man said, "I once had such a son…but he is long gone. Gone with most of his brothers. He left me, and now I have no one."

Still standing outside the tent, Nahor said, "I did not leave you, Abba. You left me. In Raqmu, with the sculptor, Aslah. It was very hard for a while. But the man taught me much. And I no longer hold it as debt against you. May I enter, to see your face once more?"

"You are really Nahor? When I left you there…I thought you were gone from the world. Gone from this life. You are Nahor?"

"Yes, I yet walk this world. May I see your face?"

"I will not turn a guest from my tent. You may enter."

Nahor lifted the tent flap and entered his abba's home. The tent lay almost empty, but for a small worn rug, nearly covered with sand, and one sullied cushion, upon which the old man slouched. A waterskin and a small pile of threadbare clothing lay heaped in a corner.

The man struggled to sit upright and said, "Are you really him? Please come closer, that I may see your face clearly."

Upon seeing Nahor's face, his mouth fell open, exposing the lack of all front teeth. He cocked his head right and left, and said, "I try to see my boy in the man, but cannot. I am sorry—it was so long ago. Are you here to take your revenge on my flesh, or to take all that I own? You can have all you see...take what you will. Just leave me to my own infirmity."

Geram cringed and shrank away into a corner. Nahor sat on the rug.

"No, Abba. I come here not for vengeance, but to tell you the wonder that has happened to me."

He paused long, glancing about the tent, before starting again.

"After you left me in Raqmu with Aslah, he trained me to be a master mason, and I was on my way to becoming a sculptor. But this young man was filled with foolish ways. Through accident, and my own follies, I fell from where I was. And I traveled to the farthest reaches of the world, searching for something I had all along. I threw away great gifts that had been given me, and lost ones I thought were in my grasp. In the end, I lost my soul. I lost myself, and I was given over to a great evil..."

Geram dropped his shoulders, and pity for his son filled his eyes.

"I was without hope. But by chance, or grand design, I met a man on the shore of a great lake to the north. And though curses spewed from my mouth against him, with a single word he rescued me from my hopeless state. His name was Yeshua. And he said I should go back to my family and tell them the great things his god—my God, Yahweh—did for me. That is why I am here. This Yeshua was used by his god—the one I now call the Great Mercy—to deliver me from the grip of demonic powers. So now you know."

The old man's eyes widened. He slapped his own face with both hands, and tearing the collar of his dirty robe said, "So you have now taken a new god—a foreign god? Dushara is no longer good enough for you? We Nabatu have worshipped him, and the others, since our beginning. Why would you take a foreign god when you do not even live in the land of this god?"

"Abba, I did not say I worship him...yet. But I may. I believe I know more about him, than I ever knew of the old gods—those of the Nabatu. The power of this god has touched my life in a potent —and wondrous—way. And he not only displayed his power in my life, but he did so simply because...he cares for me. I could not even cry out for his mercy, and yet he poured it freely upon me. And he somehow used this man, this Yeshua, to deliver me."

Nahor shrugged his shoulders and then stretched out his arms to both sides. His own face was filled with questions as he said, "I can explain none of this. I can only report what has happened to me."

Geram lowered his head and looked at the dirt covered rug before him. He said, "When my last son was born, I dreamed he would prosper and honor his family—as did his brothers. But then, I had to put him away. And so, I dreamed he would yet prosper, in a place far from here. I oft poured out wine to Dushara for his safety, and that he would become a man of honor. And now this..."

They sat in silence for a long time. And Nahor asked, "What of my six brothers—do they live? Where can I find them?"

"Your brothers? You are dead to my sons, as you have been to me. My youngest, Wahab, has a large family here. He holds many herds of sheep and now breeds camels as well. While he is often away supervising his shepherds, he returns to Hegra once or twice a month, to care for his family and to lie with his wife."

The old man recounted the list of his other sons, their accomplishments, their families, and their whereabouts. When Geram had finished, Nahor said, "I am pleased to have seen your face again, Abba. And I thank you for telling me of my brothers. May the Great Mercy find you, as he did me."

He rose to leave Geram's tent, and the old man struggled to his feet. Nahor helped him stand and then steadied him. Geram wrapped his feeble arms around his son and said, "I wish you no ill. I never did. I only sought to uphold our honor. Since you left us, I have been alone. Every day, I have longed for my Elanat, your Amma."

And Nahor answered, "As have I."

He gripped Nahor even tighter and wept. When he finally released his hold, Nahor kissed his cheeks and left the tent to find his brothers.

59

THE SUN ROSE TO light the path of Nahor as he sought out his brothers. Starting with Wahab, the youngest, and then seeking the next older, he told each of them, as he did Geram, the great things done for him. And like Geram, each brushed aside his words, and upbraided him for his apostasy from the gods of his fathers.

In the tenth month of his task, he sought the last, and eldest son of Geram—Nashgu.

Nahor jumped across the small brook running from a ravine between two grassy hills. He followed the trickle of water to an expansive opening beyond. In the distance, scores of horses dotted the rolling landscape, heads down, grazing. Between the ravine and the field, a group of six men and a boy looked up from their work of castrating a colt to see Nahor's approach. Two unsheathed their janbiyas as they walked toward him.

"Stop! Who are you—and why are you here?"

He stopped and said, "I am Nahor, son of Geram. I look for my eldest brother, Nashgu. Do you know of him?"

They slowly returned the weapons to their scabbards.

"This is Nashgu's herd. The boy is his third-born son. You will find him just beyond the hill below the sun."

"I thank you for your help, my brothers."

He paced across the field, and nearing the boy, he said, "I am your father's youngest brother, Nahor. And what is your own name?"

The boy's eyes followed him, but he said nothing.

Nahor headed toward the sun and climbed over the low hill. Descending the far side he saw a small tent pitched near the brook, its flap partly open, waving in the breeze. With no one in sight, he neared the tent and said, "Nashgu? I am your youngest brother. Nahor."

He heard low voices speaking to each other inside the tent—one a young woman. Then, a man's voice—"You may come in..."

Nahor lifted the flap and stepped into the dim interior. A young woman with long, black hair trailing down her back sat on a rug. A bearded man of about forty sprawled on cushions behind her, his arm encircling her waist. Moving his head to look around his companion, he said, "They told me I should expect you—that you would be here."

"They?"

"My brothers...they said you started with the youngest and were making your way through the family. That I would probably be the last. So here you are..."

Nahor studied the face. Sharpened, creased, and darkened by the savage, unceasing desert sun, it bore a stark contrast to the milky complexion and soft features of the girl. Nashgu continued.

"They said you spun a wild story of madness and *djinn*—of some sorcerer and his foreign gods. Is that so?"

His brothers' rejection of him still stung, but he determined to complete the task put before him by Yeshua. So he opened his mouth for the seventh time, to relate the events of the past few years. He finished by saying, "So now you have heard, yourself, the wonders done for me, through this man Yeshua. And now I have done as he said."

He turned, to leave his brother to his afternoon's entertainment, but Nashgu stopped him, saying, "Wait—there is something you should know..."

Nashgu ascended the girl's arm with kisses, then stopped to speak again to his brother.

"...much of my business involves trading horses with those Iudaeans—they have a love for fine horse-flesh, you know. About a month back, I heard from several clients that quite a stir happened in Yerushalayim, their capital—around the time of their spring feast."

"A stir?"

"They told me the story of a traveling preacher—held by some there to be someone of note, and approved by their god. They called him...*Yeshua*. Same as your magician. And they say he mostly worked up around the northern lake. The place you met your own Yeshua."

"So, you had already heard of him..."

"Yes, but...you have yet to hear the most important part of the story."

"There is more?"

He sat up and gently pulled the girl back, to lie in his lap, and said, "He rode into their capital. Acclaimed and cheered by many as their new king..."

Nahor's face brightened and a smile came upon it. "Yes, I can see that they would!"

"...but...a few days later, their Roman overseer condemned the man to death. My clients were not clear on the specific charges against him. So their governor's soldiers tortured the man until he hung dead, on a wooden post."

Nahor's face blanched. He stammered, "They...they turned against him? Against Yeshua? No. That simply cannot be. Dead?

You must be mistaken! They must have invented such a foolish tale…"

Nashgu caressed the young woman's face. And then her neck. As she closed her eyes, he bent down and touched her lips with his. He sat upright again, and with a slight grin, said, "Oh, I am quite certain those are the facts in the matter. I have now heard this from three separate sources. They bored me with the same old news, over and over. But it seemed very important to them, and they were quite worked up about it. I simply thought you should know, since it concerned your man."

He bent down again, and returned to kissing his paramour. Nahor's face sagged, and his heart felt pierced by his brother's janbiya. He turned to leave the tent—the last of his kin—and his eyes began to melt with tears. He dropped the flap, and behind him, the pair's quiet conversation resumed. Then, laughter and giggles.

With enormous effort, Nahor commanded his feet to take him away from his brother's revelations. But he walked toward nothing. He trudged on, as if wading through deep mud. Strength left him and he felt he could not walk on. But greater strength would be required to sit, and think on these matters.

60

AND SO IT WAS that many years later, arid desert winds dried the full heads of spelt and barley, blanching the fields to nearly white—the signal they stood ready for spring harvest. The heavy heads bowed the stalks into nodding arcs. Puffs of light breeze rustled the standing grain and sent waves undulating across the field.

Nahor entered the field near Gaia, east of Raqmu, with a dozen others dressed in rags like his. The early sun's heat lifted an aroma of cereal from the waist-high grain, reminding him of the void in his stomach. In one hand he gathered a few heads of grain, and with the other he cut the stalks with a borrowed sickle, laying them in neat rows, for those behind to gather and tie them in sheaves. After a few days' final drying in the field, they would return and gather them to a threshing floor of the man who owned the crop.

Grasp, cut, lay. Grasp, cut, lay. Grasp, cut, lay—ten thousands of times in a day.

What am I doing? Why am I cutting barley? Should I not be cutting stone? I remember...cutting myself. Has it truly been six years since my eldest brother told me of the horror of Yeshua's death?

Grasp, cut, lay...

I have thought of his death a thousand times over—will this never stop? He released me from my own living death—could he have not saved himself? Stop thinking about it, Nahor!—you cannot change a fragment of what has happened—please, let it go!

Grasp, cut, lay...

Grasp, cut, lay...

He stopped for a moment to wipe the sweat from his brow with the back of his hand. The brilliance of the sun climbing in the blue of the morning sky made him squint as he glanced at it. Looking down again, he saw a few drops of blood on his left hand—a finger cut by the razor-edge of the sickle. He touched the minor wound with his tongue, to staunch the bleeding. The blood tasted of salt and iron. Images of cutting himself by intention poured from his memory.

The sheaf-gatherer behind him shouted. "Stop your day-dreaming, man! I have nearly caught up to you! We need to finish this field by sunset—or lose our wages!"

Nahor shook his head and slapped his own face to jolt himself back to the matter at hand.

Grasp...cut...lay...

With the sun standing just beyond noon's high point, a loud whistle from the harvest's overseer pierced the dry air, his indication the field hands could take their only rest of the workday. Ten men and three women collapsed in the shade of a small shelter at the field's edge.

The overseer put a pot of stale porridge in their midst, and a dozen hands competed for advantage to dip out portions to their hungry mouths. Still preoccupied with his thoughts of the morning, Nahor hung back from the crowd, sitting at a short distance. A hand tapped his shoulder.

He turned to see who sought his attention, and a man of about thirty years raised his bushy eyebrows above his large eyes and nodded in greeting. He held out a full water-skin to Nahor, and said,

"Take—drink—slake your deep thirst."

Nahor took the skin, loosened its opening, and let the cool water trickle into his mouth, down his throat. While he quenched his thirst, he eyed the man—bald, with dark eyes, and sharp features. A black beard bristled his chin. The knee-length tunic made his stubby frame appear even shorter than it was. His clothing, manner and speech clashed with the harvest setting. The man looked out of place. Nahor struggled to make sense of it, and said to him,

"I have not seen you before. You seem not a field hand, nor an overseer for that matter. And you are not from here—your speech gives you away…"

The man chuckled to himself. "No, I am not. The good question would be—where *am* I from?—but the answer to that might be a bit complicated."

"*Are* you a field hand—or should I be calling you *sir?*"

"I am neither. Although I *am* someone's servant."

"Then why are you here, if you are not joined to the harvest?"

"Oh, I am, indeed, joined to the harvest—but not this one."

"I am sorry, but I do not follow you in this. Why are you here?"

"I was told you were thirsty. And I had the means to quench it for you. So here I am…"

"You, sir, are a peculiar fellow—going to a place not your own, to serve someone to whom you are not bound—neither by blood, nor hire."

Nahor took a long draft from the water-skin and closed his eyes as the fluid cooled his throat. The man said, "He is not dead, you know…"

Nahor choked on the last swallow of water, sputtering as he struggled to catch his breath.

"Wh—what?"

"I said, he is *not* dead as you suppose."

"Not…dead?…Who?"

"The one you have troubled yourself with, these half-dozen years."

Nahor looked both ways, wondering who else was privy to this conversation. But the others lay sated in the shade, resting before the return call to work. The porridge pot lay empty in their midst. He looked back to the man and whispered,

"Who are you talking about?"

"I believe you already know the answer to your own question. And I know this can be quite a shock. It was certainly so when I first found out myself."

I cannot believe what I am hearing! Is he talking about who I think he is talking about?

"You said he is not dead—so the story about his...terrible death... was made up? A fable?"

The man shook his head and said, "Oh no, it was most certainly *not* invented. The story is quite accurate. He, indeed, died a death. Even more ghastly than either you or I can possibly imagine."

"But you said...he is not dead. I do not understand."

Nahor's head churned with the news. He could not decide whether the man was an apparition or a delirium from the heat of the field. He looked both ways again, and whispered, "You *are* speaking of...the one who called himself...*Yeshua?*"

"Of course. The very one."

The overseer again shattered the air with his shrill whistle, calling the hands back to their labor. The other dozen helped each other to their feet and dragged themselves back into the field. The man said to Nahor, "I have much more to tell you. At the sun's setting, and the end of your toil, find the maker of tents. Near the pottery works. I will give you a hot meal, and a place to sleep in the shelter of my tent."

Nahor kneeled before him, to kiss his hand. The man raised him back to his feet, saying, "Do not do that—I am only a man like yourself—prone to weakness and my own set of follies. I will see you later."

He watched as Nahor entered the field again, to grasp, cut, and lay...

61

THREE RAVENS CHASED THE receding sun, their black wings brushing the sky's rose-blush. Not far from the field, now shorn of its barley, dozens of tents stood sprinkled across the outskirts of Gaia. Nahor stopped at the first and inquired of the old man who sat before a fire.

"Sir, do you know the whereabouts of the tent-maker?"

The old man looked up from the scrawny carcass of a pigeon he roasted at the end of a spindly stick. He squinted one eye, and examined Nahor with the other. He said,

"Tent-maker? The man fell dead three months ago!"

"Dead? He spoke with me this afternoon...short, balding...bushy black beard?"

"You mean that Iudaean he was training in his skills?"

"Perhaps. He did have the speech of one."

"A distance beyond the pottery furnaces. If he still lives at the tent-maker's old place."

He pointed to the north, where a lone cloud towered from the horizon like a great column, its top catching the sun's final rays of vermillion. The man looked back to his pigeon, browning at the end of the stick. Nahor thanked him and walked on.

He passed the pottery works, where a pair of men worked in the waning light. They spun eggshell-thin bowls on whirling wheels. Yellow incandescence from the blazing furnace reflected from glossy-wet clay between the potters' hands. Radiant heat from the furnace lit their faces in amber glow and warmed Nahor's exposed skin as he walked by. Crossing a small, stony brook, he continued to the north and left the hamlet of tents and the pottery works.

The first three stars glimmered into view in the darkening sky and he came to another pair of tents. He called out, "Halloo—is this the place of the tent-maker?"

In the dimming twilight, a man emerged from one of the tents, wiping his hands on a towel. He returned the greeting.

"Welcome, welcome to the tent of your humble servant! I have lentils and a bit of goat meat steeping in a pot by the fire, so our meal is not far off. Please sit at the fire and I will join you in a moment."

Nahor sat on a flat rock near the fire, and watched the few, low flames flicker and waver, occasionally touching the blackened surface of the pot. The fire consisted mostly of coals glowing a deep red, but they surged orange as a breeze wafted over them. Other than the promise of hot food, and sleep under the shelter of a tent, he wondered why he was here.

This man greatly perplexed me earlier, telling me of things I had not even dreamed. Could they be true? Or is the man insane?—as I often fear am I. But he seemed to know things about me...

The man's voice startled him—

"I am so glad you came tonight. You might have thought me addled, saying the things I did. But I have so much more to tell you —things you cannot have imagined. But first, you must be hungry, so let us give thanks and eat, shall we?"

The man raised his eyes to the starry sky, and stretching his arms out wide, said,

"Blessed are You, O Lord our God, King of the Universe—Who brings forth bread from the earth. It is truly so!"

He put a bowl and a piece of flat bread into the hands of Nahor, and then ladled a portion of the lentils and meat into the bowl. He did the same for himself. They feasted on the simple meal in silence, enjoying the savor of beans and bread. With the pot empty and the last of the lentils sopped up with a final scrap of bread, the man said, "I will be right back."

He returned from the tent with a skin, and pulling its stopper, said, "I have yet a few splashes of wine with which to wash down our meal. Hold out your bowl."

Nahor lifted the small bowl and a stream of red liquid filled it to the brim. The man then half-filled his own bowl with the dregs from the skin. He lifted the bowl to the sky, now dusted with countless stars, and said,

"Blessed are You, O Lord our God, King of the Universe—Creator of the fruit of the vine. It is certainly so!"

Nahor watched him in silence, wondering at these two invocations as the man drank. The man encouraged him, saying, "Please, drink up! Enjoy with me this wonderful substance, provided by the One who created us, for his own good pleasure."

Nahor tasted wine for the first time in many years. And not since his time on the sea with Zabibe had he felt so warmly received—as almost a brother. And by this foreigner—this Iudaean—men not known for their hospitality to those outside their nation. He said to the man,

"I thank you for the treasure of your hospitality to me...to a stranger."

His host said, "We are all strangers in this world, are we not? We may not have met before today, my brother, but you are certainly not a stranger to the One who has followed you all these years. I have heard from him that you met him once before—on the eastern shore of that lake, well to the north. And that he delivered you there, from a perilous state."

Nahor, perplexed yet again by the man's words, said, "And how do you know matters such as these? These things happened long ago, and are known only to me, and to the few who witnessed them."

"It would now make no sense to you, to attempt a mere explanation of this. And I know I have jolted you with the glimmers of what I have already said. So let me start at the beginning..."

62

THE MAN STOKED THE fire and added a little more fuel. He stroked his bushy black beard and said, "I am Sha'ul—a Iudaean born in Tarsus of Cilicia, but I was brought up in Yerushalayim. I conformed to the strictest sect of our religion, living as a Pharisee. I studied under Gamaliel, a man of accomplishment and some fame, and was thoroughly trained in the law of our fathers.

"I had heard many stories of this one called Yeshua. The rabble in our nation proclaimed him a righteous, holy man, someone of note. Perhaps, someone great. But to my peers and my superiors, and to myself as well, the man was obviously a blasphemer—one deprecating our law, and the Temple itself. Some even said he made himself out to be equal with our Great God.

"And beyond all this, our law and our fathers' traditions hold that anyone hung upon a tree is accursed by the Divine One. So when the Roman torture of hanging him on a gibbet stopped his beating heart, the issue was finally laid to rest. Or, so it appeared...

"But his followers, or the Way as they called themselves, did not fade. So I attended Yerushalayim's Synagogue of Cilician Freedmen, where they frequently gathered. There I heard a Hellenistic Iudaean—by the name of Stefan—vigorously declare the dead man Yeshua to be alive. And more, that this Yeshua was none other than our long awaited Meshiak—the Son of Dawid—the one chosen by our Holy God to rescue us from our oppressors, and from all unrighteousness."

Sha'ul shook his head vigorously and raised both hands, as if amazed himself by what he just said, and then continued.

"We knew this to be an absurd impossibility—how could our righteous God choose, as our deliverer, one he had so obviously condemned? So we delivered this Stefan into the court of the Sanhedrin, as we did their Yeshua years previous. Because the charge leveled at Stefan was blasphemy against the Temple, the capital crime lay within the bounds of our sovereign jurisdiction. And since the defendant directly and vehemently provided testimony against himself, the case was clear-cut and no other witnesses were necessary.

"With the verdict decided out of righteous fervor, the court laid aside their outer garments, the better to propel their instruments of execution upon the condemned man. While I guarded their cloaks, Stefan lifted his eyes to the skies, and a mixture of awe and joy filled his face—as if heaven itself had been opened to his view. While stones pummeled him—breaking bones, smashing his face—he strangely spoke forgiveness upon his executioners with his dying breaths."

Sha'ul shook his head again. He lowered his voice and said, "I was zealous for our God, and convinced that I ought to do all that was possible to oppose the name of Yeshua of Nazareth. And that is just what I did in Yerushalayim. On the authority of the chief priests I persecuted the followers of this Way to their death—arresting both men and women and throwing them into prison. And for the verdict of death, I cast my vote against them. Many a time I went from one synagogue to another to have them punished. And I tried to force them to blaspheme."

He stopped for a moment and looked at his hands, turning them from palms to backs, to see if they yet betrayed him with the stain of blood. He then looked to the ground before starting again. Nahor squirmed where he sat, wondering if he should flee, before the man discovered his own sympathies for Yeshua.

"Our pursuit of them was so extreme, many fled to Cilicia and to Syria to hide from our judgements. I was so obsessed with persecuting them that I even hunted them down in the foreign cities to which they fled. I obtained letters from the high priest and the Council, to their associates in Damascus, and went there to bring these people as prisoners back to Yerushalayim, to be punished."

He again paused in the narration, closed his eyes and drew in a deep breath. Nahor sat before him, wide-eyed, ears pricked, hanging on every word. Sha'ul let out the long-held breath and resumed his account.

"And as it happened, I was on one of my journeys to Damascus, armed with the authority and commission of the chief priests. About noon, as I was on the road, I saw a light from heaven—far brighter than the sun—it blazed around me and my companions. We all fell to the ground, and I heard a voice saying to me in Aramaic—'*Sha'ul, Sha'ul, why do you persecute me? It is hard for you to kick against the goads.*'

"My companions were speechless—they saw the light, but did not understand the voice of him who was speaking to me.

"Then I asked, '*Who are you...Lord?*'

"The answer came back to me—'*I am Yeshua...whom you are persecuting.*'

"Of course, such words stunned me beyond all understanding. The darkest, inmost thoughts of my heart, and every vain imagining I ever held, were laid bare in the bright light—publicly exposed—before myself, and more importantly, before the Great God I claimed to serve with pure intentions. The knowledge turned my life inside-out—like skinning a goat.

"Then I asked, '*What shall I do...Lord?*'

'*Now get up and stand on your feet,*' the Lord said, '*and go into Damascus. There you will be told all that you have been assigned to do.*'

"Because the light's excessive brilliance had blinded me, my companions led me by the hand into Damascus, and they left me at the house of a man named Iudas.

"For three days, touching neither food nor water, I lay abandoned in that darkness to meditate on the terrible and merciful truth revealed to me—terrible, because what I thought was my own righteous zeal, in capturing men and women to be put in chains, was, in fact, a horrendous crime against the living leader of their sect, who loved them so. And merciful, because he called me to himself, to make me also one of this Way, rather than to simply slay me on the road, as I so deserved."

He covered his mouth with a hand, and then closing his eyes, rubbed his face with his palms. Nahor leaned close to the Iudaean, devouring his words. Sha'ul sucked in a full breath, letting it out slowly, and said,

"While I sat in that darkness, I had a vision of a man named Ananias, who would lay his hands on me and restore my sight. Unknown to me then, the same Lord, at the same time, spoke to this man named Ananias in private, telling him exactly where to find me, and that he should heal my sight. The man protested to the Lord that I, Sha'ul, was known to them as a relentless hunter and persecutor of his brothers and sisters in the Way. But in the end, the Lord convinced him to find me and release me from my blindness.

"And so the man came to see me. He was a devout observer of the law and highly respected by all the Iudaeans living in exile in Damascus. He stood beside me, and laying his hands on me, said, '*Brother Sha'ul, the Lord—Yeshua, who appeared to you on the road as you were coming here—has sent me so that you may see again, and be filled with his Holy Spirit!*' And at that very moment, something like scales fell from my eyes and I was able to see him.

"Then he said: *The God of our ancestors has chosen you to know his will. And to see the Righteous One, and to hear words from his mouth. You will be his witness to all people of what you have seen and heard. And now what are you waiting for?*'

"I got up, and was immersed in water as an outward sign of his washing my guilt away. And I called on his name—the name of Yeshua. He joined himself to my life in a profound and elemental way. After taking some food, I regained my strength.

"Then, led by his Spirit, I came into your own land, for a season of instruction by him, for meditation on his word, and for transmitting this astonishing and excellent news to whomever might cross my path. And just as he said, he has made known his will for me. I have heard words from his own mouth, revealing the depths of marvelous truth laid down so long ago through his law, his prophets, and the sacred writings."

Both men sat in silence before the dwindling fire. Sha'ul waited for his words to sink into Nahor's understanding. Nearly whispering, Nahor said,

"You have...seen him yourself? And heard him speak?"

Sha'ul leaned closer to him and said, "Yes, it is as you say. And I am not the only one. Our Meshiak—Yeshua—died for the sake of *our* wrongdoings, just as it was written. He was buried, and came to life again on the third day, according to what was written. He appeared first to Kepha, and after him, to the rest of his twelve followers. After that, he appeared to more than five hundred of our brothers and sisters together. Then he appeared to his brother Ya'akob, and then to all the leaders of the Way. But last of all—as if to one untimely born—he appeared also to me. For I am the least of his followers and I am not worthy to be called by him, because I hounded and woefully mistreated the ones he loves. But by this undeserved gift of God, I am whatever I am."

A loud *pop!* in the dying fire burst a flurry of sparks upward into the darkness. Nahor's pulse raced and he felt as if his head would lift from his shoulders.

376

63

NAHOR FELT THE STONE of his heart crack, as if dropped from a great height, to crash upon a huge and impervious boulder. What he *thought* was his life, drained from the broken fragments of his core, like dark blood running in streams, down over the great rock, seeping into the earth. He sensed his old life ebbing away. He lay upon the rock, dying.

And he heard a voice—not that of Sha'ul, but one he recognized from many years previous. The voice said,

I told you then, I would not forsake you and we would meet again. That our fellowship would be sweet. As you trusted me then, so trust me now. I have accomplished all, so you may enter my rest. You have yielded up your broken nature—you have given up that death you once thought life—so now be filled by my own True Life, and walk in its newness, forever.

Tears of astonishment, and of joy, fell from Nahor's eyes. His physical strength drained from his body and he dropped from the stone on which he sat, falling to the ground. The rich, crimson blood of new life surged into him—it filled his empty heart, brimming over. He stammered,

"Yeshua—*my Yeshua*—I had not an inkling of who You were. You are certainly the Mercy—that *Great Mercy*, of whom my master Aslah spoke with reverence. My life is now in You. And You in me. Do with me as You will. Make of me what You desire."

He felt a hand on his shoulder, and then it gripped him under his arm. Sha'ul lifted him to his feet and embraced him as a long-lost brother. He said,

"Welcome to the family of those purchased from death with the costliest substance in this universe—the life-blood poured out by Yeshua! He has given you a heart of flesh, for your heart of stone. And more than that, you have been adopted by the Great-and-Only-God-of-All-That-Is, to be one of his children—and an adopted brother of your Lord, Yeshua."

Over the next seven days, Sha'ul poured into Nahor an understanding of the oracles entrusted by The Mercy to the children of Abraham. The oracles of more than a thousand years testified to the Coming One, who would rescue the sons and daughters of flesh from their broken lives. On a warm afternoon, at the end of the seven days, Sha'ul said,

"Now is the time for me to return to Damascus. These two years, I have stirred up enough trouble among the religion of your people here. Yeshua's Spirit has shown me I must go back to where he first apprehended me, to continue in earnest the path and the work he has laid out for me. And you must begin your own pursuit of his will for your life. There is much to be done, as the crop waits ready in the field, already heavy with the fruits of harvest."

The pangs of parting jolted Nahor, and he felt his heart would break. A stone lodged in his throat and he could not speak. Sha'ul saw his distress and, gripping his shoulder, encouraged him.

"Though of different peoples, we are now of one brotherhood— the same blood flows within our veins. We are captives and servants of the same Merciful One—the Most High—who will never let go of us. We may never meet again in this life, but he will certainly gather us together when he makes all things new at the end. The same Lord Yeshua who commands my life, will command your own. He will guide and protect, and provide for your every breath. He will take you places yet undreamed by you, and bless your life in ways unimagined."

A peace rapidly replaced fear of abandonment and Nahor said, "I will dearly miss your companionship, brother Sha'ul, but I know he will continue to walk with me. He has not brought me this far, to let me fall again. And may he guide and use you, as you trust in him. May his face continue to shine upon you, and may he grant you his peace."

Sha'ul looked to the heavens and grinned as he received the blessing pronounced upon him. He gestured behind him and said,

"These two tents and everything in them are now yours. Do with the property what you will. The man who, for two years, instilled in me the practical skills of making these portable dwellings, left me his property as he lay dying. And I now leave it to you. Inside, you will find two testaments—the first is the tent-maker's witnessed document, leaving the properties to me, the second is mine to you. As you gain this, all I ask is that you remember the poor."

Nahor said, "Having walked among them, and shared in their distress, I cannot but help to remember those poor souls. I will certainly serve them as he leads me."

The two men embraced long. Then Sha'ul slung a water-skin over his shoulder, and on his back, a bag holding a few loaves of flat bread and some scrolls. He walked off to the north, to Damascus, as Nahor watched with tears.

64

AND SO IT WAS, that just as the Nabatu take their name from the *waters bubbling up* in the desert, so living waters bubbled up afresh within Nahor. Without a family to call his own, and now at odds with the religious foundations of his countrymen, he set out to find the path his Rescuer had blazed for him.

Selling one tent and its furnishings, he prepared to use the gain for assisting the unfortunates he would meet. The other tent he would use as his home base, while he learned to lean upon his Great Benefactor and Mercy, and as he learned to listen to the Spirit of his Lord and Rescuer.

He also soon learned that his proclamation of the rescuing work of his Yeshua—and his life beyond the grave—would most often be met by sneers and jeers. But unlike the time he sought out his six brothers, the living Spirit of Yeshua now surged through him, to encourage and carry him forward.

Nahor found the greatest openness to the message he carried, among those living on the bare margins of his people—the widows, orphans, and destitute; the blind, the maimed, the dying. He tended to their needs, and told them of the One who loved them, and who offered them true and unending life.

Within a month he sold the second tent, to disperse the money among the needy, and to throw himself fully upon The Mercy—taking to the road to be led of his Spirit.

Somewhere east of Raqmu, and hours before the sun's rising, Nahor sat on the ground with his head bowed, speaking with his Great Mercy.

"I can never know the depths of Your great love for me, but what I know fills me beyond myself—it overflows what I can hold! And yet, I want to know more. I still see Yeshua's face, with Your own glorious radiance pouring out of him. He is the essence of this love from You. May I, also, be an expression of this great love."

He continued sitting in silence. And in the center of the silence came a quiet voice—a whisper—saying,

Set out...

"Set out, my Lord?"

Yes, set out...on the road north from Raqmu, toward Madaba. East of the Salt Sea.

"East of the Salt Sea?"

Engage there a caravan. Led by a man in a green cap. I will then tell you the rest.

He put on his sandals, girded his cloak about him and slung a water-skin and bag on his back. The bag held some dates, a lump of goat cheese and three pieces of flat bread. He set his feet upon the road leading north and in three days' time made his way to the region east of the sea.

At dawn, with the food consumed and only a splash of water left in the skin, he sat and asked his Merciful Abba what he should do.

"I have done as You said—and I wait here for further word. I have no more food, and I will soon thirst, my Lord. Will You bring me more sustenance here, or should I go elsewhere?"

He sat in the sun until it stood straight up in the blue sky. He pulled the hood of his cloak over his head to shade it from the merciless heat. And the small voice returned.

The time is now full. They come from the west—from the sea. Greet the man in the lead with your peace. In the sand before you lies a silver coin. It will glimmer in the noon's bright light. Take the coin and offer to buy as much of their product as it will bring.

In a short time, a fine gray horse rounded the base of a hill near the road. On its back rode a man wearing a cap the color of new spring grass. A train of camels trailed behind him, two-dozen in length. As they came to the road the man raised his eyebrows and nodded his head on seeing Nahor. Drawing near, he slowed his horse and held up his hand to halt the caravan. The camels' handlers whistled to stop their animals. Nahor stood and said, "Peace and mercy be upon you, and upon your company!"

The man in the cap said, "You are out here alone, young man? This is not the place for idle pursuits. Only cobras, coneys, and scorpions call this place home! Do you request transport from us?"

"I look not for a ride—but for something to buy."

The man shook his head and said, "To buy? We have nothing you need. Only the Egyptians buy what we carry—the makings of eternal life, or so they say. We could spare you a few morsels of food, and a skin of water, if you have need."

"I have had no instruction concerning food, but yes, I do intend to buy your goods. Whatever it is you have to sell."

The man tilted his head, narrowing his eyes. "Now this is a peculiar matter—you know not what we transport, nor have a use for what we sell—yet you are ready to purchase. I fear the sun has poached your wits, young man!"

Laughing, he turned to his companions and they laughed with him. He faced Nahor again and said, "How much will you buy, then? We deal in luxury goods, and our product is dear. I hope you have plenty of silver in your sack, there."

They all laughed again. Nahor looked at the sand before his feet, and saw the merest glint of sunlight. He bent down and raked his fingers through the sand, dredging up a large silver coin—worth four drachma. His heart leapt at the vision of silver shining in his palm. He held it up for the horseman to see and said,

"What will this tetradrachm buy me?"

"What? Did you drop that coin earlier? A lucky find to come upon it again! Four drachma? Let me see it..."

He dismounted his horse and took the coin from Nahor. He studied it carefully, and slightly bit the edge with his back teeth.

"Seems genuine enough. And all the way from Syracuse. I always liked this face of Arethusa—enough beauty to give a man dreams out here in the desert. Well, let me think...four drachma...hmmm... you know, this bitumen fetches a high price in Gaza and Rhinocolura...even more in Alexandria. But for a fellow traveler...follow me."

He returned the coin to Nahor, walked back to the nearest camel and told its driver to kneel the beast. He opened the lid of the basket bound to the camel's saddle. Irregular chunks of bitumen filled the container—sand, grit and gravel embedded in their black-tar surfaces. He grabbed the apex of a large, triangular piece, and twisting it round and round, tore off a piece about the size of a walnut. The fresh-torn surface hung the pungent aroma of tar in the air. He turned to Nahor and extended the piece to him.

"Here—this is what your tetradrachm will bring. It does not appear to be much, but I am actually giving you quite a bargain—I could sell this piece for much more at the coast."

Nahor extended his hand to take the piece, but the man said, "I will hold your silver—with the face of the beautiful nymph—before I hand over my merchandise."

He gave him the coin and the man laid the ball of tar in Nahor's empty palm.

"Are you sure we cannot give you transport to the nearest caravanserai? Or do your plans take you the other direction?"

"I have no plans. I have not yet heard which way I should go."

The man looked up and down the road, and seeing no one, said, "Not heard? From whom? You will be waiting a long time, to hear from anyone out here. But I suppose that is your own business."

The man mounted his horse, straightened his green cap and shook his head. He leaned in the saddle toward Nahor and said, "I have met many a strange man out here among the dunes and rocks, but none have matched the oddity you possess. May that black goo serve you well. And go in peace—wherever that may be."

He gestured forward, and the camel drivers whistled their animals to proceed. Nahor looked at the piece of bitumen in his hand and wondered how it would fill his belly. Before he could ask about it, the whisper returned.

Tuck your cloak in your belt and run to Madaba. Go in haste and do not stop until you find the slave market.

Carried on the strength and sustenance of the Great Mercy he ran until the sun set at his left hand. He continued running through the night, and beyond the dawn. He ran the next day until mid-morning, when he approached the city of Madaba. At the edge of the town he encountered some men and asked them the way to the slave market.

"Go to the city's center and take the Straight-street south. You will come to an open square with a small cistern, the market to one side. Merchandise may already be on the block. The lower quality flesh is offered first, with the best goods held until later. But you don't look as if you could afford either—perhaps, you wish to sell yourself!" They laughed.

He thanked the man for his guidance and rushed to the market.

65

A DUSTY, GRITTY PLAZA emerged from behind mud-plastered buildings along the street. In its midst lay a pool about four-paces square, bounded by a low wall of dressed stones. A woman lowered a large, clay jar into the cool water, to fill it.

On the far side of the plaza gathered a group of about thirty men. Voices rang out, echoing in the plaza, and the salesman ratcheted the bidding upward. A few buyers responded, but the bidding soon ceased. Nahor drew near the back of the crowd.

"Come, come, brothers—you act as though I have nothing of value here! Yes, I will grant you she does not look like much at the moment, but with a minimum of care and cleaning, she could serve you well. The bidding now stands at the embarrassing low price of just a hundred and fifty drachma. Who will start the bidding again —at a more reasonable price?"

A man near the front said, "I can go a hundred and fifty-five."

"A hundred and fifty-five it is...now who will counter?"

"One hundred and sixty. And not a bronze coin more."

"Brothers, you insult me, and clearly have no understanding of the quality I offer you."

Nahor pushed his way into the middle of the crowd. Between the heads of the men in front of him, he saw glimpses of the auctioneer and the item for sale. Next to the man, a woman stood on the stone auction block. She wore filthy rags, her dull, black hair tangled about her like a dust storm. Her grimy, sooty face looked down. A stout cord of palm fiber bound her hands together at her waist.

One man said, "You talk a good sale, but we don't see much here. Conclude the sale and let's move on to better merchandise…"

"Oh, my brothers, let us not be too hasty—the day is yet young, and we have plenty of time to linger over the value of my offerings. Give me a moment…"

He stepped down from the platform and jerked the cord binding his captive. She stumbled from the block and struggled to keep up as he pulled her to the square's cistern. He grabbed a handful of hair on the back of her head and forced her down, submerging her head in the water. She bucked against his effort, bubbles rising and breaking around her head. With his other hand he thoroughly scrubbed her face underwater and then lifted her up. Water streamed from her face and sprayed from her mouth and nose. She gasped, lungs heaving, desperate for air. The man dragged her back to the auction and prodded her to stand again on the block. Grabbing a fistful of her dripping hair, he pulled her head back, offering the gathered buyers a view of her face.

"Now, what do you think, brothers? She has not too bad of a face, does she? And I hear she once came from a noble family to the south —silk merchants, they say—a woman of fine breeding. Now what do you offer? Two hundred?"

The woman's face, now somewhat cleaned of grime, displayed a purplish bruise ringing one eye, and the lower lip swollen and red.

"I could maybe go…two hundred."

"That is more like it! Do I hear two-fifty?"

The men mumbled to each other, discussing the merits and flaws of the woman before them. One spoke up.

"She may be good for grinding grain and washing my feet, but my wife is old and worn out. I look for one to warm my bed and cheer my nights."

"Ah, brothers—you have come to the right place—and at just the right time! I acquired her recently from a brothel near Bostra, where she had been sold into captivity for the great debt she incurred there. The master of the house said she served him well while in his employ. And he said she could sing like a bird! Now what am I offered?"

Nahor looked closely at the slave-woman's face. Behind the swollen and beaten features he thought he saw a face he once knew.

Could it be? Is this the face of...The Song? Is this Margani? She cannot be a slave! I cannot allow this to continue...but what can I do?

He jerked his head to the left and to the right, but there was no one else to intervene on her behalf. He felt his blood surge into his face, he clenched his fists, and his pulse pounded. He was desperate to flee with her, to take her away from such humiliation, such shame.

A man near the back of the crowd said, "I will buy no swine-in-a-sack—show us what we are buying!"

The auctioneer grasped the front of her threadbare tunic in his hands, and rent the garment from top to bottom, splitting it open and baring her body to the buyers. She fought to turn her body away from the crowd but his tight grip restrained her, forcing her to remain exposed in full public view. She turned her face away so as not to see the eyes of the crowd of men, their stares roving over her most private features.

"Now imagine this face without the bruise—atop the flesh you now see—can you not imagine the pleasurable moments you will enjoy? Now what am I offered?"

"I will give three hundred."

"Four hundred over here!"

"That is more like it, my brothers! What else do I hear?"

"I have five hundred, in Roman coin!"

"I want her for six!"

In great distress, Nahor looked down and opened his hand that held the ball of bitumen. The quiet whisper came again to his mind.

Break open this piece of tar, which lay so long in the depths of waters, hiding its treasure. For this is why you are here…to buy back another treasure, that lies hid in this heart now broken…

His pulse raced as he began pulling away the tar, tearing open the lump. In its center hid a small, hard object. As he tore away the remaining black bits, a greenish-white, stone ring emerged—a dark green nugget its carved gem. His heart sped, and he held it high above his head, shouting,

"This is a ring of royal pedigree—made in the farthest east for the finger of a queen! I offer this jewel for the one on the block!"

The man next to him said, "May I have a look at it, sir?"

The man inspected it and declared to the crowd, "My trade is in fine things, and this article is one of a kind. I will offer nine hundred drachma for it."

Others shouted out ever higher bids for the ring, taking their attention from the sale of the woman. The auctioneer rapped his mallet repeatedly to reclaim their attention and shouted,

"No, the ring is mine! He first offered it for this woman—you all heard him. Is that not true, sir?"

Nahor acknowledged the offer, and so the exchange was made. Nahor used the salesman's janbiya to cut away the cord binding his purchase and he removed his own outer cloak to hide her nakedness, to cover her shame. He helped Margani down from the block and escorted her from the market. Behind them, the auctioneer held the ring high, saying,

"This is truly a remarkable piece—the only one like it in the world! Look at it closely—it bears the marks of royal provenance. Who will start the bidding at one-thousand drachma? What do you say?"

66

AND SO IT WAS, that Nahor hired out his services of a strong back and shoulders to a businessman in Madaba. The man needed to move his products—lubunah and myrrh—from the packs of camels into the security of his warehouses. In return, Margani would enter the care of the man's household. They would dress her wounds, clothe and feed her. In a week, Nahor returned to her.

The man's wife showed him to the courtyard of their home, where Margani was sitting in the morning sun. As they entered, the woman said to her,

"The man who bought you and paid for your care has come to see you."

Margani rose from where she was seated, and bowed, waiting for Nahor to seat himself on a bench nearby. He said,

"Please—sit. You look much better now. I trust your health is returning with good care? And I see your beauty returning as well."

She hesitated before sitting again, and then, with her eyes cast down, said,

"I thank you for taking me from that place. And I appreciate your kindness in providing for my care here. I will serve you well. Will you take me into your service here in Madaba, or elsewhere?"

Nahor shook his head as he said, "Into my service? So you think I own you?"

His words bewildered her. She raised her gaze but looked at him only from the corners of her eyes, and said, "Of course, you own me. I heard the seller-of-flesh strike his gavel, and you took me from the market. Are you trying to trick me?"

He lifted a hand to his mouth to stifle a laugh and said, "You were bought, not with my own riches—for I own little more than nothing—but you were bought with the same riches of the one who purchased me—that Great Mercy."

She pursed her lips and opened wide her eyes, looking directly at him.

"So then, you are a slave, also?—just acting in your master's name, to buy me for himself?"

Nahor laughed out loud, "Yes, that is *exactly* it! I had not quite thought of it in those terms, but you have said it yourself better than I."

With the knowledge they were on equal footing, she raised herself up a bit, and spoke more forcefully. "And what is your master—*our* master—like? Will he act cruelly toward me, like those who owned me before? I suppose that name you use—Great Mercy—is one of irony?"

"Oh, no—to say he is the Great Mercy has barely begun to describe his gentle and tender ways. He has bought you—and bought me—simply because he loves us."

She tilted her head sideways, questions in her eyes.

"You mystify me with these words! You say he loves us? Yet he buys us and keeps us as his slaves—because he loves us?"

"No, no…you do not understand—he did not buy you to *keep* you a slave—but to set you free."

"To set me free? I have not heard of such a thing! You mean he wastes his wealth, to simply let his property go?"

"He considers it no waste—though the price was far greater than you can know—to buy the freedom of those he loves. I know it makes no sense, but nevertheless, there it is."

"You say he bought me for my freedom. You mean I can just walk away—of my own free will?"

"Yes, that is exactly what I am saying."

"I can just walk away, and he will not pursue me, to reclaim his property?"

"No, if you walk away, he most likely *will* pursue you—with his love for you."

"It sounds as if...I am still a slave then."

"Well...yes...and no. He buys us back, to turn us loose, so we will continue to turn to him of our own free will and love."

She raised her hands, shaking her head, then turned her eyes to the sky and said,

"This is more than I can understand..."

"Margani, you are not alone. This is more than *anyone* can understand. All one can do is simply receive it. We will speak again of these things, another time."

She dropped her shoulders and lowered her head. After a time of silence, she lifted her face, looking directly at Nahor. In a low voice, she asked,

"And did you call me Margani? How do you know that name? The slave merchant did not use it of me...and you have not asked me."

Nahor looked at the ground and spoke in a soft voice to her. "I know that name—your name—because I once knew you. For one, brief night. And then you were gone..."

Her eyes blinked and opened wide, as if she awoke for the first time that day.

"...and I last saw you from the height of the unfinished work at the crossroads in Raqmu, when you rode your roan horse at a fast sprint north—to Bostra. Your abba said you would start a new and prosperous life there. I borrowed a horse to pursue you, but I took a wrong turn and came to a dead end—where I began to realize the fool that I was."

Her heart skipped a beat, and then sped faster. Her voice breaking, she asked,

"You are...Nahor?...son of Geram?"

"I am...or was. Then I became Shamir, son of Aslah. And now I am—and always will be—Nahor—adopted son of the Great God and Mercy.'

Knowing with whom she now spoke, her breathing shallowed and accelerated. She could not catch her breath. Her mind staggered, and finally recovering enough to speak, she said, "I left my home in such haste...because you affected me...profoundly. I knew I could not control my feelings for you. So I left my heart behind in Raqmu, fleeing with my body and mind to a new place, hoping to drown myself in my business, and in the life of the royal court. But I could not."

She bent over from her waist and buried her face in her hands. Nahor closed his eyes and sat back against the wall of the courtyard. He paused, thinking, before speaking again.

"Margani, you have long been in my thoughts—and yearnings. Though I fled to the farthest ends of the world to rid myself of your memory."

He stood, and with a gentle touch, laid his hand briefly on her shoulder. "Farewell" he said, and left the courtyard.

67

NAHOR VISITED MARGANI DAILY, and she inquired more concerning this Great God and Mercy whom he claimed as his master. By the end of a week, she claimed this Yah'weh—the Self-existent One, and Abba of Yeshua—as her own Lord and master, yielding her life to the will of his love. Together, Nahor and Margani rejoiced in the newness of her life.

At the end of the following week, Nahor took her hand in his, and before witnesses they pledged their devotion and unyielding commitment to each other. They set out for Raqmu, to see what their Lord had for them in that city, and to tell her own abba of her rescue, and of the great mercy visited upon her.

In the third month of the intermingling of their lives, Margani sang a new song. Her womb blossomed, and carried the fruit of a new life. The life grew, ripening within, and her song became a praise to the One who delivered her from desperation and bondage, into the light of freedom and joy. It became a lullaby to the life she carried and sustained. She sang,

"O, blessed be You, O Light and Life

*Who hides Your treasure in secret places
and waters in the sand.*

*You find the one lost in the waste,
Your little lamb a-wandering,
      and carries her out to peace
      and safety and fields of grazing.*

*O, High and Blessed One,
      Who satisfies my soul,
May I never forget
      the beauty of Your face,
      the love of Your heart,
      or the strength of Your right arm.*

*O, blessed be You, O Light and Life,
Who hides Your treasure in secret places
      and waters in the sand."*

But in her sixth month, the season changed and an unexpected storm assailed the home of Nahor and Margani. A wind rose up, rushing upon the sheltering boughs of her womb, which cast its fruit before its time. Great sorrow filled both their hearts as they buried the tiny child in the hills east of Gaia, trusting her brief life to their Lord. Nahor pulled Margani close, and she buried her face in his chest. She wept freely, her bitter tears wetting his robe. She cried to him,

"Oh my Love!—though I had been through much pain before I knew you, I did not know how terrible it could be...loving, and then losing someone! How will I ever continue?"

He pulled her closer and smoothed her hair. He looked up to the sky, trying to see some blue in the gray slate above them. But the clouds did not part. He whispered her name,

"Margani, *My Song*...this will always be the great cost of love—the breaking of one's heart. The Mercy himself knows this all too well. His heart now breaks with ours. And his great heart of love will heal your own. Let's go to our home."

The next day, upon returning from his work at the quarry, Nahor found a small desert rose sprouting from the crevice in a rock, and blooming out of season. He picked the bloom, as scarlet as a brilliant sunrise, and carried it home to Margani. Without a word, he watched her from behind as she ground barley on a stone before their tent. After several strokes of the grinding stone, she paused. He saw her head drop and her body heave with silent sobs before she continued. With a quiet joy in his voice, he said,

"Look what has grown from the crack in a rock—it is a small token of his love for you. A small mercy from the Great Mercy."

She turned to see the flower, caught her breath, and carefully took it from his hand. She held it to her breast and wrapped her other arm around him, weeping tears of joy, mixed with those of grief.

In time, her grief began to subside, but the womb of Margani would not be opened again.

Into a light blue sky, the morning sun rose with promise in its wings. On the earth far below, Margani emerged from the cleft of Raqmu's Grand Thaniya and continued her walk to the public fountain, south of the royal palaces. She carried two water-skins for lugging a day's worth of water back to their tent near Gaia. Though a spring and its cistern lay closer to home, she used the journey to make new acquaintances in Raqmu. She eagerly sought every opportunity to serve others with the Great Mercy's love.

Twenty women already waited their turns to draw out water in double-handled ceramic amphorae, or in waterproof bags made from the skins of young goats. Blocks of white stone formed the waist-high walls of the octagonal pool, and a stream of water gushed from a ceramic pipe, splashing and gurgling. The fountain's overflow filled the water system's cisterns and pools farther downstream. A few of the women rested, sitting on the walls, sharing with each other local news and gossip.

The Roman merchants living in Raqmu called the fountain the *nymphaeum*—the local abode of the water-nymph Undine. But the Hellenes in the area disputed the claim and attributed the flowing water to the *naiad* Castalia, who, they said, bored a subterranean channel all the long way from her primary fountain at Delphi.

Dressed in black from head to ankles, a woman sat in the dust a short distance from the fountain. Her cheeks and mouth sagged, her eyes dull and without the sparkle of life. Though women walked in front of her, she looked straight through them as if they did not exist. She lifted her hand and slowly stroked her face from brow to chin.

Margani gradually moved forward with the line, her attention fixed on the woman.

Is she ill? Or hungry? How may I help her, my Lord?

As she drew nearer the woman, deep crevices and wrinkles in her face betrayed her age, and life of sorrow. Margani left the line and stooped down by the old woman. She asked her,

"Can I help you in any way? How may I serve you?"

The woman slowly turned her face toward Margani, surprised that a young woman addressed her. Words, dragging themselves up through layers of pain, finally found their way through her parted lips.

"Help...me? No one...can help...me. They are gone. Both gone. Now they take everything else."

"Who is gone?"

"Wagilu...gone twenty-two years. No husband these twenty-two years. But I feed and raise my son—my little Amiri—by weaving rugs every day. We kept our tent those twenty-two years."

"Does your boy still honor his amma, does he yet provide for you in your age?"

"He cannot. His body lies buried. Somewhere in the sand to the north."

Margani sat in the dust beside the woman, and wrapped her arm around her. She looked into the old woman's face and said,

"Your grief becomes my own. It is too much to carry on your shoulders alone. Please tell me what happened to your Amiri."

She looked away from Margani into the distance, and said, "When that Iudaean Antipas dishonored the daughter of our King by taking his brother's wife—Herodias, they call her—our King, He-Who-Loves-His-People, took up arms against him. He won the battle for the honor of his daughter, and the honor of his people... but my son lay dead on the field of battle. A mighty victory for the kingdom. A great loss for me—and for the young woman to whom he was betrothed. So now...I wait for death."

Margani pulled the woman closer and encircled her with her other arm. "You said, *They take everything else.* What did you mean?"

The old woman took in a deep breath and let it out in pulsing sobs.

"My husband's brothers have now taken my tent, without taking me—violating our law. And I have nothing left with which to take them to the judge. My husband and my son are gone! My home is gone...and justice flees from me. I long for death's sweet embrace."

Margani leaned her head on the woman's shoulder, and said, "There *is* One who yet loves you, and will take care of you. And he now whispers to my heart that I will become like a daughter to you, and my husband will be your son. You will live under the protection of our tent, and live out your days as our own Amma. What is your name?"

"I am Hina."

The woman's frail body shuddered, then relaxed into Margani's embrace. Her chest convulsed as if sobbing deeply, but no sound came from her.

"That is a beautiful name, *Hina—an unexpected gift.*"

She helped the woman to her feet, and filled the two water-skins. As they returned to the tent of Nahor, the old woman wept freely and clung to Margani.

68

AND SO IT WAS, in three months' time, Nahor walked into Raqmu on his way to the quarry beyond the Head-of-the-Camel. He made a modest income by selecting stone for various projects, and by hiring crews to cut and dress the stone to specification. On this morning, he passed near one of the refuse dumps on the edge of the city, and saw some movement near the base of the pile. Though the stench of carcasses and rotting scraps of food nearly overwhelmed him, he stopped and watched again for the movement.

For a while, he saw nothing. Then a small, grimy face peered around the edge of the pile. And upon seeing him, hid again. The process continued several times. Like stalking prey, Nahor crept silently around the far side of the garbage dump. From there, he saw a tiny, naked girl, of no more than three or four years. Her filthy, skinny body was strewn with scrapes and scabs, her hair a tangled chaos. Unaware of his presence, she stretched out her neck, looking around the pile, trying to see where Nahor had gone.

"Little girl—you must be hungry."

Startled, she jumped, stumbled, and fell into the stinking pile. She scrambled to her feet and retreated to the far side, again playing a game of hide-then-peek.

"I will be back, little girl. If you wait here, you shall have your fill of food."

Nahor returned to his tent, to tell Margani of the lost girl. She said, "If you continue to your work at the quarry, I will go to the garbage heap alone. She will more likely come to a woman than a man. Amma Hina—will you wait here for me?—I may be returning with a granddaughter for you!"

With two loaves of flat bread and a small water-skin, she went to the midden and found the little girl, peering from behind the pile, just as Nahor had said. Margani sat on the ground nearby and hummed a lullaby, pretending not to see the girl. Knowing the girl watched her every move, she nibbled at the bread and said,

"Oh, such tasty bread—on such a fine morning! It is a shame I have to eat alone. Won't someone share it with me?"

She cast a piece of it in the child's direction, the morsel landing halfway between them. Again she hummed the soothing melody. From the edge of her vision, she saw the tiny form dart from the pile, retrieve the scrap, and scamper back.

Over more than an hour, she repeated the process many times, leaving each morsel closer to herself. Finally, she held a piece out in the open palm of her hand, and in moments it was snatched away. She said,

"Little Talia—my little lamb—can you sit in my lap, and enjoy this bread with me? I have cool, clean water here, also."

There was no movement for a long time. Then, with Margani looking away from the place of hiding, the girl emerged and crept toward her. She stood beside the seated woman for several minutes, until she gradually slid into her lap from the side. Margani said nothing, but held out another morsel to her, and then offered her sips from the water-skin.

"We need a little lamb at our house, Talia—will you be our little lamb?"

The girl said nothing, but curled up in her lap and fell asleep. Margani cradled her arms around the scabby little body and rocked her as she slept. From Margani's eyes, tears of joy fell upon the sleeping child, washing away some of the dirt.

In the tent of Nahor and Margani, Talia grew and thrived. The family rejoiced the day she first smiled, and then laughed. On another, they celebrated again as she began to speak.

Over little more than two years, the small family continued to grow as Nahor, Margani, and Hina rescued five more children—orphans, runaways, and abandoned. Each child brought their own troubles, and each time, the family's Divine Provider brought enough love to cover them all.

At the beginning of their third year, at the half-year autumn pilgrimage of 'umrah, Nahor took a shortcut through the edge of Fortune Hill. He was on his way to inspect a project near the summer palace, perched atop the high mountain west of Raqmu. As he passed behind the fine estate of a wealthy Roman merchant, a muffled, nearly inaudible whimper floated on the air.

He stopped to listen, but the sound faded. Hearing nothing more than the low whisper of a light breeze, he continued on his journey. But in two more steps, the sound returned. He looked in all directions, but saw no one, and nothing of note. Then it came again, this time more of a cry. Walking this way, and that, he stumbled along, desperate in his attempt to locate the cry.

The sound seemed louder as he neared a good-sized, lidded clay pot sitting on the ground. Hoping to not be accused of stealing or tampering with someone else's property, he looked all around him before stooping to lift the pot's lid.

As soon as the pot was open, the cry stopped. Peering into the contents, all he could see was something like a pile of dark, bloody meat. And then, the pile moved. He jumped back, dropping the lid, which clattered and broke on a rock. The muffled cry began again.

He stared more intently into the pot, and saw a wee, bloody face, nearly hidden below the bloody mess. A tiny hand poked out of the pile, struggling with desperation. An infant, only hours old, fought for its life, nearly buried below the mass of its own afterbirth.

Nahor reached into the pot, carefully searching below the afterbirth for a secure grasp on the child's body. He lifted the blood-streaked baby girl from the pot, her life-cord still dangling from her belly and yet attached to the afterbirth. He snatched his janbiya from his belt and severed the cord. A fold of his cloak formed her first blanket as he tucked her close to himself and raced home.

"Margani! Amma Hina! We have another child! I found her in a pot—abandoned to exposure."

The family ran from the two tents, gathering to see the bloody infant, bawling and cradled in Nahor's right arm. Margani nearly wept, saying,

"How can they throw out a treasure like this?—to die from exposure, or hunger—or to be torn by animals!"

Hina shook her head, and said,

"I have heard some say they even resort to the brutality of slaying them through horrors unspeakable—as they yet grow in the *safety* of their ammas' wombs. Can there truly be a Great Mercy if he allows such atrocities?"

Margani implored Nahor with her eyes, asking,

"The child is so young, how will we care for it? How will we stave its hunger?"

He stood silent, having no answers, but Hina spoke up.

"I know of a woman we can hire to nurse the babe for now. In order to pay her, you need not feed me in the meantime—I will manage somehow. And I will show Margani how to suckle the child to bring in her milk. In a few weeks, she will be able to nourish the child, as if she birthed this tiny daughter herself."

Nahor assured her,

"No, Amma Hina, you will continue to eat in our household—we will make do with what our Lord provides, as he always has."

In time, the child thrived at the breast of Margani, who raised her as if born from her own womb.

In all, they raised thirteen children in the nurture and admonition of their Lord. The children grew and prospered, finding their own mates and founding their own families, producing for Nahor and Margani, sixty-five grandchildren, and an untold number of great-grandchildren.

Amma Hina grew old and died, surrounded by the many who loved her. Her family mourned her loss and they buried her east of Raqmu.

Several years later a fever passed through the region and Margani succumbed to its claim on her life. Her thirteen children gathered around her death bed, and she pronounced upon them blessings of the Great Mercy, and she committed them to his care. At her final breath, Nahor kissed the lips of The Song for the last time. He wept greatly at the passing of her spirit from this life, into the glorious one to come. But he wept not as those who have no hope. And he buried his wife in the soil, east of Raqmu.

And so it was that Nahor grew old and full of years. He outlived twelve of his thirteen children, and half of his sixty-five grandchildren. He watched generations come, and generations go.

69

SABAH CLOSED HIS MOUTH, and the echoes of his last words died away between the rock walls of the thaniya. Amru prodded the dying fire with the end of his staff, sending a shower of sparks into the night sky. Timrah asked,

"Are you done for the night, Sabah?"

The old man closed his eyes as he drew a deep breath, and let out a long sigh.

"I am...entirely done."

Amru glanced up from stoking the fire, and Timrah's eyes bugged out.

"Entirely done? What do you mean? You cannot truly be finished. That was the end? Your ending was no more lively than the beginning! Although I must say, once you were in the middle of things, this was one of the more engaging epics I have heard over the years. Which of the traveling poets recited to you this wonderful yarn?"

Before the old man could respond, Amru interrupted.

"No, no, dear brother—Sabah told the tale with too much feeling for it to simply be the retelling of another's epic!—it is of his own invention—is it not, Sabah?"

The twins looked at the man, waiting for his answer. After a long pause, he opened his eyes and said, "It is neither of my own invention, nor that of some other man more clever than myself."

Speechless, the two stared at Sabah, then at each other, then back at the old man. With one voice they asked, "What?—how can that be?!"

The old man smiled. "The Great Mercy wrote his own story upon my life—for, *Man of the Tombs...I was.*"

As the truth of the matter seeped into the brothers, silence fell heavy upon them. No one spoke, or moved, for some time. Amru finally noticed flames growing from the end of his staff, so he jerked it from the fire, beating it on the ground to quench the flames. He sputtered, "You, then...are Nahor?—Shamir? No, you just say this for dramatic effect!"

"I assure you, my brothers, this was truly the sum of my life—just as surely as I sit with you now at the hospitality of your fire."

Timrah stroked his beard a few times, then turned his head to look at Sabah out of the corners of his eyes. He turned back toward the old man, cocked his head and said, "But surely, you made up the parts about the demon Ashmedai...and about this rescuer—what did you call him? Yeshua?"

Nahor's smile grew to a wide grin as he said,

"Of the entire story, those portions stand apart as the *most* true and significant. As I stood on the shore of that lake, wrecked in my hopeless plight, Yeshua stood there with me, and with a word, rescued me from that sad state."

Amru pulled hard at his beard, tearing some of the hairs from his chin.

"But...you said the man was killed...at the hands of the Romans—and who knows killing better than they? And, then...that the man was later found to be alive? Hah! That is surely an invention for a twist in the plot!"

Nahor's smile faded, he leaned toward his hosts and lowered his voice, speaking with all gravity.

"*That*, my brothers, is the most wondrous matter of all—truly a twist in the plot of all history—that the Great Mercy, the Great God Who-Created-All-That-Is, should send the One from the very center of his heart—the One Son who he loves perfectly—to suffer and die the horror I deserved, and then, to live again, that I might live in, and through, this one called Yeshua. No one could make up such a thing."

The twins knew nothing more to say. Nahor lay his back against a large stone and closing his eyes again said,

"I tire my brothers. I will sleep well tonight, this story now brought full-circle. Think upon these things, and consider them carefully. I believe tomorrow will be a beautiful day. Dawn comes quickly!"

With no words spoken between them, both Timrah and Amru remained awake, long into the night.

With a golden glow clothing the dawn, the sun rose in the east as it did every morning, needing no help from the two brothers. But having found little sleep the previous night, they did not greet the sun's appearance with joy. The sun's first rays penetrated the length of the thaniya, and they blinked and grumbled.

"Amru, will you wake Sabah while I milk some ewes for our morning meal?"

Timrah headed to the sheep-fold and Amru rolled over, to tap Sabah awake, who slept, propped up against a large rock.

"Old man, the sun is now upon us. You caused my brother and I a grievous lack of sleep last night with your revelation. He is getting us milk now. Perhaps we yet have some dried fruit with which to enjoy it."

Seeing no response, he nudged the man again.

"Sabah? Nahor? Are you awake, old man?"

He prodded him, and Sabah rolled away from the rock onto the ground. Amru shouted to his brother,

"Timrah! Come quickly! Something is wrong with Sabah!"

The man came on the run while Amru shook their guest, shouting,

"Sabah! Sabah! Wake up!"

They both looked closely at the old man, his mouth hanging agape, and dry. His eyelids parted slightly, his skin a pale gray. Timrah touched his palm to the man's cheek and coarsely whispered,

"He is cold. And without life. As he told us last night, his story was complete."

Intense sorrow came upon Amru. His breaths came in short gusts and he gripped Timrah by the shoulders, shaking him. He cried "He cannot be gone. He cannot be dead! How could he leave us?"

Timrah wrapped his arm around his younger brother.

"He was a hundred years old. How could he have even lived this long? As he said, he was surely old and full of years."

Amru wept on his brother's shoulder and asked,

"What shall we now do with him? There is no place of exposure nearby...and who would take care of the sheep if we carry him off?"

"Sabah said he buried Margani, his wife, in the soil. Perhaps that is the way of men who believe as he. We should do the same for him."

So Timrah and Amru dug a pit in the valley beyond the thaniya, and buried the physical remains of Nahor in the dry soil. Returning to their sheep, they discussed the man's life.

"Timrah, you can better think upon these sorts of things than myself. Do you believe that what he said could be true? That some Great Mercy made all that we see, and that he sent some rescuer for us? That a man could die...and yet live again?"

"I don't expect, my brother, that simply thinking about these things must bring one to the right conclusion. This sort of understanding can, most likely, only come as it is thrust upon one, making itself known, as it was to him."

Amru put his arm around his brother, looked to the sky, and said,

"Then come, Great Mercy! Reveal to us Yourself—and this One called Yeshua..."

And Timrah said,

"Indeed!"

Afterword

About forty years ago I first read the account of a man torment-
ed by demons and delivered from their influence on the shores of
Lake Galilee. The story affected me profoundly and somehow
touched a chord of identity within. While I had never been so
violently, and obviously, controlled by forces of spiritual darkness
like the man from Gadara, my life had, nevertheless, once been
directed and guided by unseen powers bent on my destruction. The
afflicted man's dramatic encounter with a deliverer from across the
lake, paralleled the essential crisis which pivoted my own destiny. As
the Light pierced the shadowy dread of his existence, so it changed
my own irrevocably.

A dozen years later I heard the lyrics of a song—*"Man of the
Tombs"*—by the consummate songwriter and musician Bob Bennett.
With a fresh power, the story of the man held captive by vile spirits
once again entered my thoughts and emotions. I knew then how
much I identified with this poor soul—a man enslaved by self-decep-
tion, tortured by forces beyond his control, and doomed to harm
himself just to feel alive. I could proclaim, alongside this now-deliv-

ered man, and my brother Bob Bennett, *"I'm telling you this story because...man of the tombs, I was."*

The song played over and over in my head—a hundred, a thousand times—and I knew that, sooner or later, I would have to do something about it. I would have to put my personal mark upon the story.

Several years ago, I returned to the song, and thought, perhaps, I might use the song itself as a springboard for bringing the story's message to a new audience. Never having written anything associated with a theatrical production (even worse, knowing nothing of dance), in my naiveté I determined to write something of a brief, choreographed "ballet" to Bob's music and lyrics. At the time, I was pleased with my effort, not so much for the quality of the work (ye gads!—the initial work of a total novice!), but because I felt I finally gave some tiny expression to the song resonating inside me. Of course, the work never saw the light of day, and I have never gone back to review it.

More recently, I found myself drawn into the unlikely prospect of writing a novel (having nothing whatsoever to do with the Gadarene demoniac). The forty-five years of my professional life had been involved in optical and human vision research, so the idea of writing a work of fiction was not only foreign to me, I had little interest, and almost no motivation to undertake such an elaborate and consuming effort. But I was sucked into the labor by the inevitable and inescapable gravity of some mysterious blackhole of creativity. For the novel, I chose neither the subject, the setting, the protagonist, nor its unfolding plot and structure. Night by night, I merely lay in darkness on my bed, awake, and watching the detailed scenes of a story play out before me. I then got up and commuted to my daily job, finally returning home and hoping to pound out the scenes on my computer keyboard before they evaporated in the evening haze.

As amazing as the process was—producing a five-hundred page novel in about six months (while continuing in my forty-hour-a-week research position)—I believe the writing of that book (*A Peculiar Darkness*) was merely preparing the ground for composing the work you have in your hands. Had I not been pushed, nearly contrary to my will, into writing that first work, I believe *The Stone Cutter* may never have come to light. The process showed me not only could I write one novel, but I could probably write a second.

While *The Stone Cutter* did not come to me fully fleshed-out, in scenes projected upon the screens of my imagination, it did come in bits and pieces remarkably accompanied by the same Author who visited me for the first work. His incredible timing of creative inspiration, and the divine appointments of other people to cross my path, sustained a kind of spiritual momentum for the project.

Because the novel hinges upon an historical event—the deliverance of the Gadarene demoniac—it was imperative to build a detailed timeline of my story which would dovetail with the event described in the Synoptic Gospels, as well as what is known of the history of Nabataea, Judaea, Rome, Syria, India, and China of that day.

A further consideration was my dramatization of the deliverance event itself. Because a great amount of detail is specified in the three accounts provided by Matthew, Mark, and Luke, I used that rich source material as the backbone upon which I built my own story leading up to it, and then the aftermath proceeding from it. With great effort, I attempted to harmonize my account with the historical records.

Over the years, some have noted what they describe as a potential conflict in the three different records of the deliverance—were there two demon-seized men, or one? While I don't personally subscribe to the idea there is a conflict in the texts, as I wrote my fictionalized account of the deliverance, an interesting possible solution revealed itself. When demonic power displaced Nahor's control over his actions, it evicted him from his physical form. In the scene on the beach, we see his body used by demons to rage against Yeshua, while the sentient part of Nahor floats along behind, attached to his body by only the slimmest of "life-threads." So we see both demon-tormented fragments of Nahor—the two, separated side-by-side, but one man. While I am not claiming this is the truth of the historical event, it was an interesting solution for the fiction.

I also identify deeply with another historical character in the book—the man Sha'ul of Tarsus, known today by most as the apostle, Paul. Although he only appears in two of the latter chapters in the work, his presence in the narrative is intensely significant. In history, as the confident and self-righteous Sha'ul made his way from Jerusalem to Damascus, his dramatic confrontation with the Living One foreshadowed my own crisis of belief, perhaps, even more so than the life of the Man of the Tombs. While I was yet a young man, full of my own "truth," like Sha'ul I also often pitted myself against followers of Christ, maneuvering mightily in my attempts to get them to blaspheme.

But this Sha'ul, who so strongly believed in his own apprehension of the truth, came face-to-face with the very embodiment of Truth. In response, he could say nothing, except—"Who are you, Lord?" And he received, what was to him—as it was to me—an entirely unexpected answer.

From blasphemer to believer in the moment of a bright flash, Sha'ul's life was changed, as was my own. When the idea first came to me of the man Sha'ul entering the story, I wondered how that might function in the narrative. The more I carried out detailed research on the culture, kingdom, and history of the Nabataeans (the people of my protagonist), and of their neighbors, the Judaeans (the people of Sha'ul), the more I saw how possible an encounter between Nahor and Sha'ul might have been.

Many who read of Paul's conversion story have been intrigued by the hints of his sojourn in Nabataea (or "Arabia" as it was called among Greeks and Romans). The story recounted by Luke in the book of Acts, as well as Paul's own three mentions of it, leave tantalizing but all-too-brief glimpses into the event. Of course, my effort here is a work of fiction, and not to be mistaken for what actually happened at this time in Paul's life. But because I drew an historical person into its pages—Paul the apostle, no less—I wanted to stay focused on the truth of his life as much as possible.

I decided, for my fictional account, that Sha'ul would tell Nahor the story of his own dramatic conversion. To that end, I compiled the words of the five separate accounts, as drawn from Luke's historical narrative (Acts 7.51–8.3 and 9.1–30), Luke's record of Paul's first spoken account (Acts 22.1–21), Paul's direct account written in an early letter to the Galatians (1.13-23), and finally in his second letter to the Corinthian church (11.31–33). These narratives tell us much (but not all) of what happened, and I built my account of Sha'ul's testimony to Nahor, based specifically on those words.

Beyond these matters, much of my own inner life's development can be found in that of Nahor/Shamir. While the specific events I have recounted in his story bear little resemblance to the external realities of my own life, I found Nahor frequently acting and reacting to his life as I would have, if faced with the same events. Many of his hopes, longings, weaknesses, and failures seem my own, and as I wrote, I sometimes wept alongside him, feeling the same things he felt.

In the end, the story is simply and powerfully that of a Deliverer from beyond this world and time, who came to us, as one of us—to live the life we would not, to bear the shame and guilt we could not, to pour out his breath and blood, that we might gain life abundant and unending.

The Stone Cutter
is book one of Brock Meier's series,

≈ *Waters In the Desert* ≈

The series explores the intersections of culture, religion, politics, and commerce in a rapidly changing world set in the first century desert Kingdom of Nabataea. The Nabataeans were as little understood at the zenith of their influence and wealth as they are today. Springing up in desert wastelands, without obvious history, natural resources, technology or military might, they wrested a culture and kingdom from barren rock and sand. As they became a powerhouse in the Mediterranean economy, the Romans despised their wealth. The Kingdom lay at the trading crossroads of Rome, Greece, Egypt, Persia, India, and China, providing a rich ferment of colliding world views and intents. Such a setting provides fertile ground for stories deep with meaning, emotion, and spirit.

For information on Brock Meier, new work, and **how to get free content and swag**, sign up for his bi-weekly newsletter at:

brockmeierauthor.com/subscribe

Please leave a review at Goodreads:

Brock Meier's work is distributed by Amazon, IngramSpark, and other online retailers, or at your local bookstore.

Five Meanings of the title,

"The Stone Cutter"

1)   *Stone Cutter* (i.e., sculptor) is the artistic profession of the protagonist Nahor.

2)   the mysterious object of Nahor's pursuit, the Shamir, is a *stone-cutting* device.

3)   refers to the ancient Asian parable, *The Stone Cutter*, as told by the Chinese pearl merchant, prophesying Nahor's fruitless pursuit.

4)   in emotional desperation and demonic torment, Nahor resorts to self-harm by cutting himself with sharp stones—thus, becoming a "*stone-cutter.*"

5)   refers to the rescuer Yeshua, who *cuts out the "heart of stone"* of Nahor, and gives him a "heart of flesh."

For a long time, "The Stone Cutter" was only a working title and simply described the story's protagonist. But as the story developed, it was clear that the title gained more and deeper meanings. With the book nearly complete, I related a brief synopsis of the story to a friend over coffee. When he suggested the final meaning I included above, I was surprised I'd not noticed it before, though I was familiar with the quotation from Ezekiel. In the end, I felt I could do nothing other than title my work The Stone Cutter.

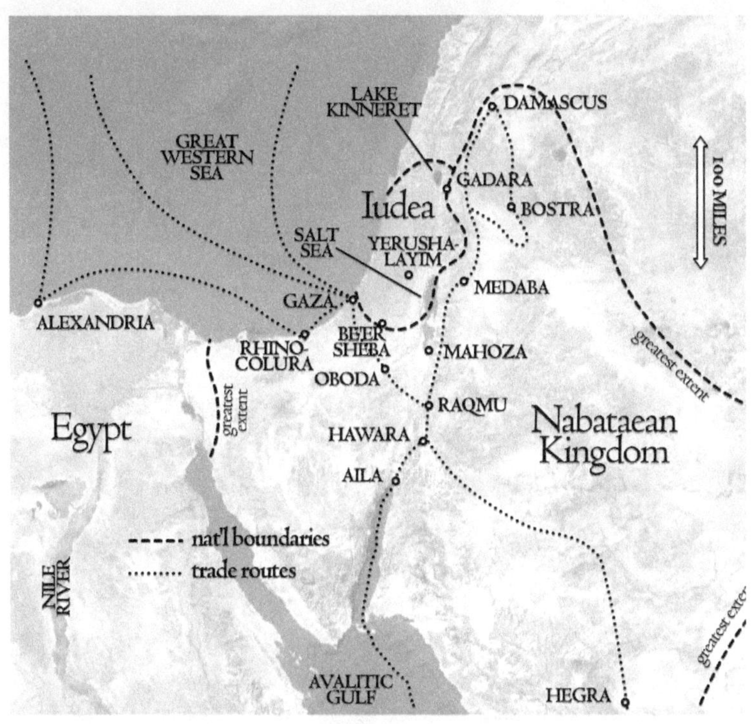

Greatest extent of the Nabataean Kingdom and trade routes

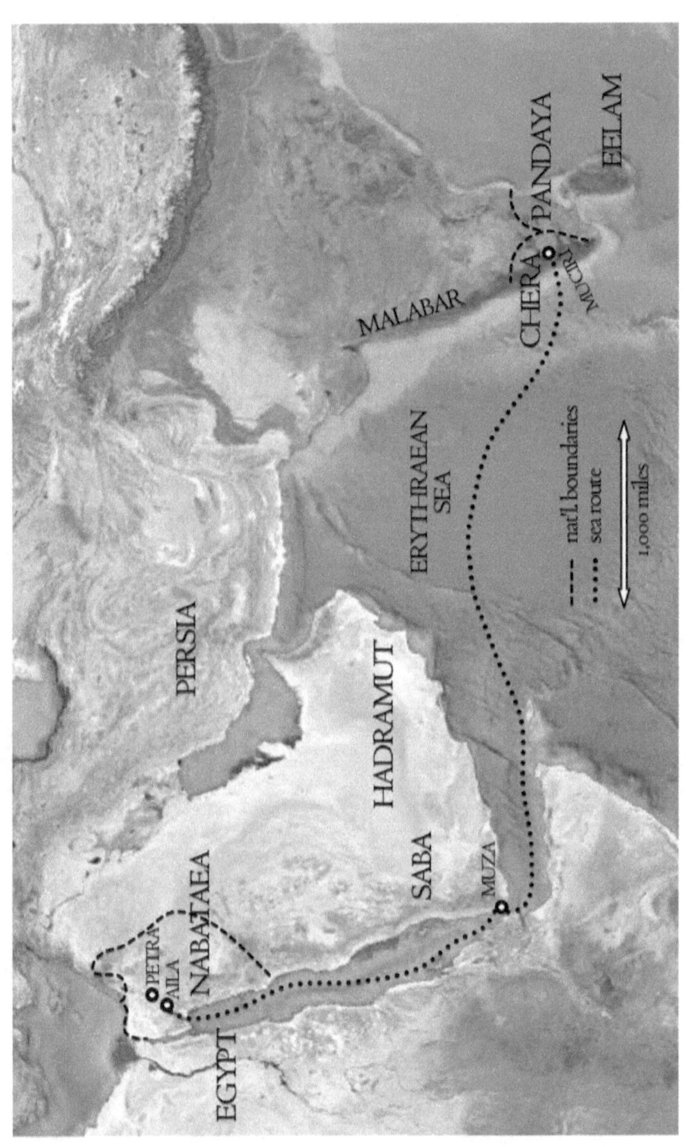

Voyage from Nabataea to Muciri

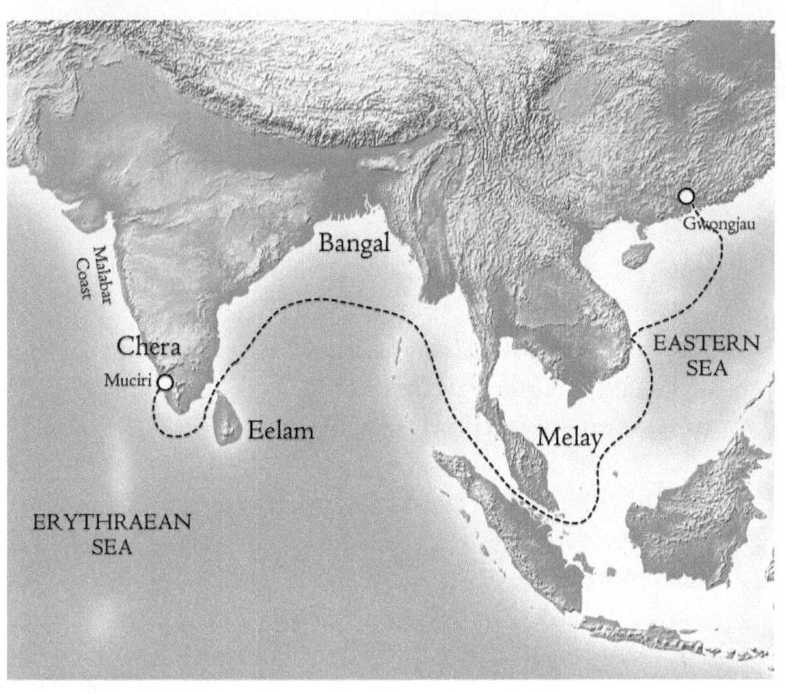

Voyage from Muciri to the Farthest East

Timeline of the story of Nahor/Shamir, a Stone Cutter

— Bold denotes actual, historical event
— ? denotes approximate date
— *Italics denotes fictional event*

169?BC—**Haretat I ascends to throne**

115?BC—**Haretat II ascends to throne**

96 BC—**Obodas I ascends to throne**

86 BC—**Obodas I dies in battle, Rabbel I ascends to throne**

84?BC—**Haretat III, son of Obodas, ascends to throne**

72 BC—Dayan born

62 BC—**Haretat III dies, Obodas II ascends to throne**

62 BC—Duvsha born

59 BC—**Obodas II dies, his son Malichus I ascends to throne**

40 BC—Dayan (28) marries Duvsha (18)

32?BC—**Aeneas (later called Haretat IV) born**

31 BC—Geram born to Duvsha (31)

30 BC—**Malichus I dies, Obodas III ascends to throne**

30 BC—Aslah born

30?BC—**Khuldu born**

26 BC— **Obodas's vizier Syllaeus misleads Romans in desert**

26 BC—Elanat born

20 BC—**Herod Antipas born**

15?BC—**Herodias born**

15?BC—Aeneas (17) and Khuldu (15) married

14 BC—Zaidan born

13?BC—**Phasaelis born to Aeneas and Khuldu**

12 BC—Dayan(60) and Duvsha (50) die

11 BC—Geram (20) marries Elanat (15)

10 BC—Nashgu born to Elanat (16)

9 BC—Ausos born to Elanat

9 BC—**Obodas III dies, probably poisoned by Syllaeus,**
    Aeneas takes the name Haretat IV (23), ascends to throne

8 BC—Walu born to Elanat

7 BC—Adnun born to Elanat

6 BC—Amand born to Elanat

6 BC—Syllaeus summoned to Rome, executed

5 BC—Wahab born to Elanat (21)

4 BC—Yeshua born in Bethlehem

4 BC—Herod Antipas (22) begins reign over Galilee and Perea

3?AD—Herod Antipas (23) marries Phasaelis (16),
           daughter of Haretat

2?BC—Shuqilat born

5?AD—Sha'ul born in Tarsus

2 AD—Margani born to Manotu's wife

7 AD—Nahor born to Elanat and Geram (last of her sons)
     —Qainu born to Hamilat (and Arwas)

12 AC—Talia born to Elanat (last of her children)

14 AD—Khuldu (Haretat's queen) (44) dies
     —Nahor given charge of Talia's (2) welfare
     —Talia is killed by black cobra under Nahor's care
     —Qainu takes blame for Nahor, she is beaten by her father

15-30?AD—Sha'ul (10-25) begins tutelage under Gamaliel in Jerusalem

15 AD—Qainu's family moves to Decapolis
     —Elanat (41) dies by her own hand
     —Geram abandons Nahor (8) in Raqmu, in the care of Aslah (45)

16 AD—Haretat (48) takes Shuqilat (18) as his second queen

24 AD—Nahor (17) meets Margaini (22) and is smitten
     —Margani moves to Bosra to help Shuqilat set up her palace there
     —Nahor pursues Margani, casts the ring into the Dead Sea
     —Nahor and Aslah gain major app't. to project planned by Haretat
     —Aslah tells Nahor of the Shamir
     —in quarry, Aslah (54) is killed and Nahor's hand is maimed

25 AD—Nahor learns more of the Shamir, and sails to the east to find it
     —Nahor meets the sailor Zabibe and hears more of the Shamir

26 AD—Nahor learns more about the Shamir from Indian gem master
     —Nahor sails to China, hears more of the Shamir

27 AD—Nahor finds love with Tenicca, but abandons her for his quest
     —Nahor sells his soul to Ashmedai to discover the location of the

Shamir

> —*Nahor follows the flight of the bird to the shore of the Dead Sea*
> —*Nahor (20) travels to Gadara in search of flawless stone*
> —*Nahor meets Qainu/Nura outside of Gadara*
> —*Arwas sets a high bride-price for Nahor's Nura*
> —*Nahor sets out to find perfect stone*
> —*Nahor hires stonecutters to cut the perfect block*
> —*Zaidan moves to Gadara and takes an interest in Qainu*

28 AD—*Arwas betrays Nahor and marries Qainu (20) to Zaidan (40)*

> —*Nahor sells the perfect stone to a cutter making a coffin*
> —*Nahor confronts Arwas about the marriage of his intended*
> —*Nahor falls into despair, wanders aimless among the tombs*
> —*Ashmedai claims Nahor's soul, subjecting him to unspeakable evils*
> —*Arwas dies and Zaidan buys a tomb and Nahor's perfect coffin*
> —*Nahor, possessed and in grief threatens Zaidan and others*
> —*people of Gadara hunt Nahor, to beat and chain him*
> —*at Arwas' entombment, Nahor confronts Zaidan*
> —*Zaidan accidentally kills Qainu, blames it on Nahor*
> —*Nahor wanders in the wilderness, cutting himself with stones*

28 AD—Nahor delivered from demonic possession by Yeshua

> —*Nahor tells people in Gadara of his miraculous deliverance*
> **—John the Baptizer beheaded**
> **—Yeshua feeds 4000 in Decapolis**
> —*Nahor travels to Hegra to tell his family of Yehshua*

29 AD—Yeshua (33) executed in Jerusalem, *Nahor's trust shaken*

32 AD—stoning of Stephen,

> **start of Jerusalem persecution of Yeshua's followers**

33-34 AD—Sha'ul (28-29) leads persecution of the Way

34 AD—traveling to Damascus to enlarge persecution,

> **Sha'ul meets Yeshua and believes**

34-37—Sha'ul enters Nabataea, deepening faith *and learns tent-making*

36 AD—Antipas divorces Haretat's daughter Phasaelis,

> **who escapes home to her father in Nabataea**

37 AD—Nahor (30) meets Sha'ul, and is changed by the living Yeshua

> **—Sha'ul (32) returns to Damascus**

—Sha'ul escapes Haretat's ethnarch there by fleeing to Tarsus

—Haretat (69) defeats Herod Antipas in battle

38 AD—Nahor (31) rescues and marries Margani (36)

39 AD—Herod Antipas and Herodias exiled to Gaul by Caligula

—Margani (37) loses her only child

40 AD—Haretat IV (72) dies, Malichus II, (his son by Chuldu) ascends to throne

—Margani meets Hina,

who believes on Yeshua and enters their household

58-62 AD—Sha'ul (63) goes to Jerusalem and then to Rome for trial

64 AD—Sha'ul (69) imprisoned in Rome and executed (?) by Nero

70 AD—Malichus II dies, his son Rabbel II ascends to throne, with his mother Shuqilat II as co-regent

105 AD—Nahor/Sabah (98) meets the shepherds, Amru and Timrah, and tells his story

106 AD—Nahor (99) dies and is buried by shepherds

106 AD—Roman Emperor Trajan annexes Nabataea/Petra

Acknowledgements

This book could not have been written, had not Yeshua Hamashiach stepped from the boat that day two millennia ago, onto the eastern shore of Lake Kinneret, and set a hopeless, wrecked man free.

And it might not have been written, had not Bob Bennett picked up the historical account, adding substance and humanity to the man's life through his haunting and hopeful lyrics and melody.

C.S. Lewis showed me, in his incomparable novel *Perelandra*, how deep truth can be communicated through the art of fiction. And I was awakened to the validity and power of taking history beyond the record and into the realm of story through Frederick Buechner's historical novel *Son of Laughter*.

Let it be known to all that I also owe a deep debt of gratitude to countless friends, family, colleagues, mentors, and encouragers, who, like Aaron and Hur, have lifted my arms up in ways both large and small. I hope you know who you are, and I trust you can take joy in this finished work, and in some way, see it as partly your own.

And of course, I have been, and always will be, forever indebted to the One Who invented creating, the One Who forever writes His own indelible story in this vast, unknowable universe, and upon the hearts of humanity—and Who has inscribed His own holy Name upon my now tender heart.

This first edition of

The Stone Cutter

is set in

Coelacanth

Produced by the American type designer

Ben Whitmore

Coelacanth is a classic revival of Bruce Rogers' legendary **Centaur**,

heralded as the most beautiful typeface ever designed.

Coelacanth is distinguished by its

rich set of glyphs, weights,

and optical sizes

to comprise

a family

of 37

fonts.

Blue Sevens Publishing
Bulverde, Texas
February, 2023